Tree-
House
[redacted]omix
[redacted]roudly
[redacted]resents

DOG MAN

WRITTEN AND ILLUSTRATED BY DAV PILKEY
AS GEORGE BEARD AND HAROLD HUTCHINS
WITH COLOR BY JOSE GARIBALDI

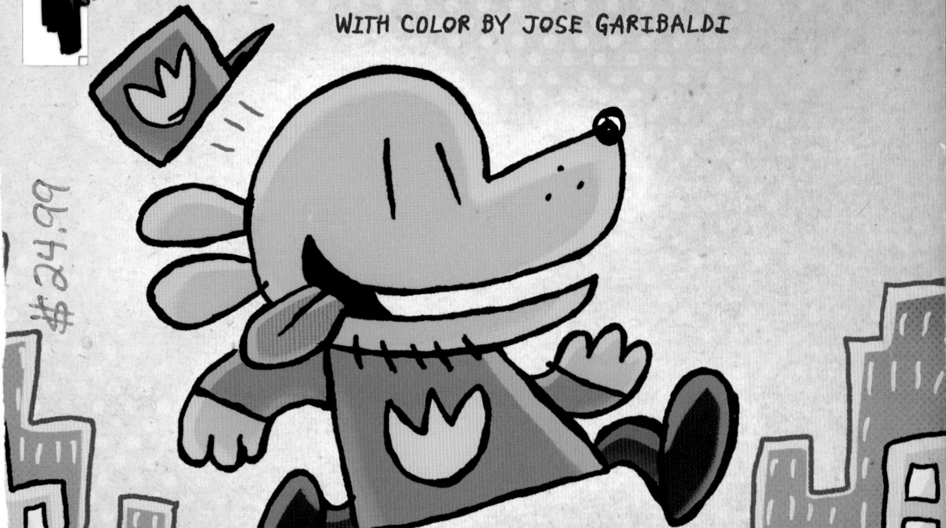

graphix
AN IMPRINT OF
SCHOLASTIC

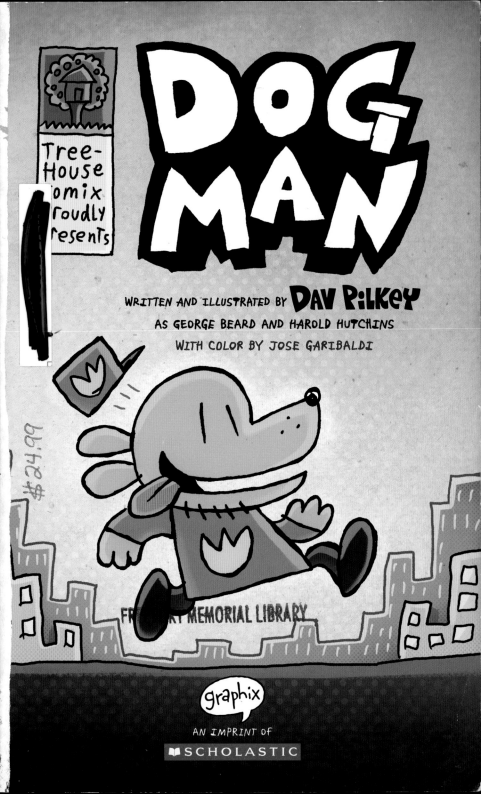

FOR DAN, LEAH, ALEK, AND KYLE SANTAT

Library of Congress Control Number 2016932063

978-0-545-58160-8 (POB)
978-1-338-61194-6 (Library)

10 9 8 7 6 5 4 3 2 1   20 21 22 23 24

Printed in China   62
First edition, September 2016

Edited by Anamika Bhatnagar
Book design by Dav Pilkey and Phil Falco
Color by Jose Garibaldi
Creative Director: David Saylor

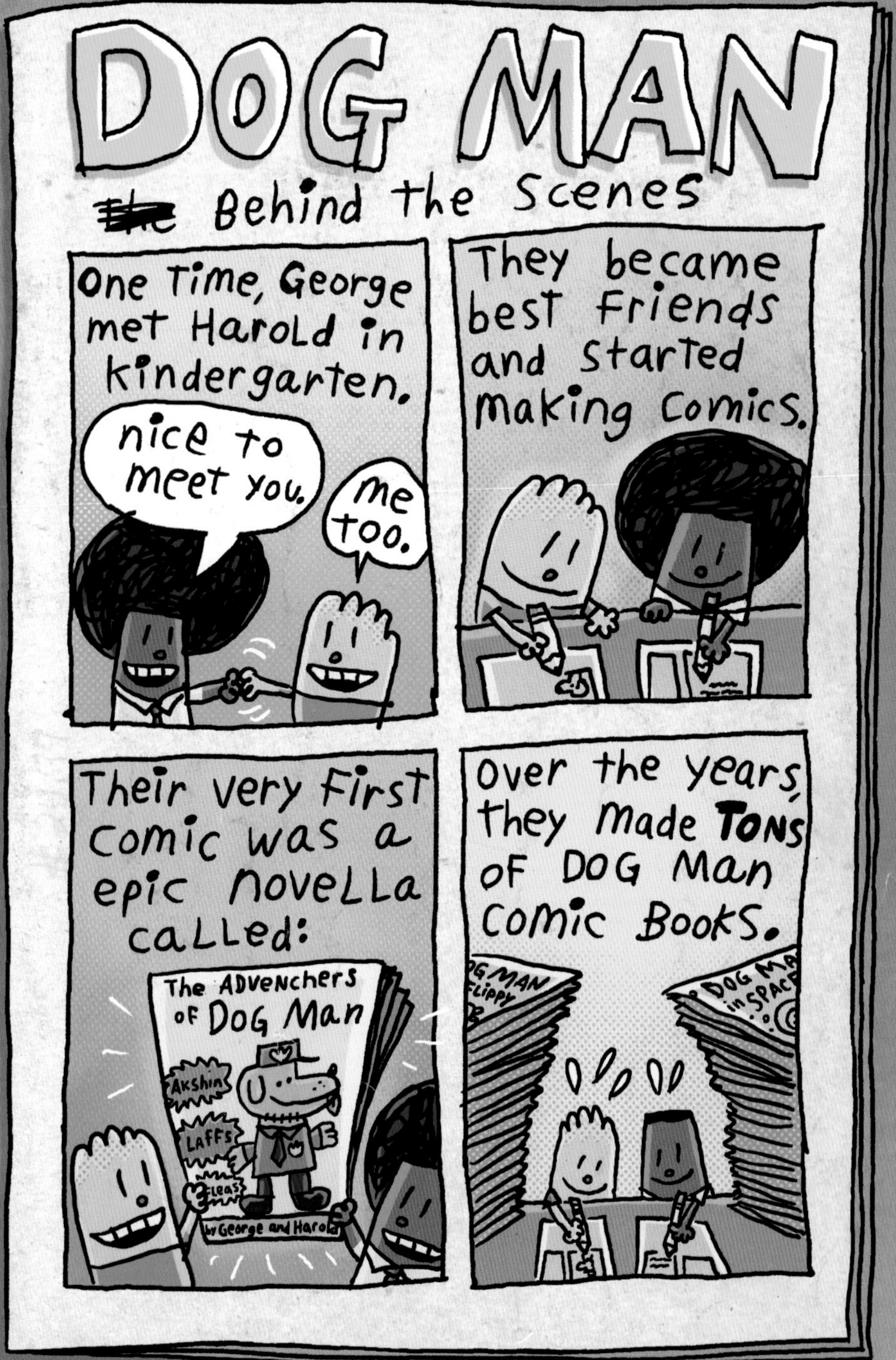
DOG MAN
Behind the Scenes
One Time, George met Harold in kindergarten.
nice to meet you.
me too.
They became best friends and started making comics.
Their very first comic was a epic novella called:
The ADVENchers of DOG Man
Akshin
LAFFS
by George and Harold
Over the years, they made TONS of DOG Man comic books.

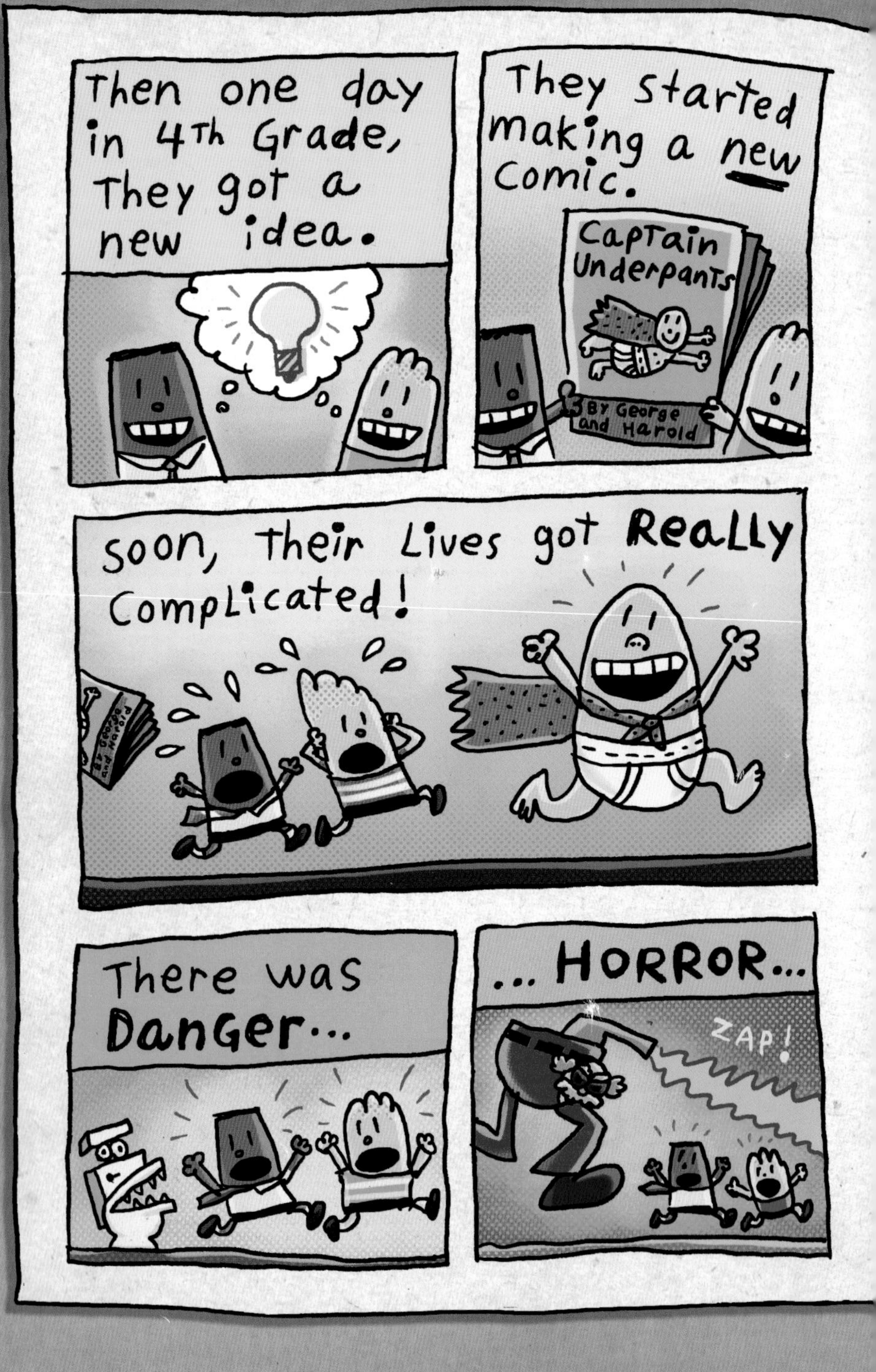
Then one day in 4th Grade, They got a new idea.
They started making a new Comic.
Captain Underpants
By George and Harold
soon, their Lives got ReaLLy CompLicated!
There was Danger...
... HORROR...
ZAP!

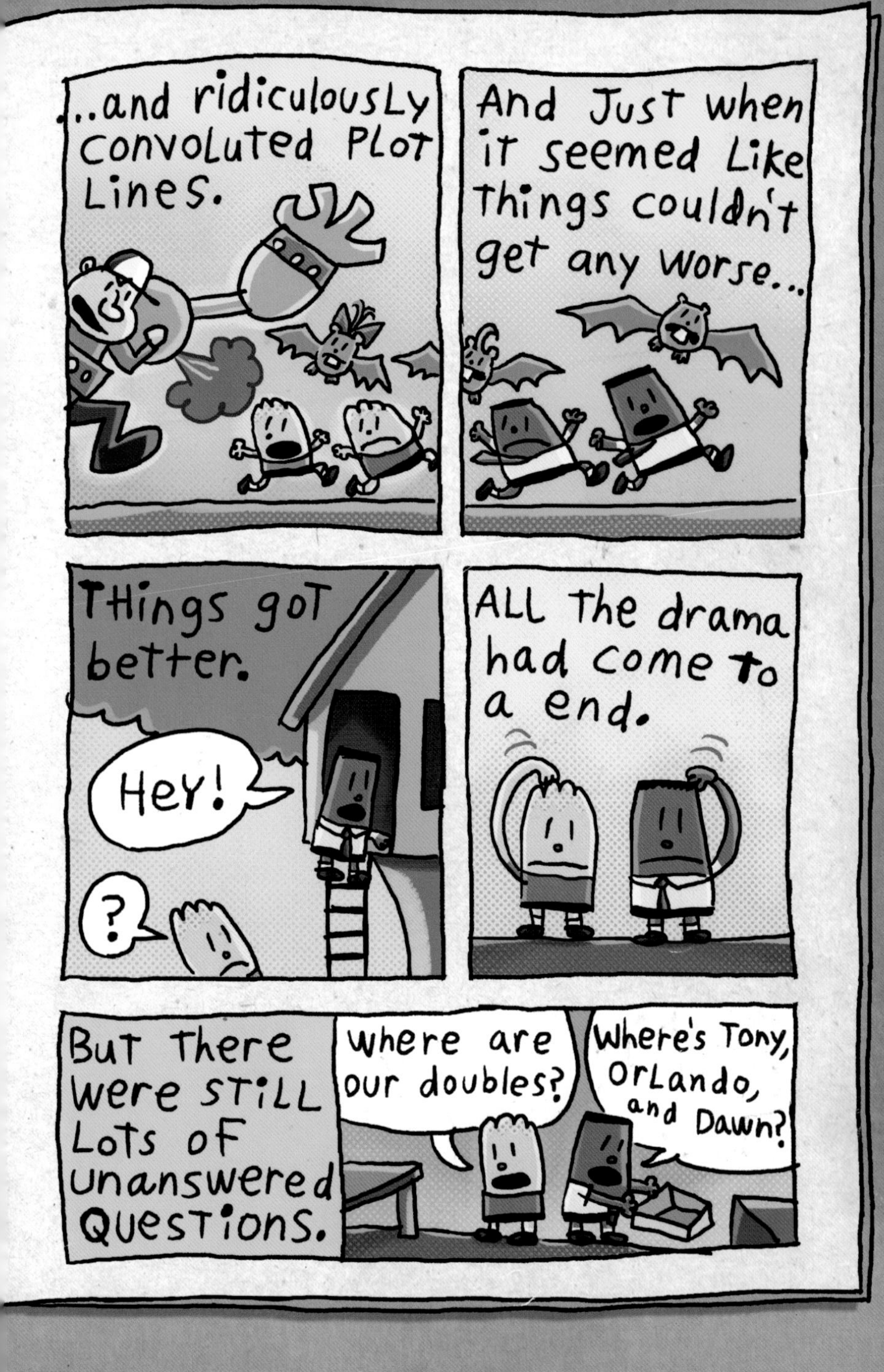
..and ridiculously convoluted plot lines.
And just when it seemed like things couldn't get any worse...
Things got better.
Hey!
?
All the drama had come to a end.
But there were still lots of unanswered questions.
Where are our doubles?
Where's Tony, Orlando, and Dawn?

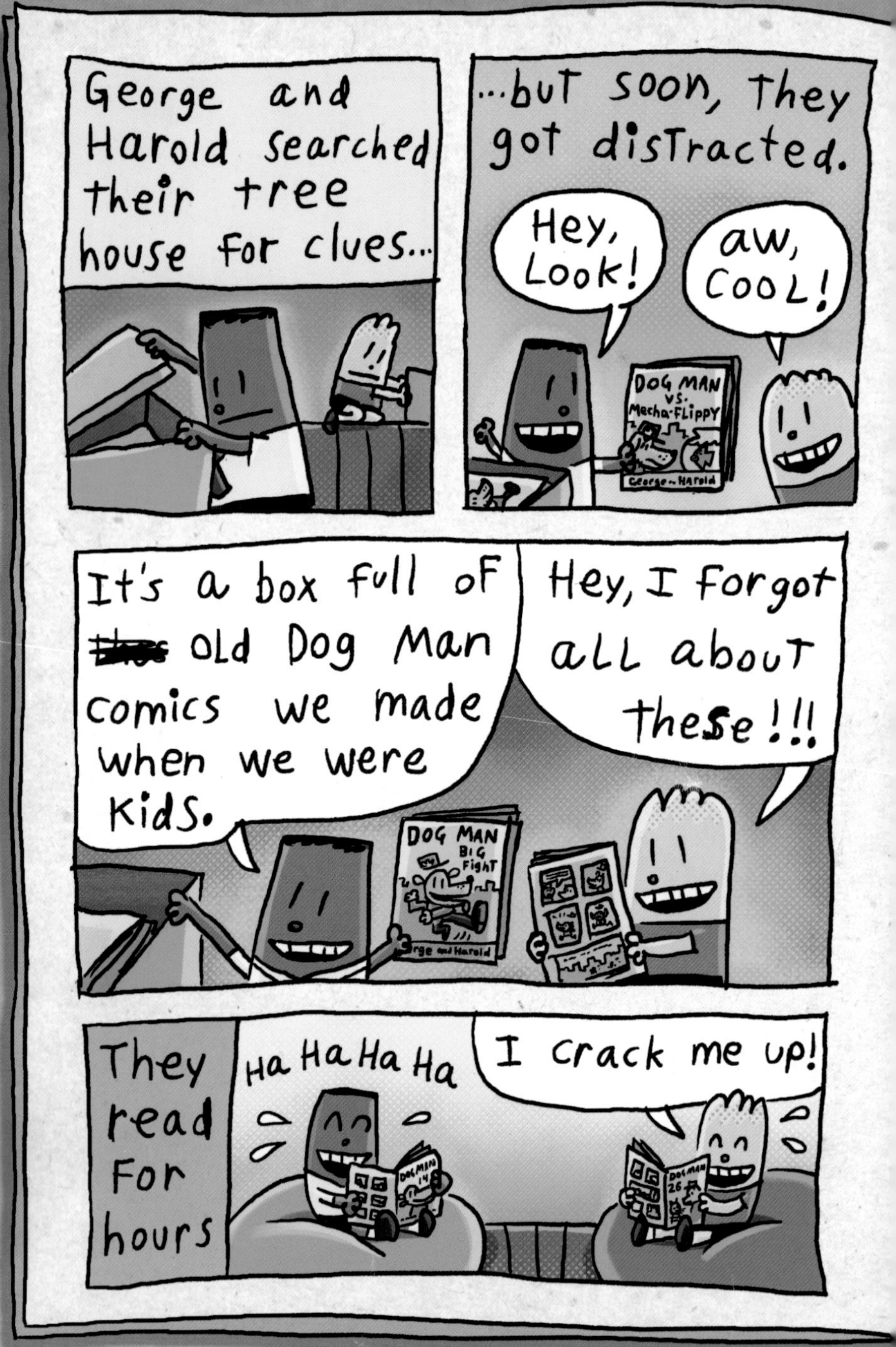
George and Harold searched their tree house for clues...
...but soon, they got distracted.
Hey, Look!
aw, COOL!
DOG MAN VS. Mecha-FLIPPY
George-HAROLD
It's a box full of old Dog Man comics we made when we were kids.
Hey, I forgot all about these!!!
DOG MAN BIG FIGHT
They read for hours
Ha Ha Ha Ha Ha
I crack me up!
DOG MAN 14
DOG MAN 26

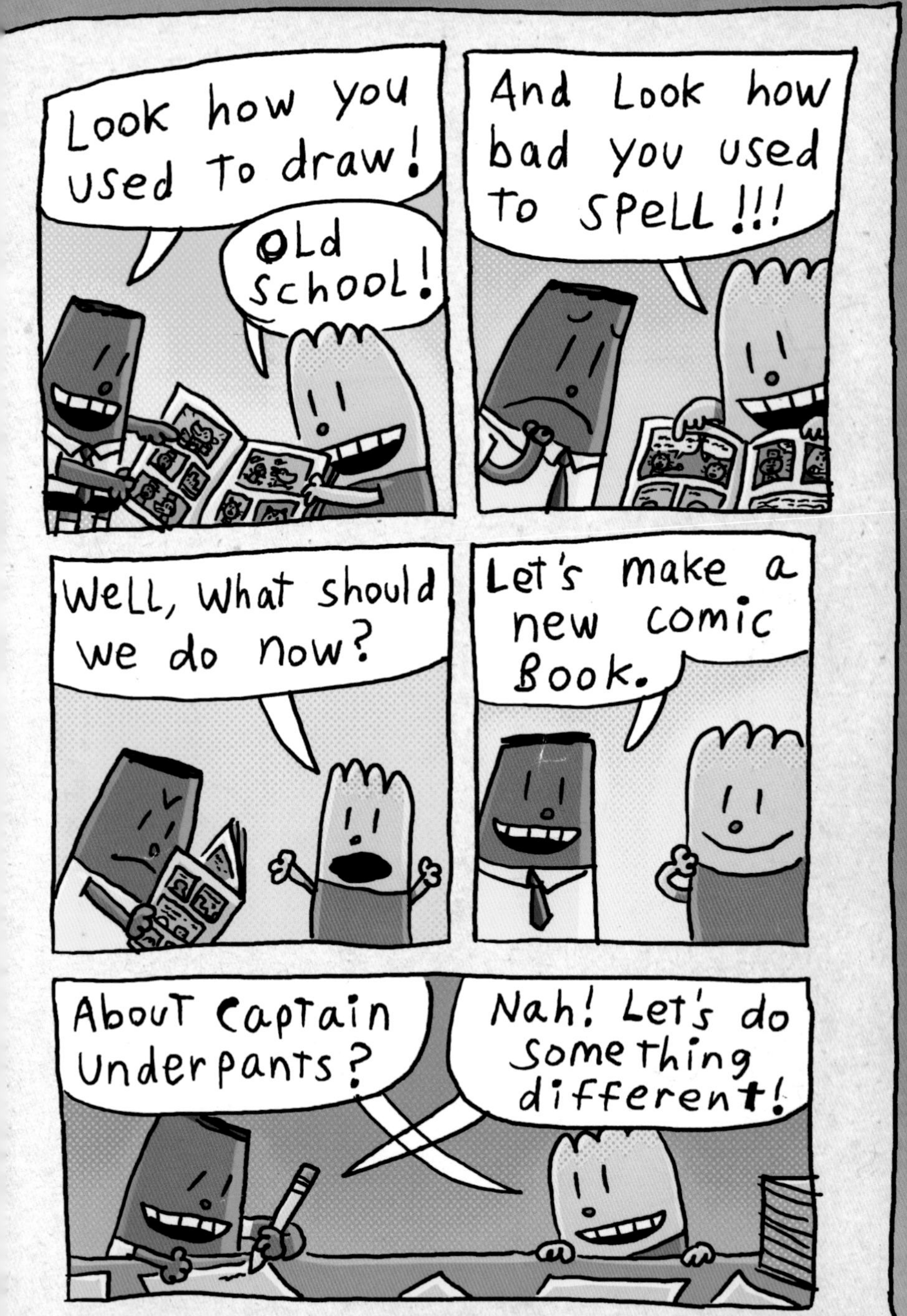
Look how you used To draw!
OLd School!
And Look how bad you used To SPeLL!!!
WeLL, What should we do now?
Let's make a new comic Book.
AbouT Captain Underpants?
Nah! Let's do Something different!

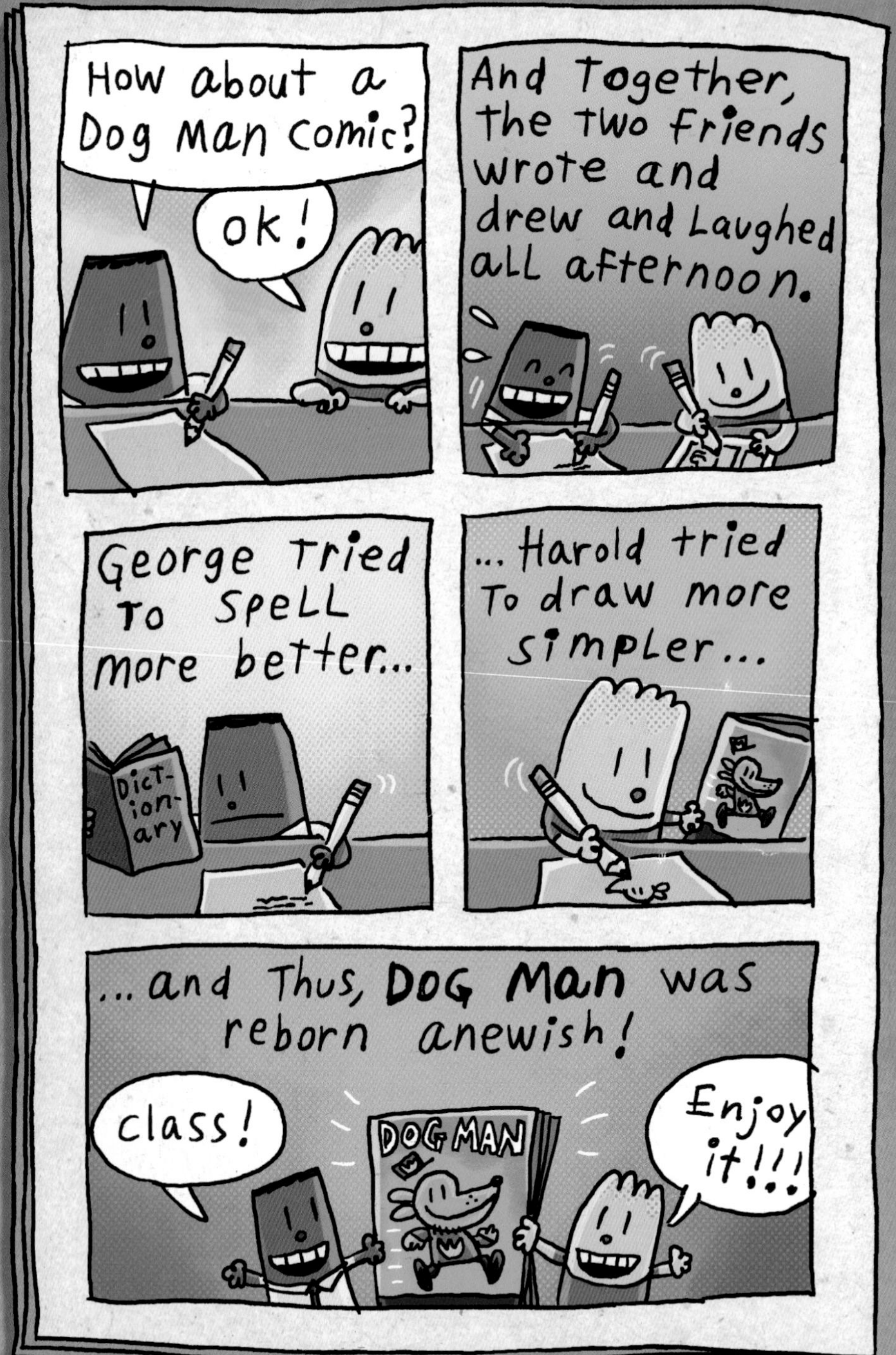
How about a Dog Man comic?
ok!
And together, the two friends wrote and drew and laughed all afternoon.
George tried to spell more better...
...Harold tried to draw more simpler...
Dict-ion-ary
...and thus, DOG MAN was reborn anewish!
Class!
DOG MAN
Enjoy it!!!

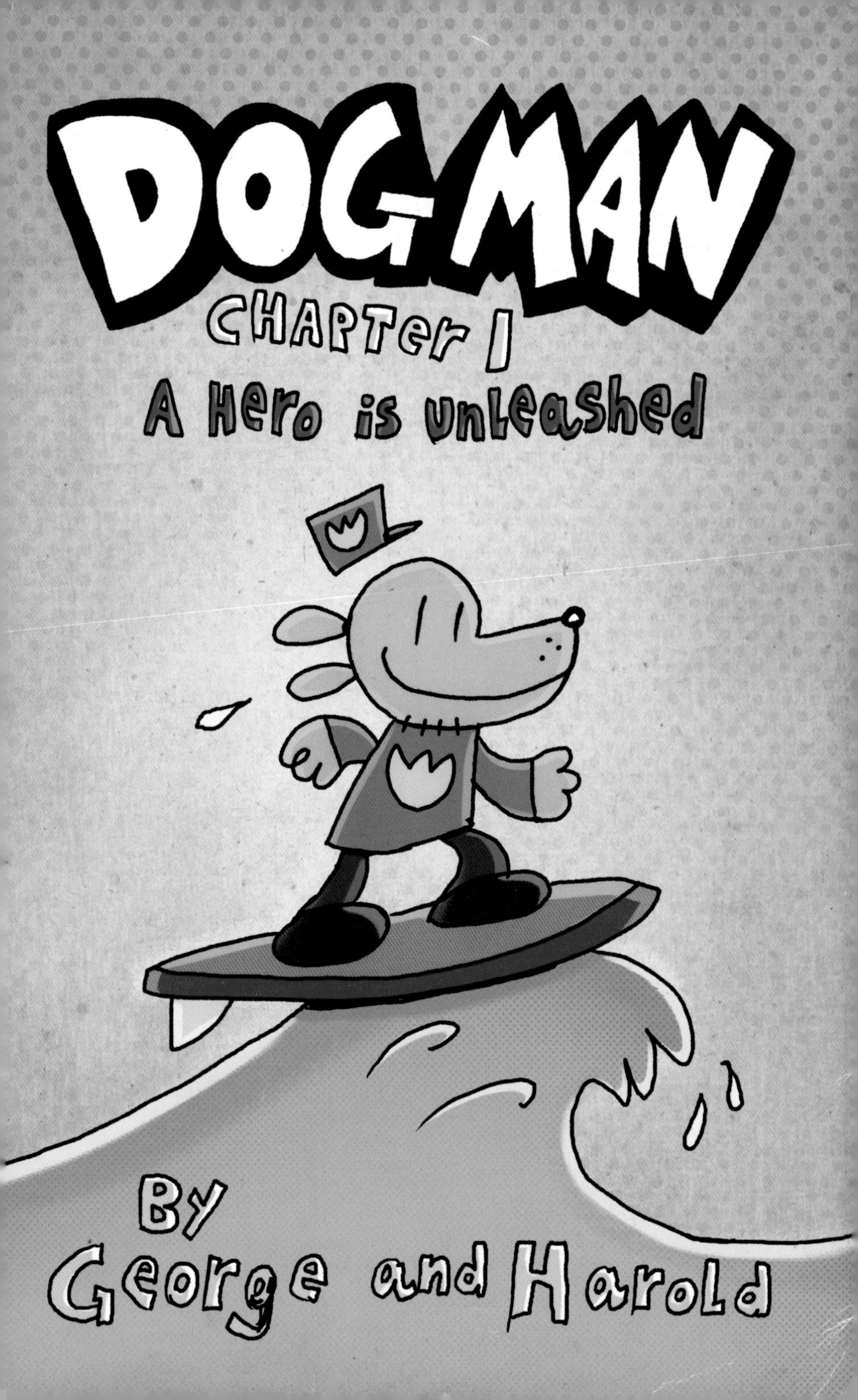
DOG MAN
CHAPTER 1
A Hero is unleashed
By
George and Harold

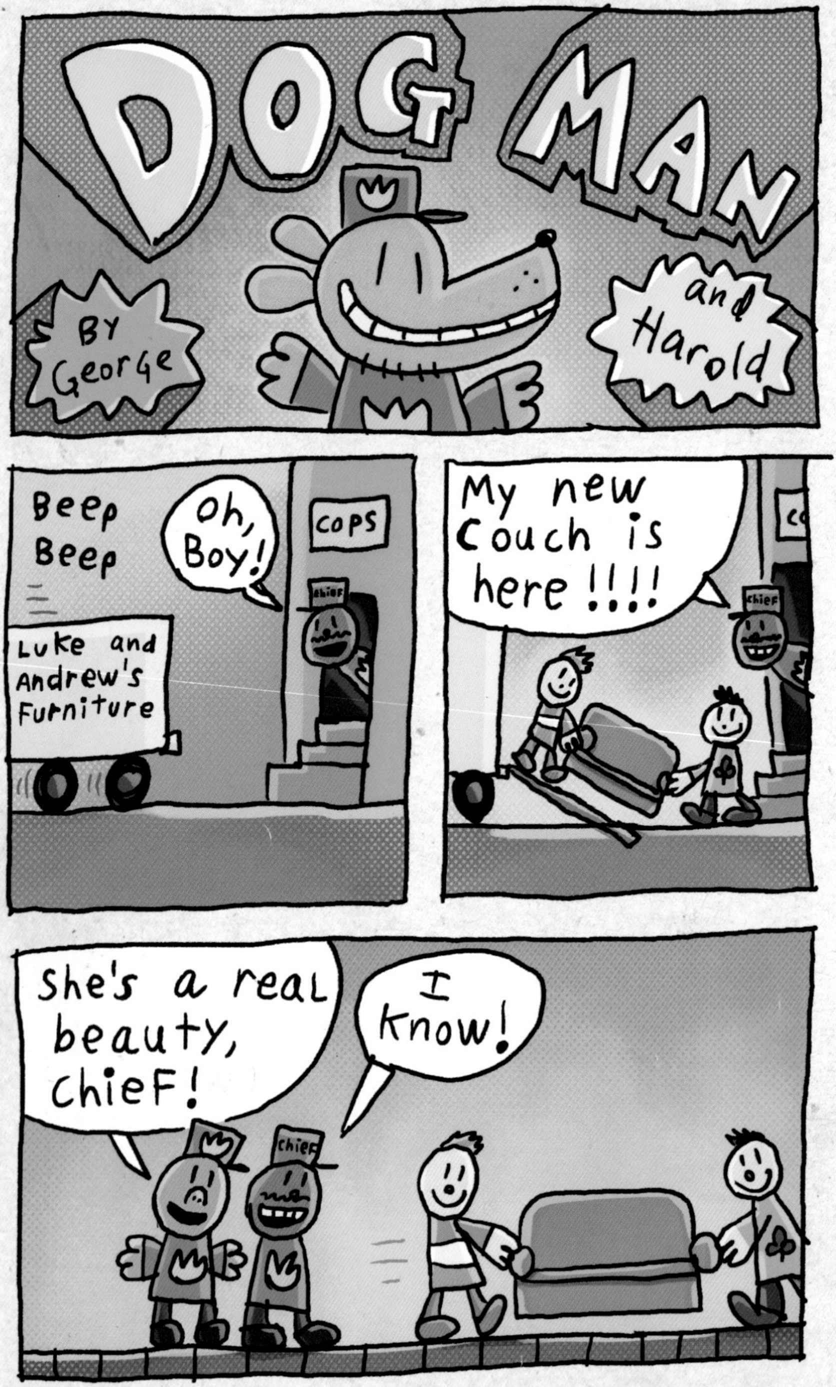
DOG MAN
BY George
and Harold
Beep Beep
Oh, Boy!
COPS
Luke and Andrew's Furniture
Chief
My new Couch is here!!!!
Chief
She's a real beauty, Chief!
I know!
Chief

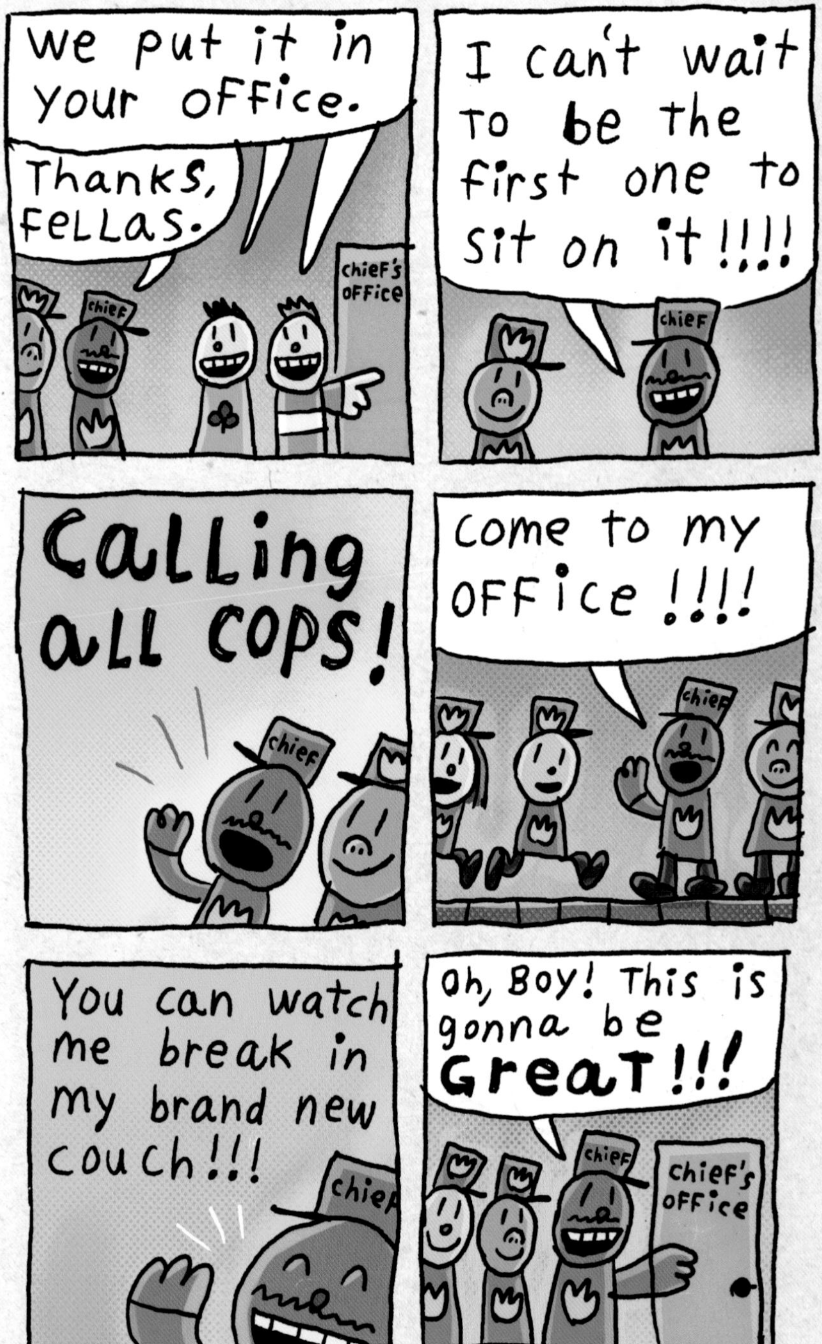
We put it in your office.
Thanks, fellas.
Chief's office
Chief
I can't wait to be the first one to sit on it!!!!
Chief
Calling all cops!
Chief
Come to my office!!!!
Chief
You can watch me break in my brand new couch!!!
Chief
Oh, boy! This is gonna be GREAT!!!
Chief
Chief's office

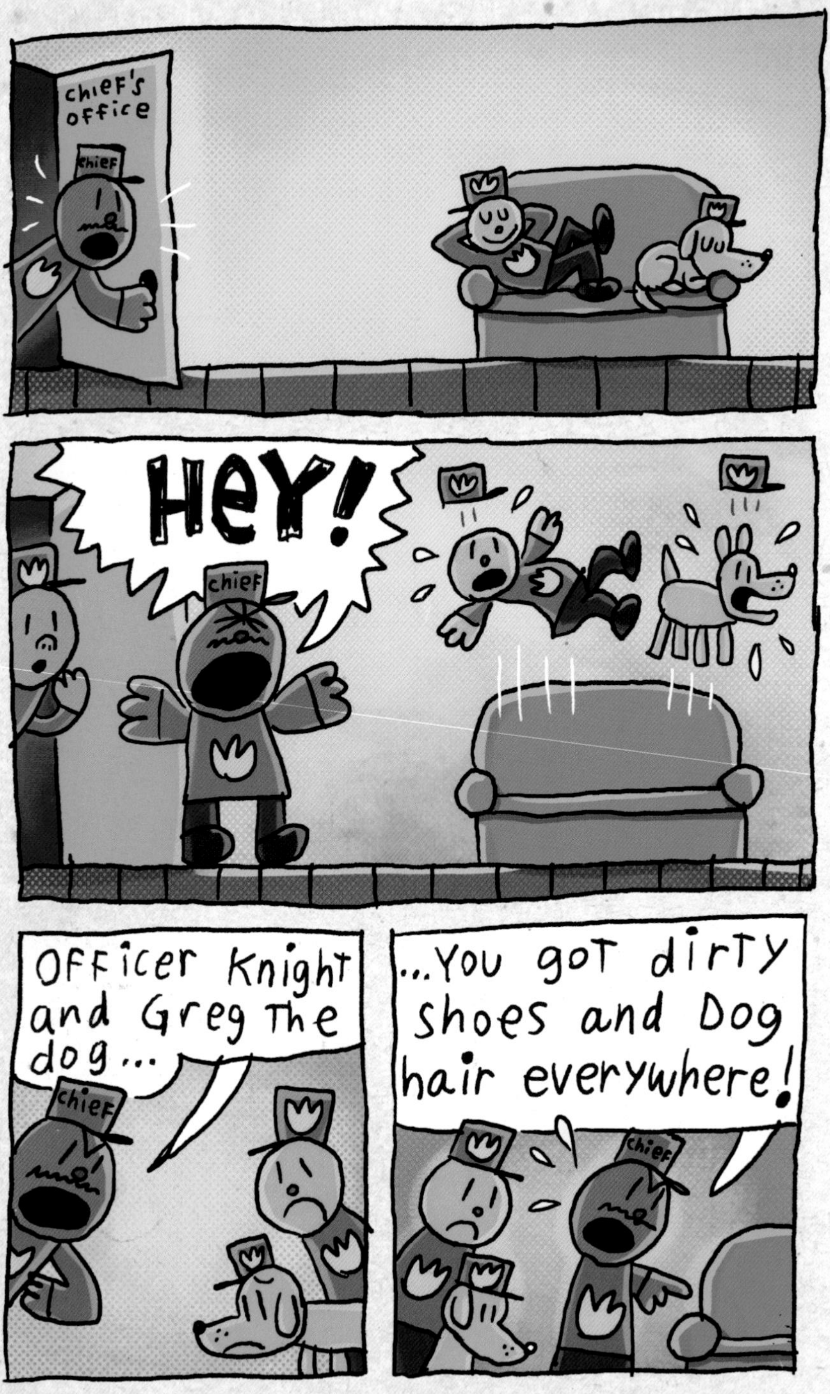
chief's office
chief
HEY!
chief
Officer Knight and Greg the dog...
chief
...You got dirty shoes and Dog hair everywhere!
chief

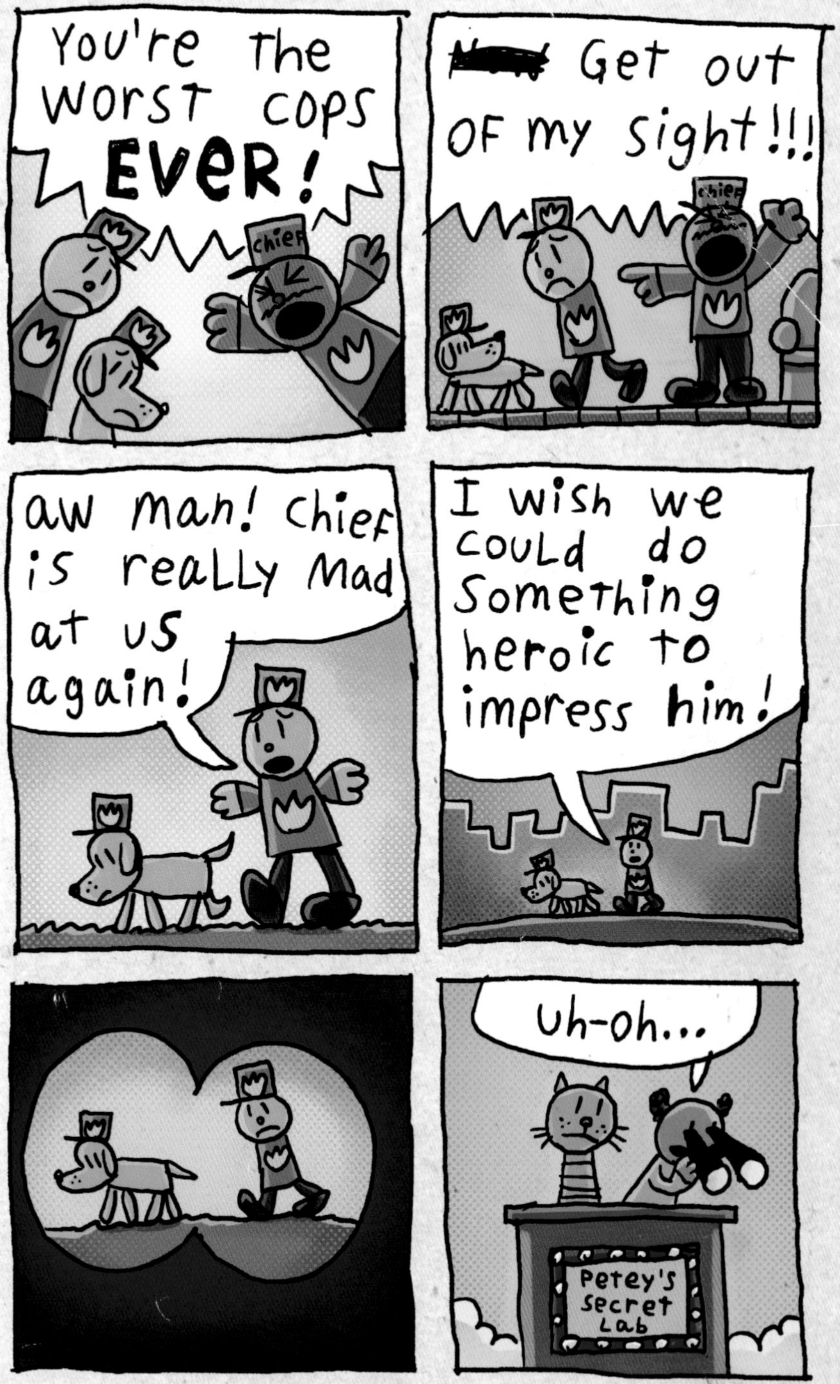
You're the worst cops EVER!
[redacted] Get out of my sight!!!
aw man! chief is really Mad at us again!
I wish we could do Something heroic to impress him!
Uh-oh...
Petey's Secret Lab

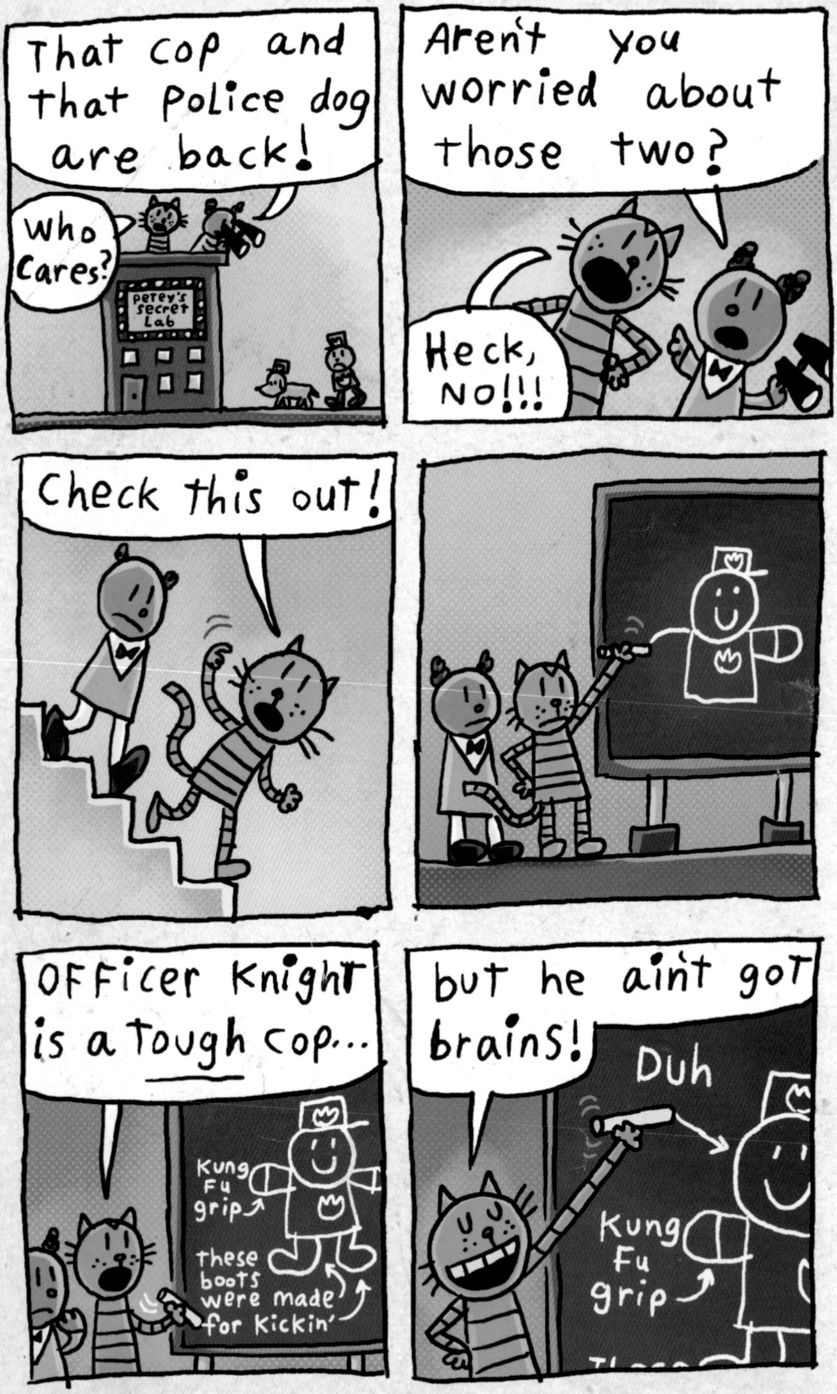
That cop and that police dog are back!
Who Cares?
Petey's Secret Lab
Aren't you worried about those two?
Heck, No!!!
Check this out!
Officer Knight is a tough cop...
Kung Fu grip
these boots were made for kickin'
but he ain't got brains!
Duh
Kung Fu grip

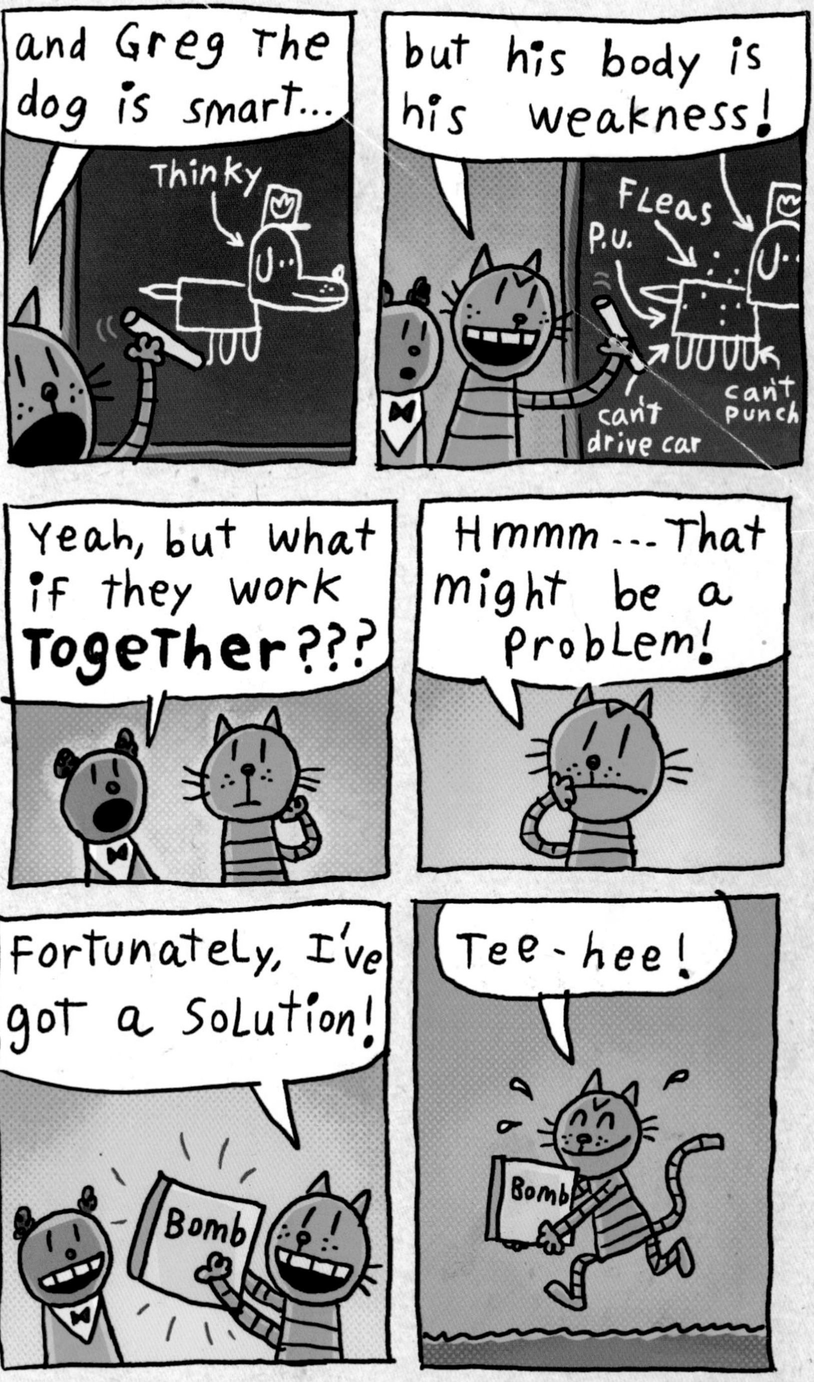
and Greg The dog is smart...
Thinky
but his body is his weakness!
FLeas
P.U.
can't drive car
can't punch
Yeah, but what if they work TogeTher???
Hmmm... That might be a probLem!
FortunateLy, I've got a SoLution!
Bomb
Tee-hee!
Bomb

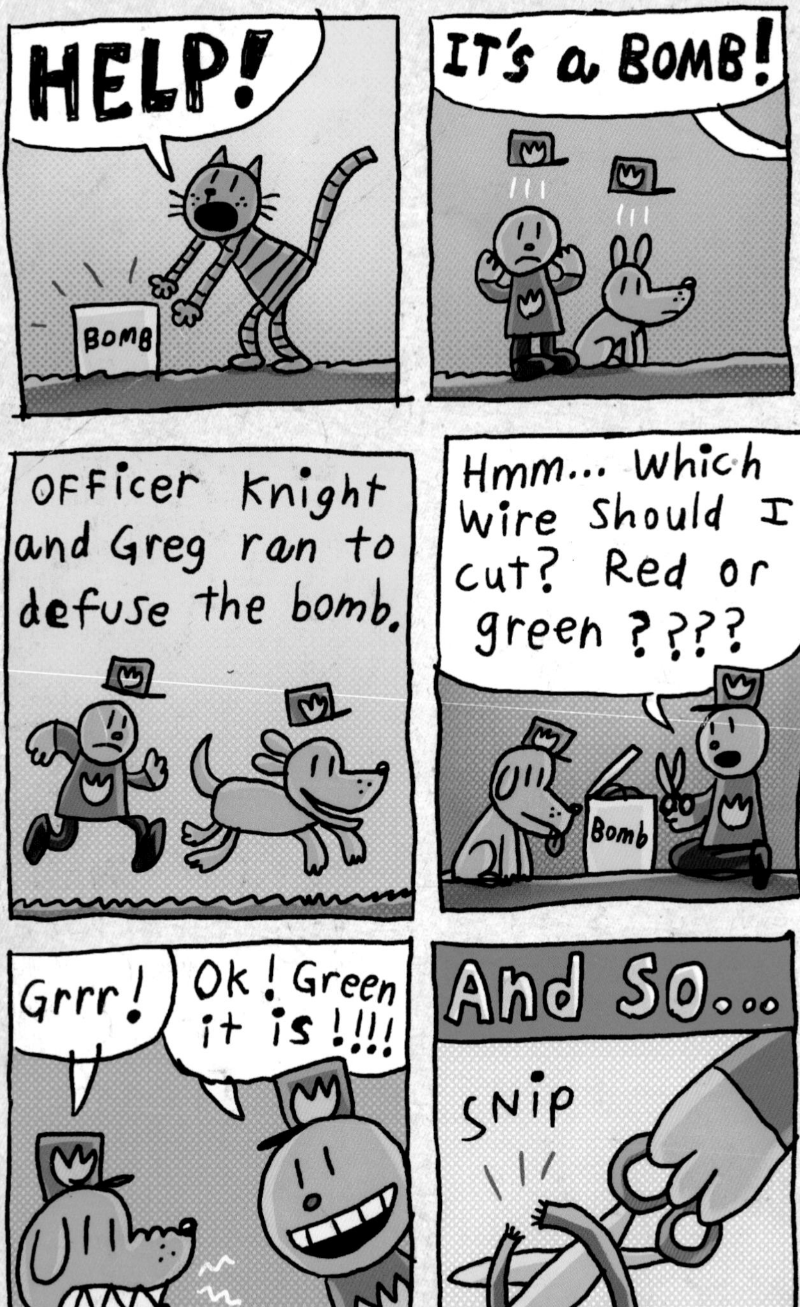
HELP!
BOMB
IT'S a BOMB!
Officer Knight and Greg ran to defuse the bomb.
Hmm... Which Wire Should I cut? Red or green ????
Bomb
Grrr!
Ok! Green it is !!!!
And SO...
SNIP

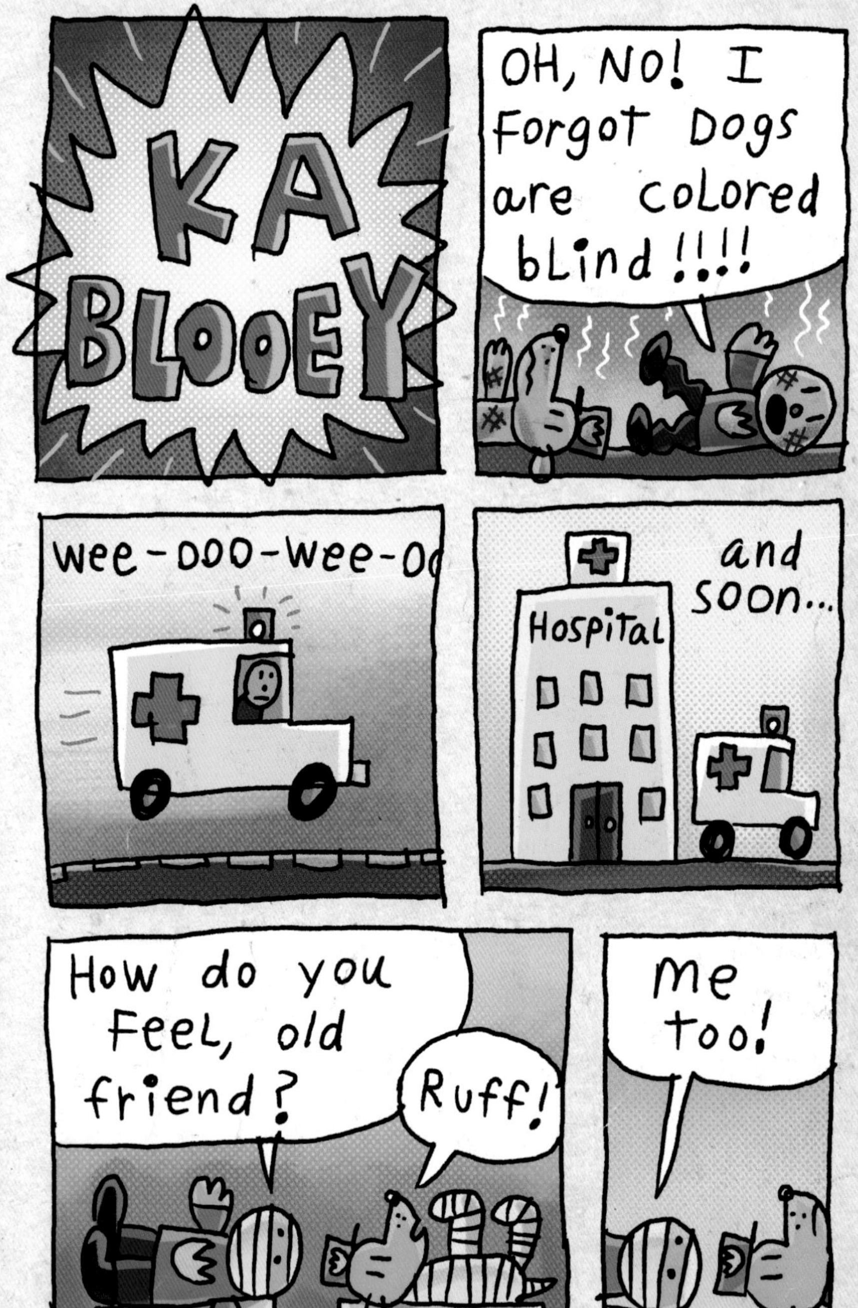
KA BLOOEY
OH, NO! I Forgot Dogs are colored bLind!!!!
wee-ooo-wee-o
and soon...
Hospital
How do you Feel, old friend?
Ruff!
me too!

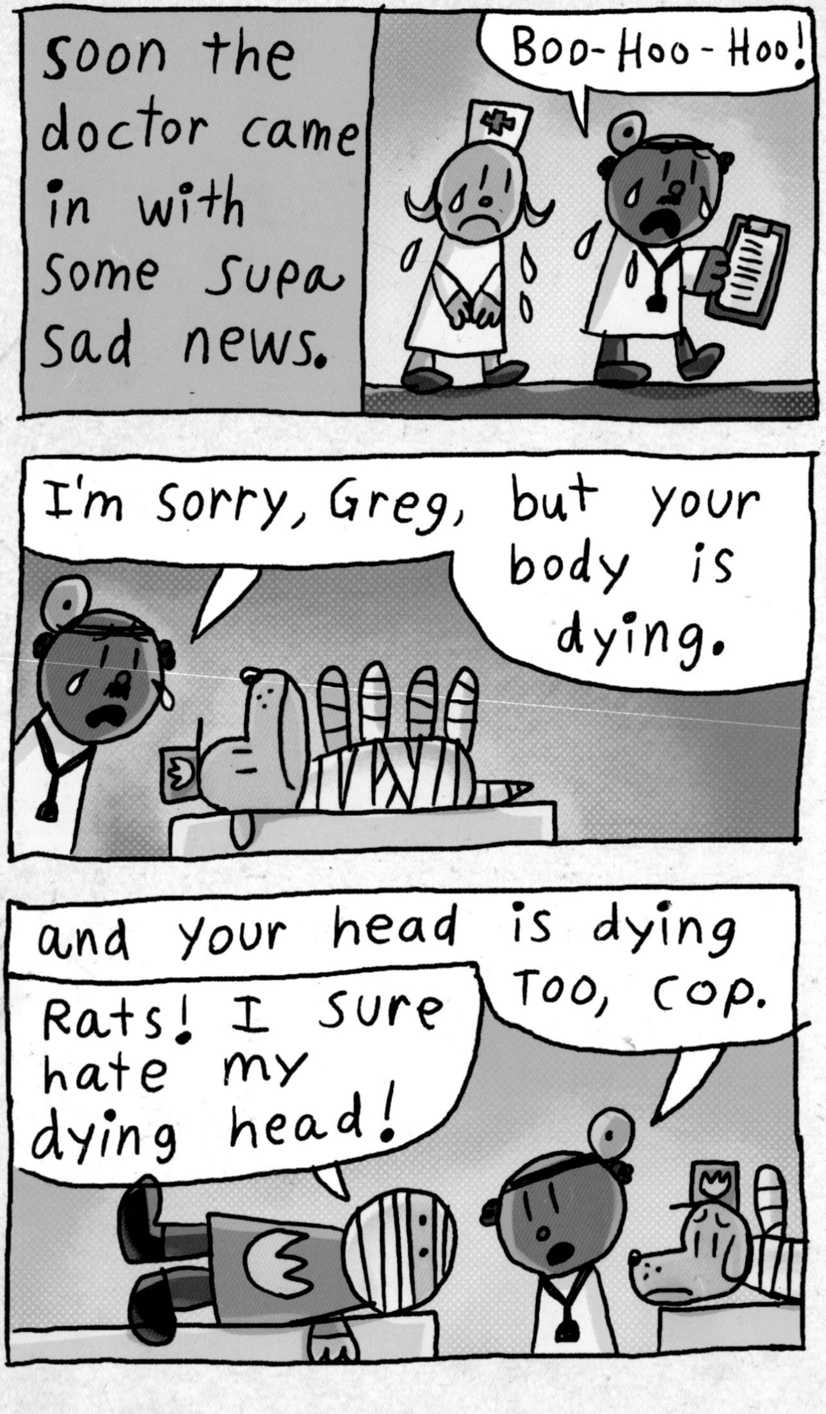
soon the doctor came in with some supa sad news.
Boo-Hoo-Hoo!
I'm sorry, Greg, but your body is dying.
and your head is dying Too, cop.
Rats! I sure hate my dying head!

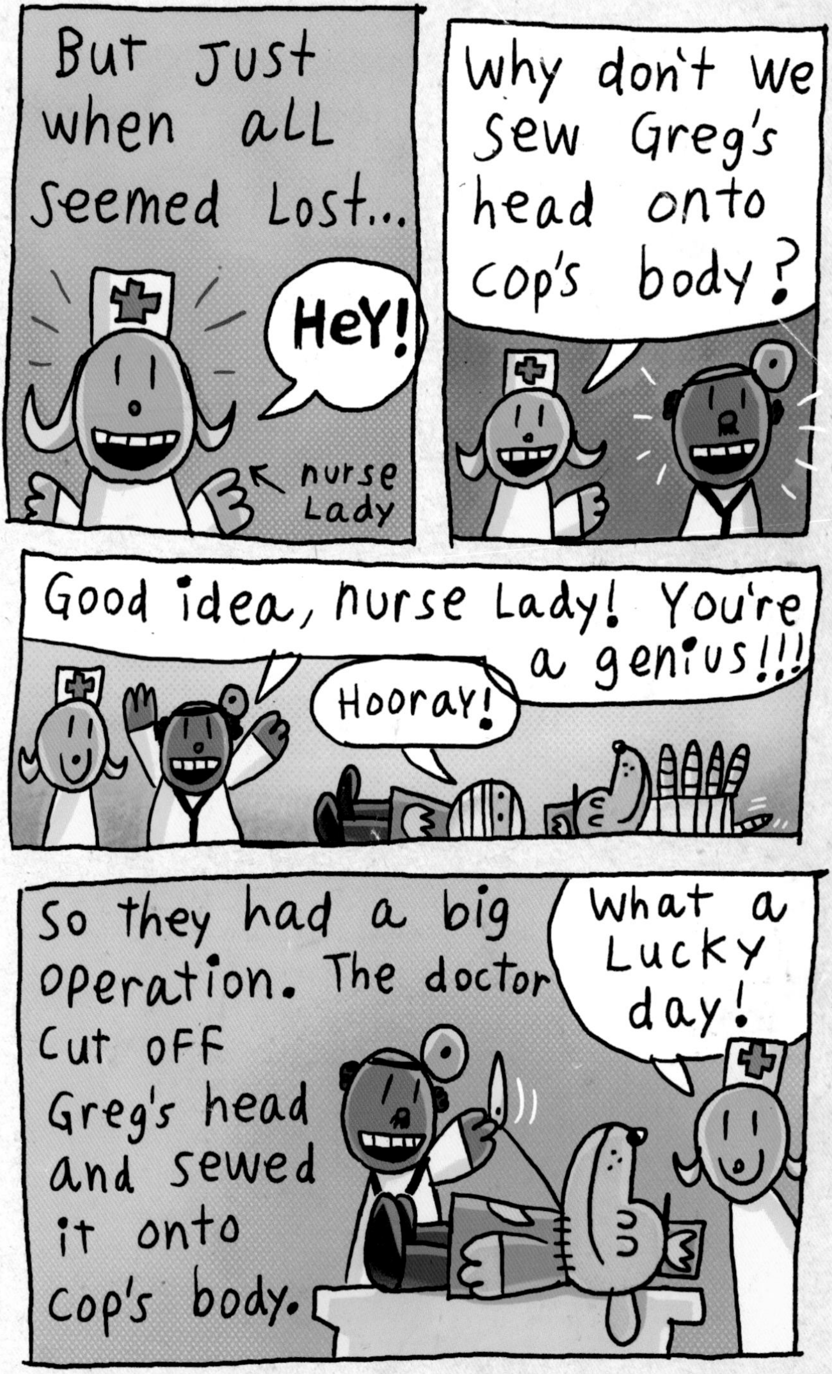

But just when all seemed lost...
HEY!
nurse Lady
Why don't we sew Greg's head onto cop's body?
Good idea, nurse Lady! You're a genius!!!
Hooray!
So they had a big operation. The doctor cut off Greg's head and sewed it onto cop's body.
What a lucky day!

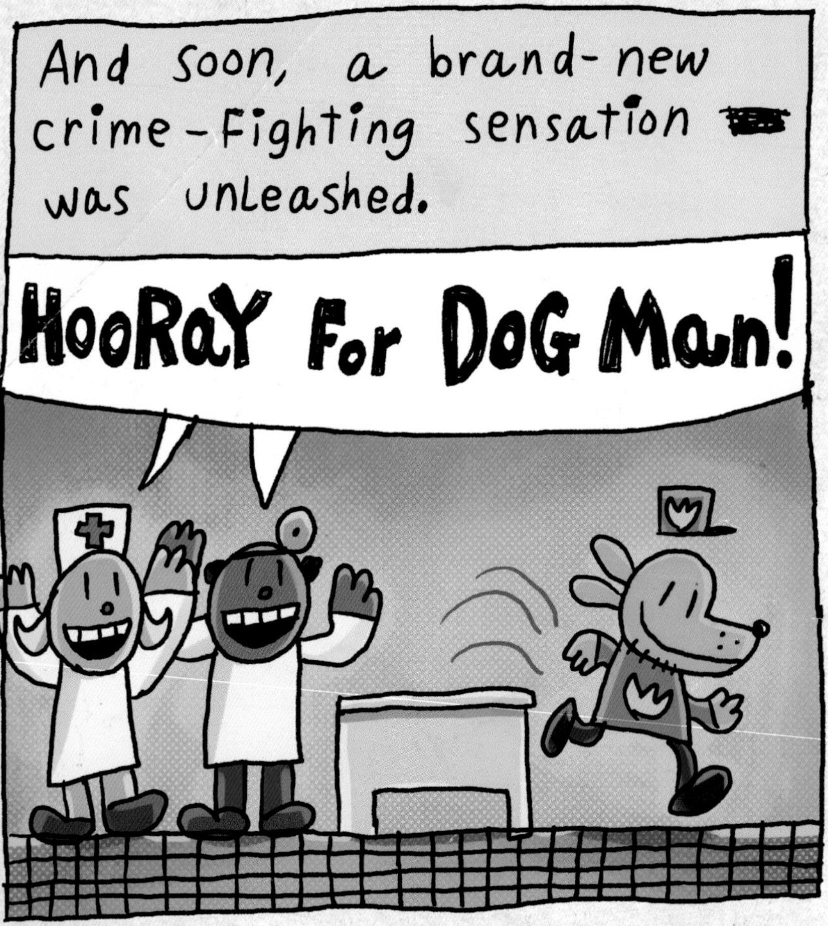
And soon, a brand-new crime-fighting sensation [redacted] was unleashed.
HOORAY For DOG Man!

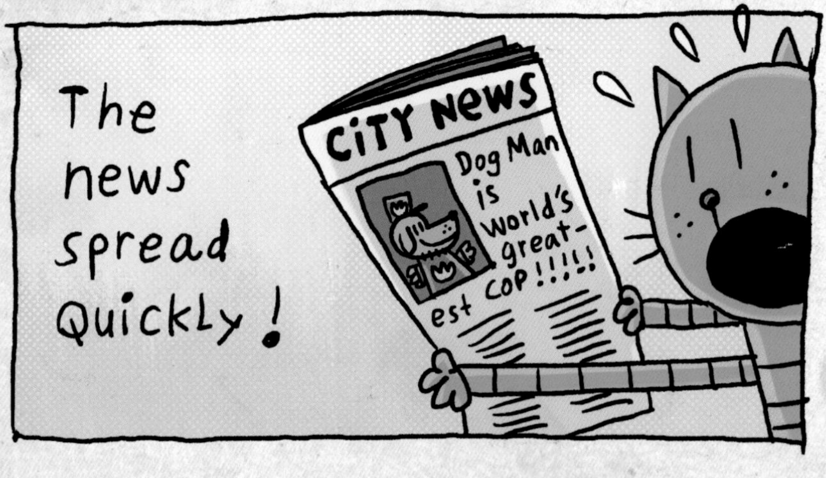
The news spread quickly!
CITY NEWS
Dog Man is world's great-est cop!!!!!

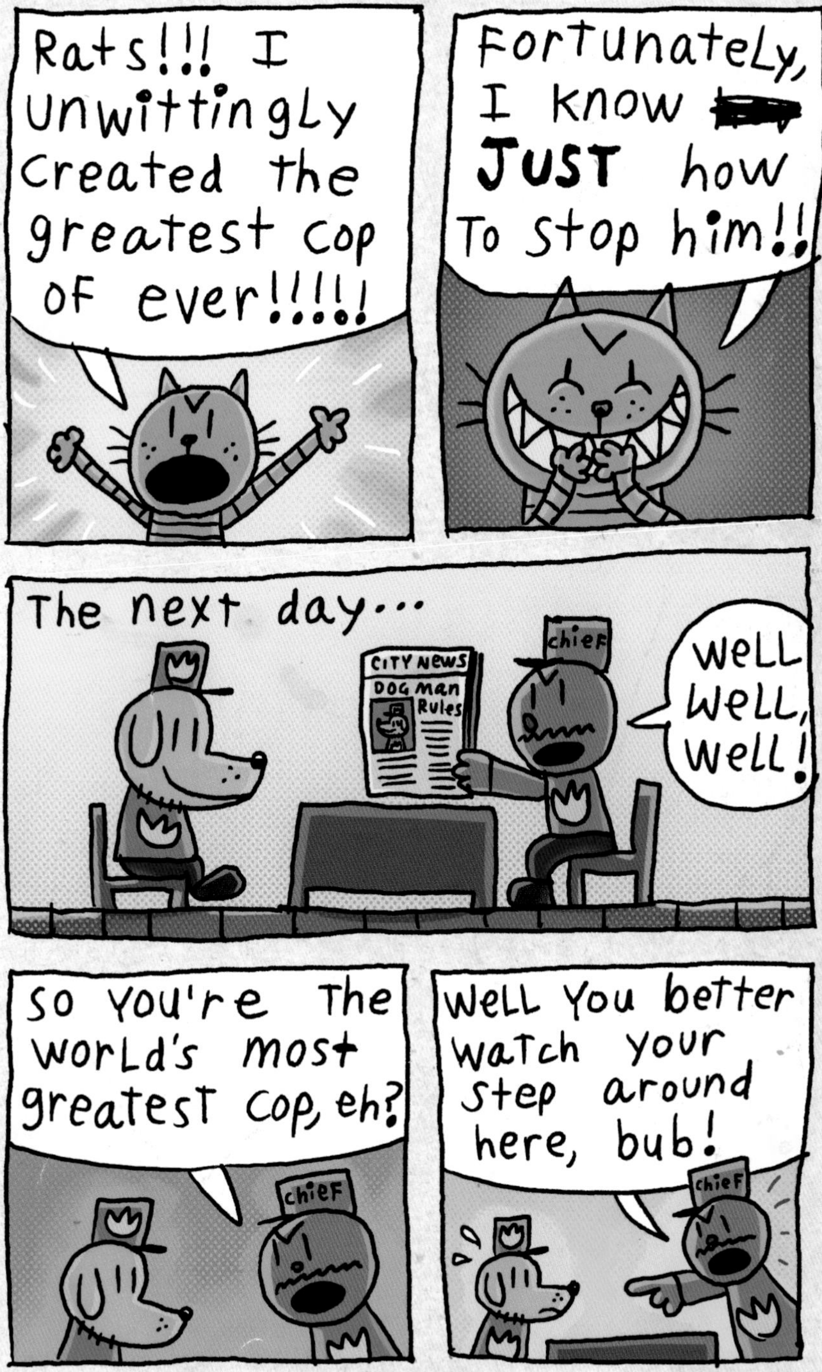

Rats!!! I unwittingly created the greatest cop of ever!!!!!
Fortunately, I know JUST how to stop him!!
The next day...
CITY NEWS
DOG MAN Rules
chief
Well Well, Well!
So you're the world's most greatest cop, eh?
chief
Well you better watch your step around here, bub!
chief

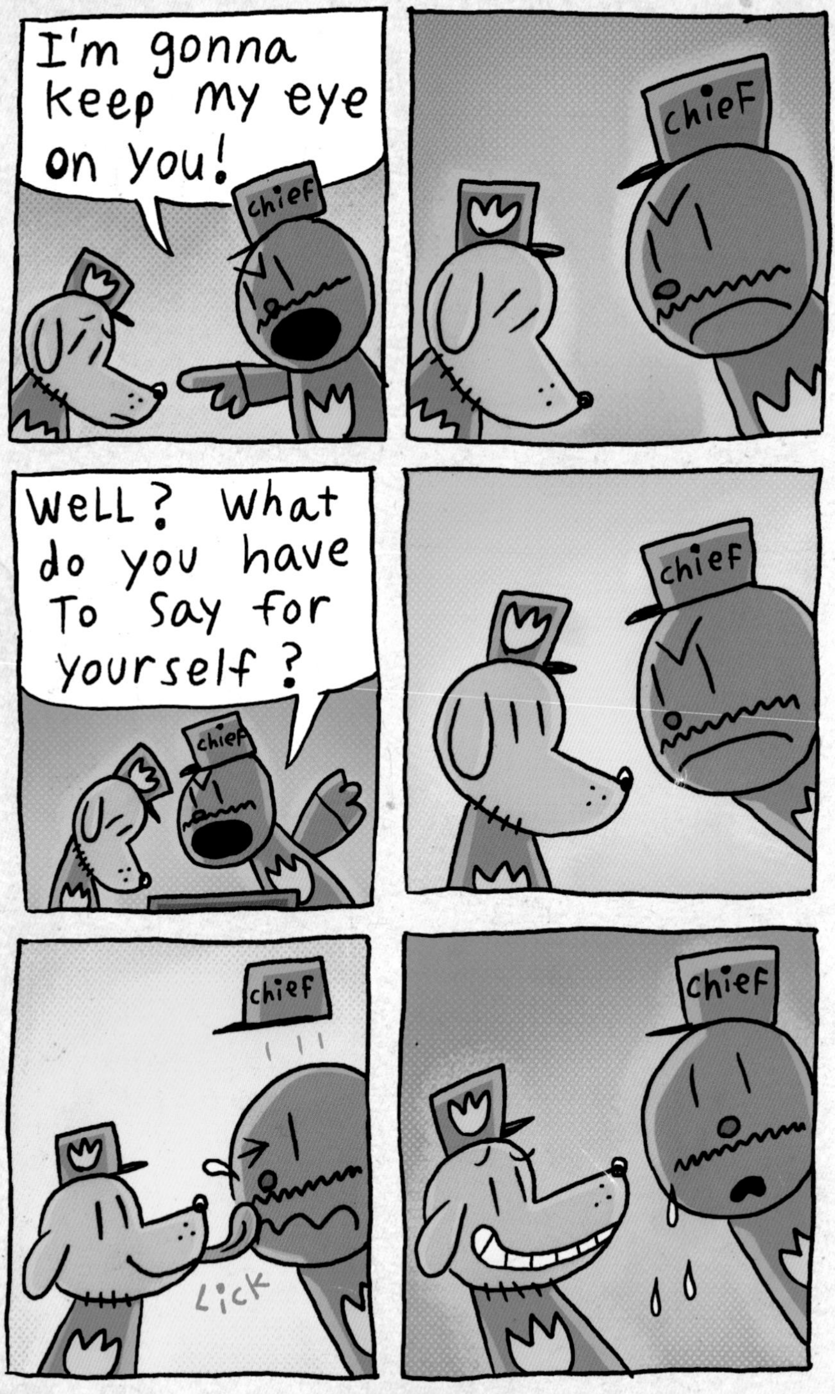
I'm gonna keep my eye on you!
chief
chief
WELL? What do you have To say for yourself?
chief
chief
chief
Lick
chief

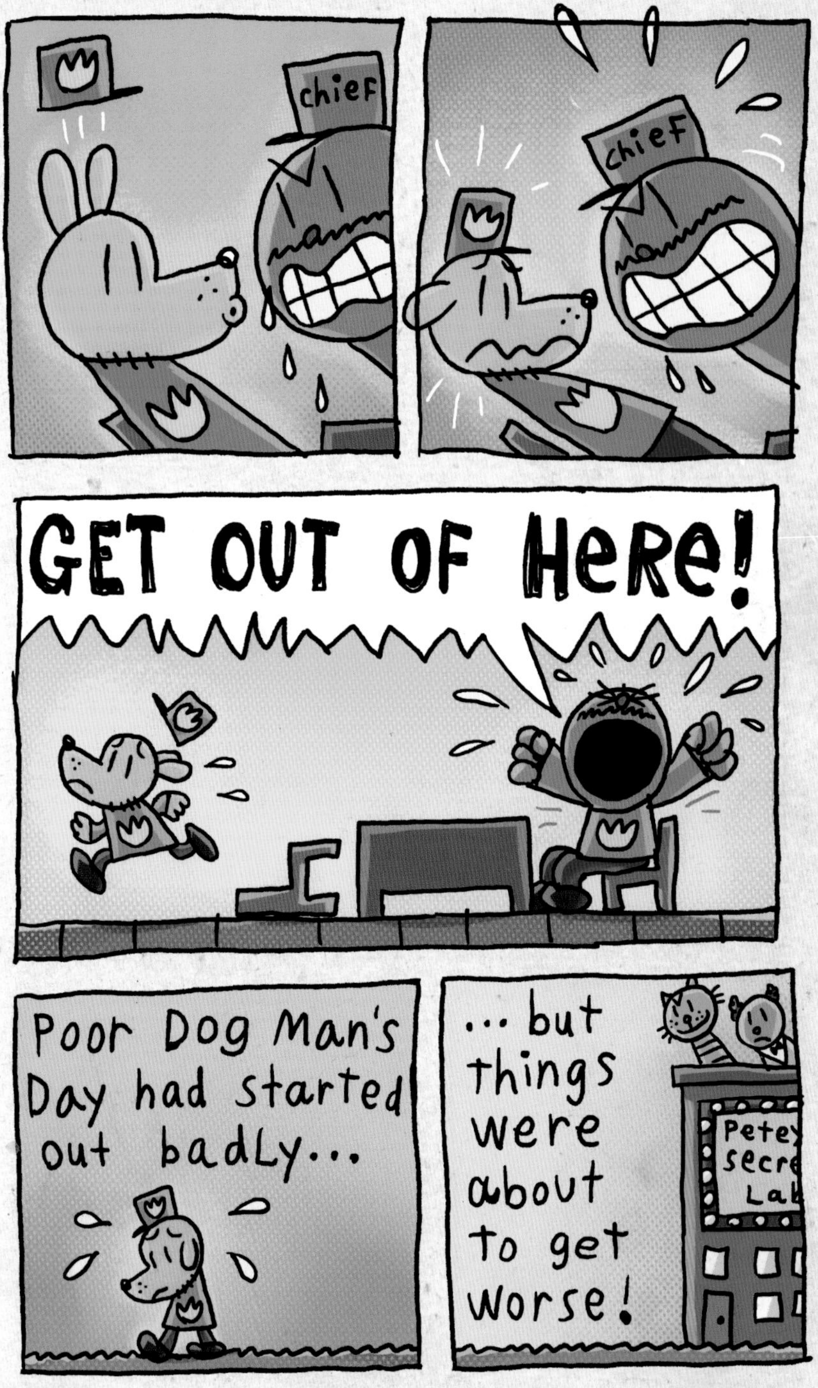
chief
chief
GET OUT OF HERE!
Poor Dog Man's Day had started out badly...
... but things were about to get worse!
Petey
secre
Lab

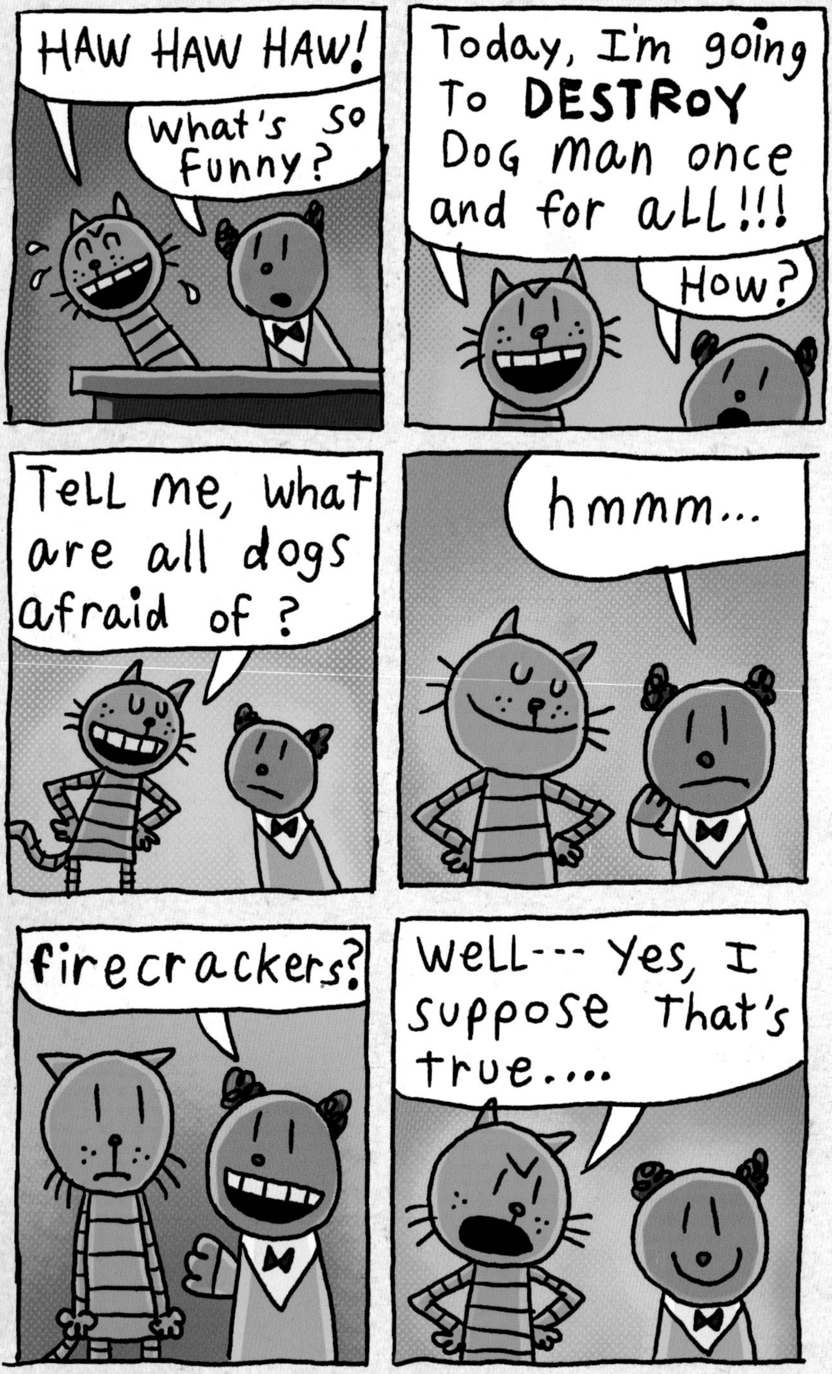
HAW HAW HAW!
What's so Funny?
Today, I'm going To DESTROY Dog man once and for aLL!!!
How?
TeLL me, what are all dogs afraid of?
hmmm...
firecrackers?
WeLL--- Yes, I suppose That's true....

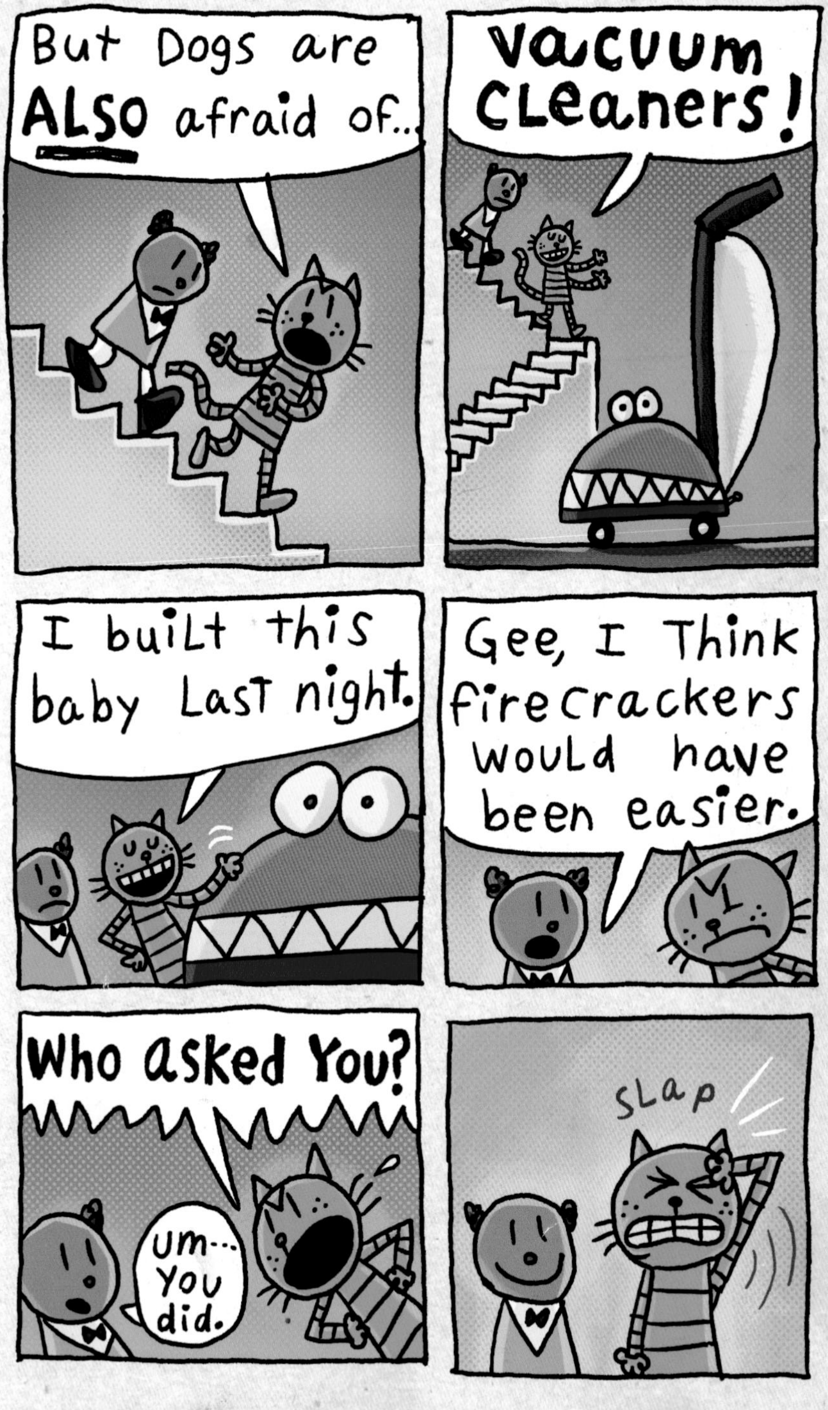
But Dogs are ALSO afraid of...
VACUUM CLEANERS!
I built this baby Last night.
Gee, I Think firecrackers would have been easier.
Who asked You?
Um... You did.
SLap

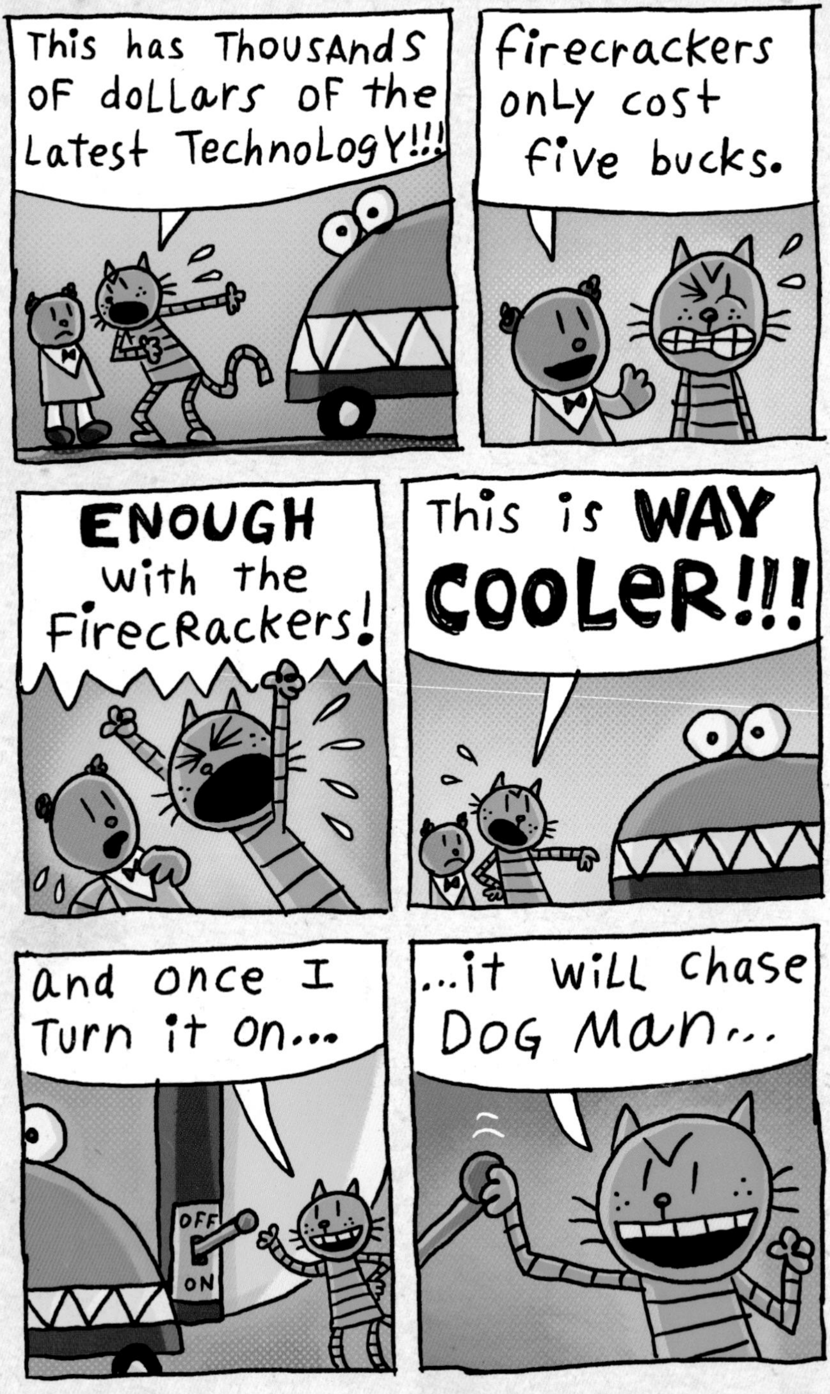
This has THOUSANDS OF dollars OF the Latest TechnoLogY!!!
firecrackers onLy cost five bucks.
ENOUGH with the FireCRackers!
This is WAY COOLER!!!
and once I Turn it on...
OFF
ON
...it will chase Dog Man...

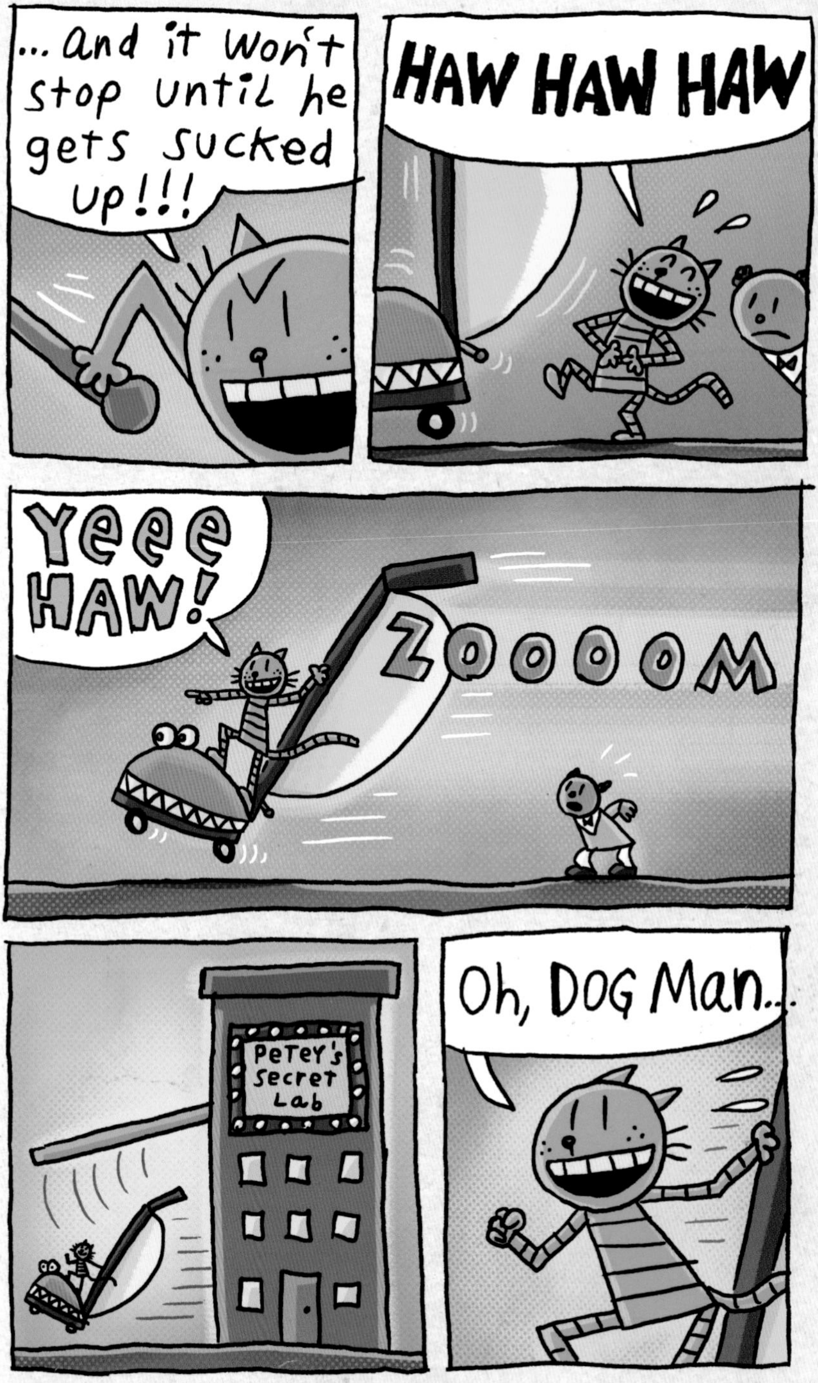
...and it won't stop until he gets sucked up!!!
HAW HAW HAW
Yeee HAW!
ZOOOOM
Petey's Secret Lab
Oh, DOG Man...

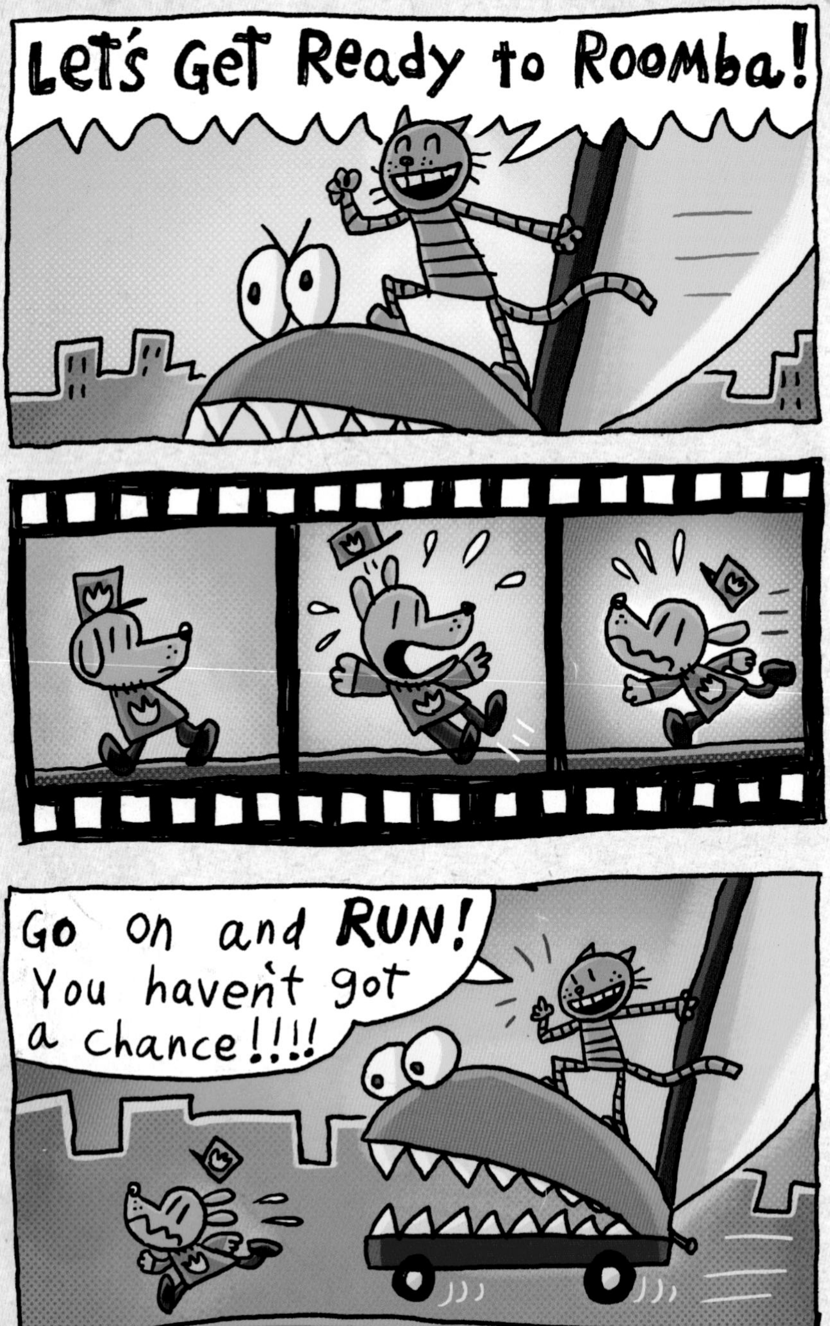
Let's Get Ready to Roomba!
Go on and RUN! You haven't got a chance!!!!

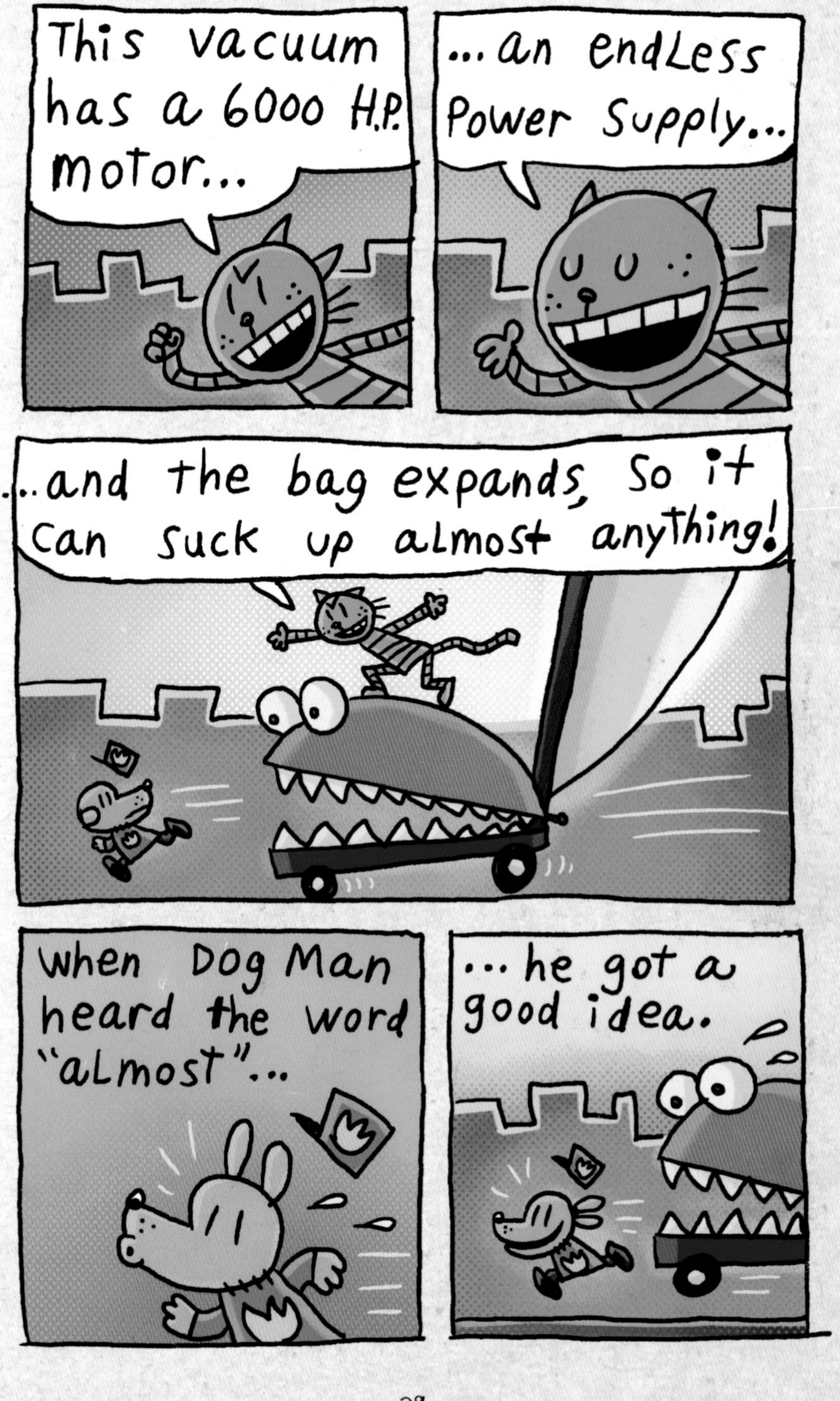
This vacuum has a 6000 H.P. motor...
...an endLess Power Supply...
...and the bag expands, So it can suck up aLmost anything!
When Dog Man heard the word "aLmost"...
...he got a good idea.

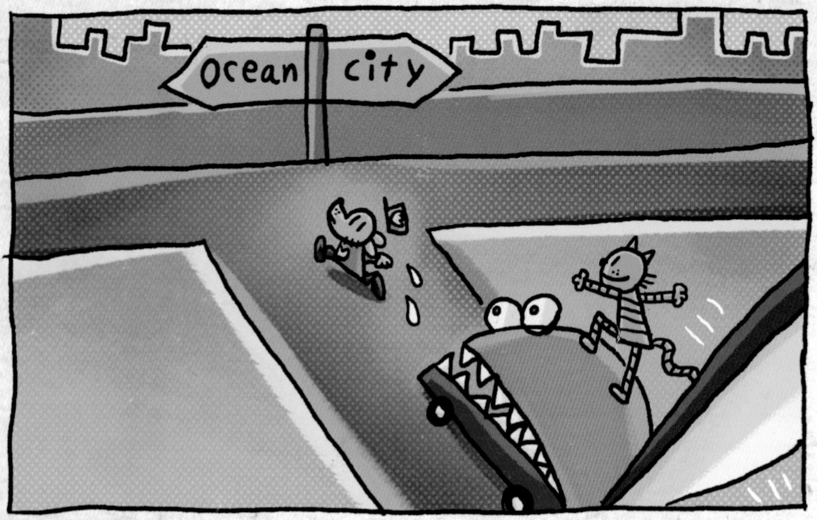
Ocean
city

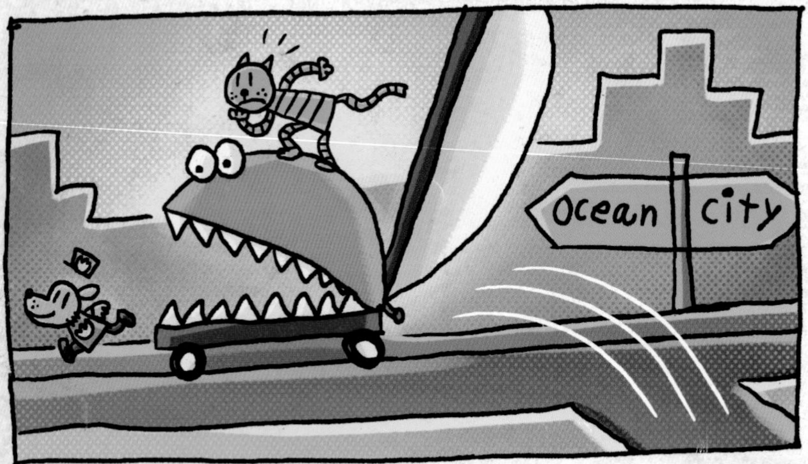
Ocean
city

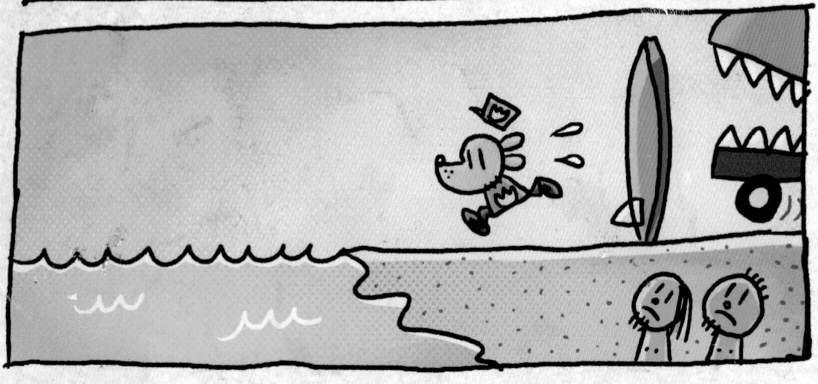

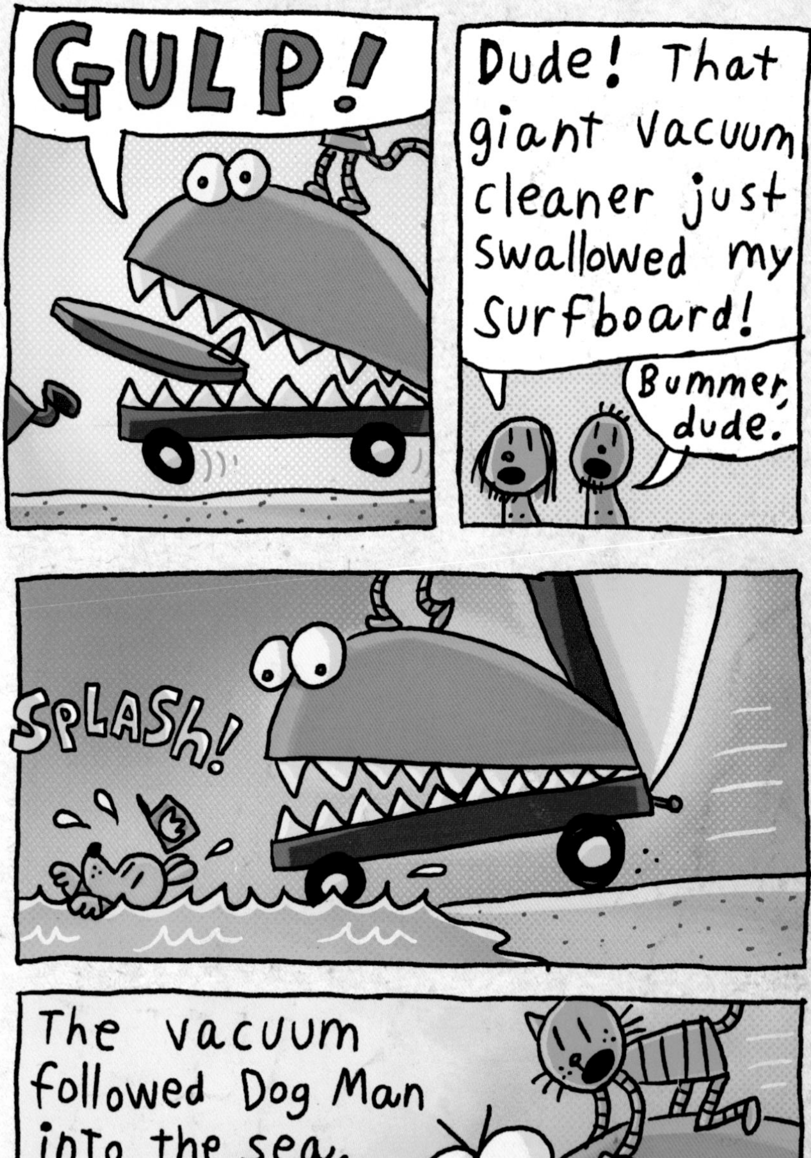
GULP!
Dude! That giant vacuum cleaner just swallowed my surfboard!
Bummer, dude.
SPLASH!
The vacuum followed Dog Man into the sea.

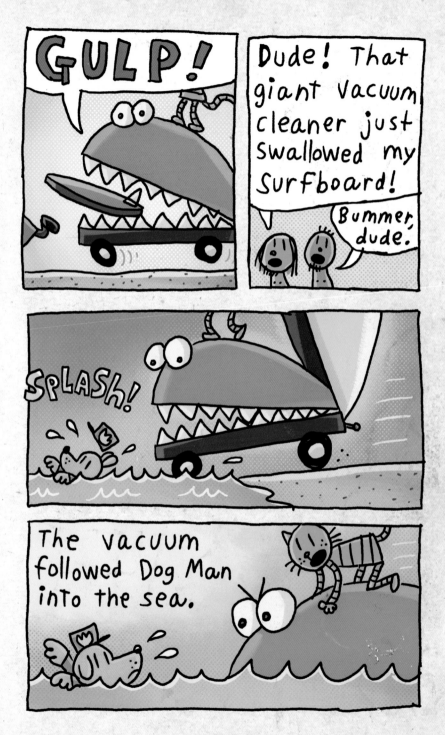

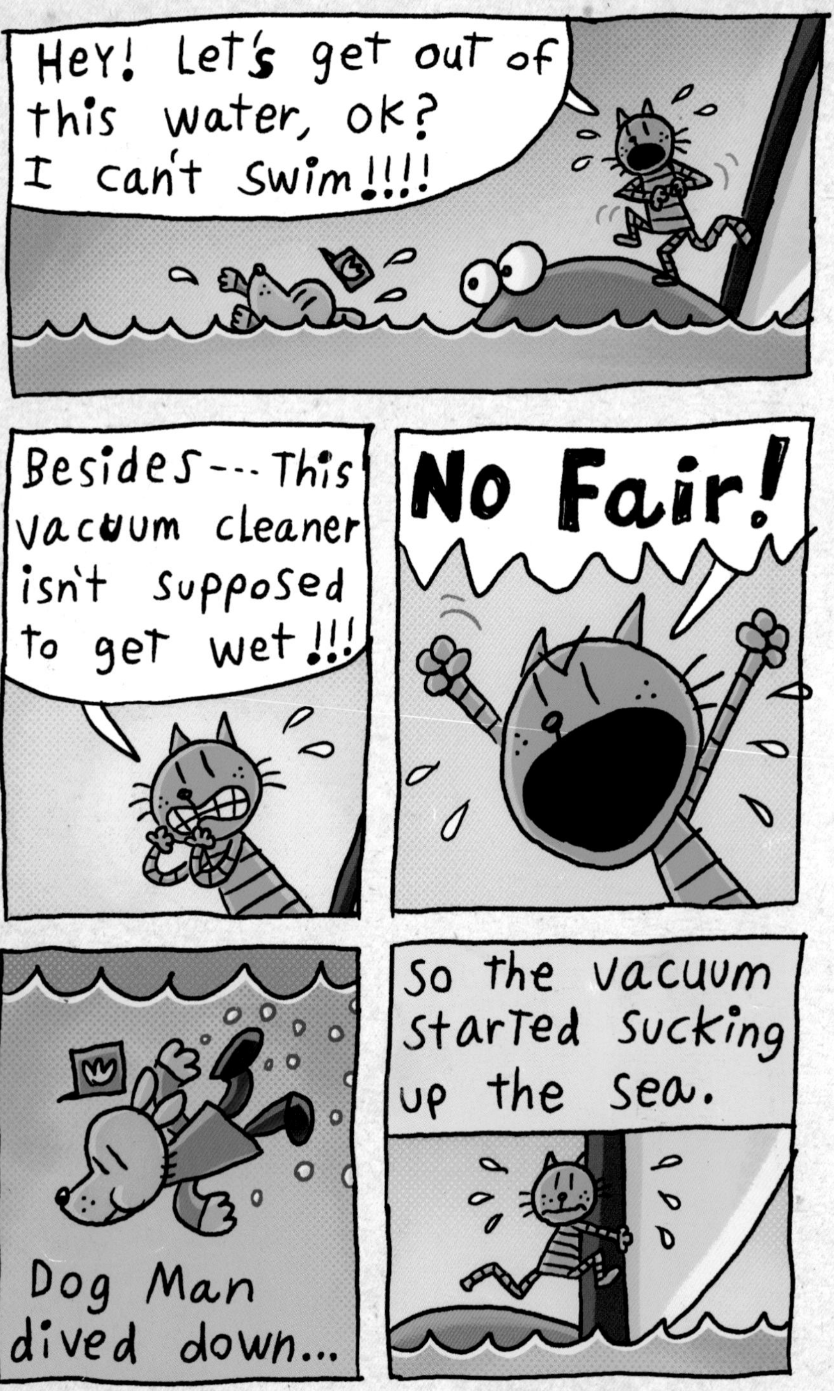

HEY! Let's get out of this water, OK? I can't swim!!!!
Besides--- This vacuum cleaner isn't supposed to get wet!!!
No Fair!
Dog Man dived down...
So the vacuum started sucking up the sea.

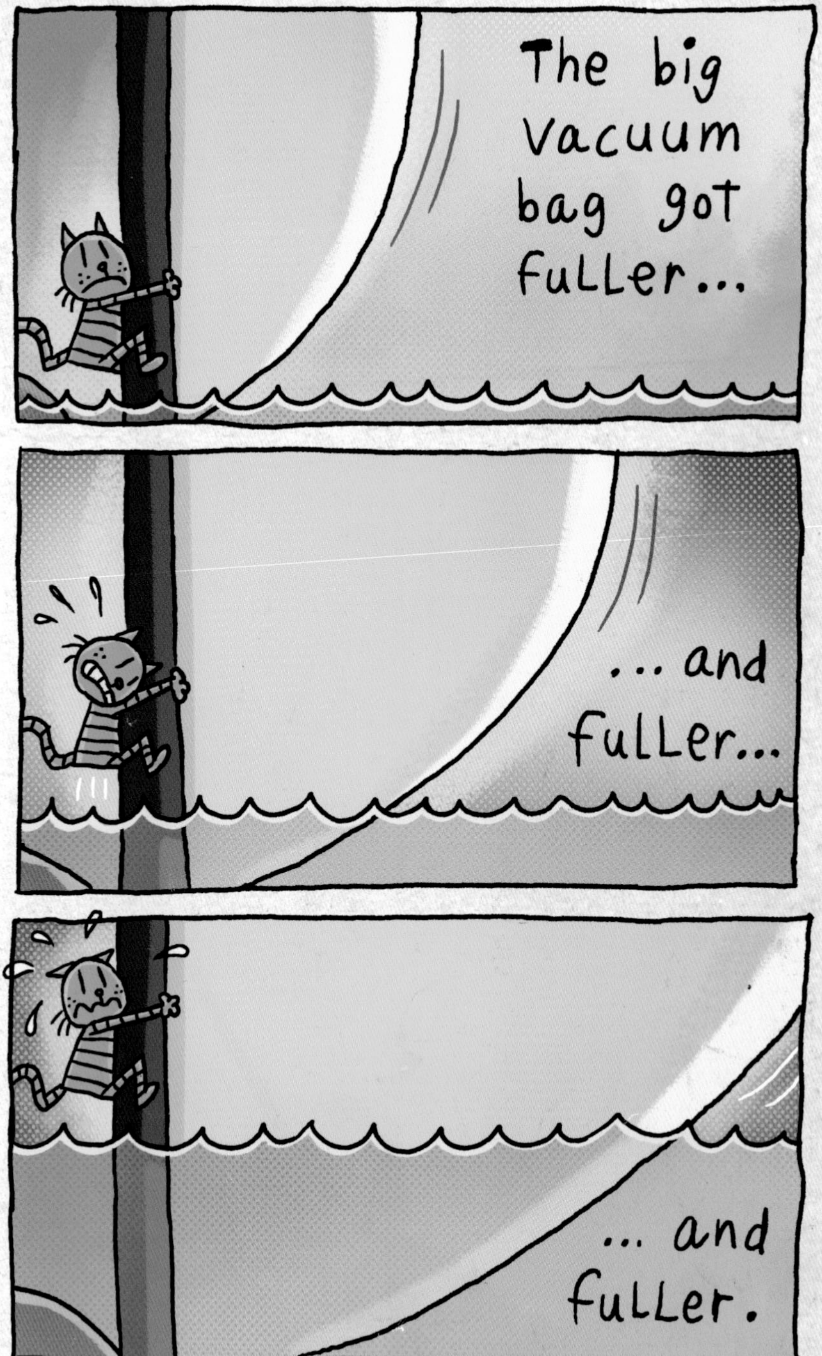
The big vacuum bag got fuller...
... and fuller...
... and fuller.

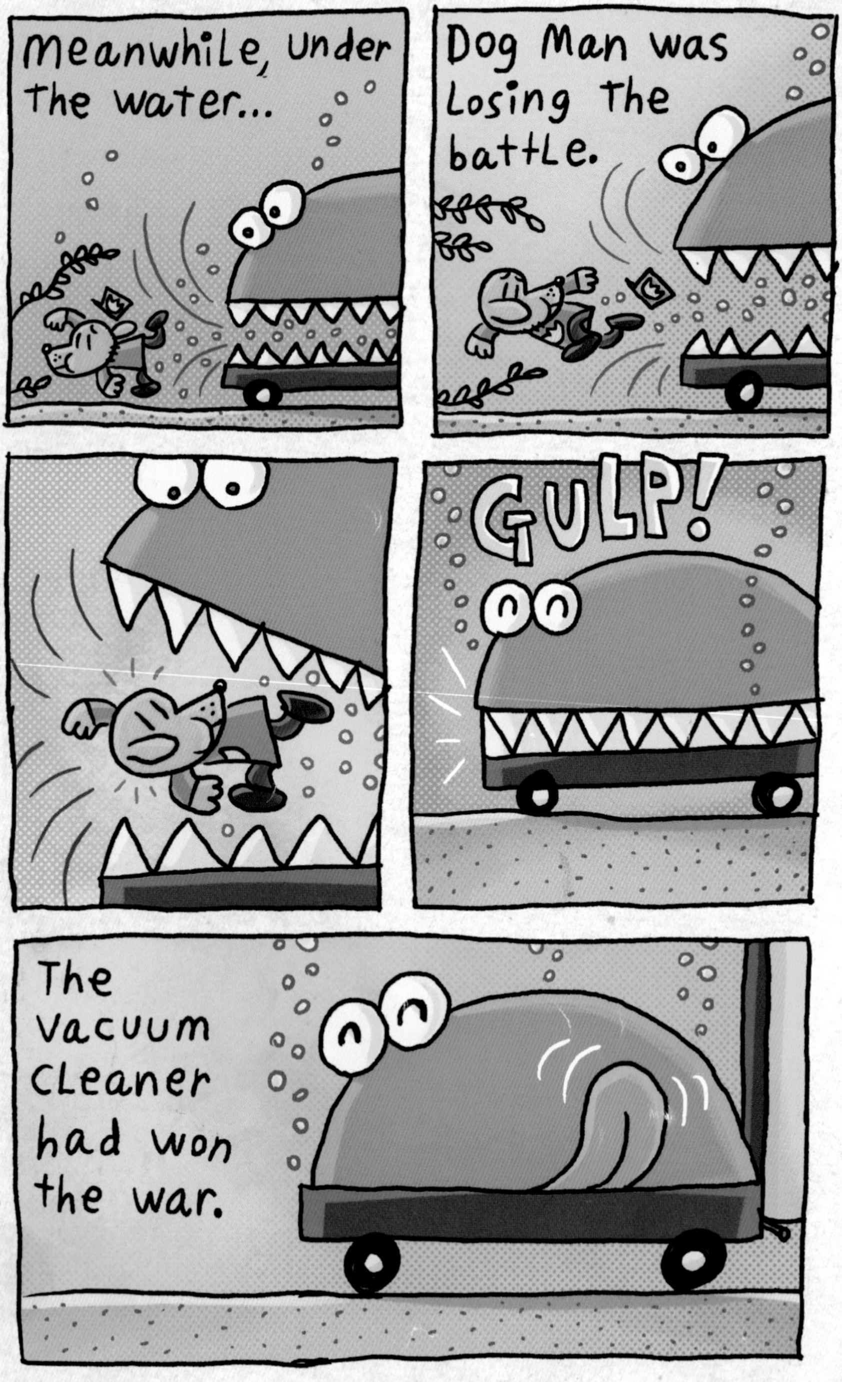
Meanwhile, under the water...
Dog Man was Losing the battLe.
GULP!
The vacuum cLeaner had won the war.

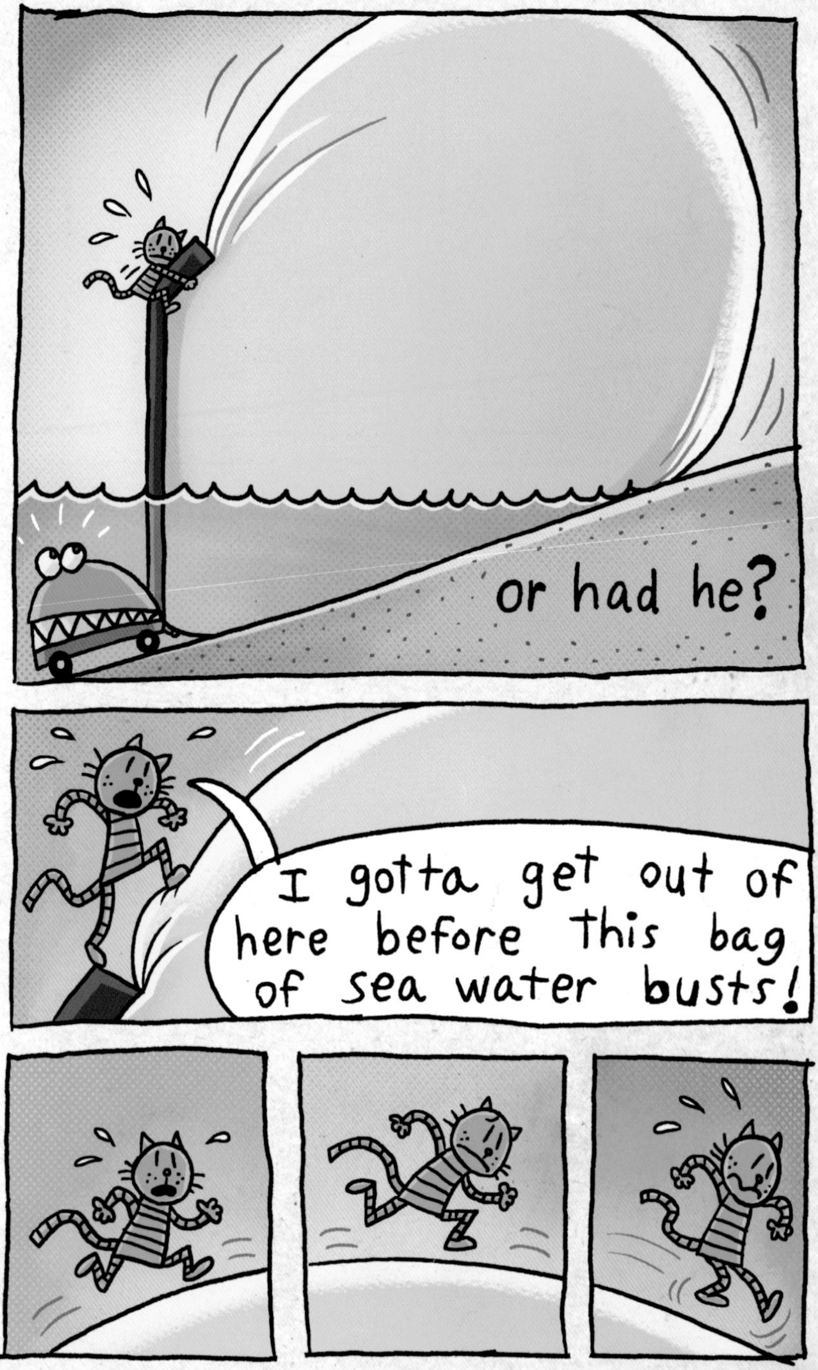
or had he?
I gotta get out of here before this bag of sea water busts!

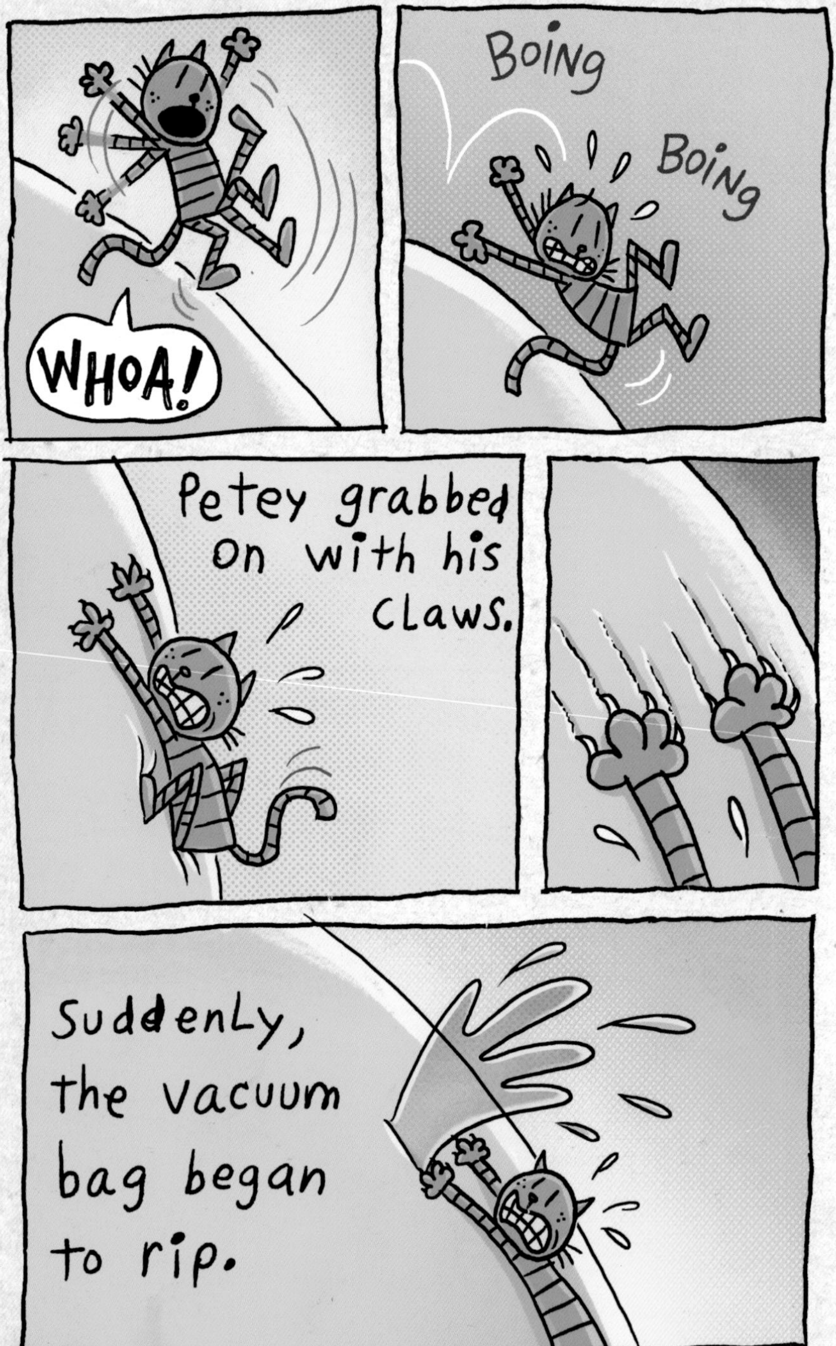
WHOA!
Boing
Boing
Petey grabbed on with his claws.
Suddenly, the vacuum bag began to rip.

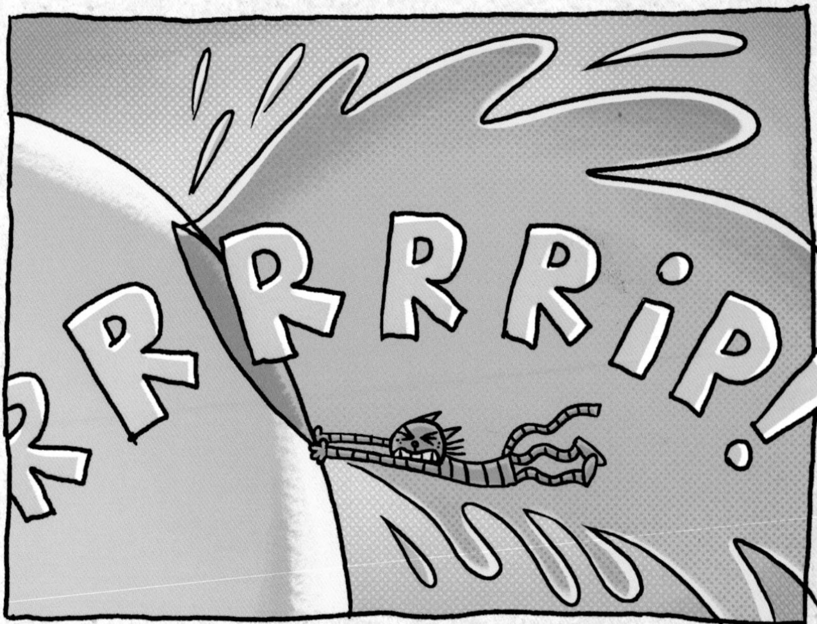
RRRRRRIP!

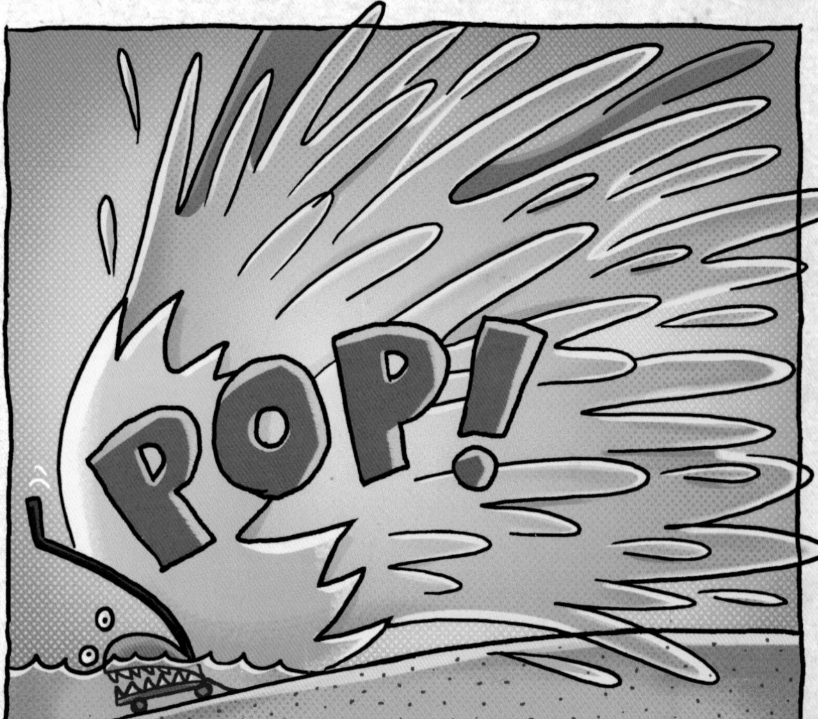
POP!

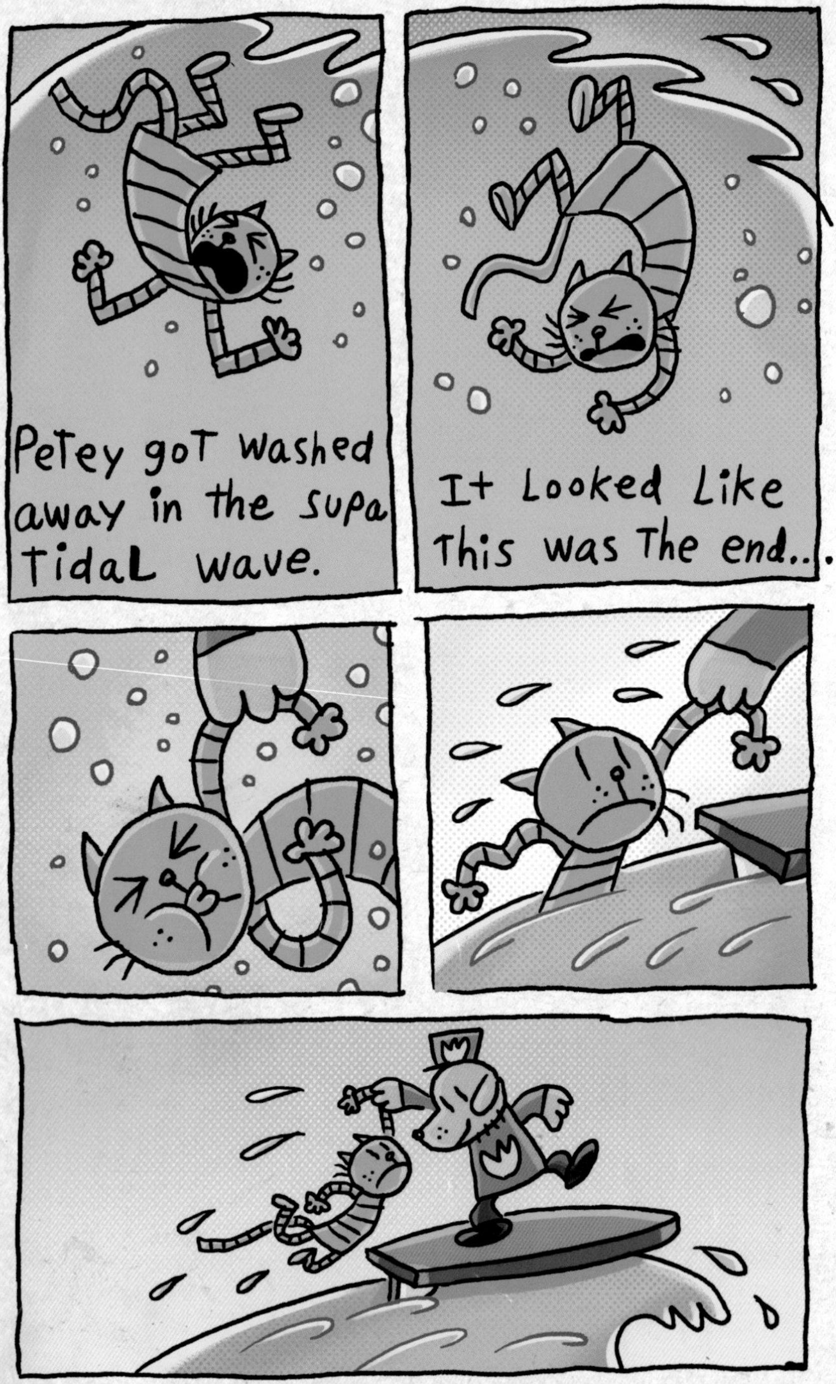
Petey got washed away in the supa Tidal wave.
It Looked Like This was The end...

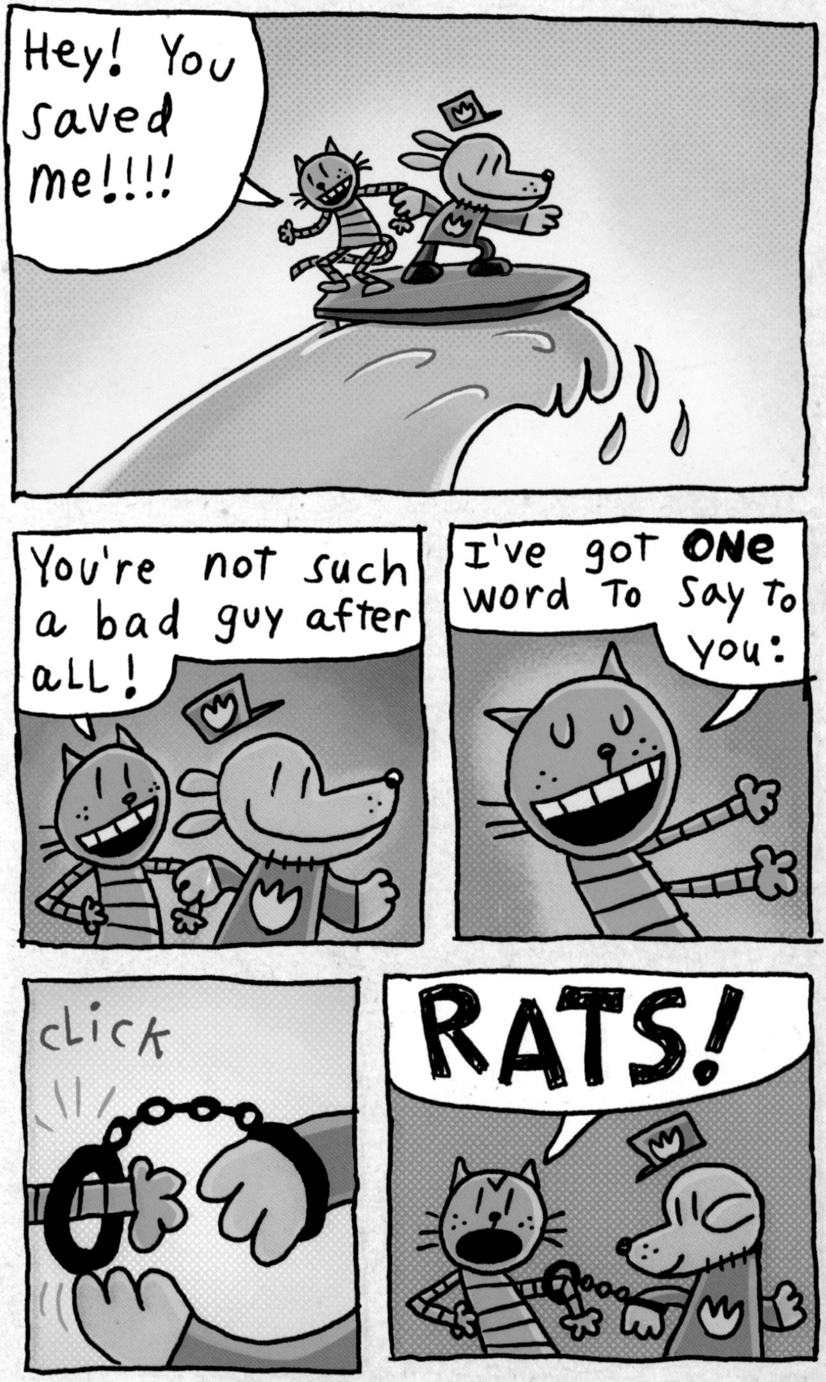
Hey! You saved me!!!!
You're not such a bad guy after all!
I've got ONE word To say To you:
click
RATS!

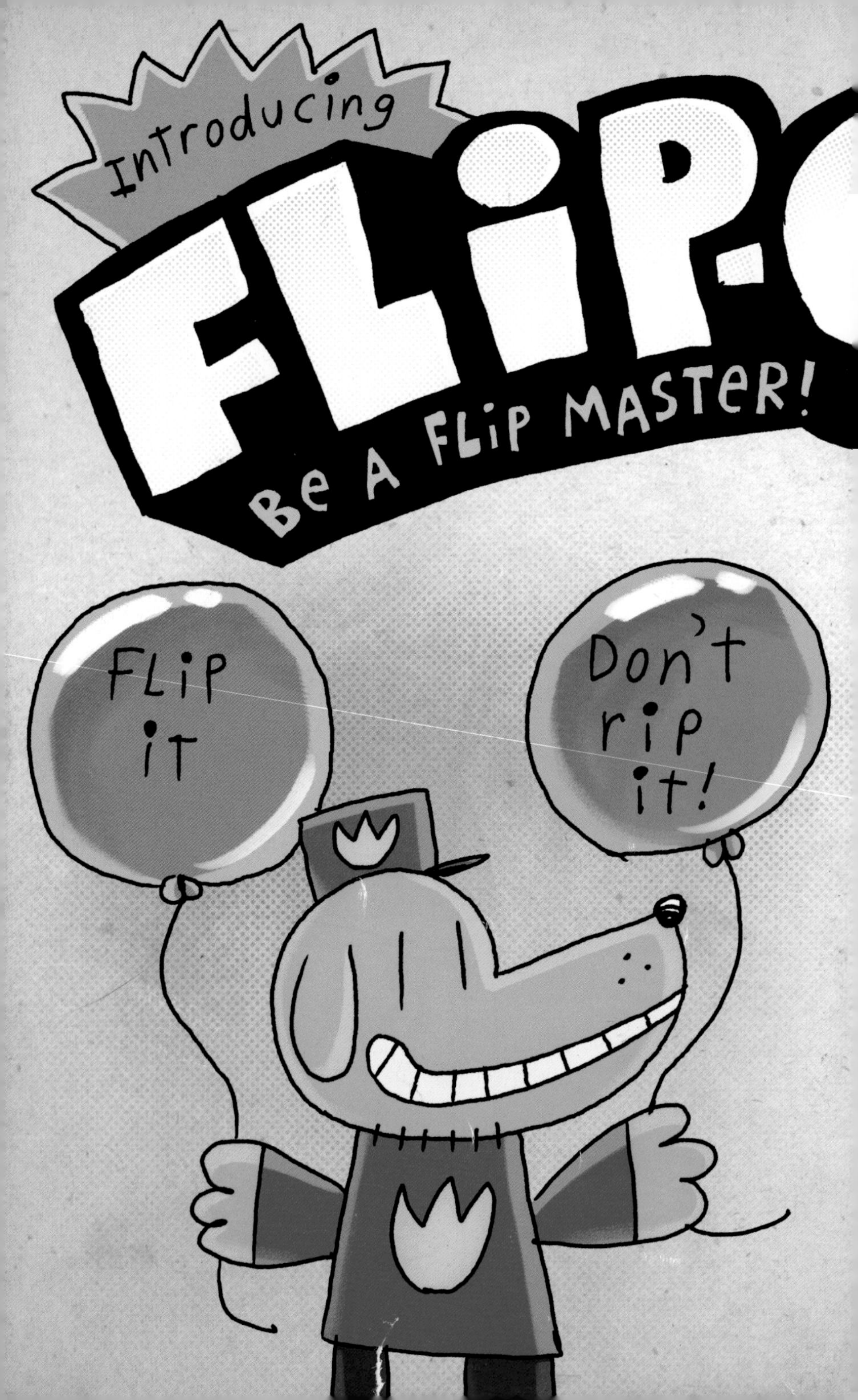
Introducing
FLIP-O
Be A FLIP MASTER!
FLIP it
Don't rip it!

O-RAMA

EXTRA CHEESY

Here's How it Works:

STEP 1.
First, Place your Left hand inside the dotted Lines marked "Left hand here". Hold The book open FLAT!

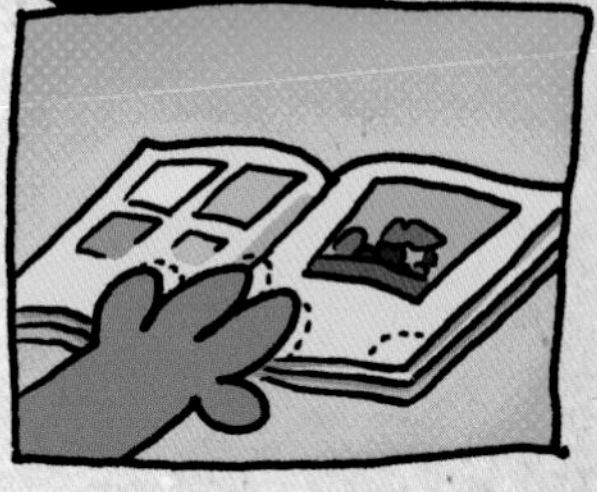

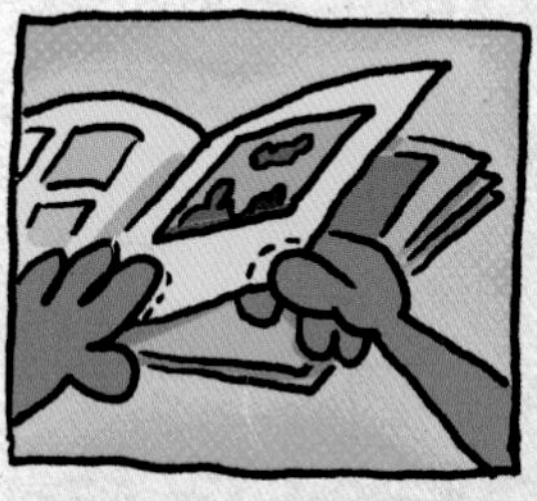

STEP 2:
Grasp the right-hand Page with your Thumb and index finger (inside the dotted Lines marked "Right Thumb Here").

STEP 3:
Now QUICKLY flip the right-hand page back and forth until the Picture appears to be Animated.

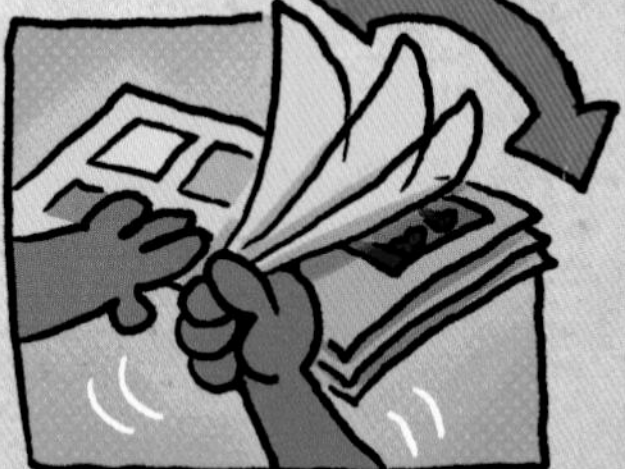

(For extra fun, try adding your own sound-effects!)

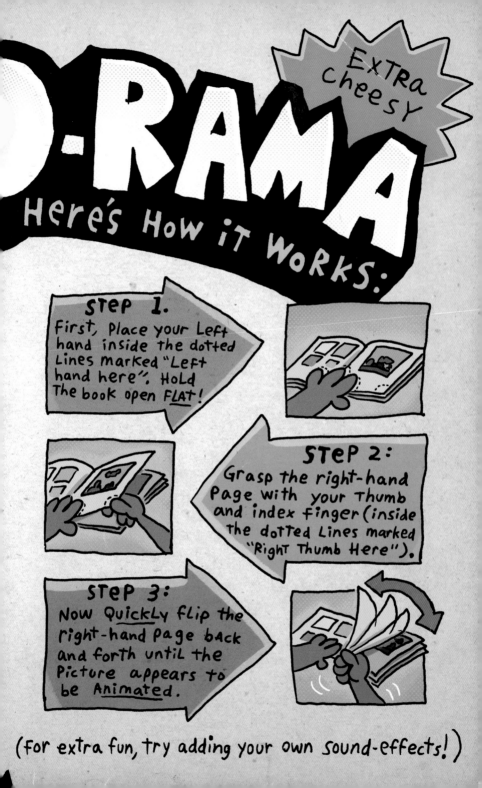

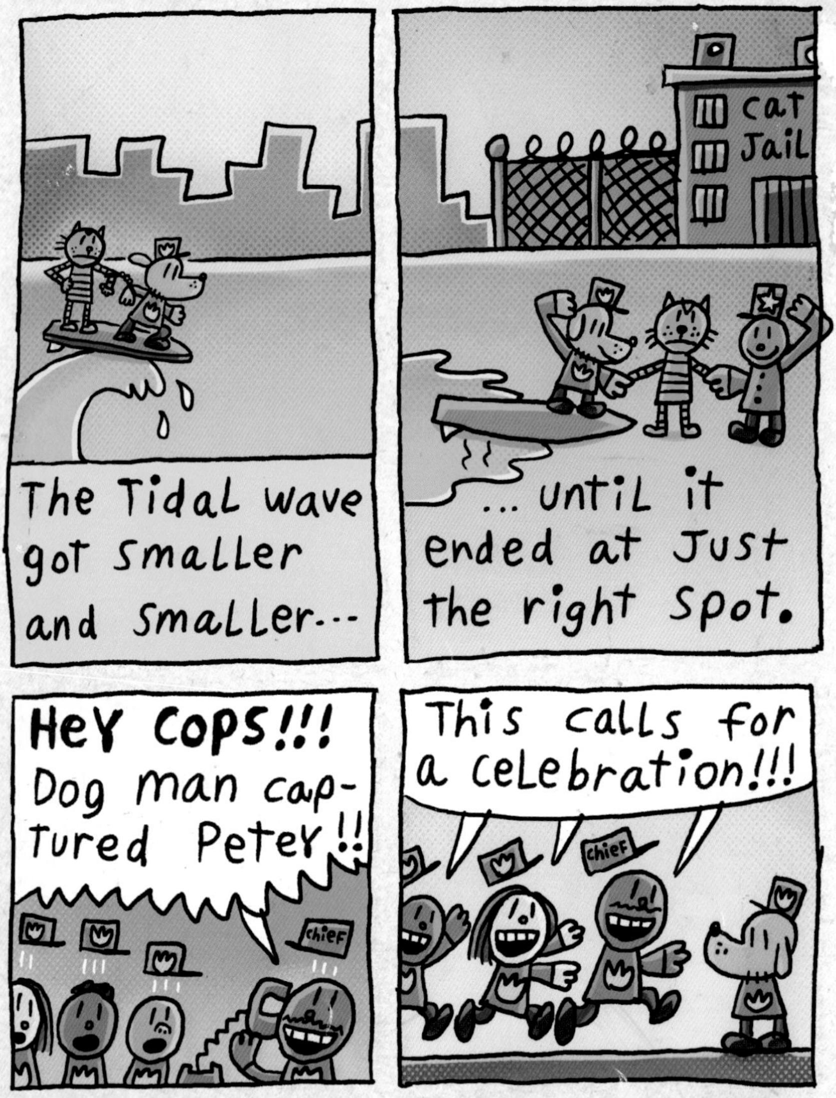
The Tidal wave got smaller and smaller...
Cat Jail
... until it ended at Just the right spot.
Hey COPS!!! Dog man captured Peter!!
chief
This calls for a celebration!!!
chief

Remember, Flip only page 43.
Be sure you can see the picture on page 43 **AND** the one on page 45 while you flip.

Left hand here.

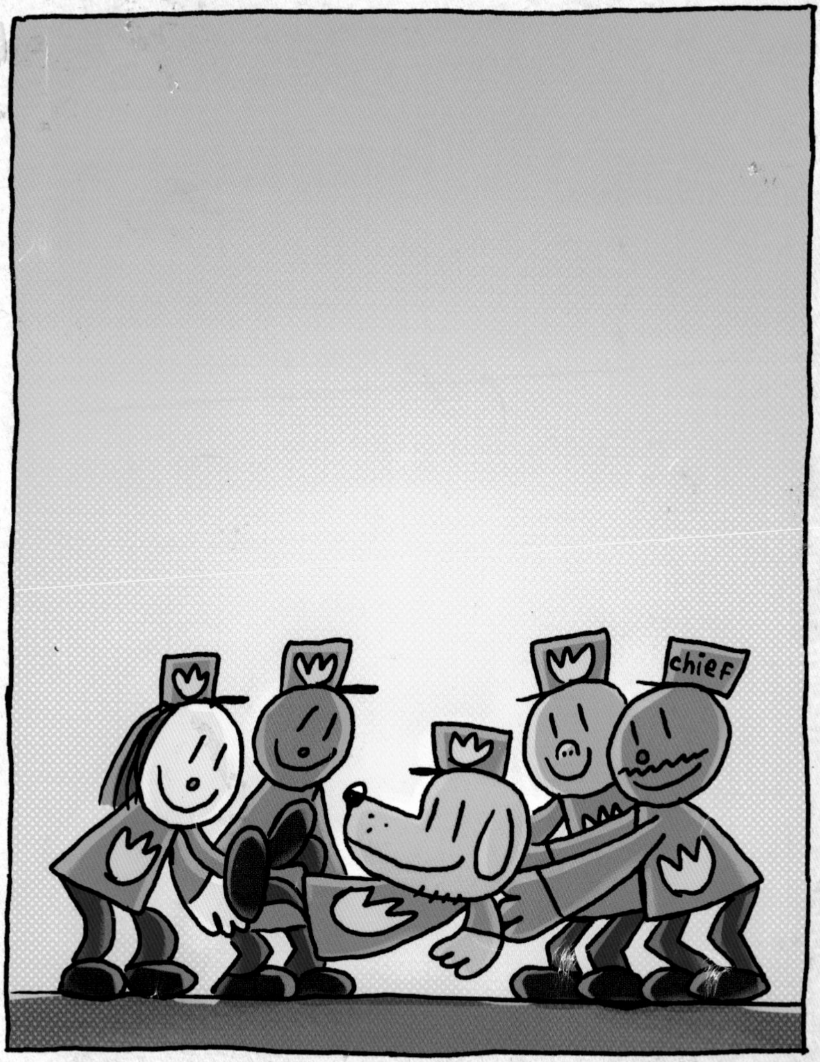
chief

For he's a JoLLy good doggy!

Right Thumb here.

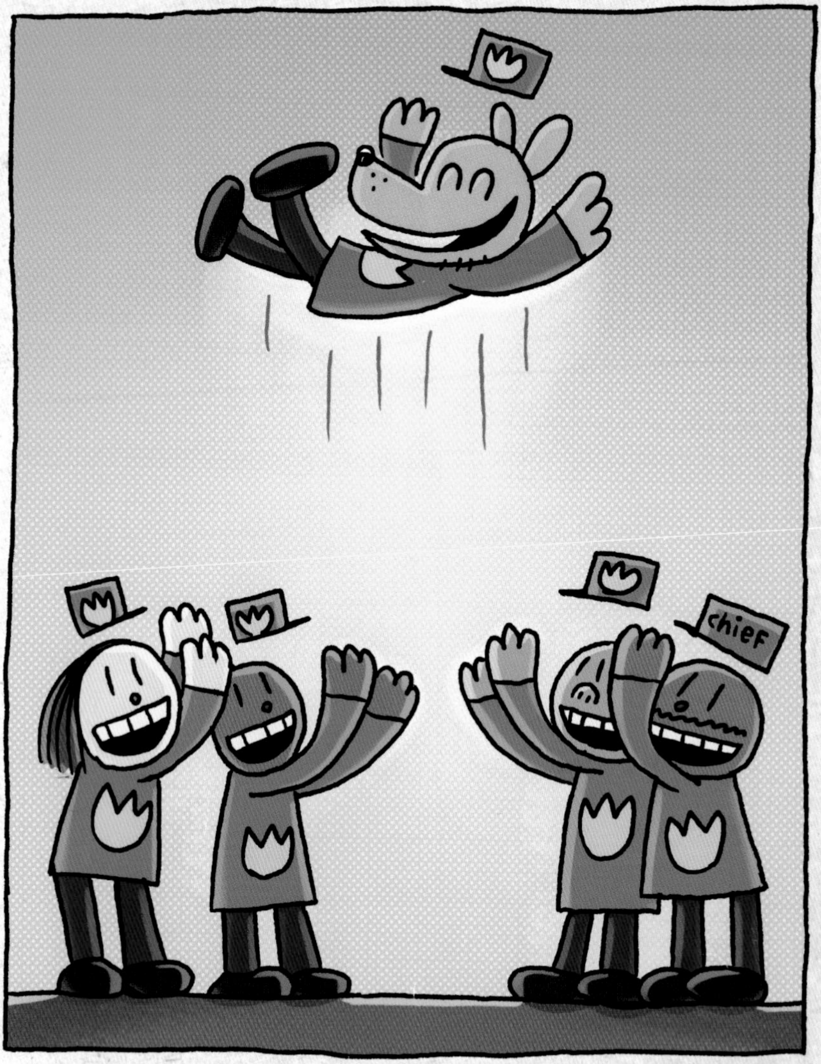
chief

For he's a
JoLLy good
doggy!

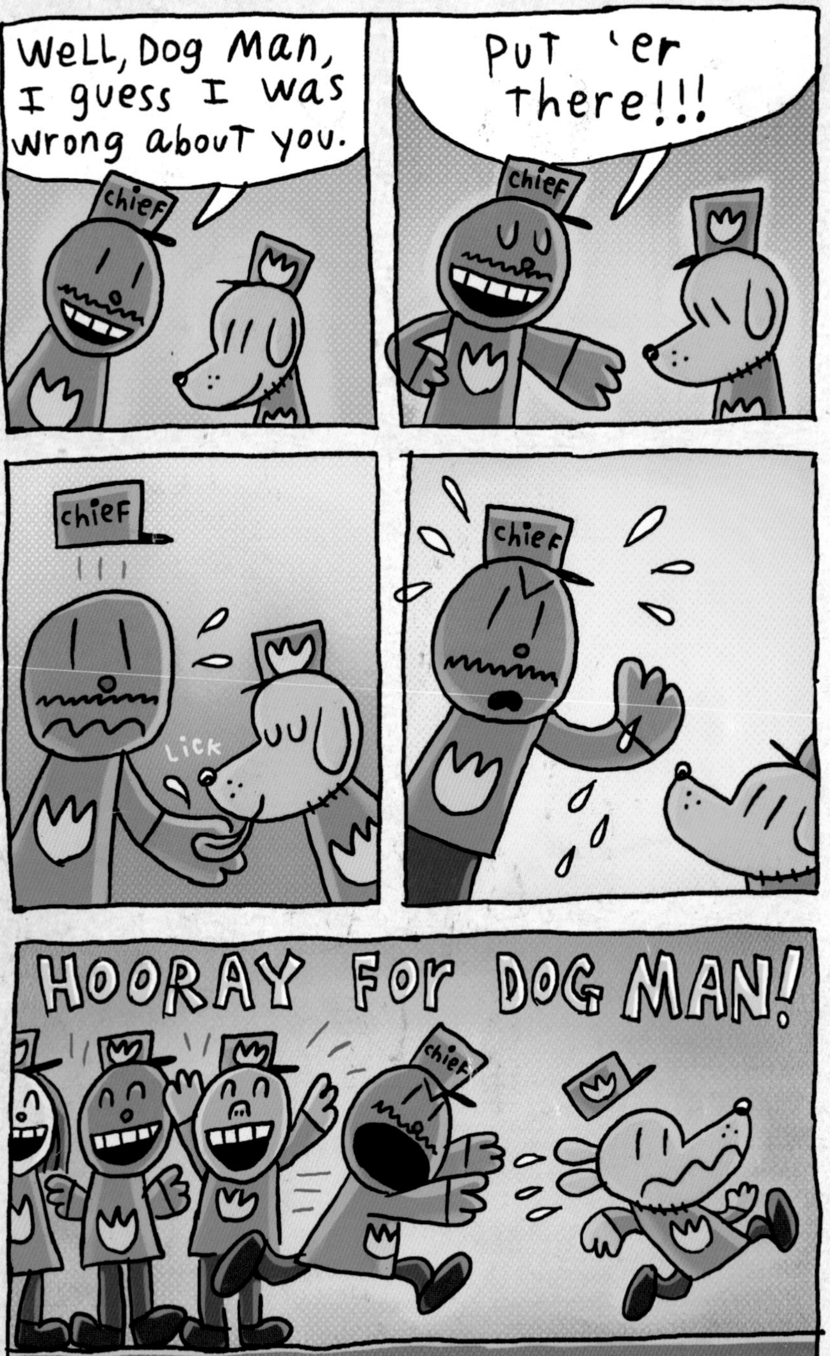
WeLL, Dog Man, I guess I was wrong about you.
chief
PuT 'er There!!!
chief
chief
Lick
chief
HOORAY FOR DOG MAN!
chief

CHAPTER 2

ROBO CHIEF

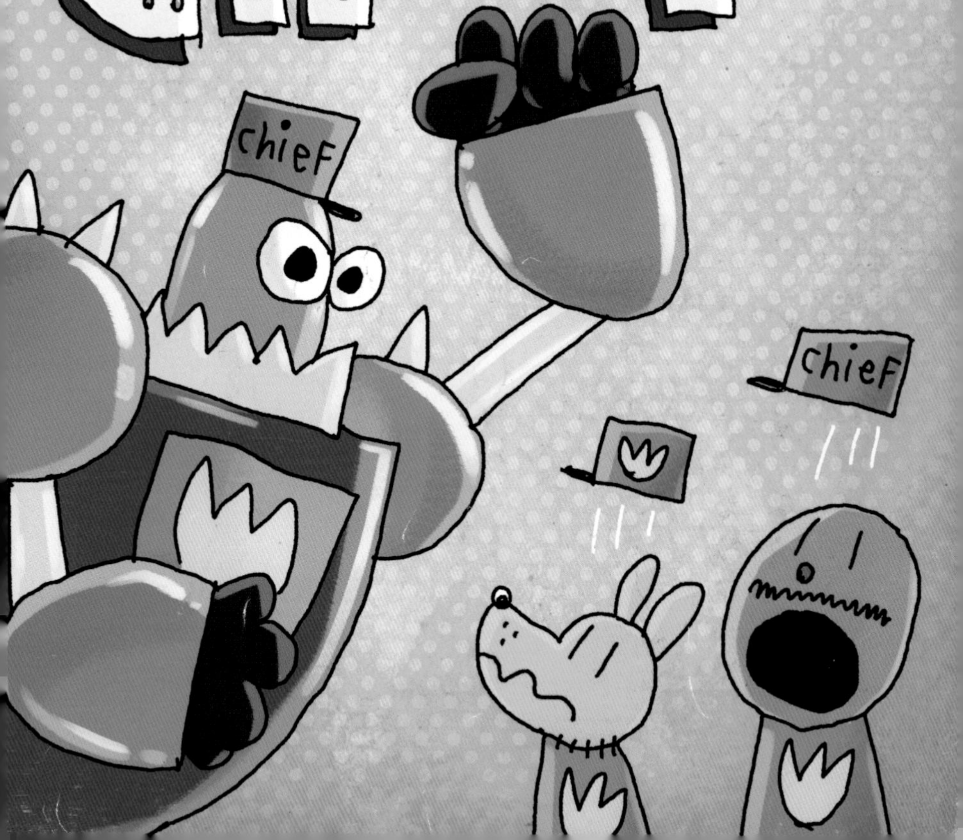
chief
chief

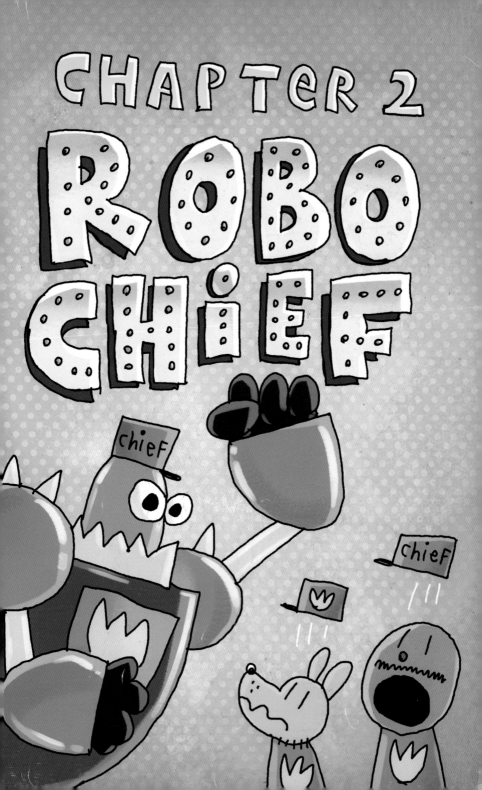

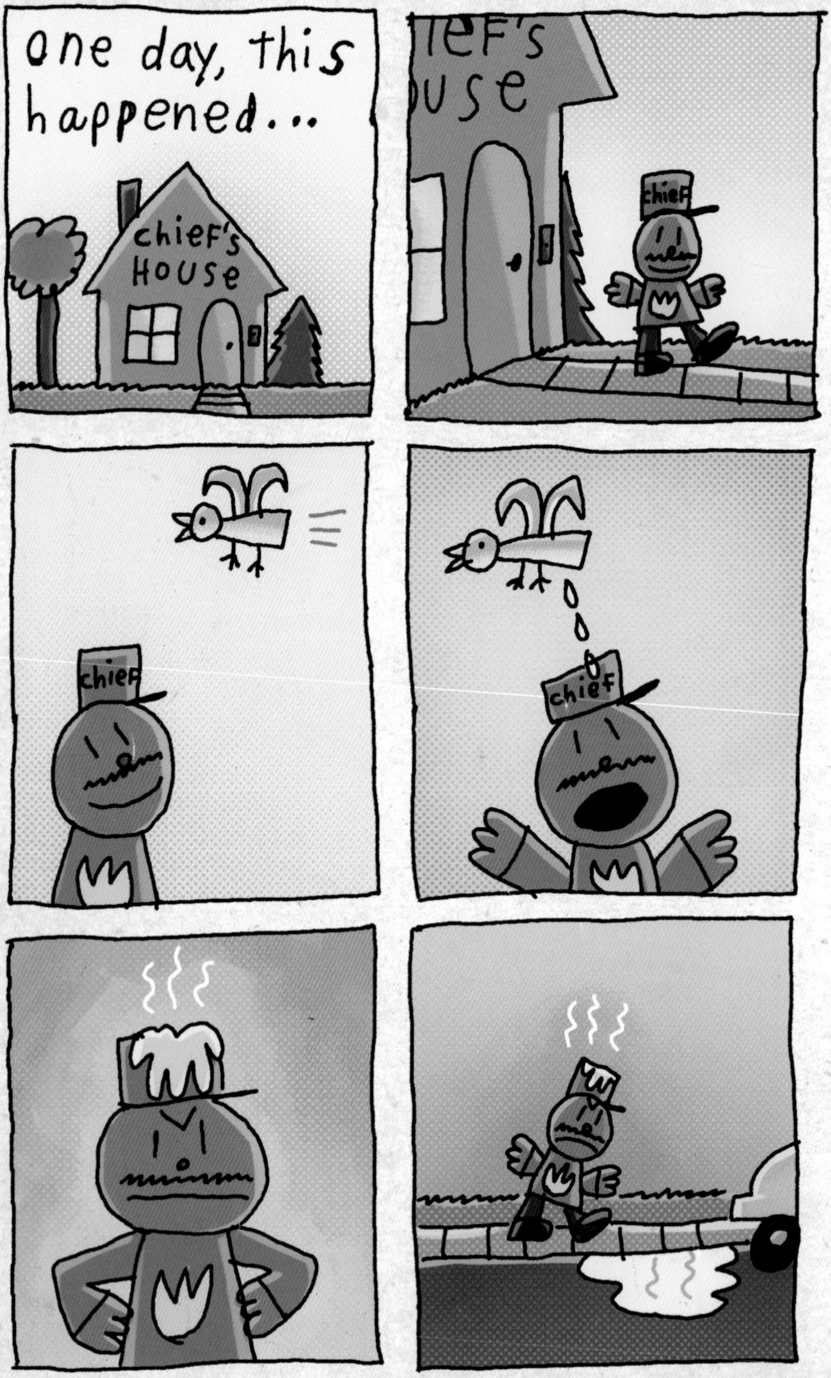
one day, this happened...
chief's HOUSE
IEF's OUSE
chief
chief
chief

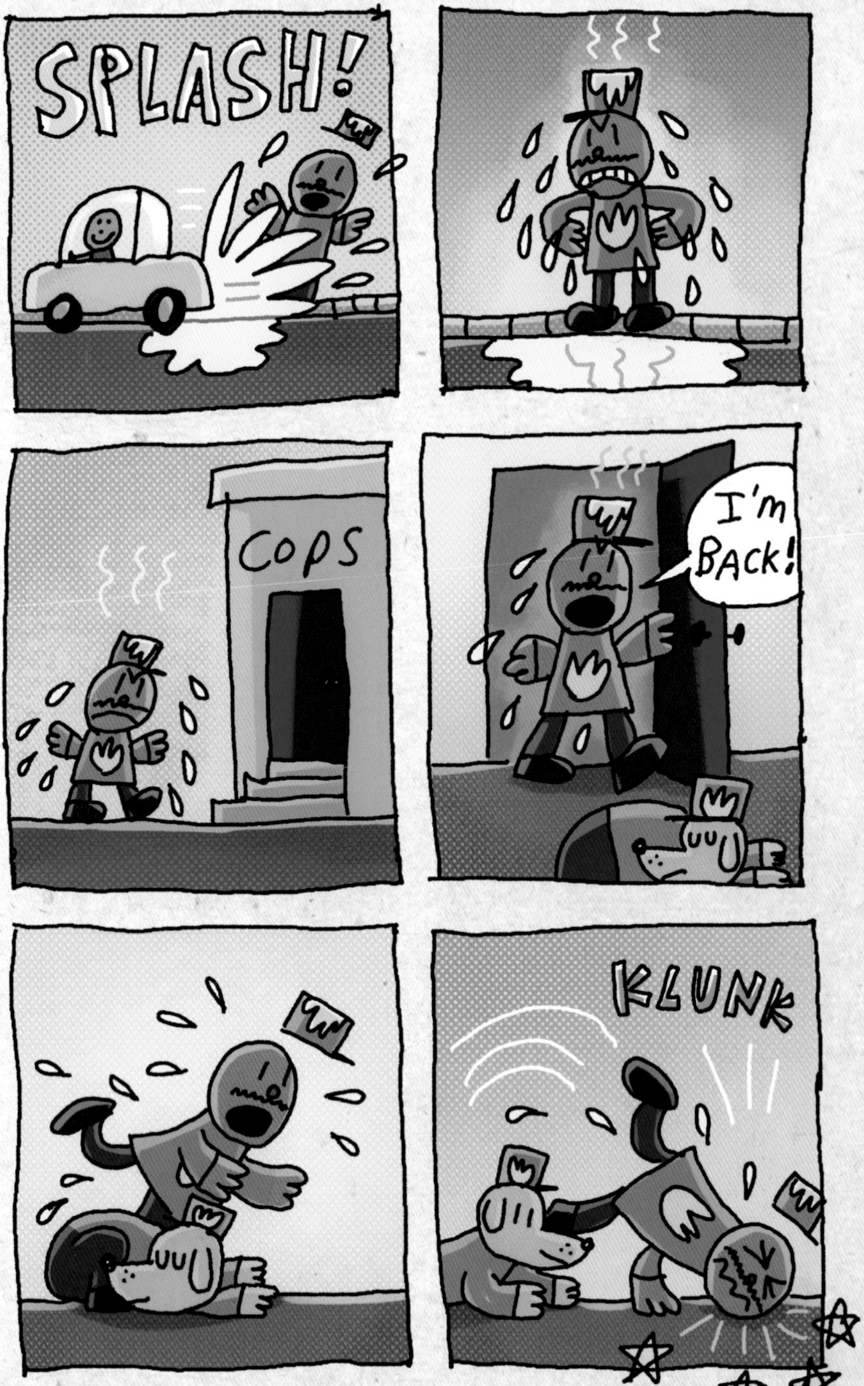
SPLASH!
COPS
I'm BACK!
KLUNK

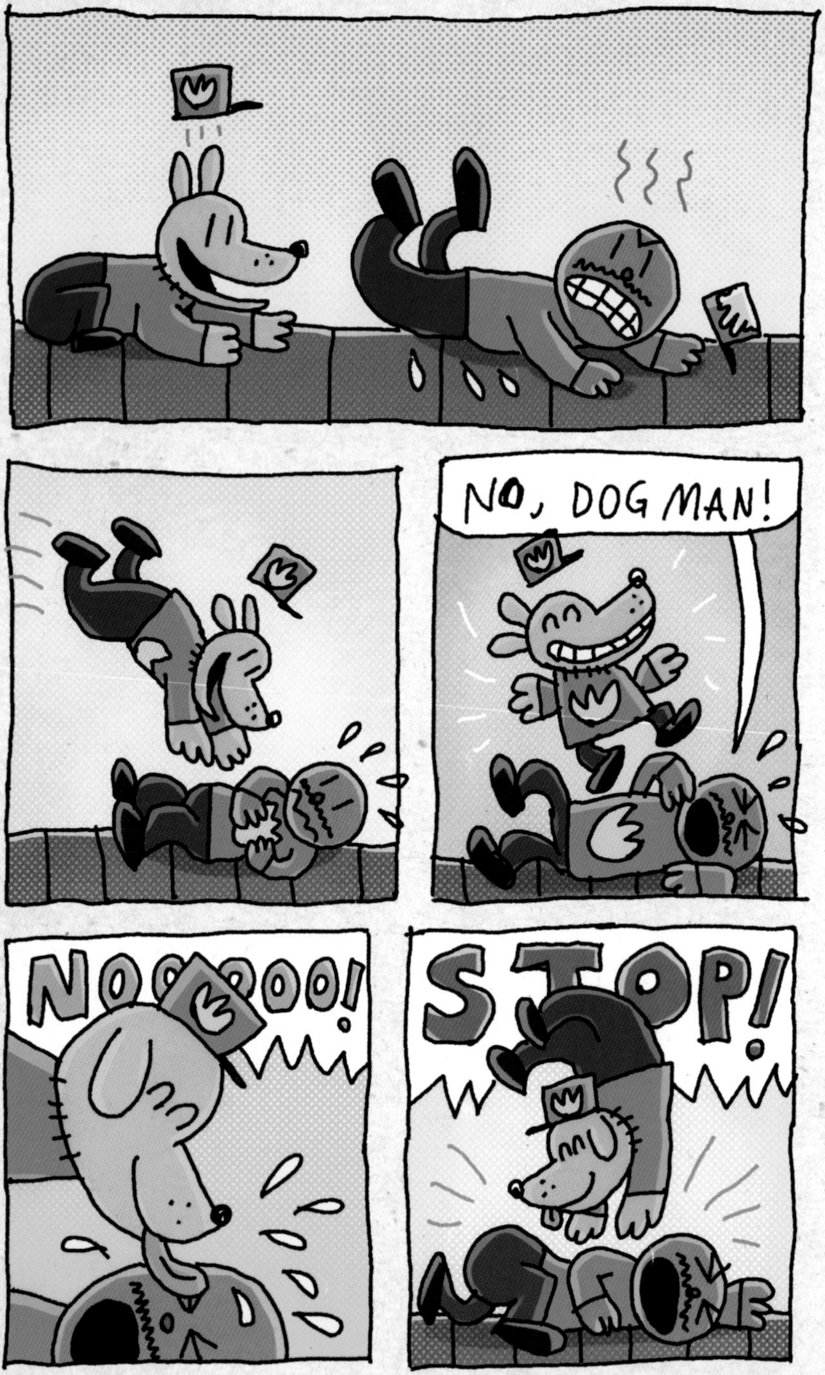
NO, DOG MAN!
NOOOOOO!
STOP!

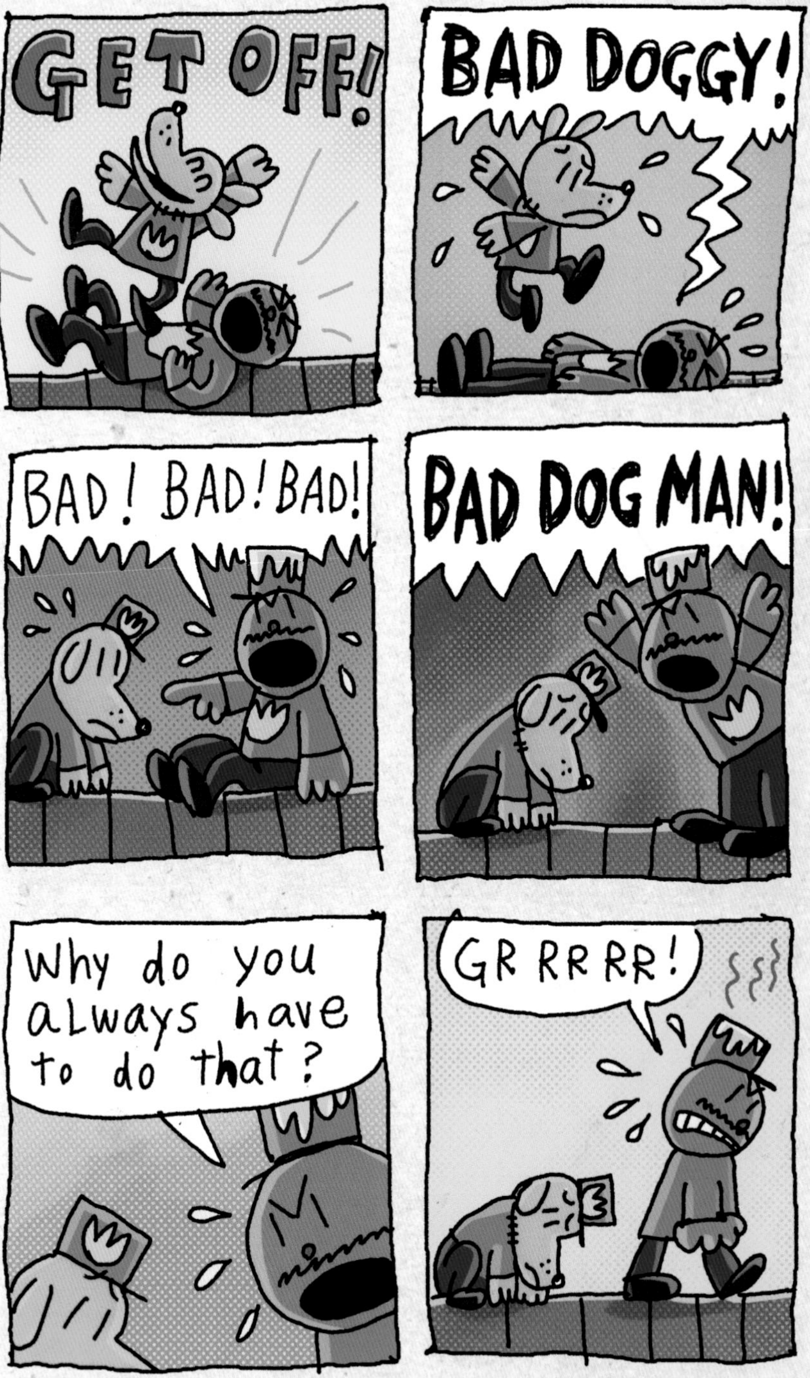
GET OFF!
BAD DOGGY!
BAD! BAD! BAD!
BAD DOG MAN!
Why do you always have to do that?
GRRRRR!

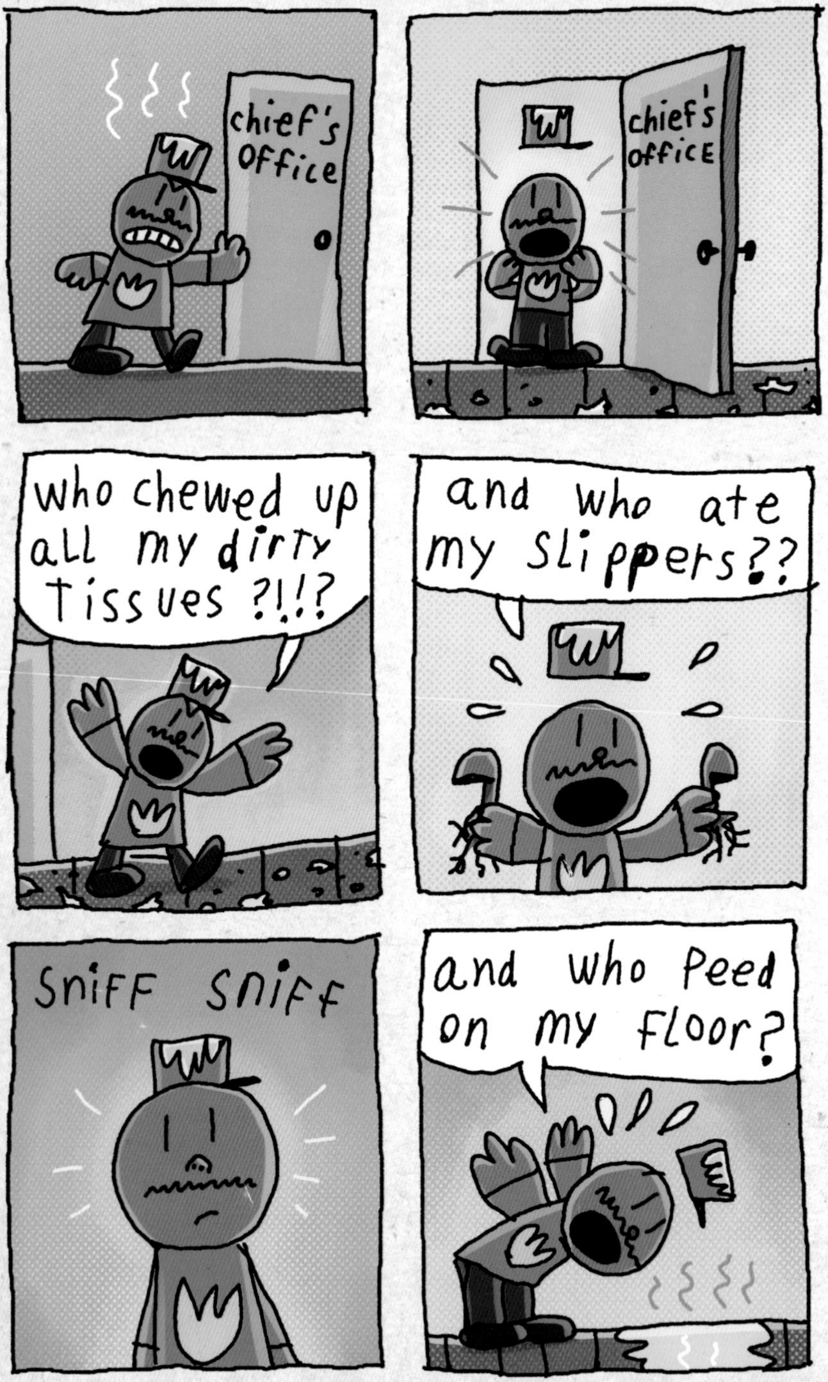
chief's office
chief's office
who chewed up all my dirty tissues ?!!?
and who ate my slippers??
sniff sniff
and who peed on my floor?

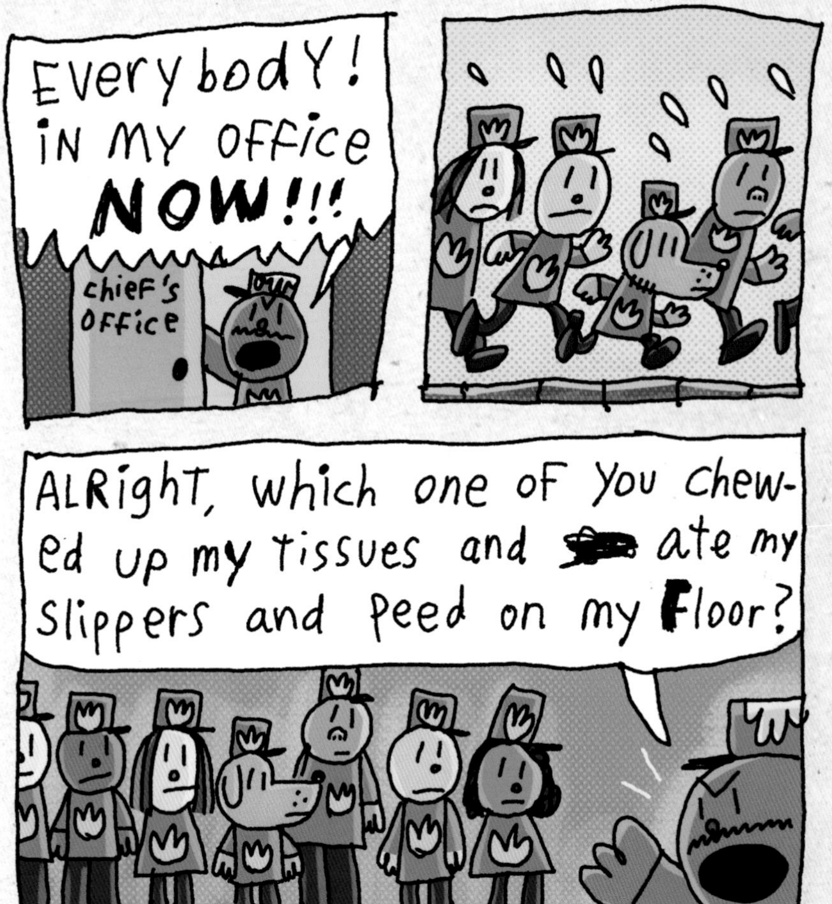
EveryboDY! iN MY OFFice NOW!!!
chieF's OFFice
ALRight, which one of You chew-ed up my tissues and ate my slippers and peed on my Floor?
Just as I SuSpected!

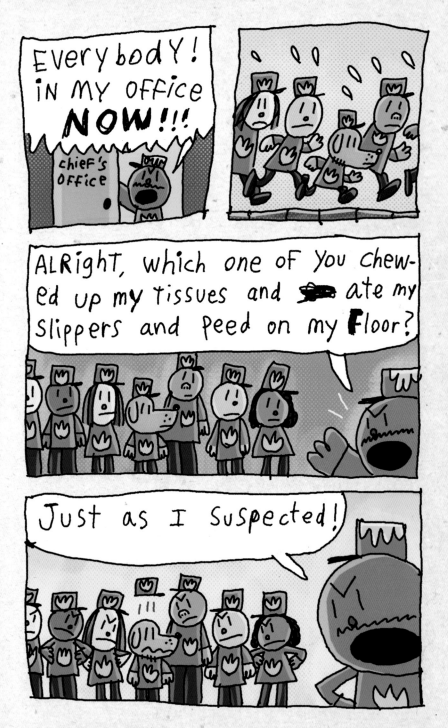

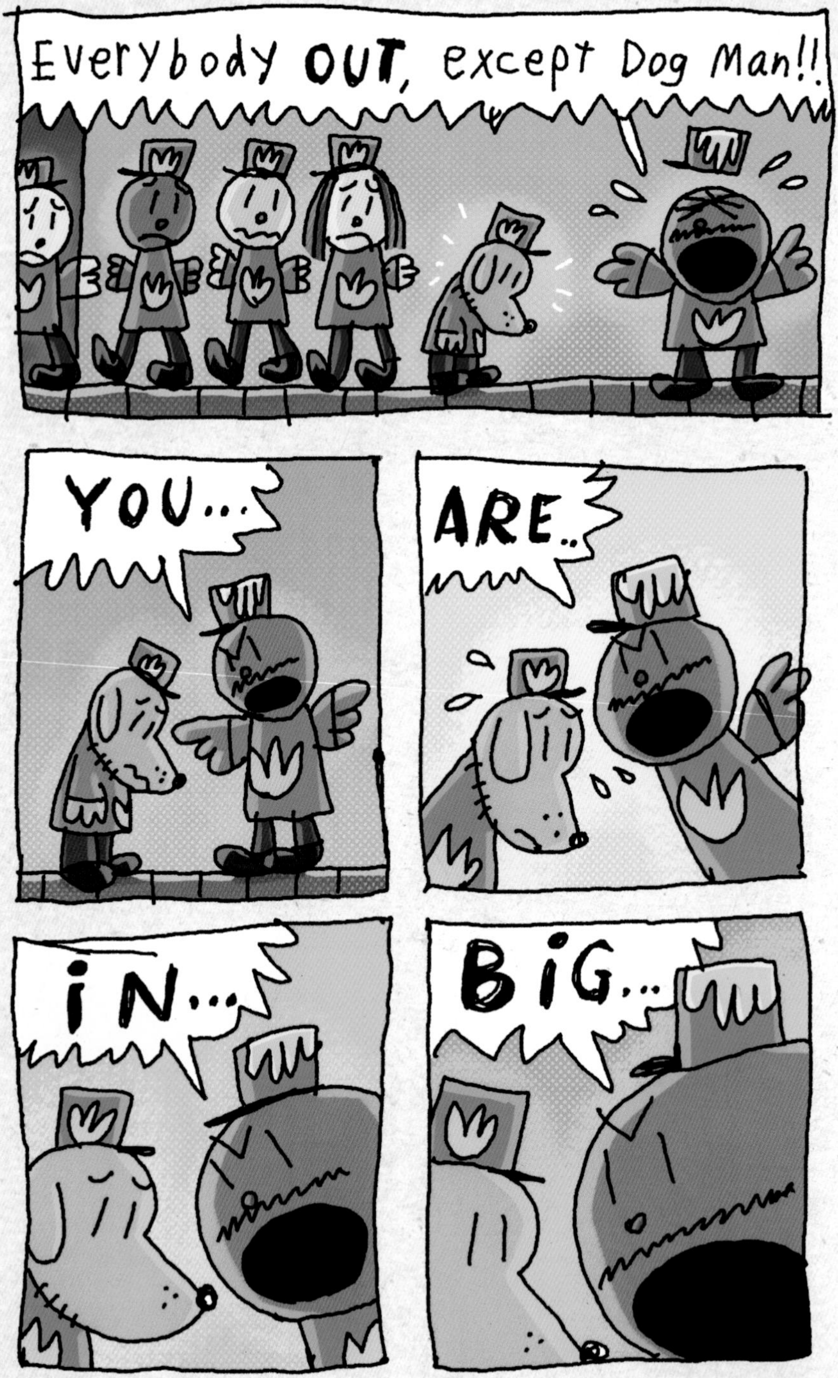
Everybody OUT, except Dog Man!!
YOU...
ARE..
iN...
BiG...

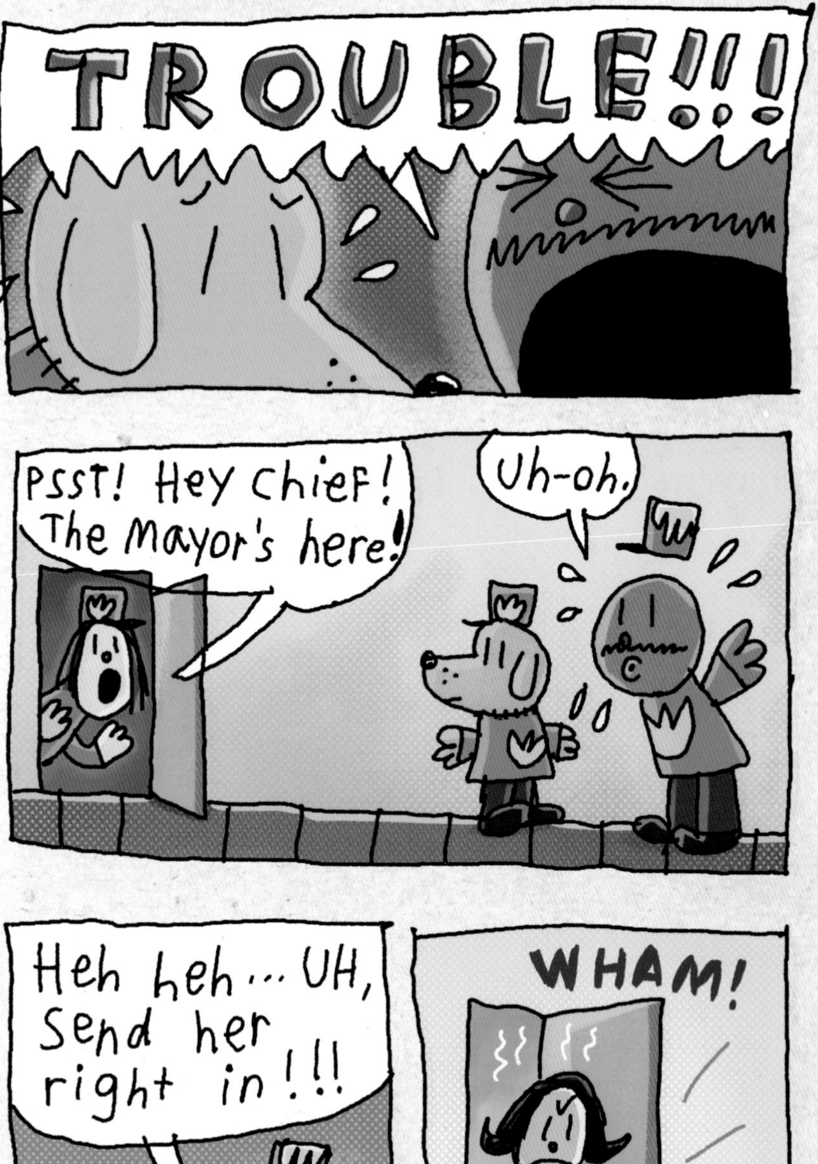
TROUBLE!!!
PSST! Hey Chief! The Mayor's here!
Uh-oh.
Heh heh... UH, Send her right in!!!
WHAM!

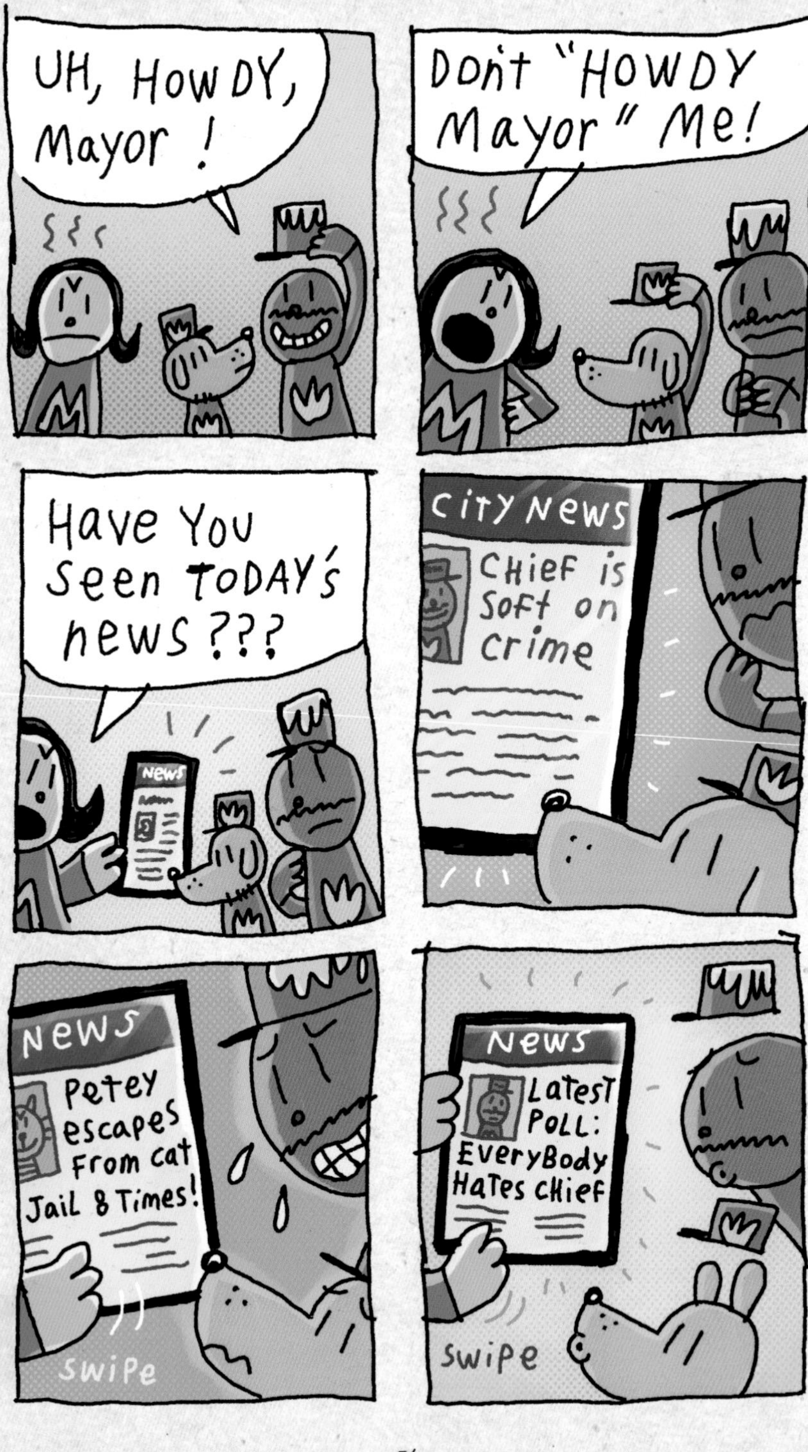
UH, HOWDY, Mayor!
Don't "HOWDY Mayor" Me!
Have You seen TODAY's news???
NEWS
CITY NEWS
CHIEF is Soft on crime
NEWS
Petey escapes From cat Jail 8 Times!
SWIPE
NEWS
LATEST POLL: EVERYBODY HATES CHIEF
SWIPE

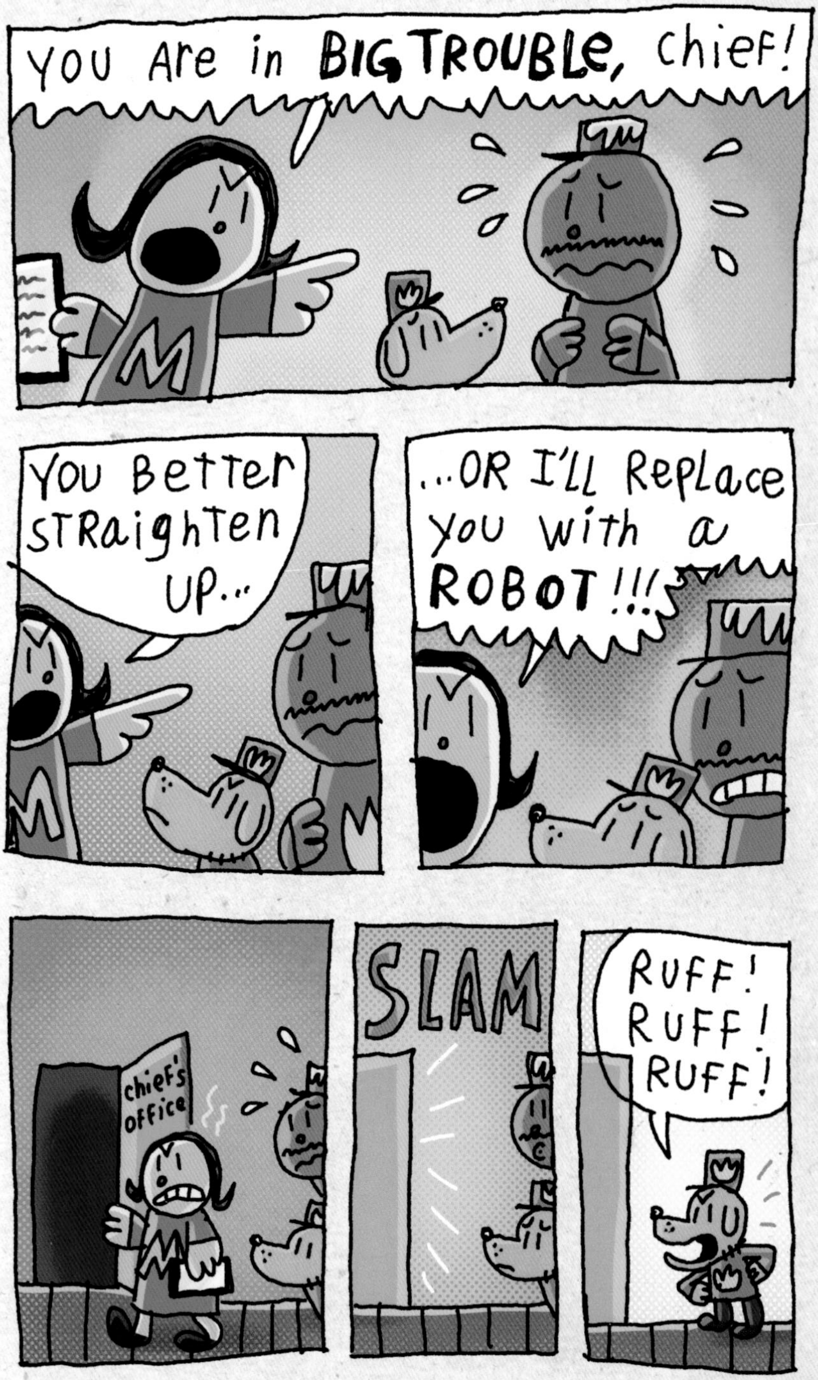
YOU ARE in BIG TROUBLE, chief!
YOU BETTER STRAIGHTEN UP...
...OR I'LL REPLACE YOU WITH A ROBOT!!!
chief's office
SLAM
RUFF! RUFF! RUFF!

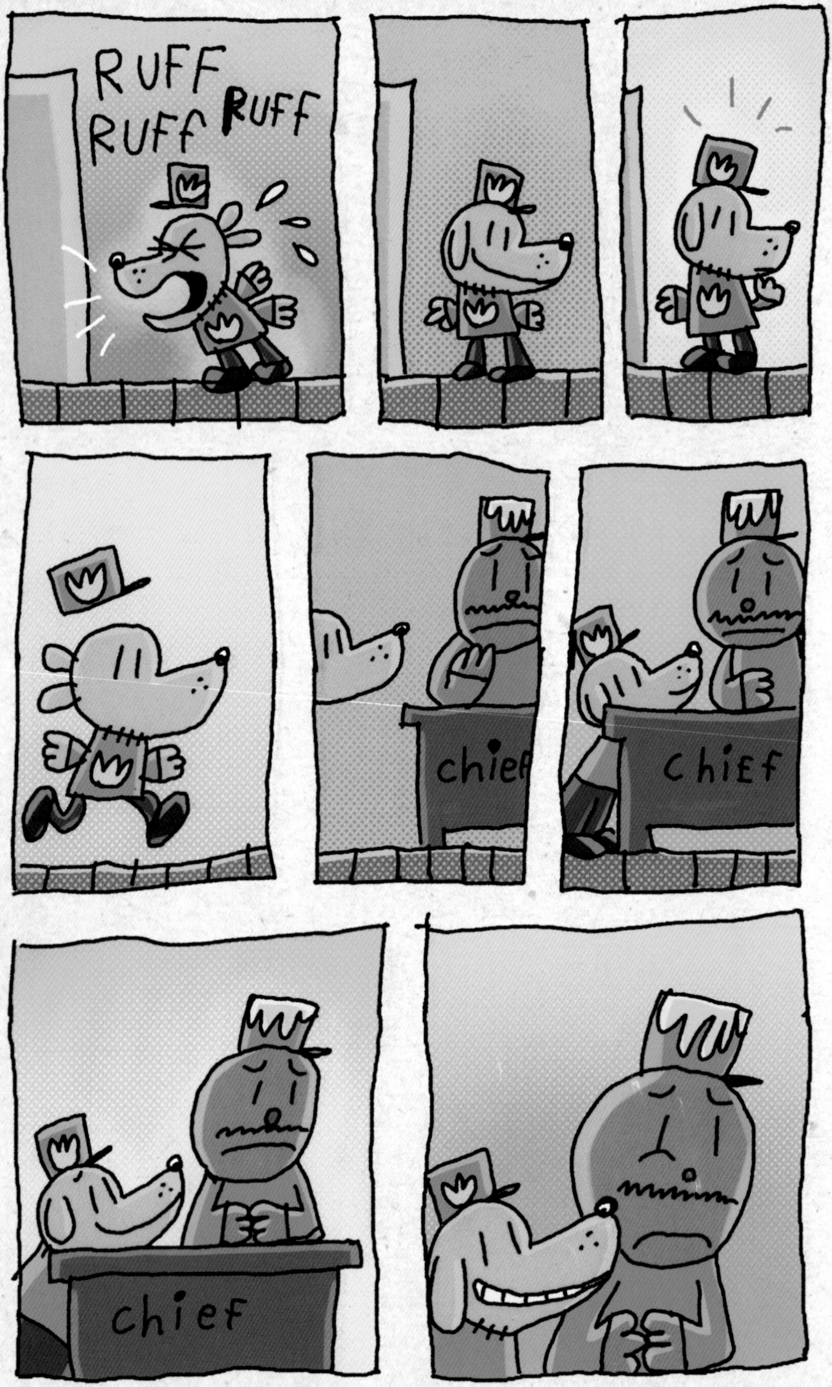
RUFF
RUFF RUFF
RUFF
chief
Chief
chief

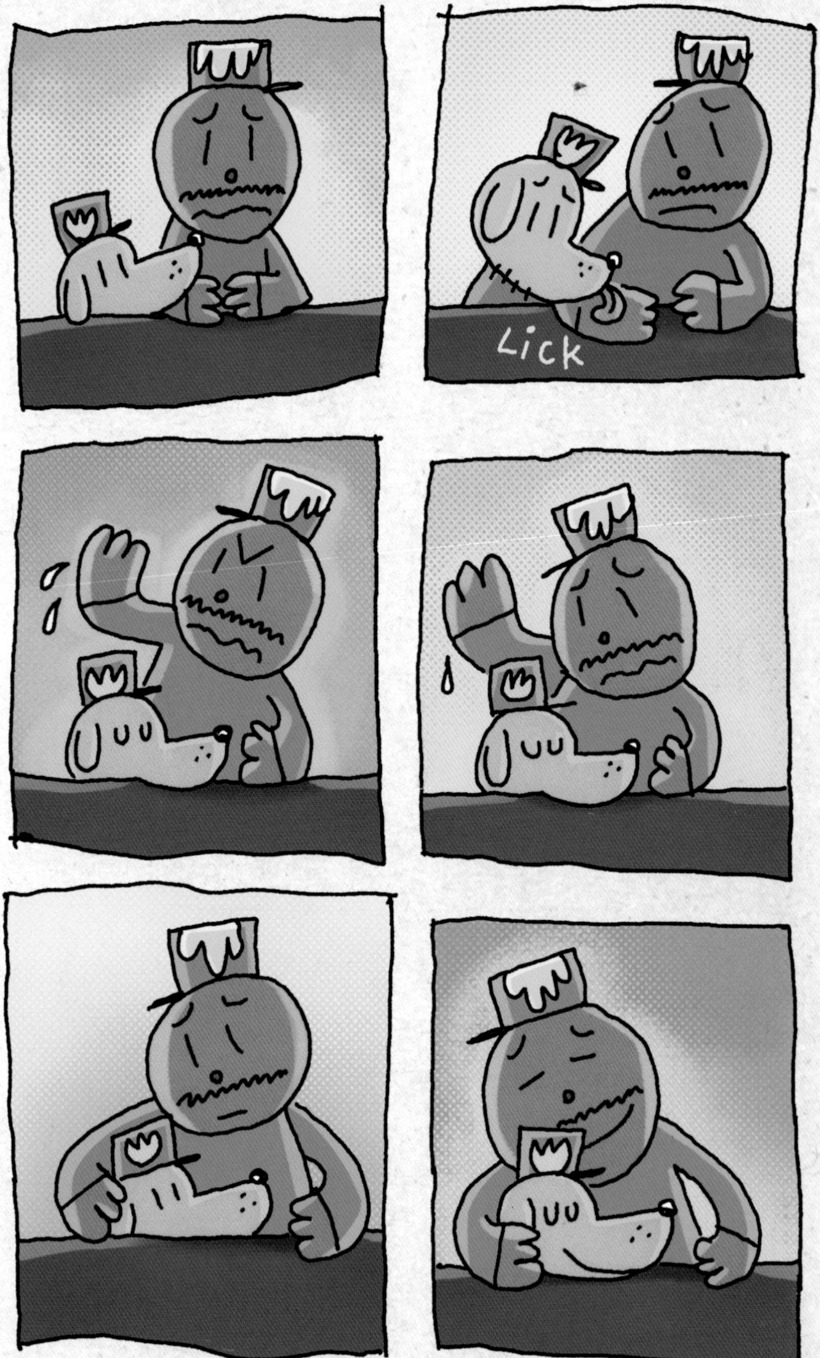
Lick

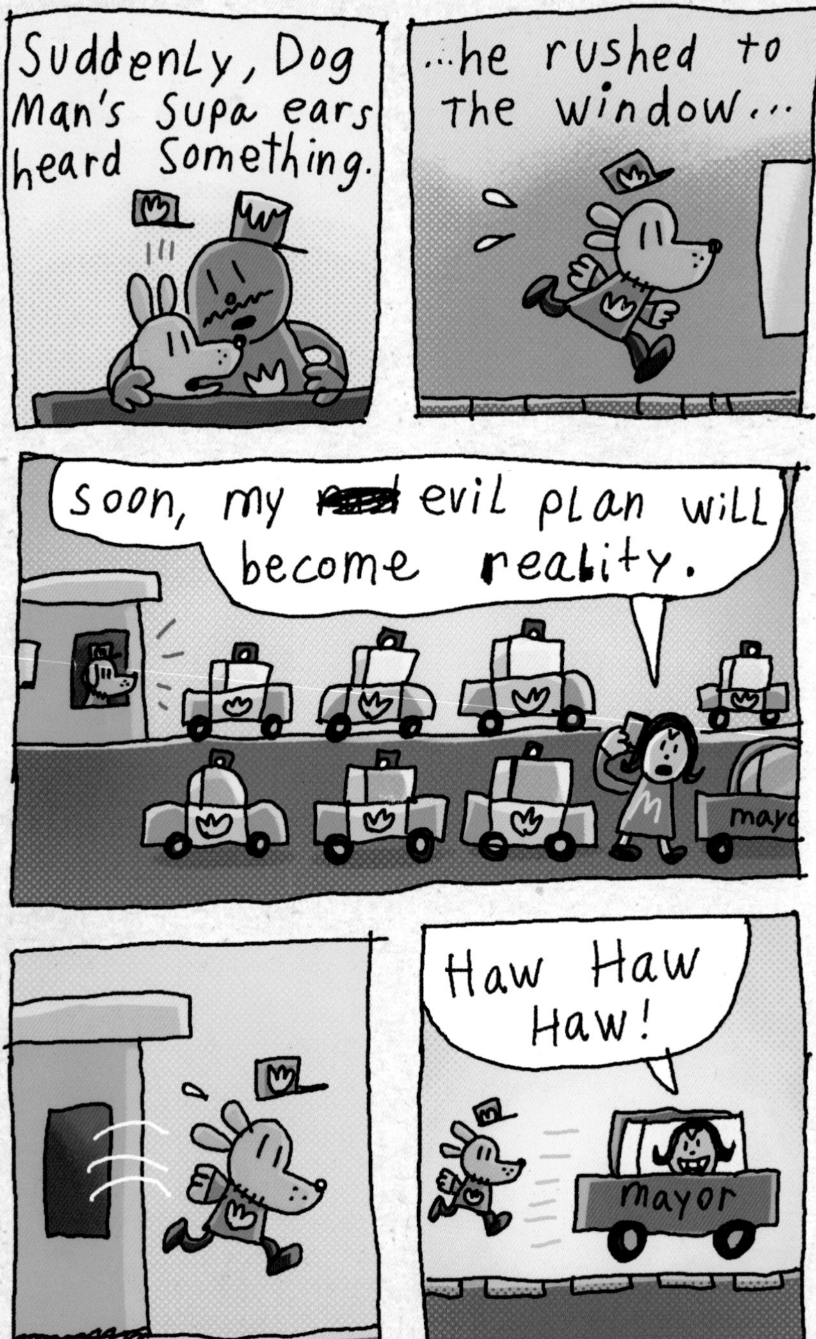
Suddenly, Dog Man's Supa ears heard Something.
...he rushed to The window...
soon, my evil plan will become reality.
Haw Haw Haw!
mayor

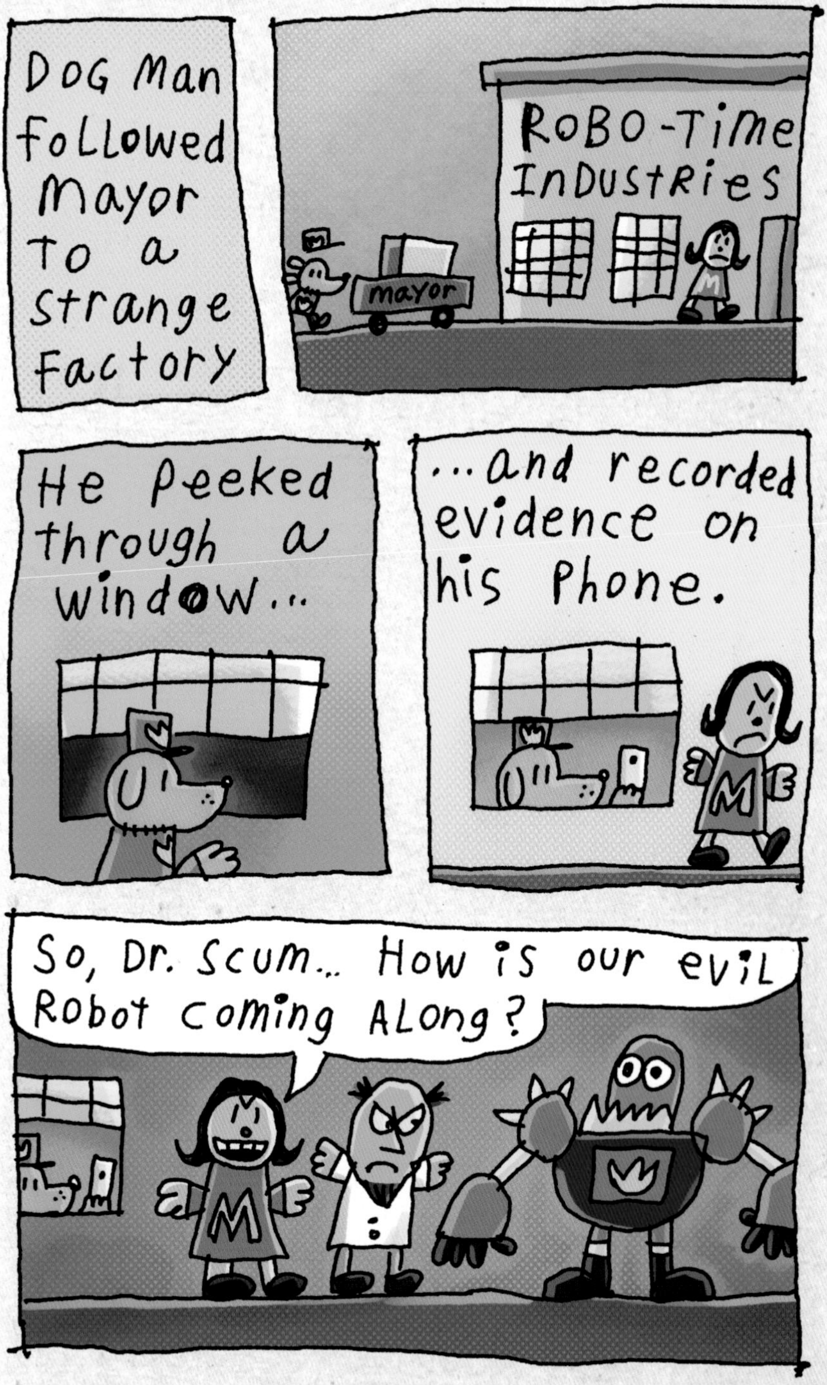
Dog Man followed Mayor to a strange Factory
mayor
RoBO-Time InDustRies
He peeked through a window...
...and recorded evidence on his phone.
So, Dr. Scum... How is our evil Robot coming Along?

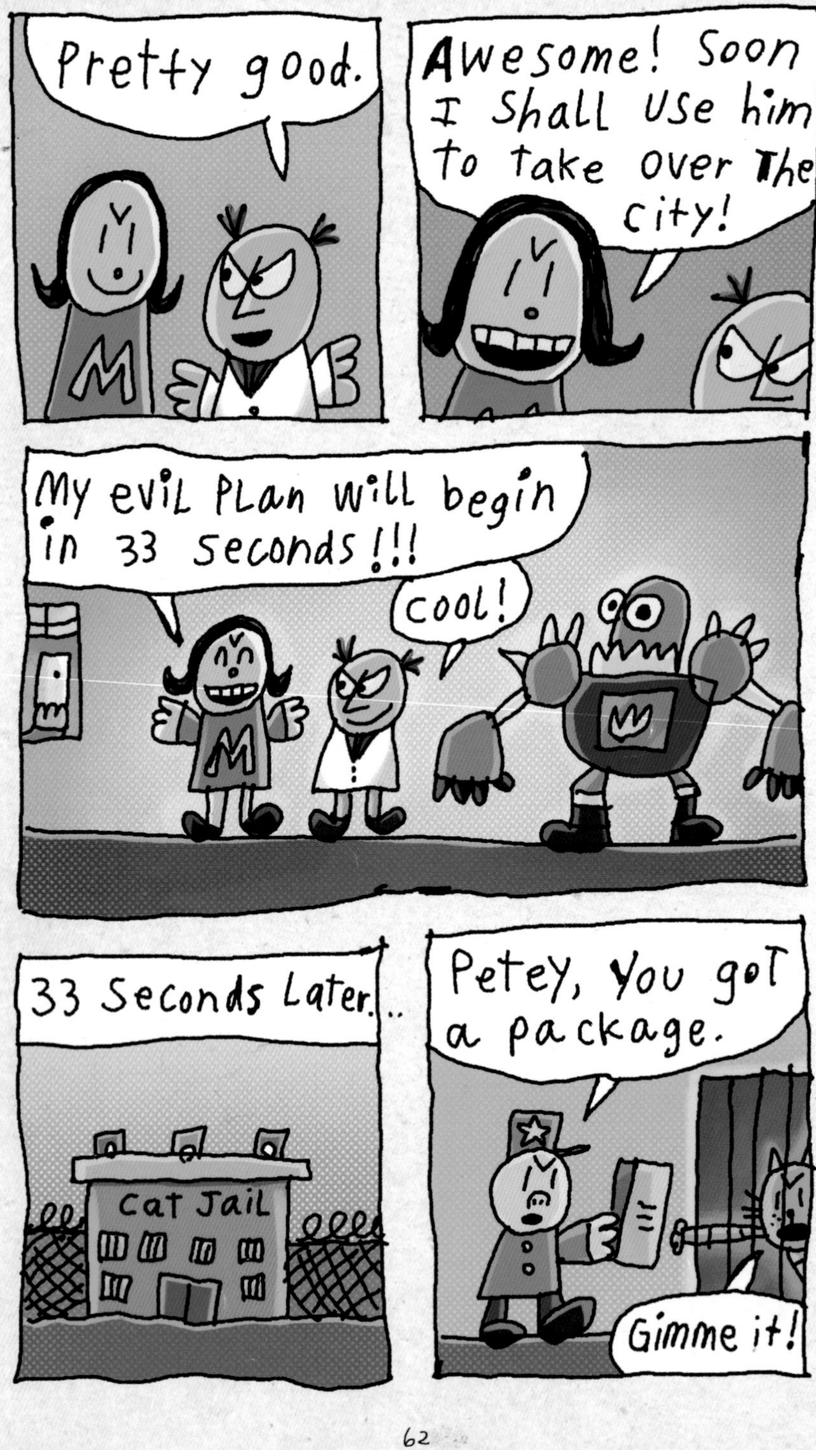
Pretty good.
Awesome! Soon I Shall Use him to take over The city!
My evil Plan will begin in 33 seconds!!!
COOL!
33 Seconds Later...
Cat Jail
Petey, You got a package.
Gimme it!

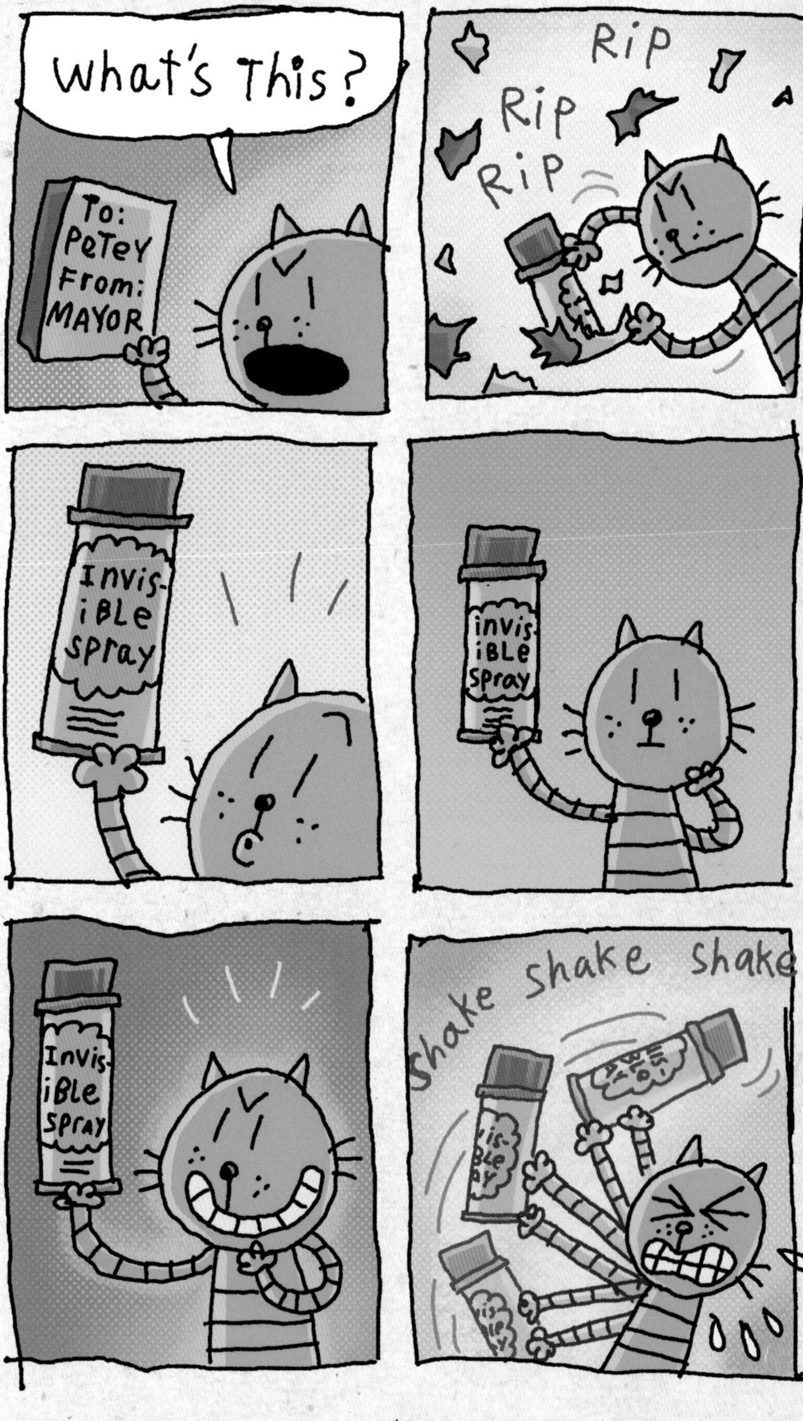
What's This?
To: PeTeY From: MAYOR
RiP
RiP
RiP
Invis-iBLe spray
invis-iBLe Spray
Invis-iBLe SPRAY
Shake shake Shake

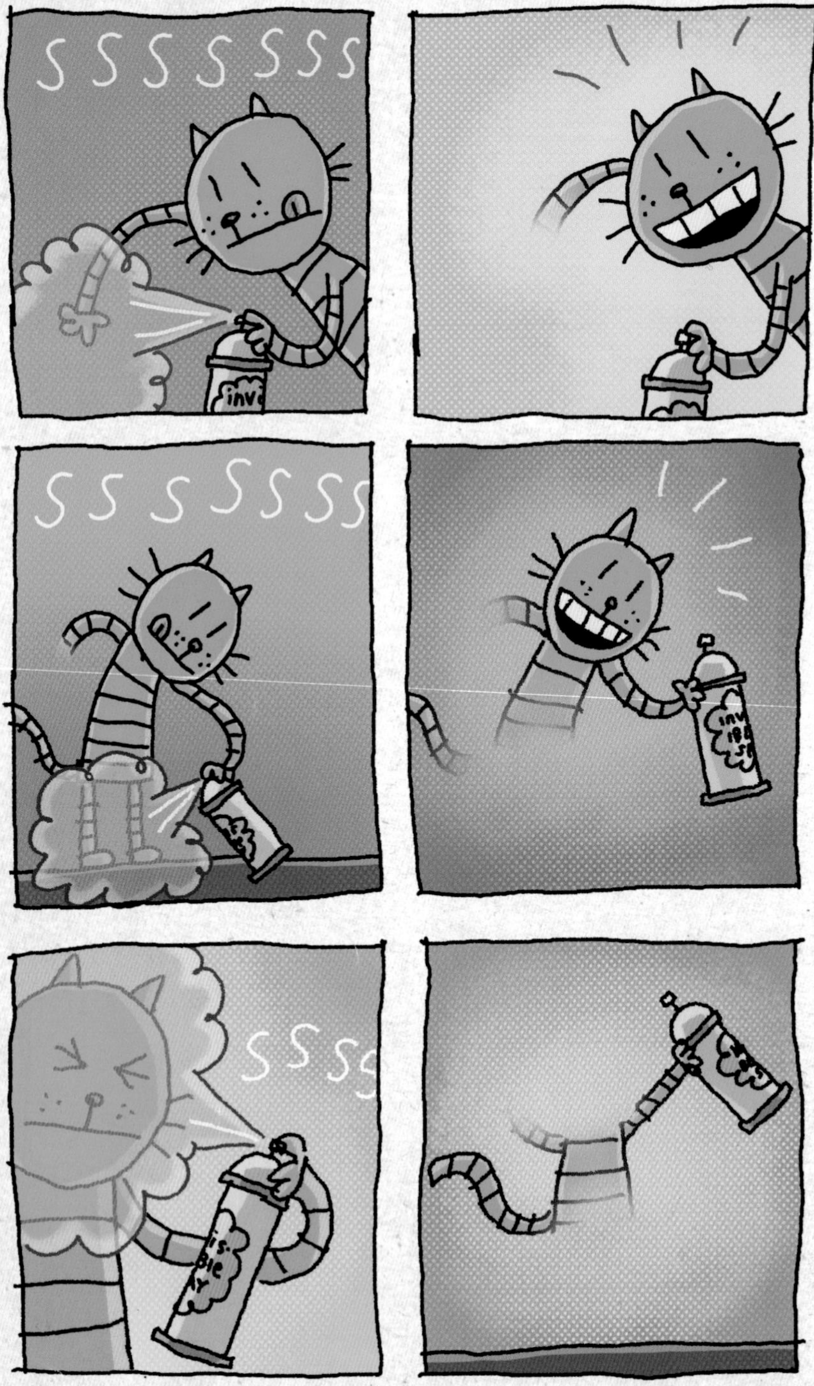
SSSSSSS
SSSSSSS
SSSS

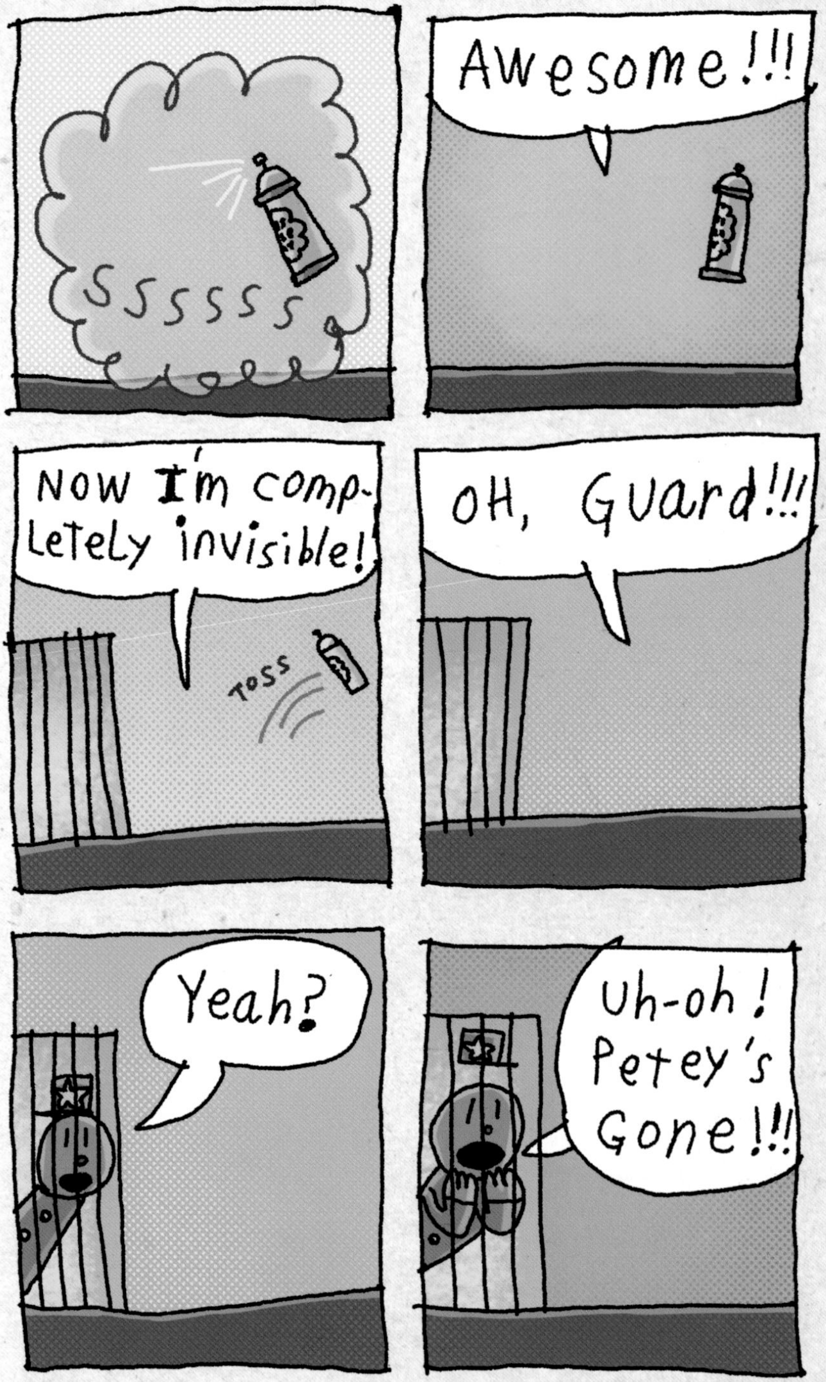
SSSSSS
Awesome!!!
Now I'm comp-
Letely invisible!
TOSS
OH, Guard!!!
Yeah?
Uh-oh!
Petey's
Gone!!!

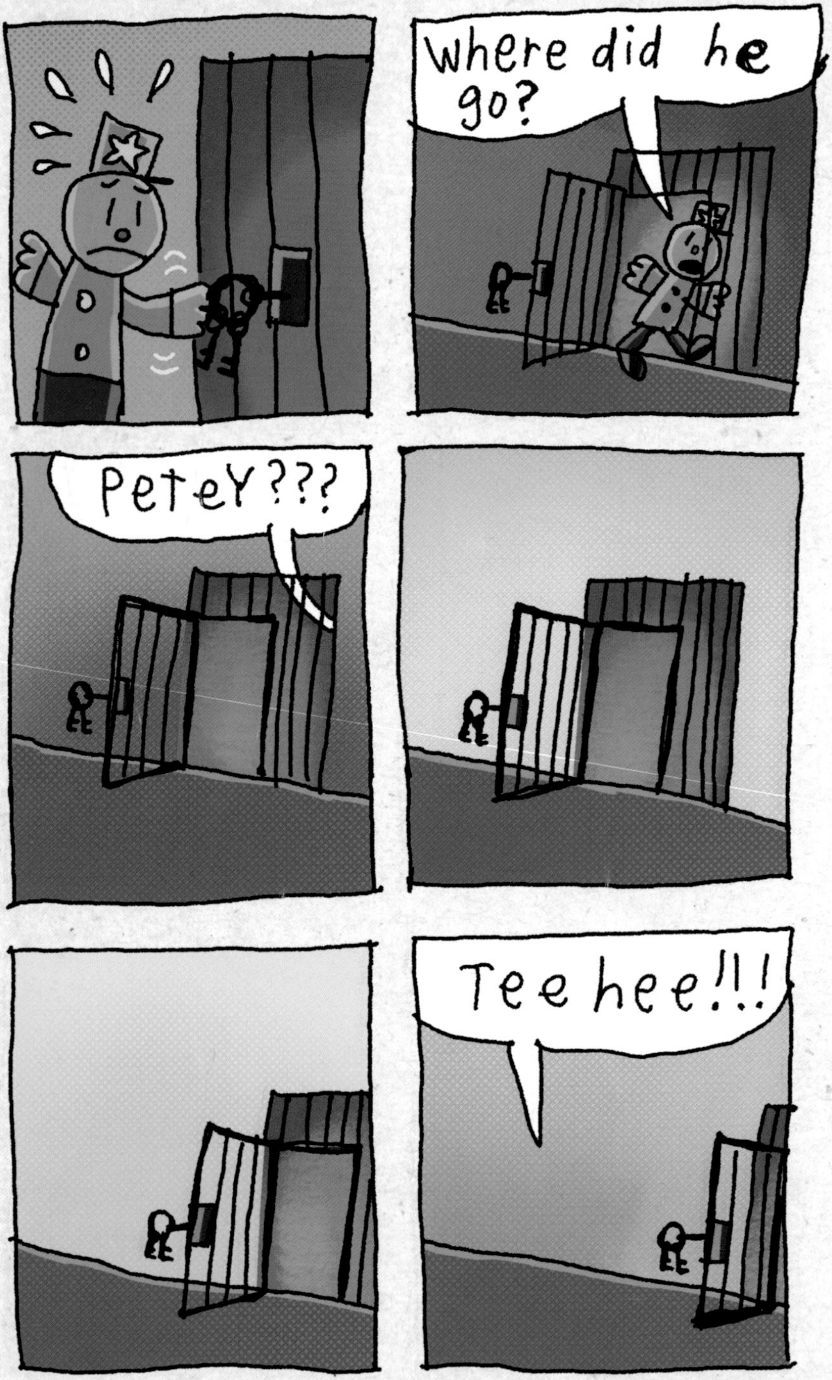
Where did he go?
PeteY???
Teehee!!!

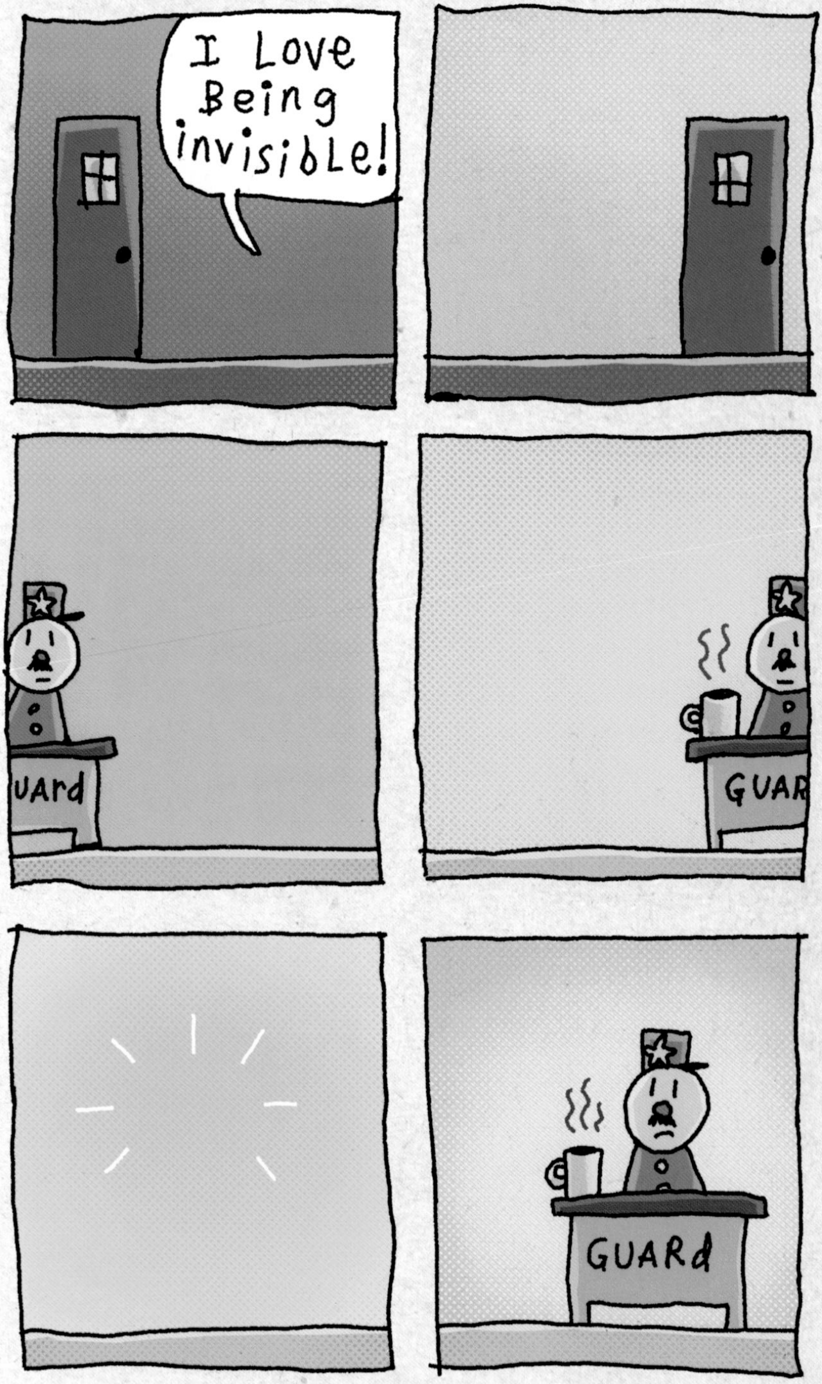
I Love Being invisible!
UARd
GUAR
GUARd

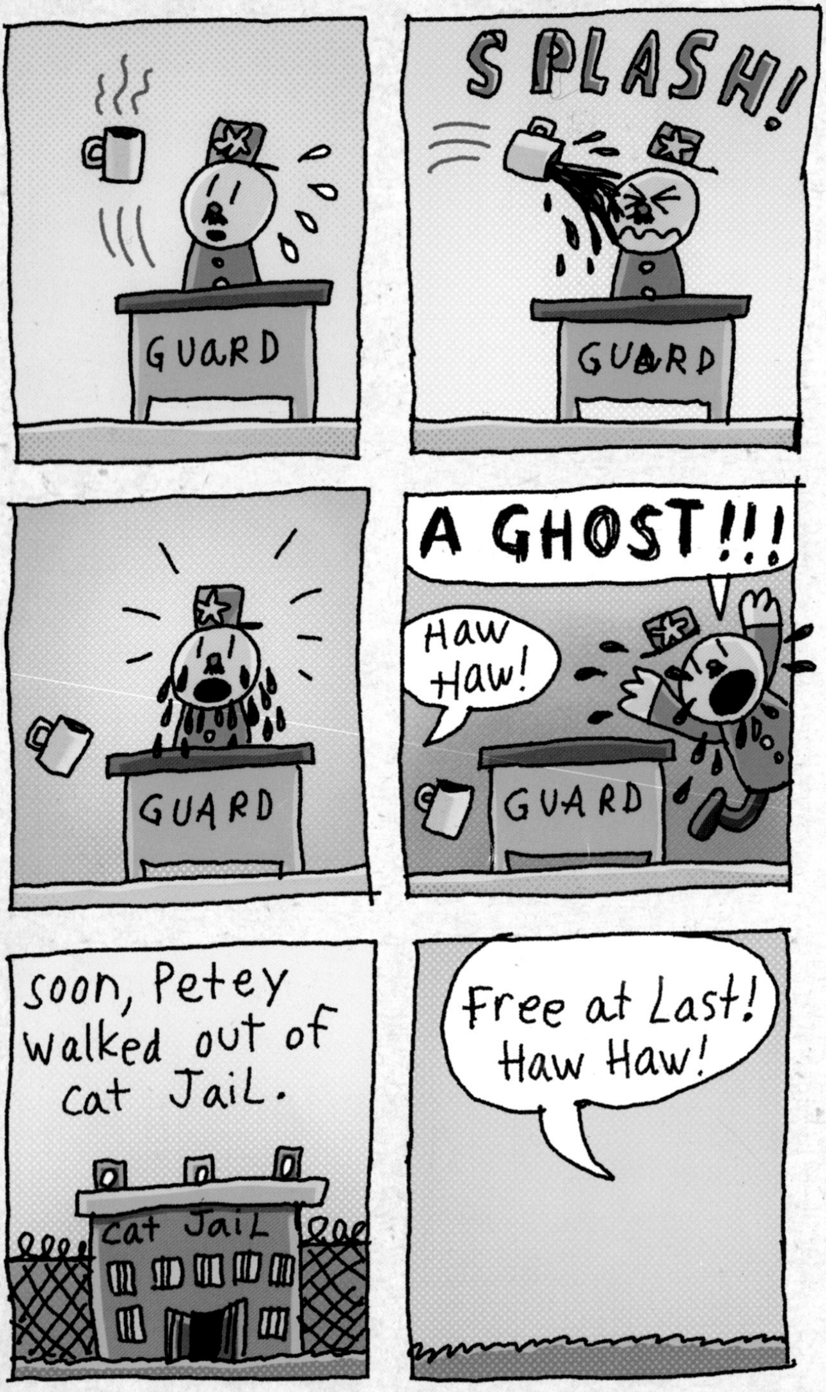
GUARD
SPLASH!
GUARD
GUARD
A GHOST!!!
Haw Haw!
GUARD
soon, Petey walked out of cat JaiL.
cat JaiL
Free at Last! Haw Haw!

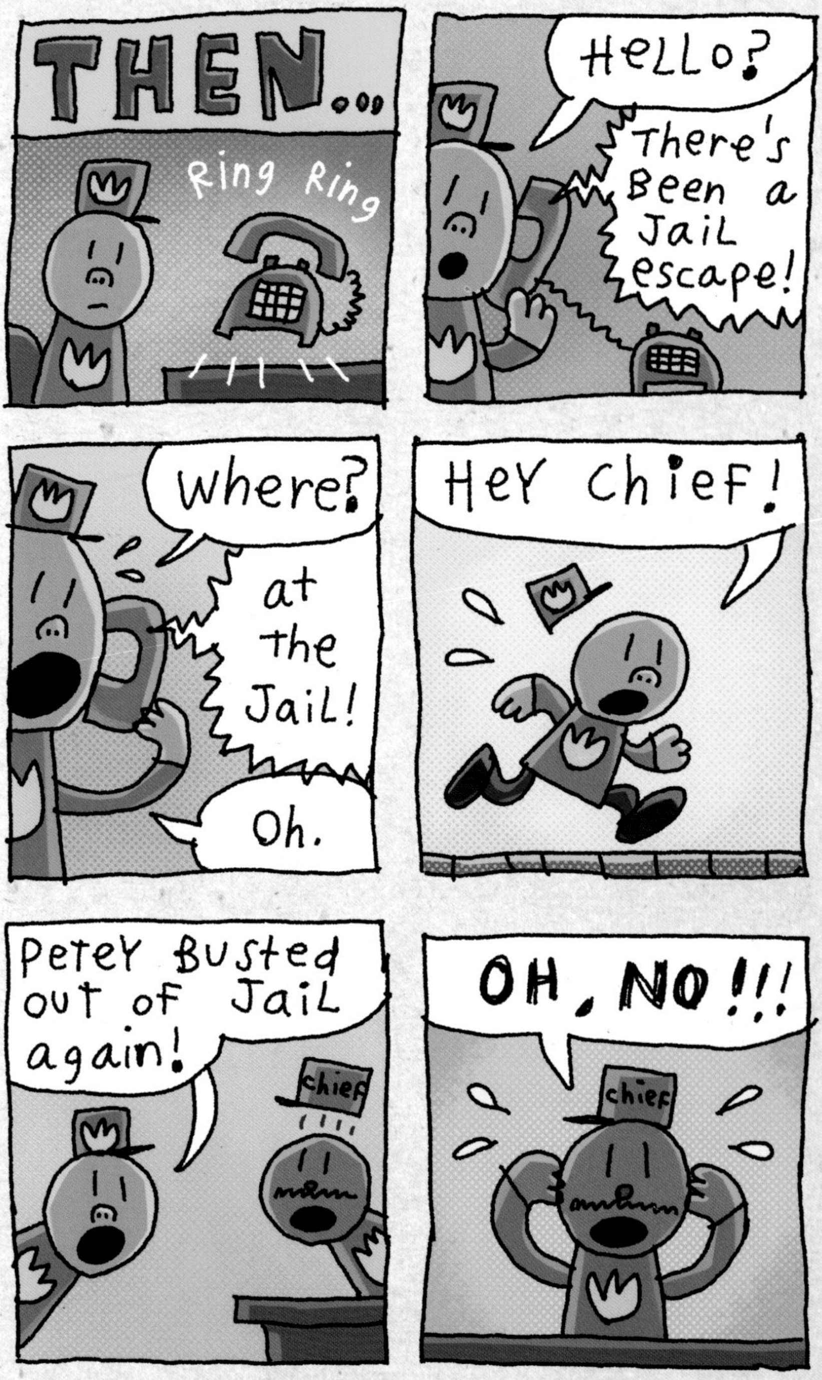
THEN...
Ring Ring
HELLO?
There's Been a JaiL escape!
Where?
at the JaiL!
Oh.
HeY Chief!
PeTeY BuSted out of JaiL again!
chief
OH, NO!!!
chief

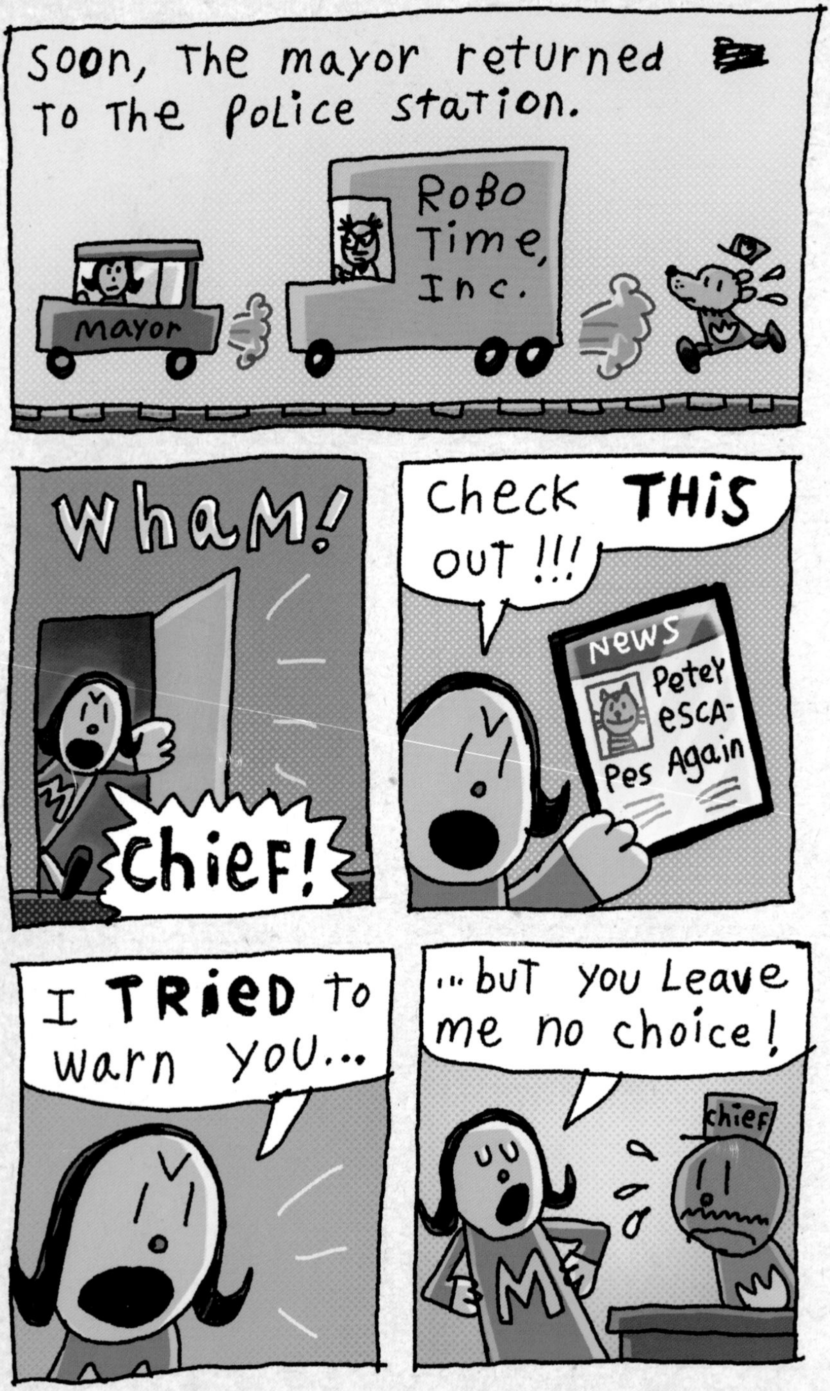
Soon, The mayor returned to The Police station.
mayor
RoBo Time, Inc.
WhaM!
Chief!
Check THIS out!!!
News
Petey esca-pes Again
I TRIED to warn you...
...but you Leave me no choice!
chief

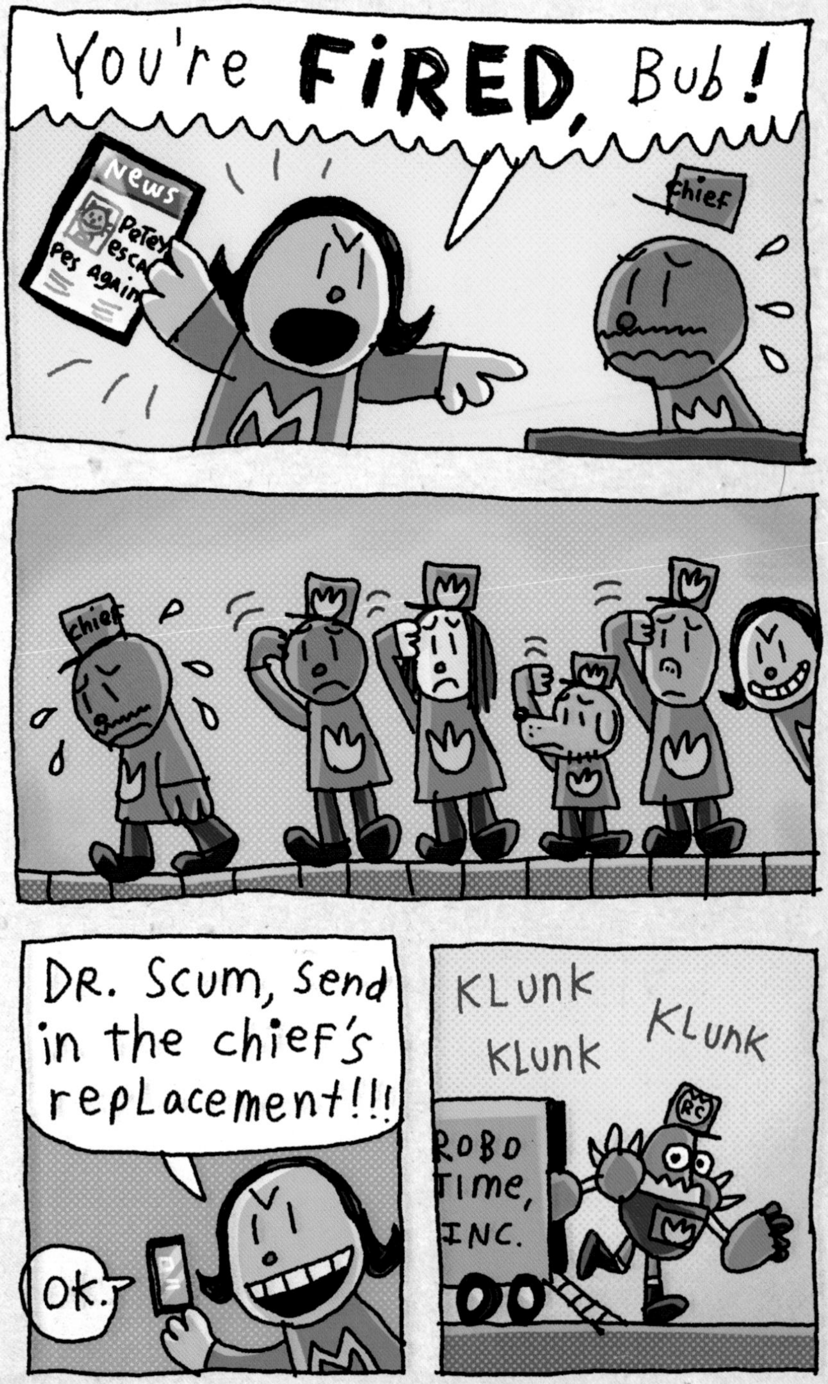
You're FiRED, Bub!
News
PeTey escapes again
chief
chief
DR. Scum, send in the chief's replacement!!!
OK.
KLUNK
KLUNK
KLUNK
ROBO Time, INC.
RC

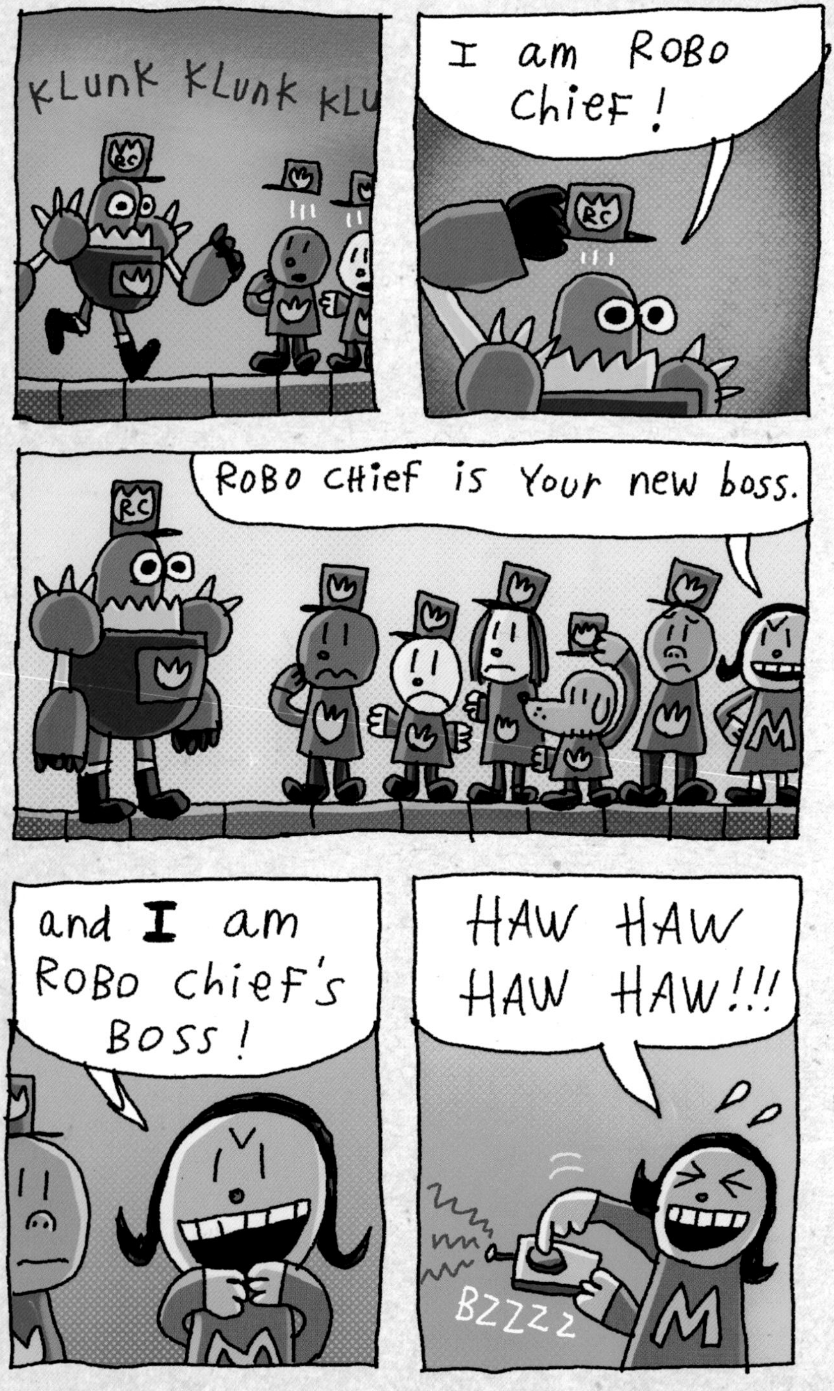
KLUNK KLUNK KLU
I am ROBO CHIEF!
ROBO CHIEF is your new boss.
and I am ROBO chief's BOSS!
HAW HAW HAW HAW!!!
BZZZZ

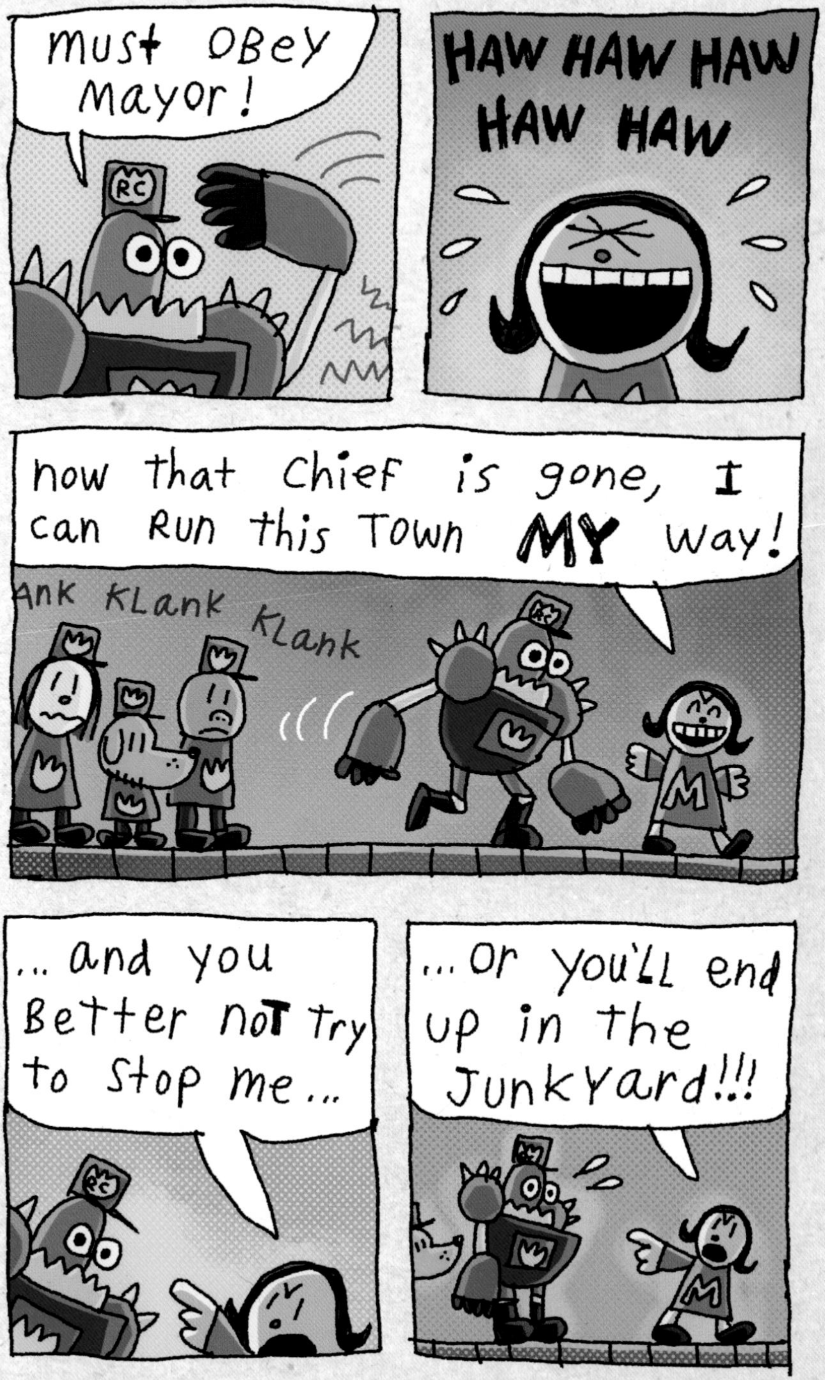
must OBEY Mayor!
HAW HAW HAW HAW HAW HAW
now that Chief is gone, I can Run this Town MY way!
ANK KLank KLank
... and you Better noT Try to Stop me...
... or you'll end up in the JunkYard!!!

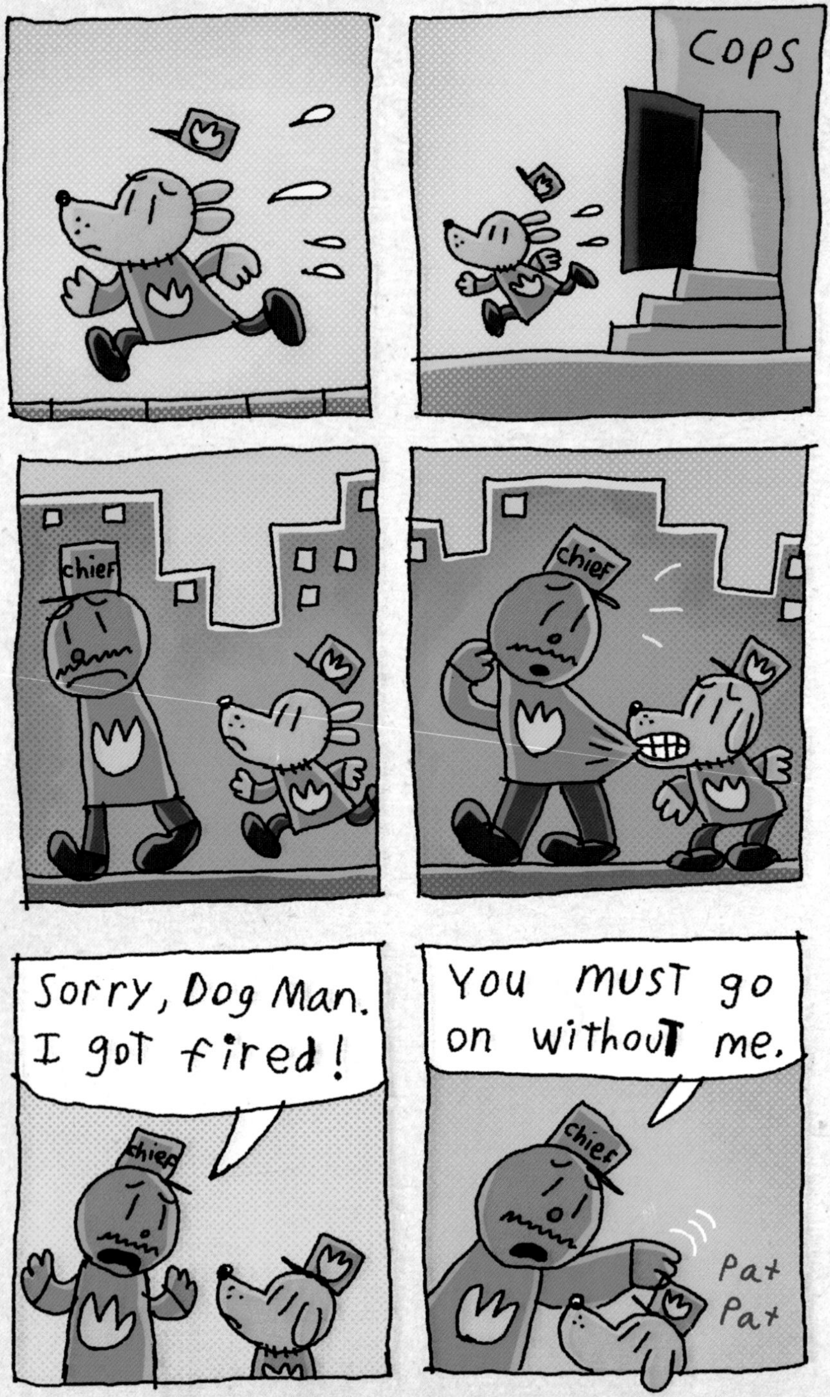
COPS
chief
chief
Sorry, Dog Man. I got fired!
chief
You MUST go on without me.
chief
Pat Pat

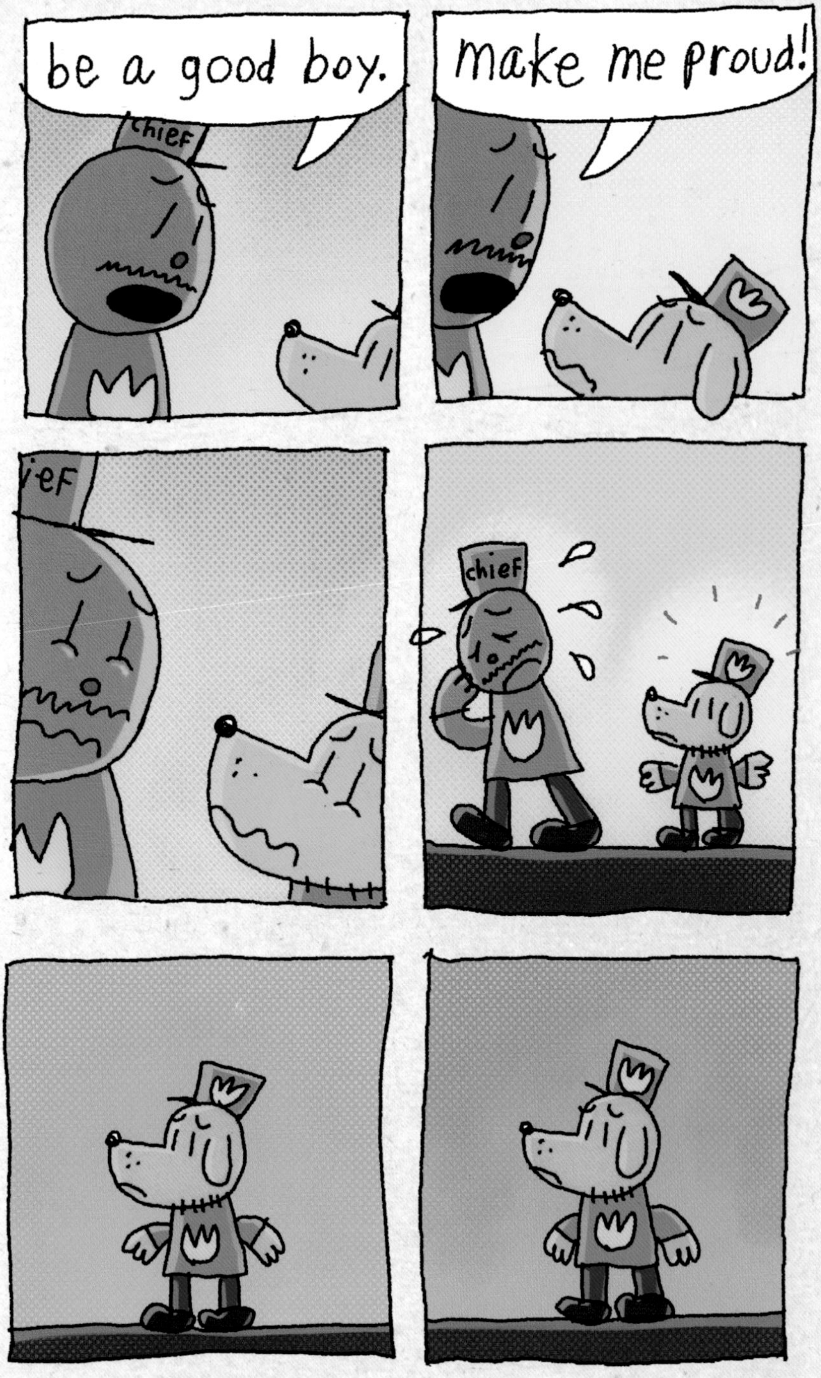
be a good boy.
chief
make me proud!
ief
chief

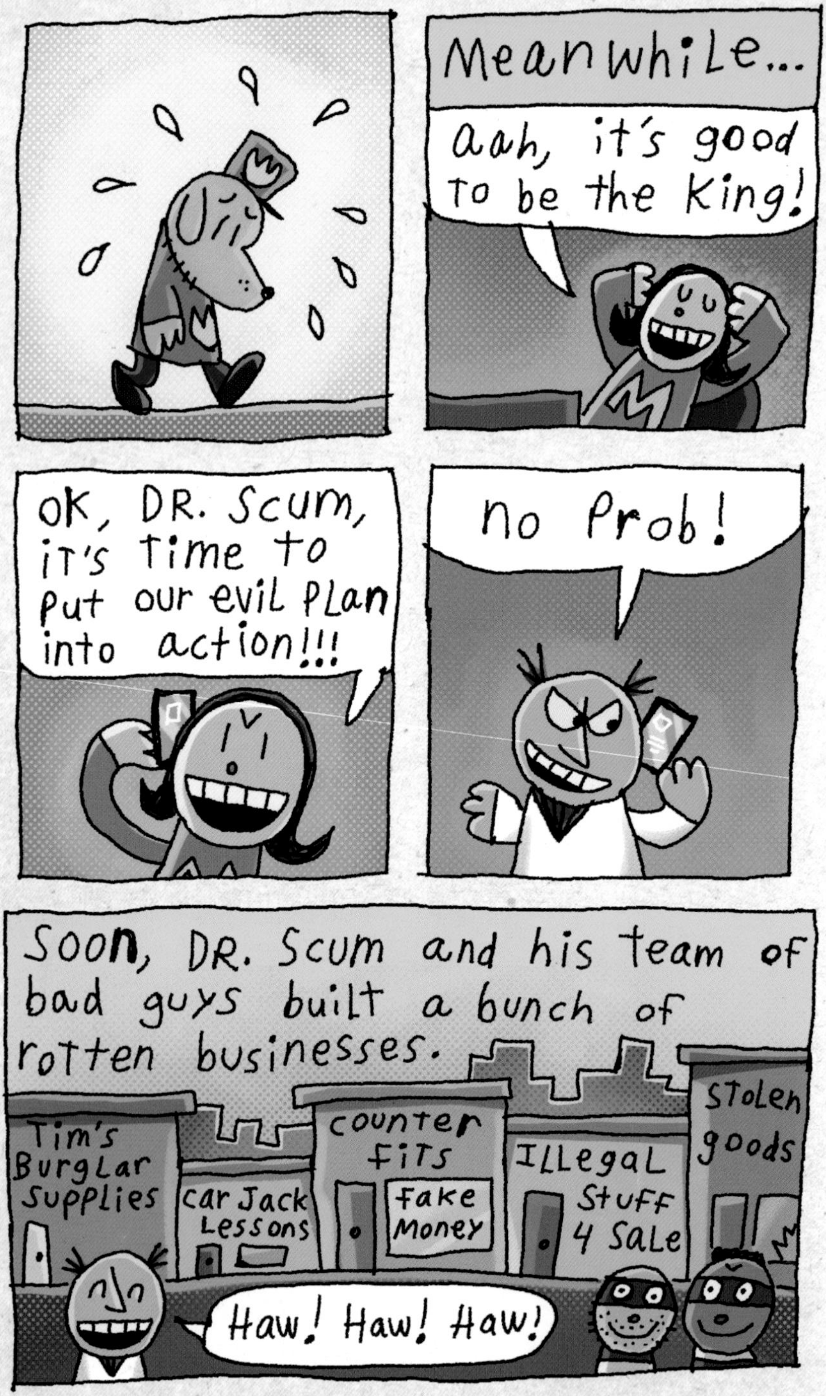
Meanwhile...
aah, it's good to be the King!
OK, DR. Scum, it's time to put our evil plan into action!!!
no Prob!
Soon, DR. Scum and his team of bad guys built a bunch of rotten businesses.
Tim's Burglar Supplies
Car Jack Lessons
counter fits
Fake Money
Illegal Stuff 4 Sale
Stolen goods
Haw! Haw! Haw!

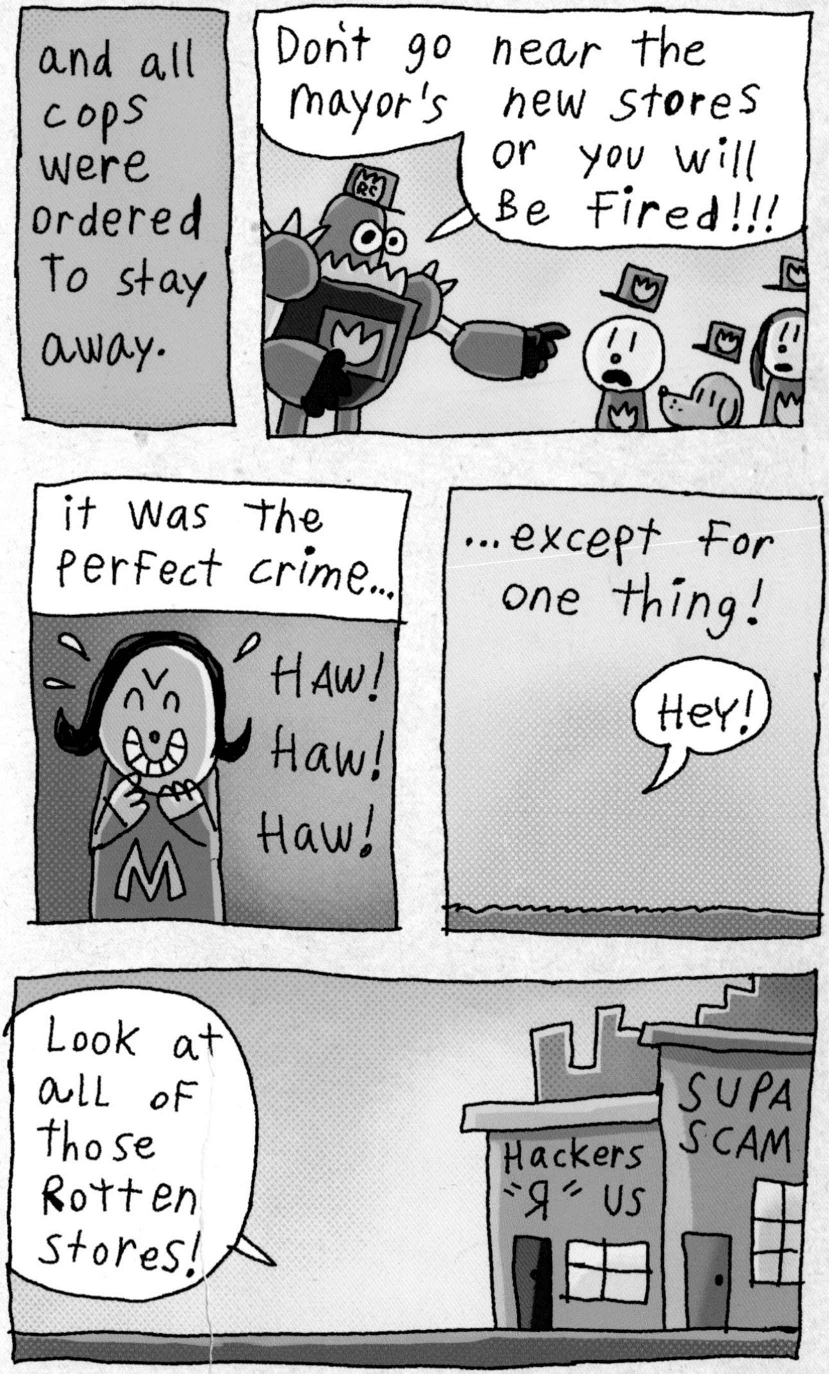
and all cops were ordered To stay away.
Don't go near the mayor's new stores or you will Be Fired!!!
it was the perfect crime...
HAW! Haw! Haw!
...except For one thing!
HEY!
Look at all of those Rotten stores!
SUPA SCAM
Hackers Я US

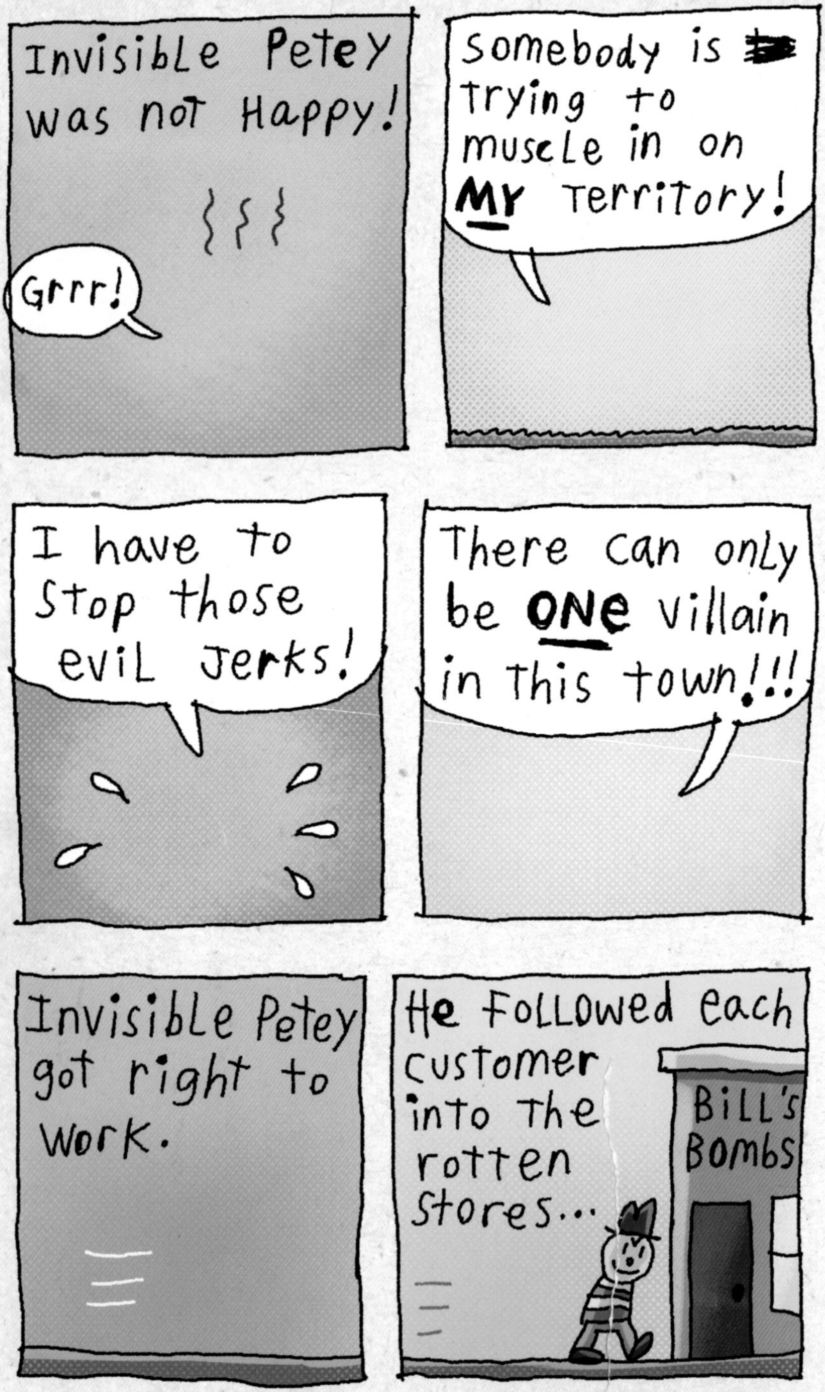
Invisible Petey was not Happy!
Grrr!
Somebody is trying to muscle in on MY Territory!
I have to Stop those evil Jerks!
There can only be ONE villain in this town!!!
Invisible Petey got right to work.
He Followed each customer into the rotten Stores...
BILL'S BOMBS

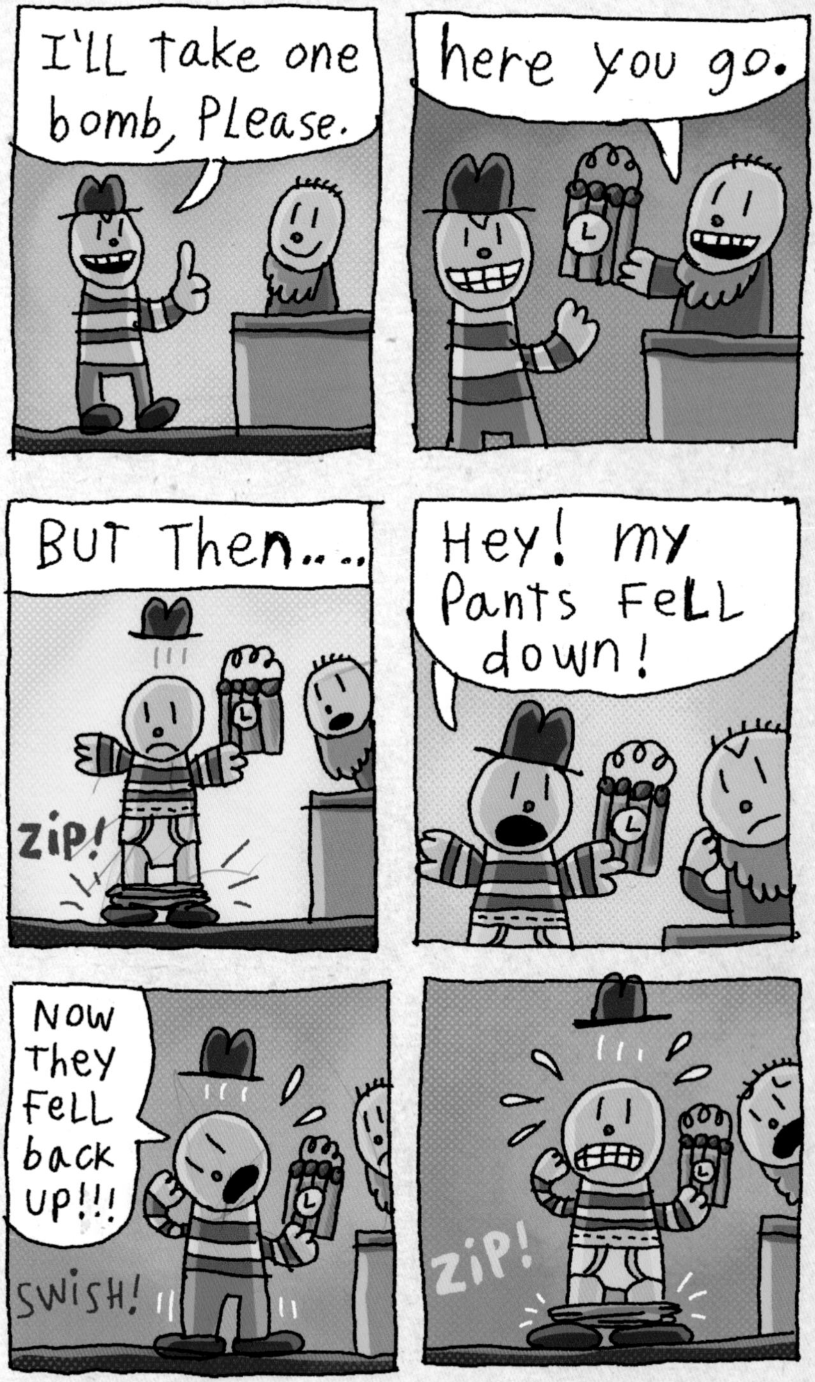
I'LL take one bomb, PLease.
here you go.
BUT Then....
ZIP!
Hey! my Pants FeLL down!
Now they FeLL back up!!!
SWISH!
ZIP!

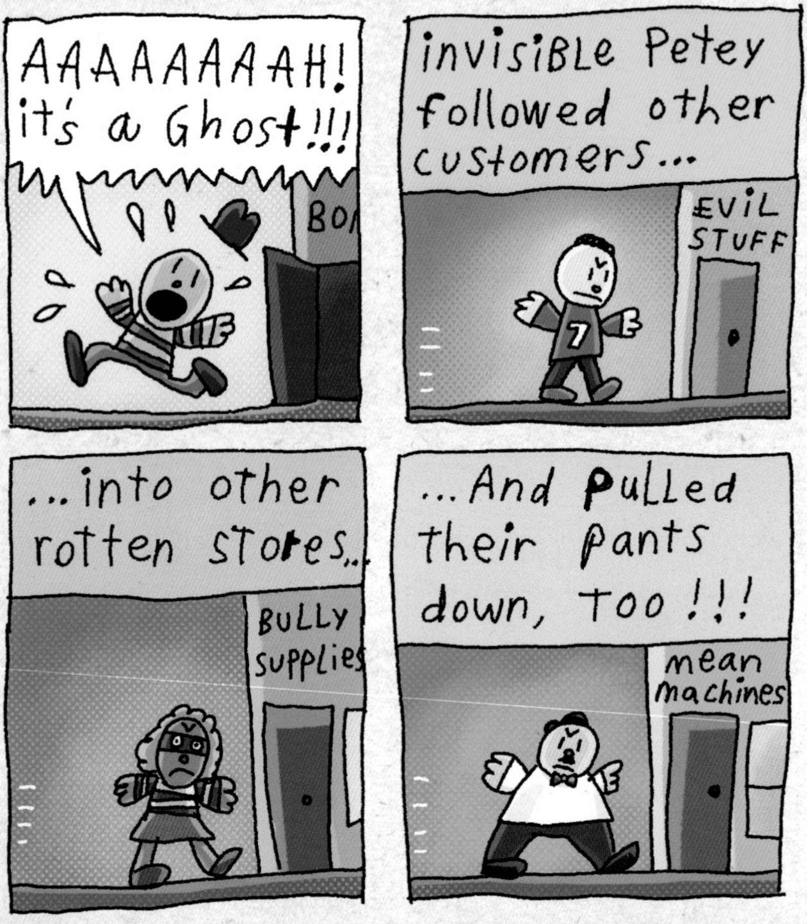
AAAAAAAAH! it's a Ghost!!!
BO
invisible Petey followed other customers...
EVIL STUFF
...into other rotten stores...
BULLY SUPPLIES
...And pulled their pants down, too!!!
mean machines

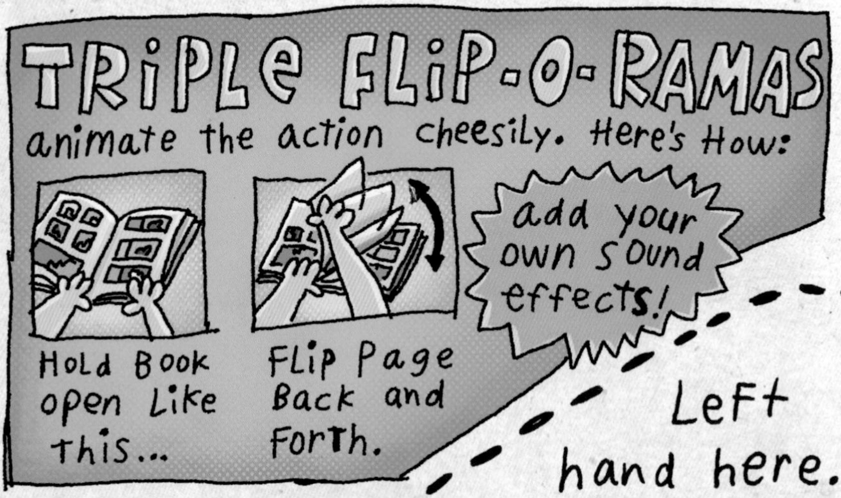
TRIPLE FLIP-O-RAMAS
animate the action cheesily. Here's How:
Hold Book open Like this...
Flip Page Back and Forth.
add your own sound effects!

Left hand here.

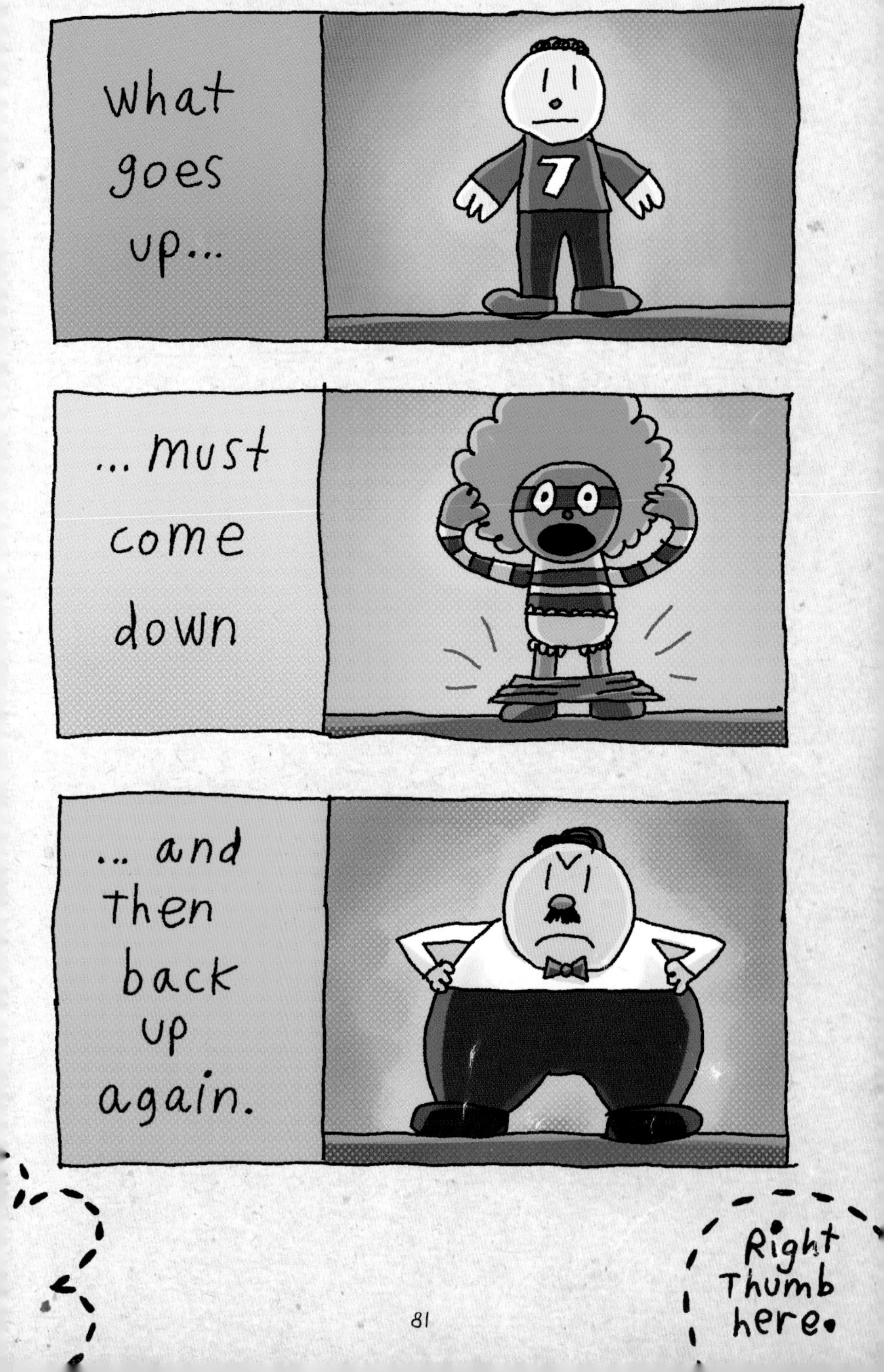
what goes up...
7
...must come down
... and then back up again.
Right Thumb here.

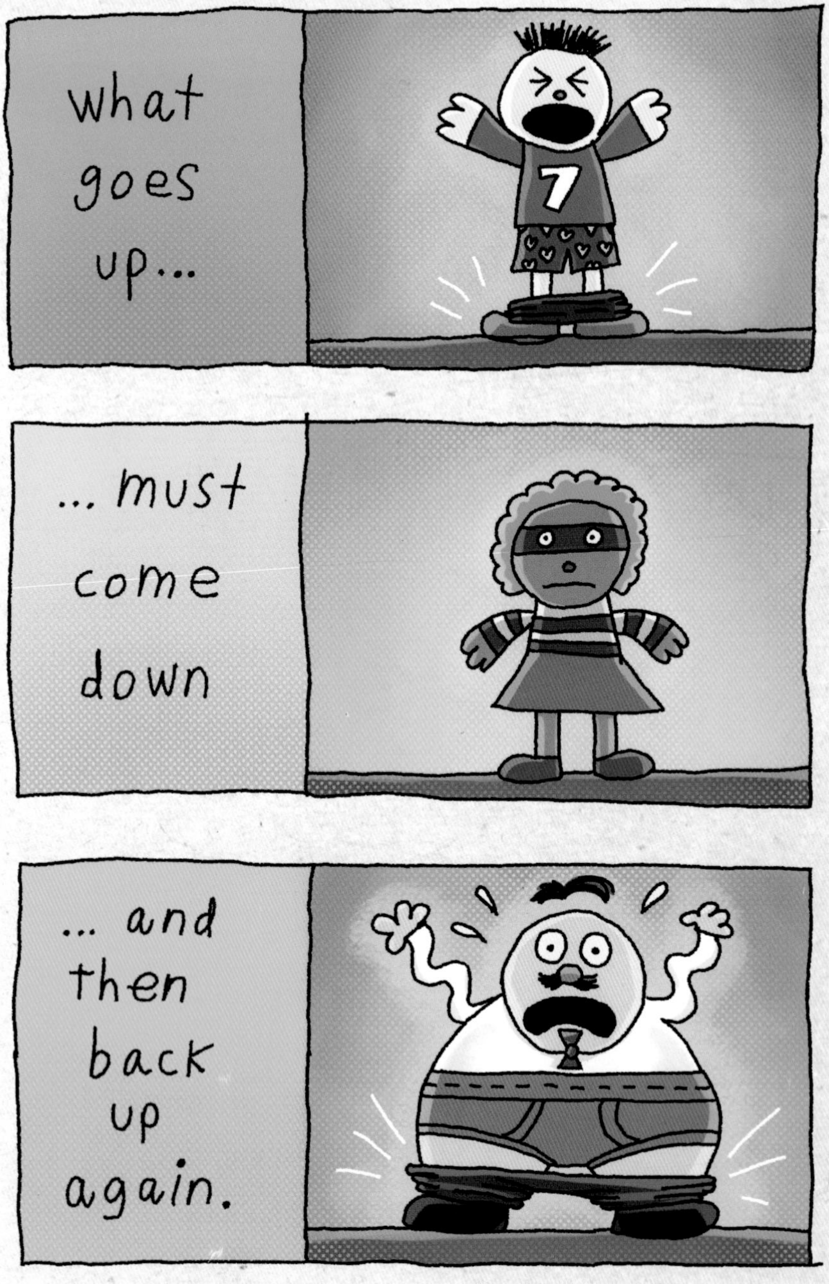
what goes up...
... must come down
... and then back up again.

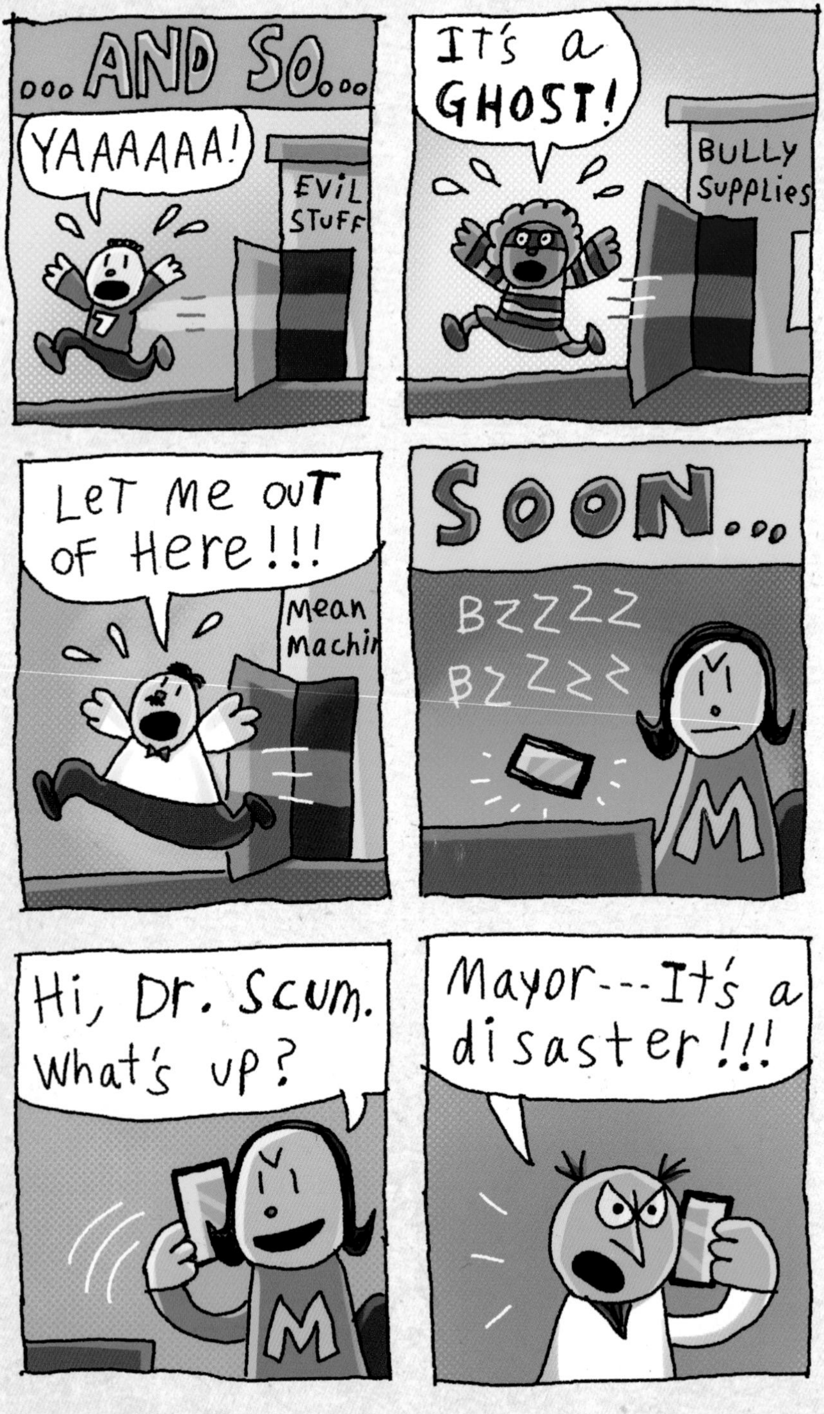
...AND SO...
YAAAAAA!
EVIL STUFF
It's a GHOST!
BULLY Supplies
Let Me OUT OF Here!!!
Mean Machi
SOON...
BZZZZ
BZZZZ
Hi, Dr. Scum. What's up?
Mayor---It's a disaster!!!

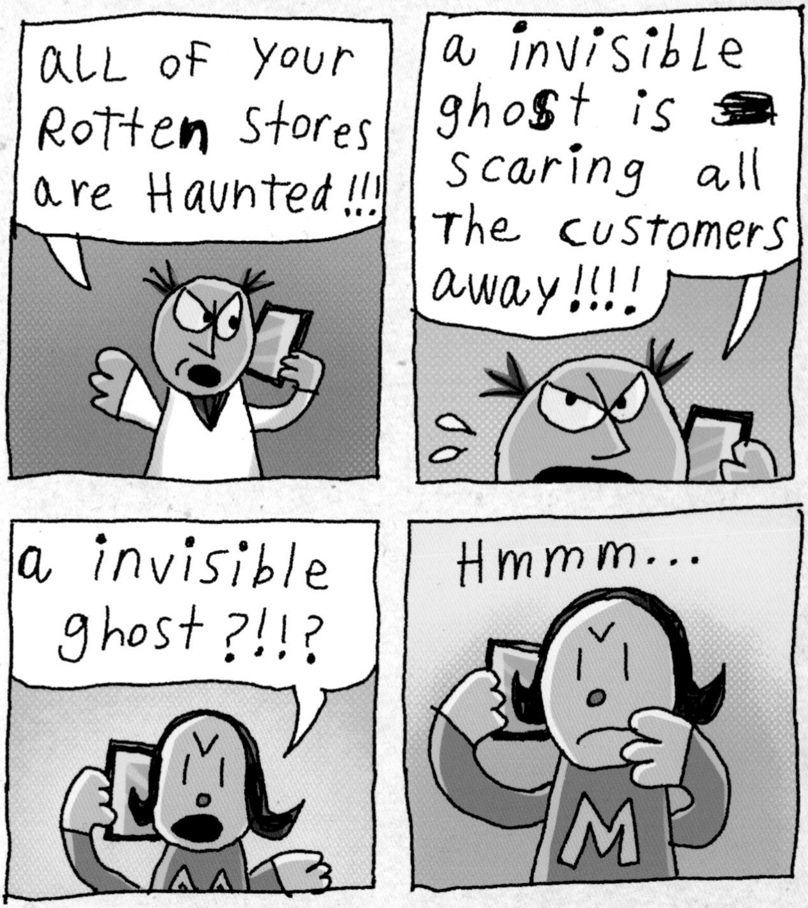
ALL of your Rotten Stores are Haunted!!!
a invisible ghost is scaring all The customers away!!!!
a invisible ghost?!!?
Hmmm...
PETEY!

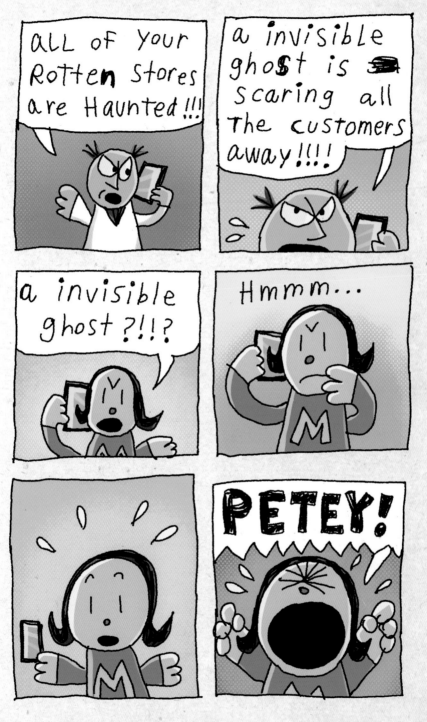

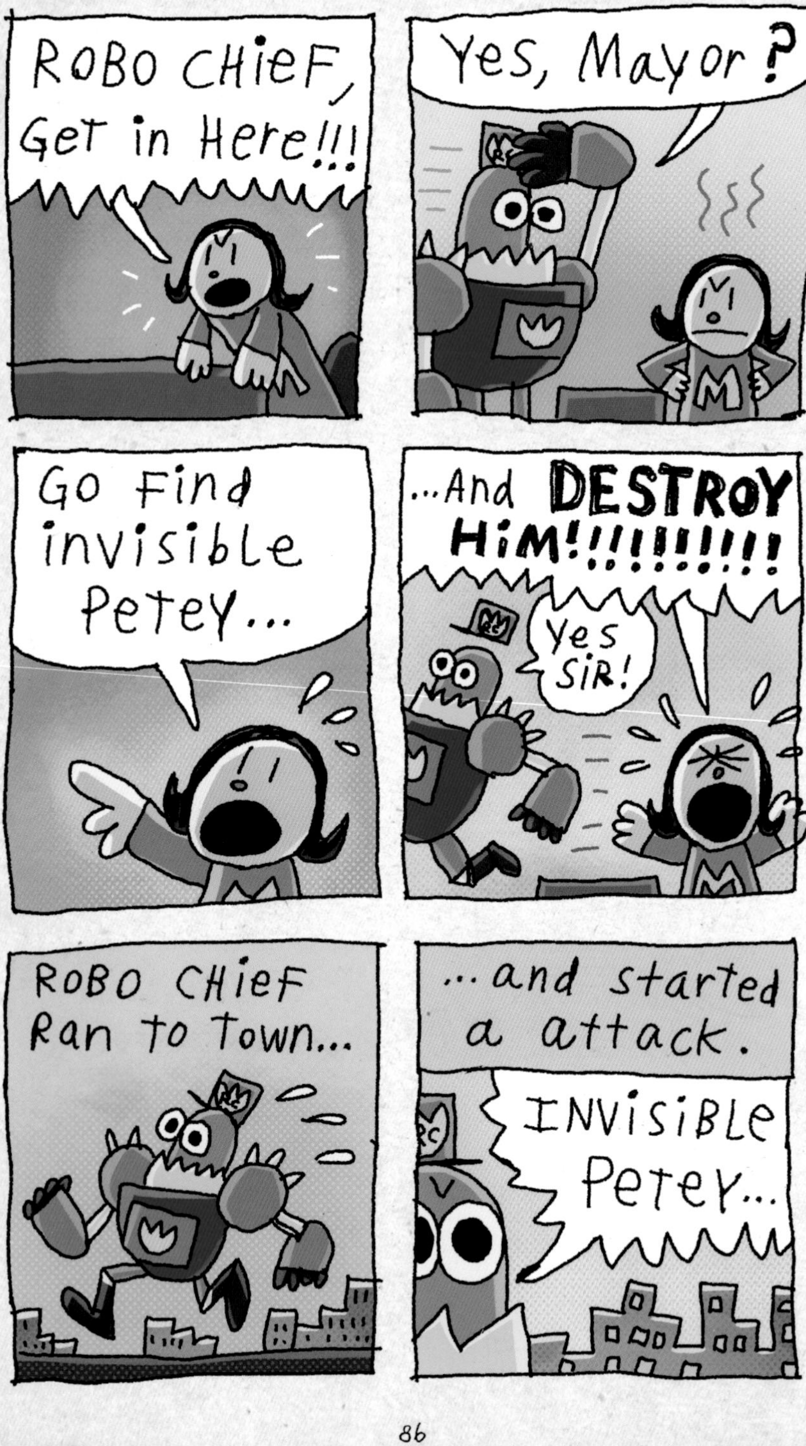
ROBO CHIEF, Get in Here!!!
Yes, Mayor?
Go Find invisible Petey...
...And DESTROY HIM!!!!!!!!!!!
Yes SIR!
ROBO CHIEF Ran to Town...
...and started a attack.
INVISIBLE Petey...

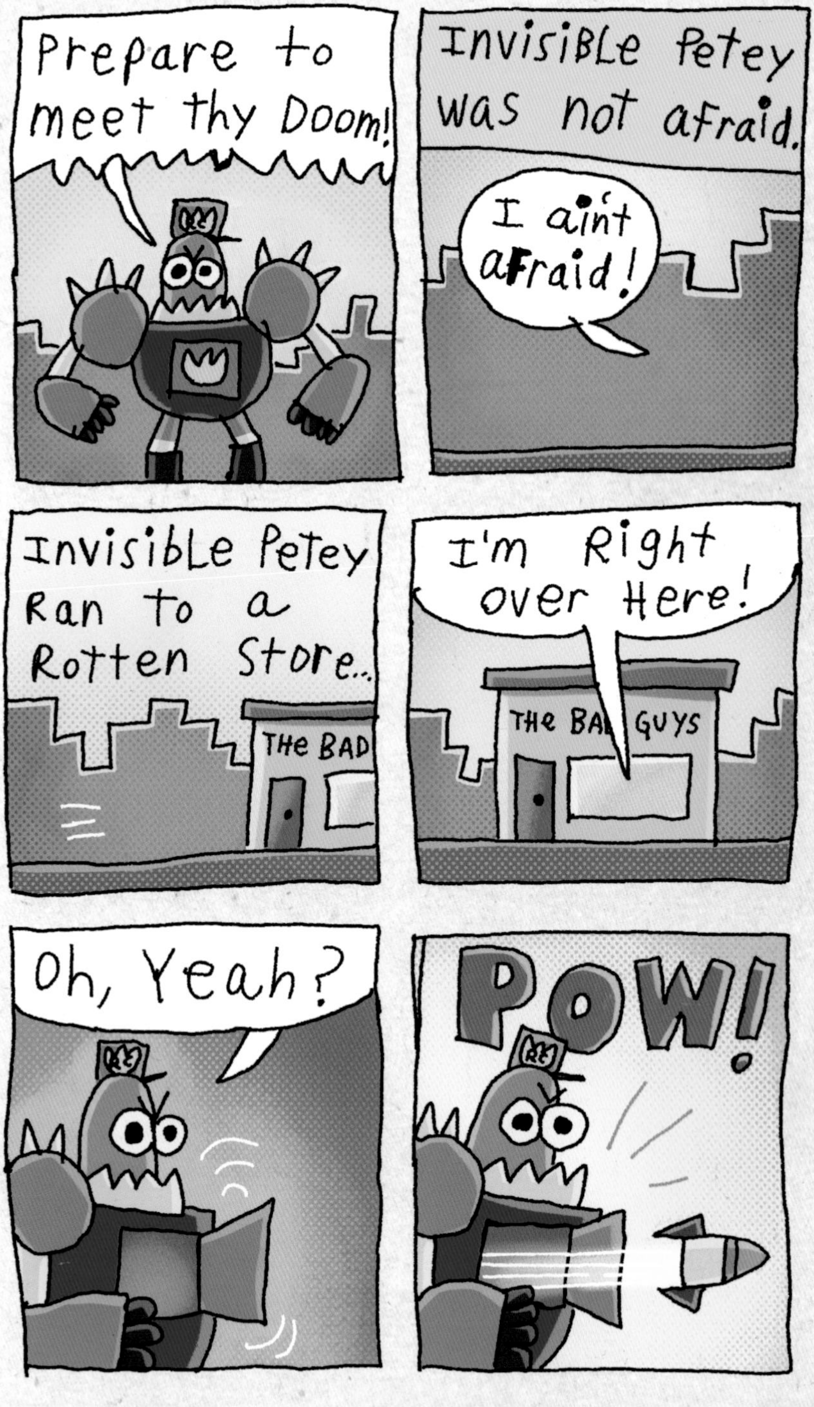
Prepare to meet thy Doom!
Invisible Petey was not afraid.
I ain't afraid!
Invisible Petey Ran to a Rotten Store...
THE BAD
I'm Right over Here!
THE BAD GUYS
Oh, Yeah?
POW!

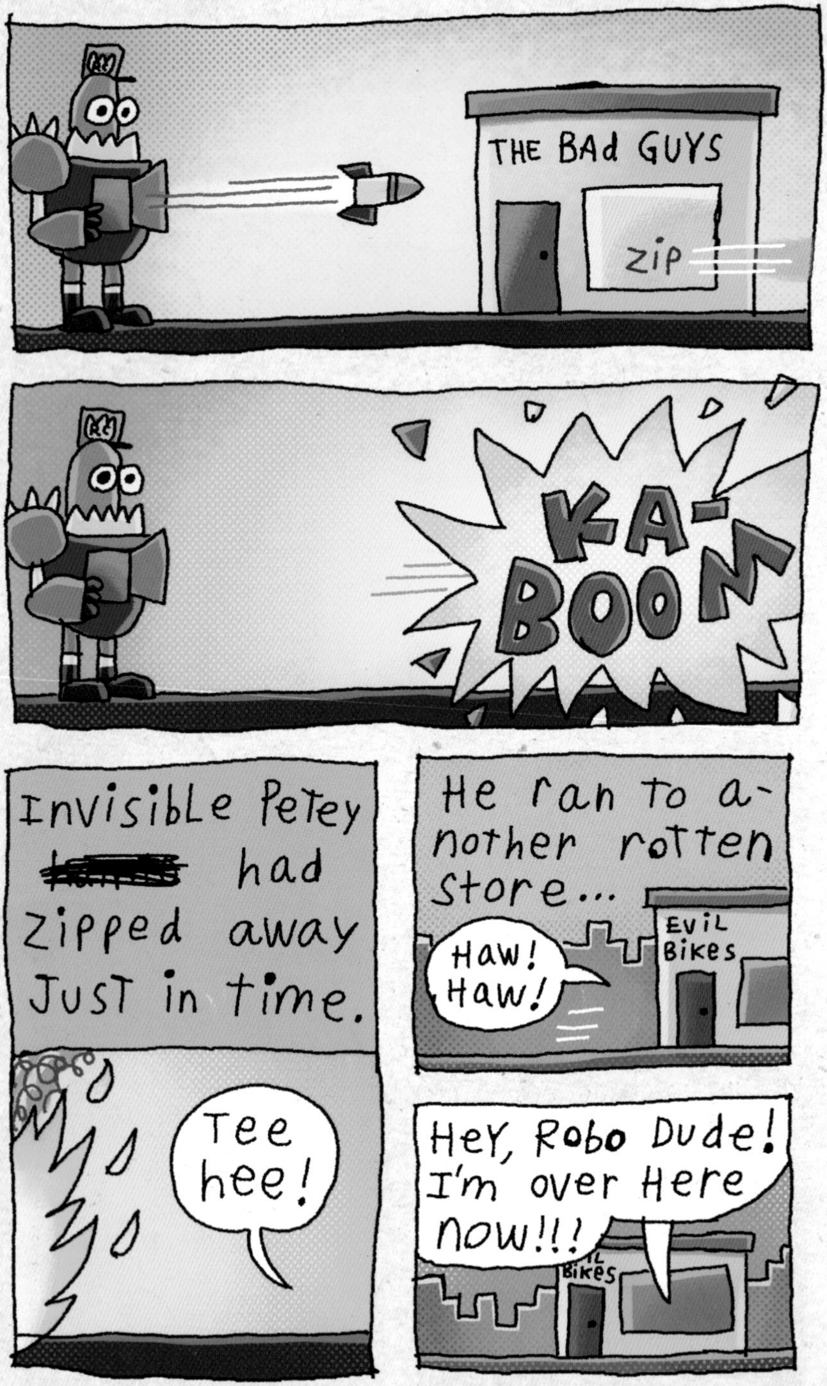
THE BAd GUYS
Zip
KA-BOOM
Invisible Petey had zipped away just in time.
Tee hee!
He ran to a-nother rotten store...
EViL BiKes
Haw! Haw!
Hey, Robo Dude! I'm over Here now!!!
Bikes

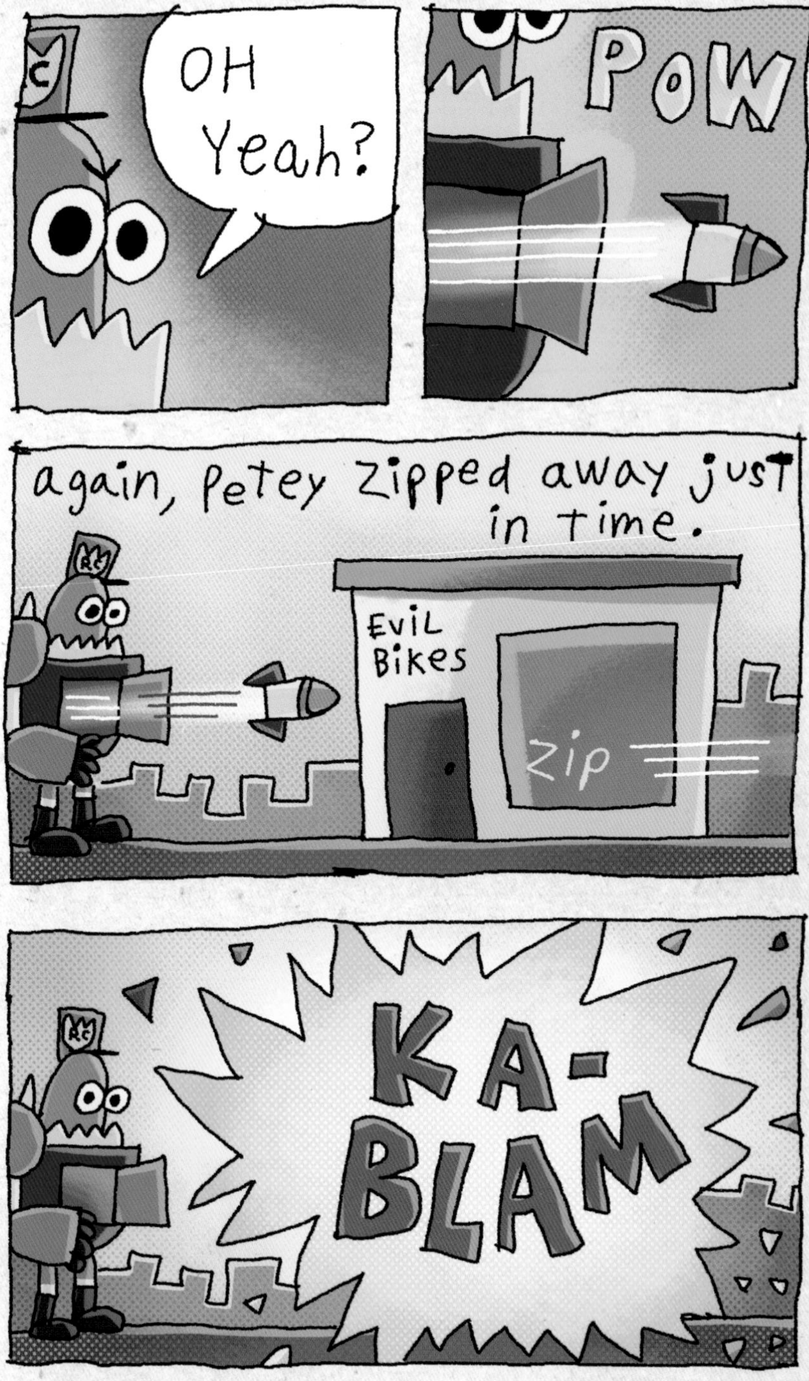
OH Yeah?
POW
again, Petey Zipped away just in time.
EVIL Bikes
Zip
KA-BLAM

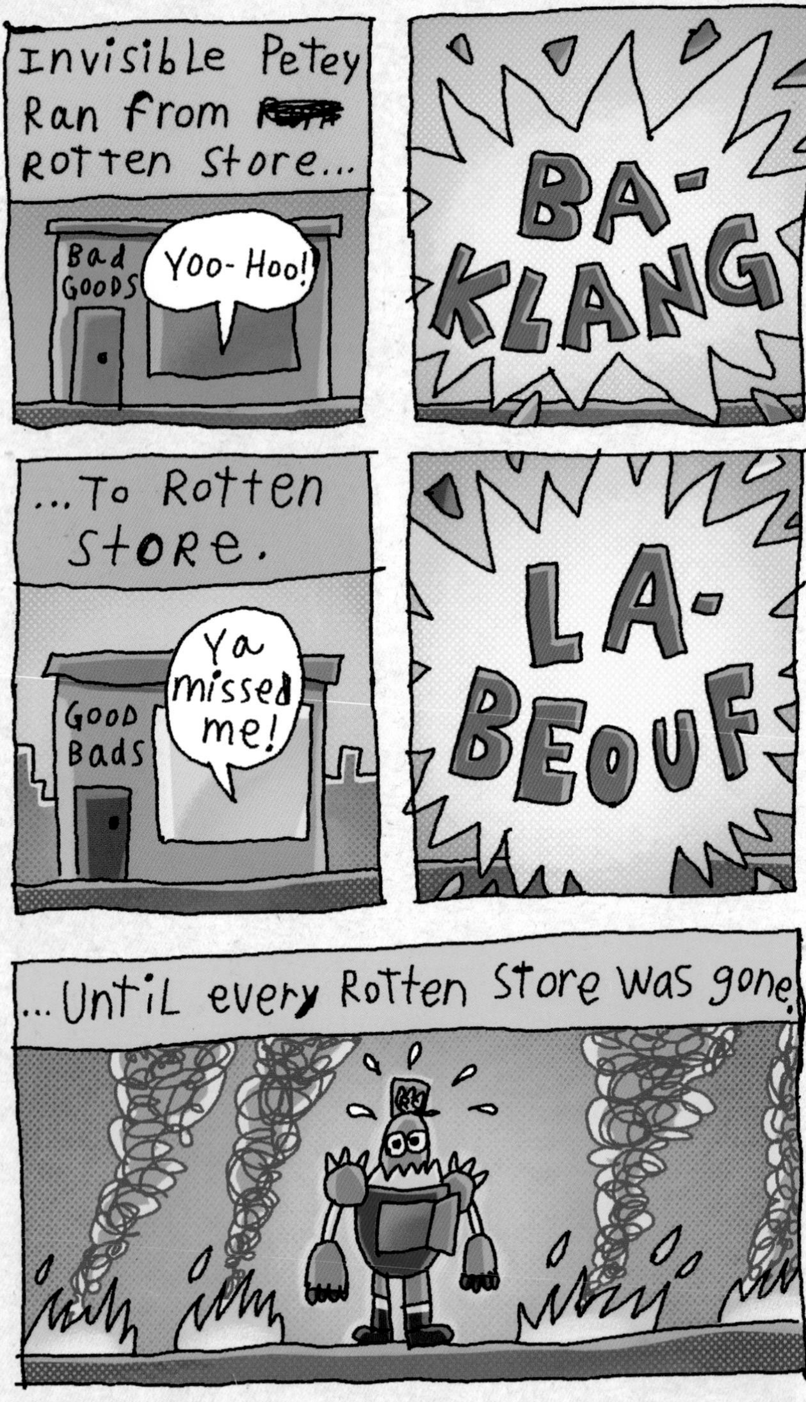
Invisible Petey Ran from rotten store...
Bad GOODS
Yoo-Hoo!
BA-KLANG
...To Rotten store.
GOOD Bads
Ya missed me!
LA-BEOUF
...Until every Rotten Store was gone.

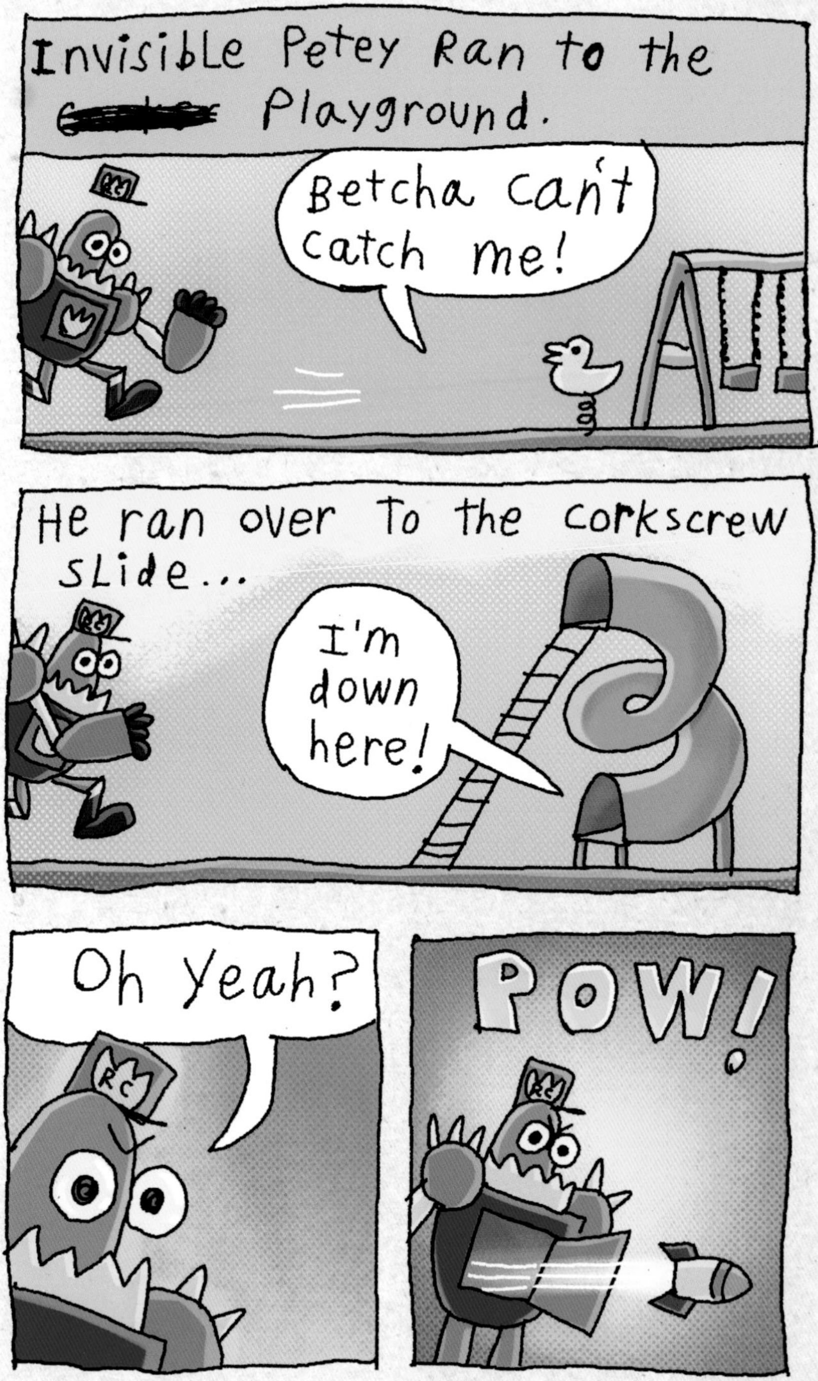
Invisible Petey Ran to the Playground.
Betcha can't catch me!
He ran over To the corkscrew sLide...
I'm down here!
Oh yeah?
POW!

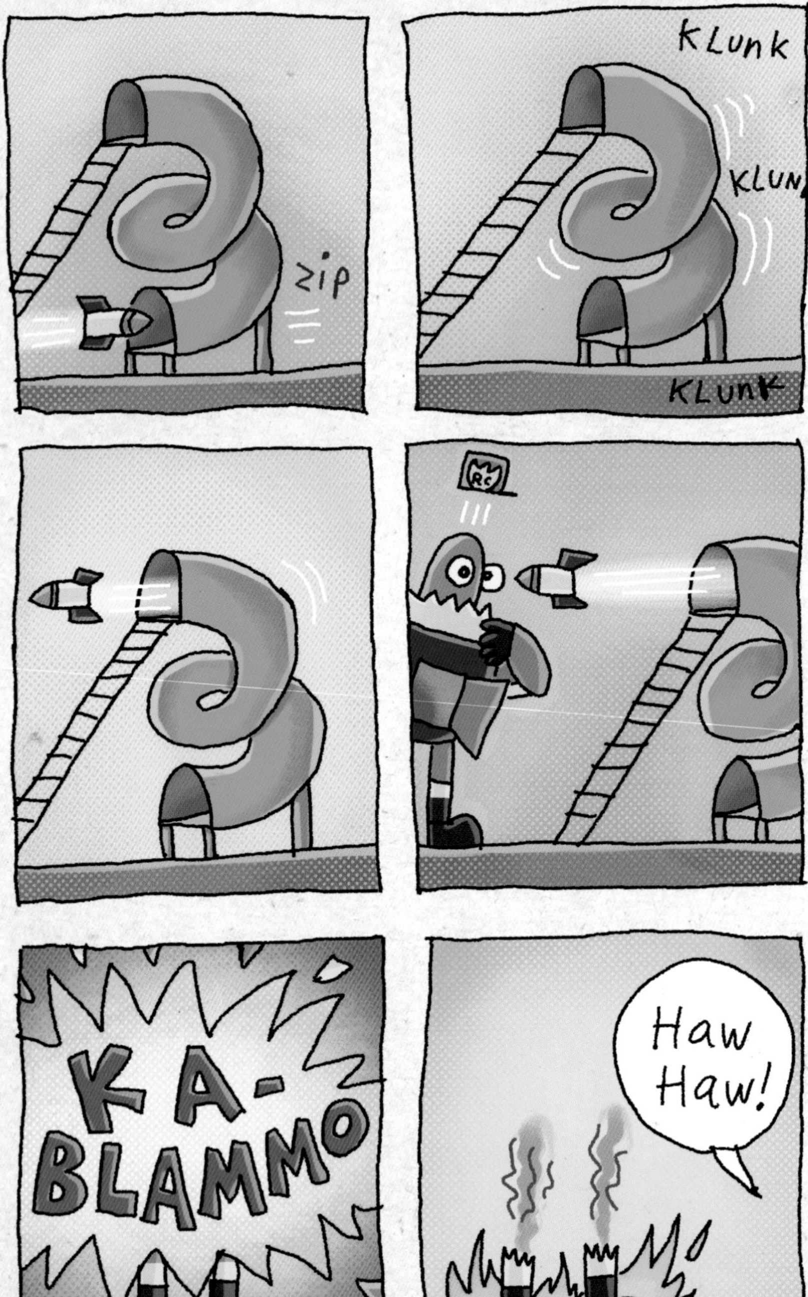
zip
KLunk
KLUNK
KLUNK
KA-
BLAMMO
Haw
Haw!

SOON... Ring Ring

HeLLo, Dr. Scum. Did RoBo chief Destroy Invisible PeTey?

Dr. Scum Told Mayor The bad news.

NOOO

Mayor had one Last plan up her evil sleeve.

She drove to the cop Station...

Mayor

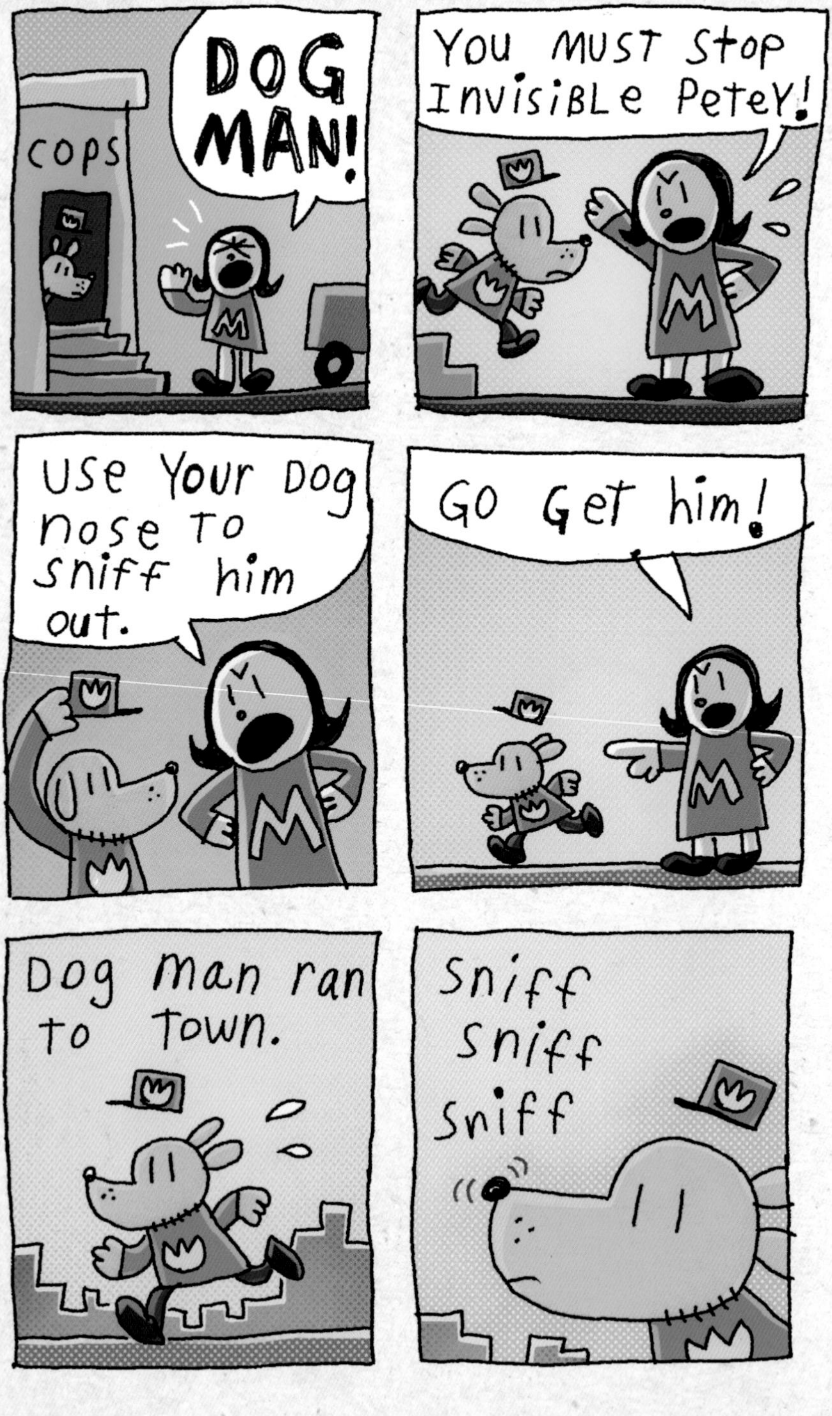
DOG MAN!
COPS
YOU MUST STOP INVISIBLE PETEY!
USE YOUR DOG NOSE TO SNIFF HIM OUT.
GO GET HIM!
DOG MAN RAN TO TOWN.
SNIFF
SNIFF
SNIFF

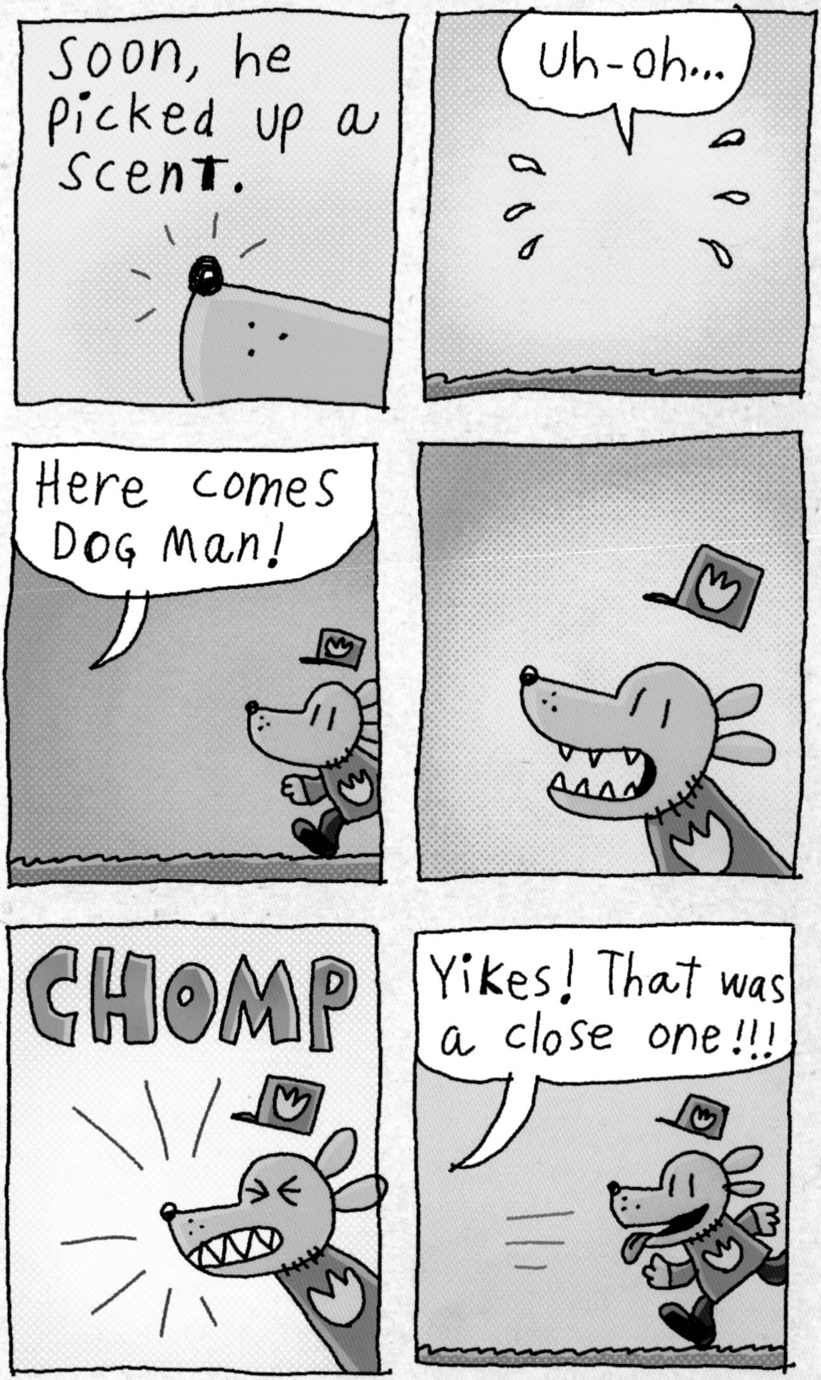
Soon, he picked up a scent.
Uh-oh...
Here comes DOG Man!
CHOMP
Yikes! That was a close one!!!

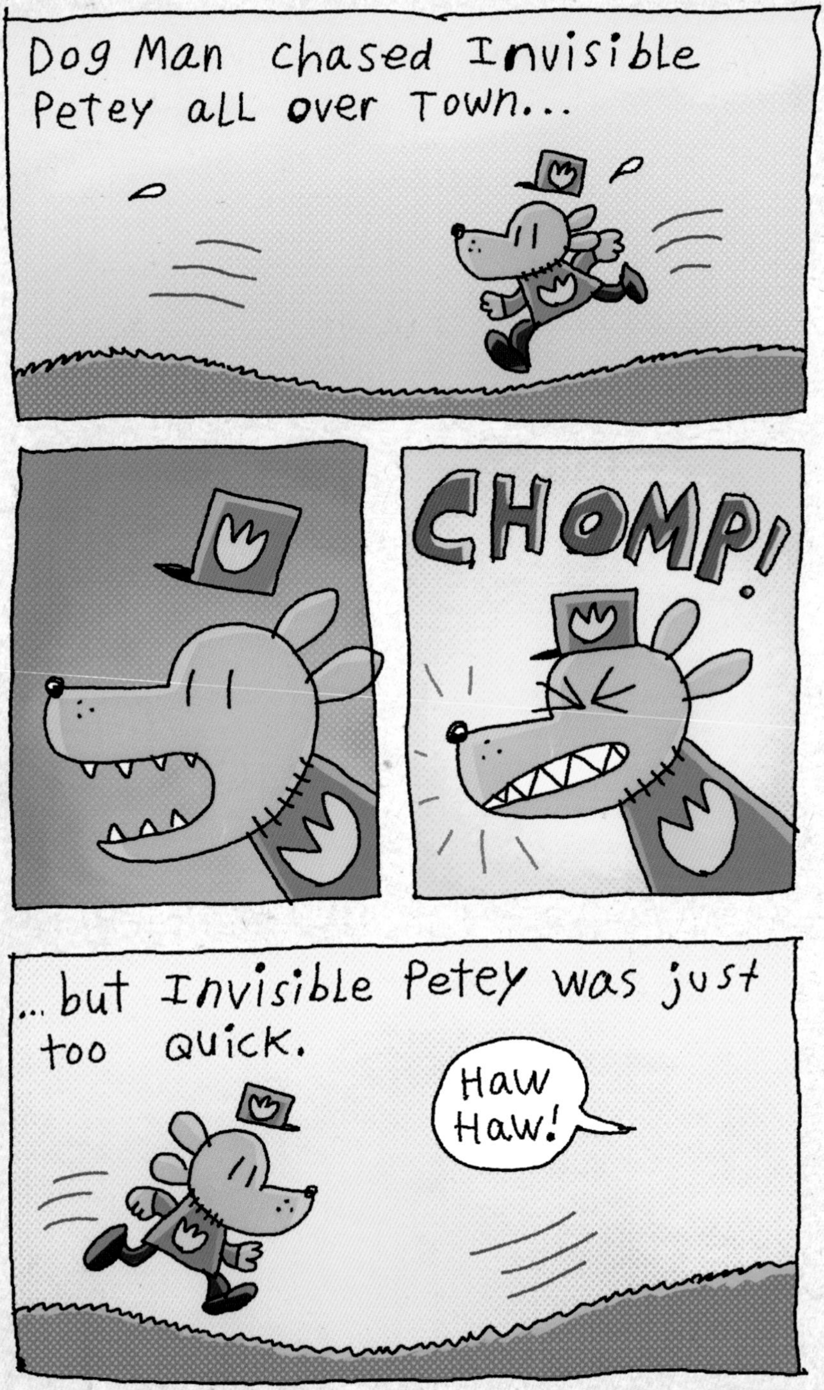
Dog Man chased Invisible Petey all over Town...
CHOMP!
...but Invisible Petey was just too quick.
Haw Haw!

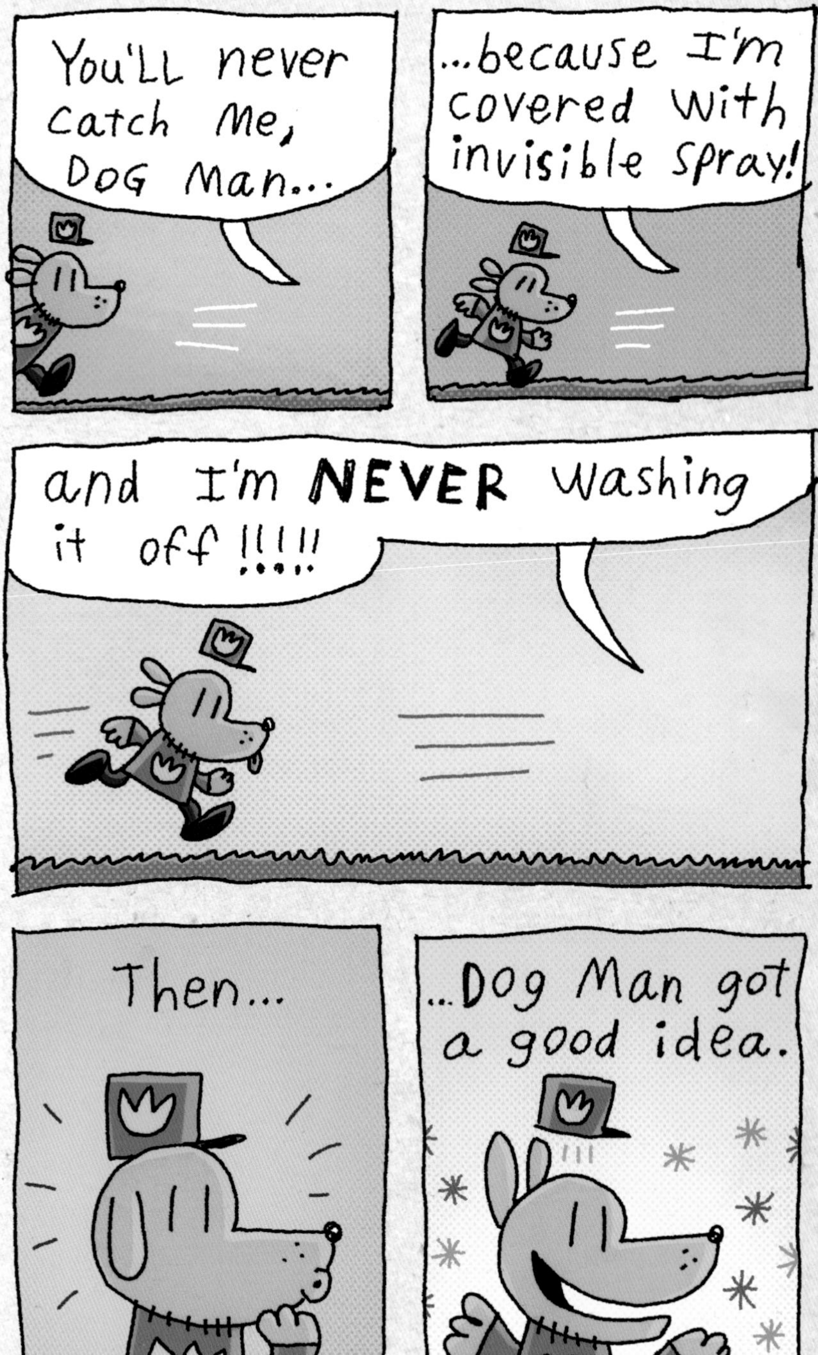
You'LL never catch me, DOG Man...
...because I'm covered with invisible spray!
and I'm NEVER washing it off!!!!!
Then...
...Dog Man got a good idea.

Supa
Soaker

Right
Thumb
here.

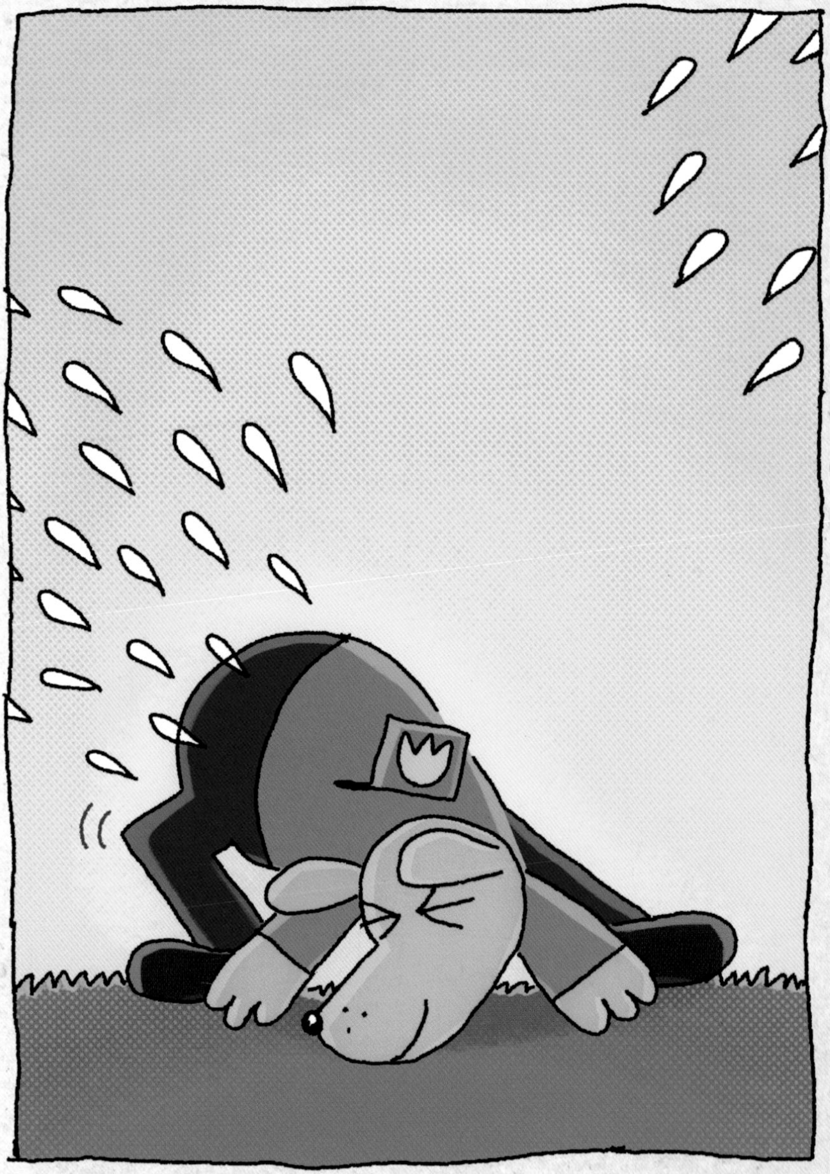

Supa
Soaker

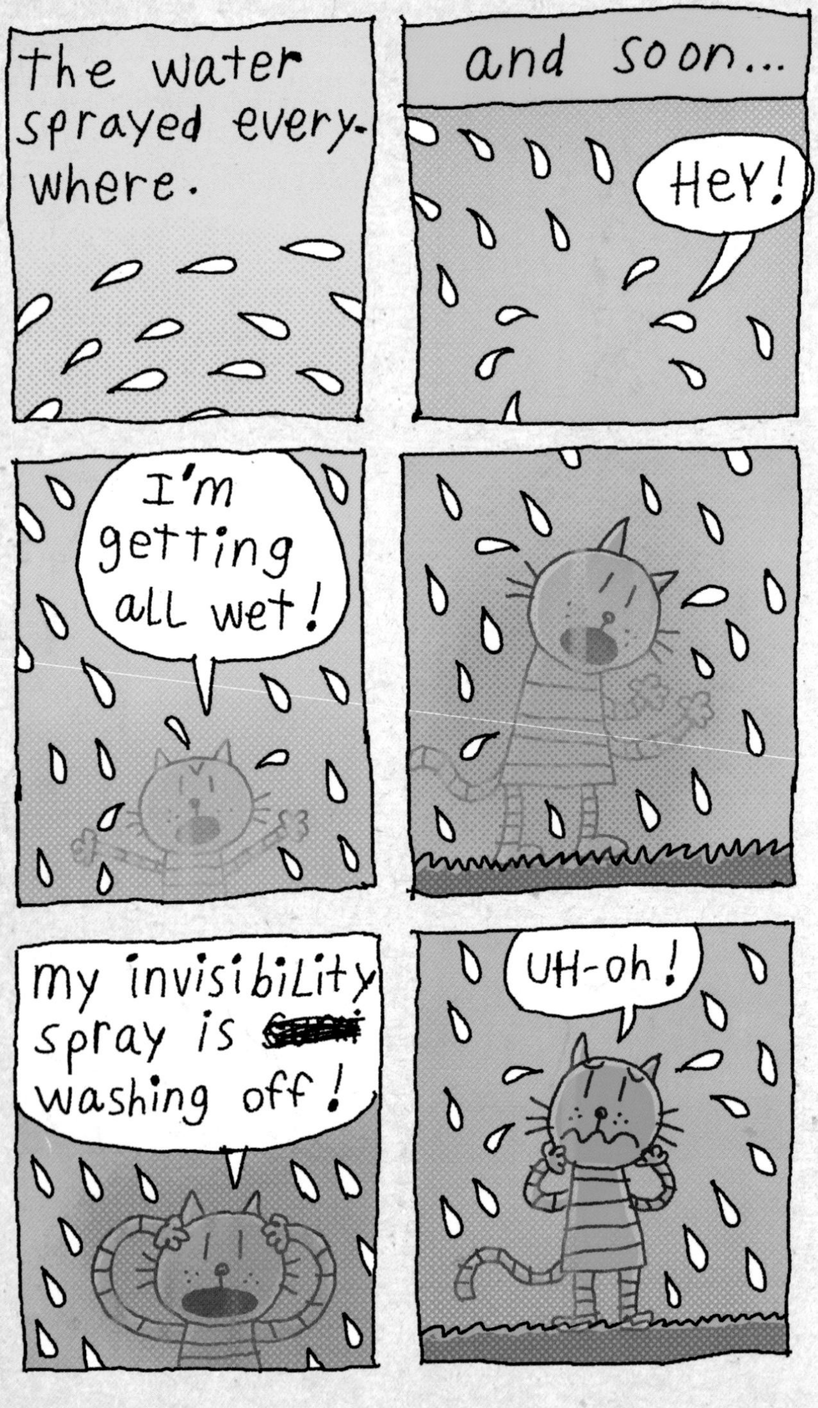
The water sprayed every-where.
and soon...
HEY!
I'm getting all wet!
my invisibiLity spray is [redacted] washing off!
UH-oh!

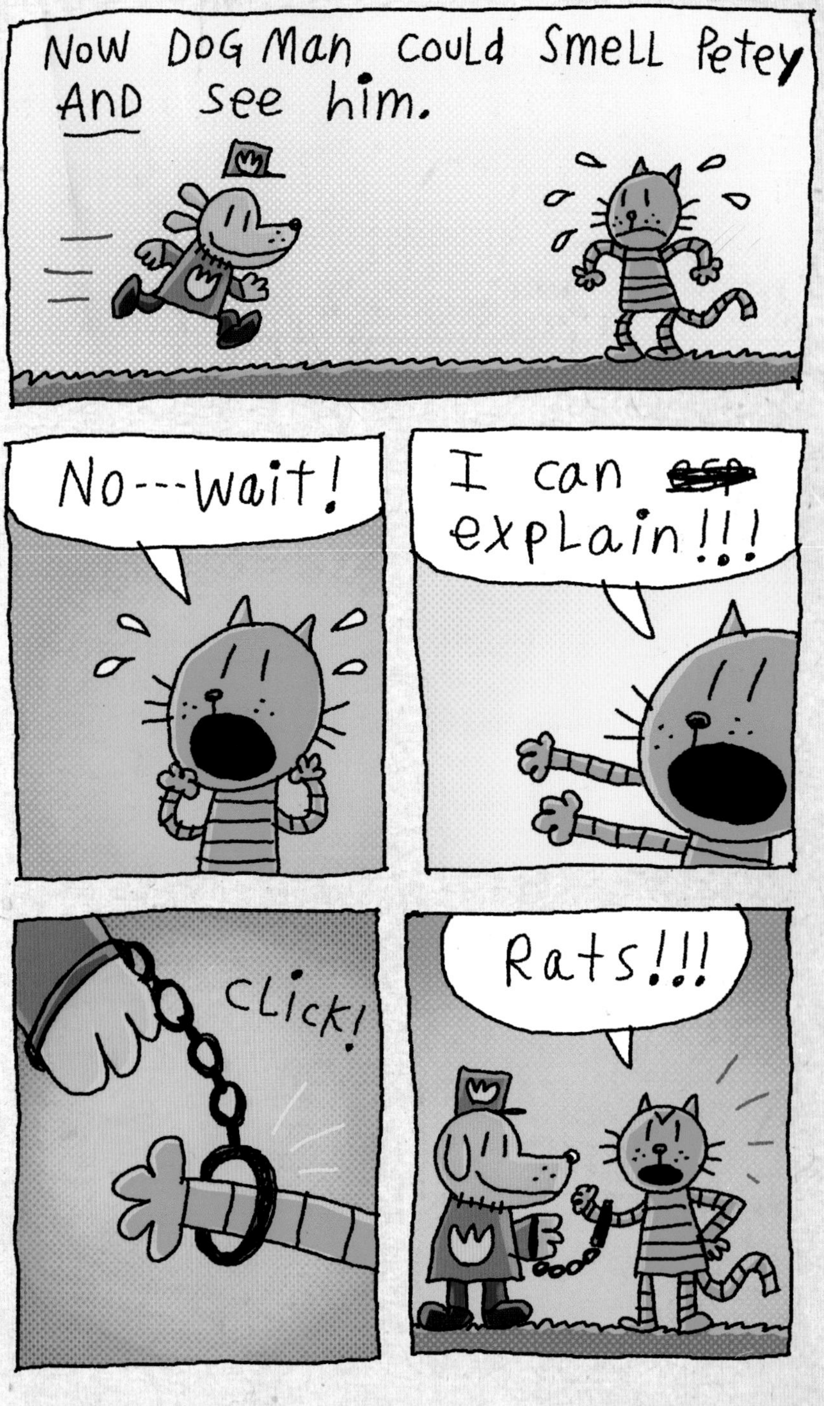
Now Dog Man could smell Petey AND see him.
No---wait!
I can explain!!!
Click!
Rats!!!

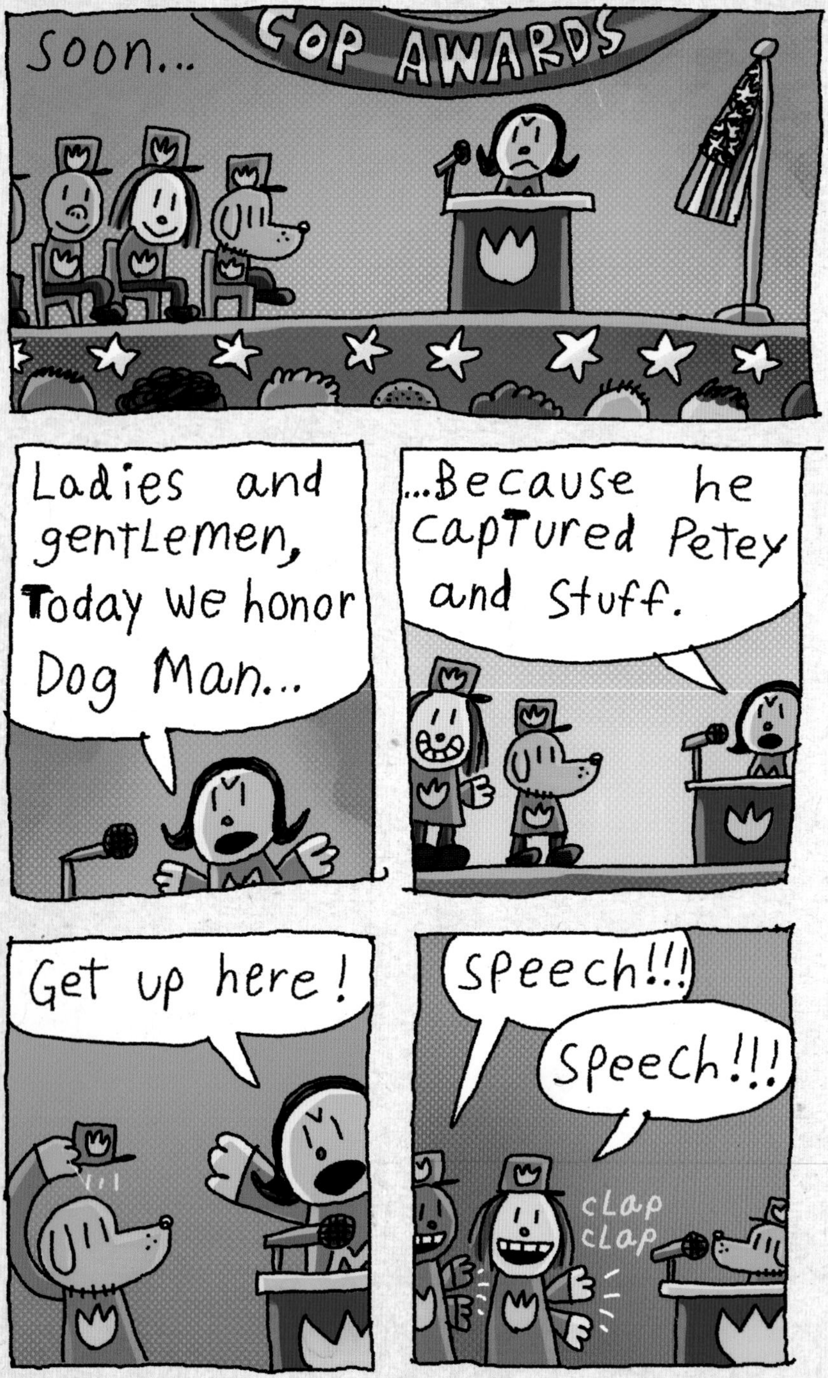
Soon...
COP AWARDS
Ladies and gentlemen, Today we honor Dog Man...
...Because he captured Petey and stuff.
Get up here!
Speech!!!
Speech!!!
clap clap

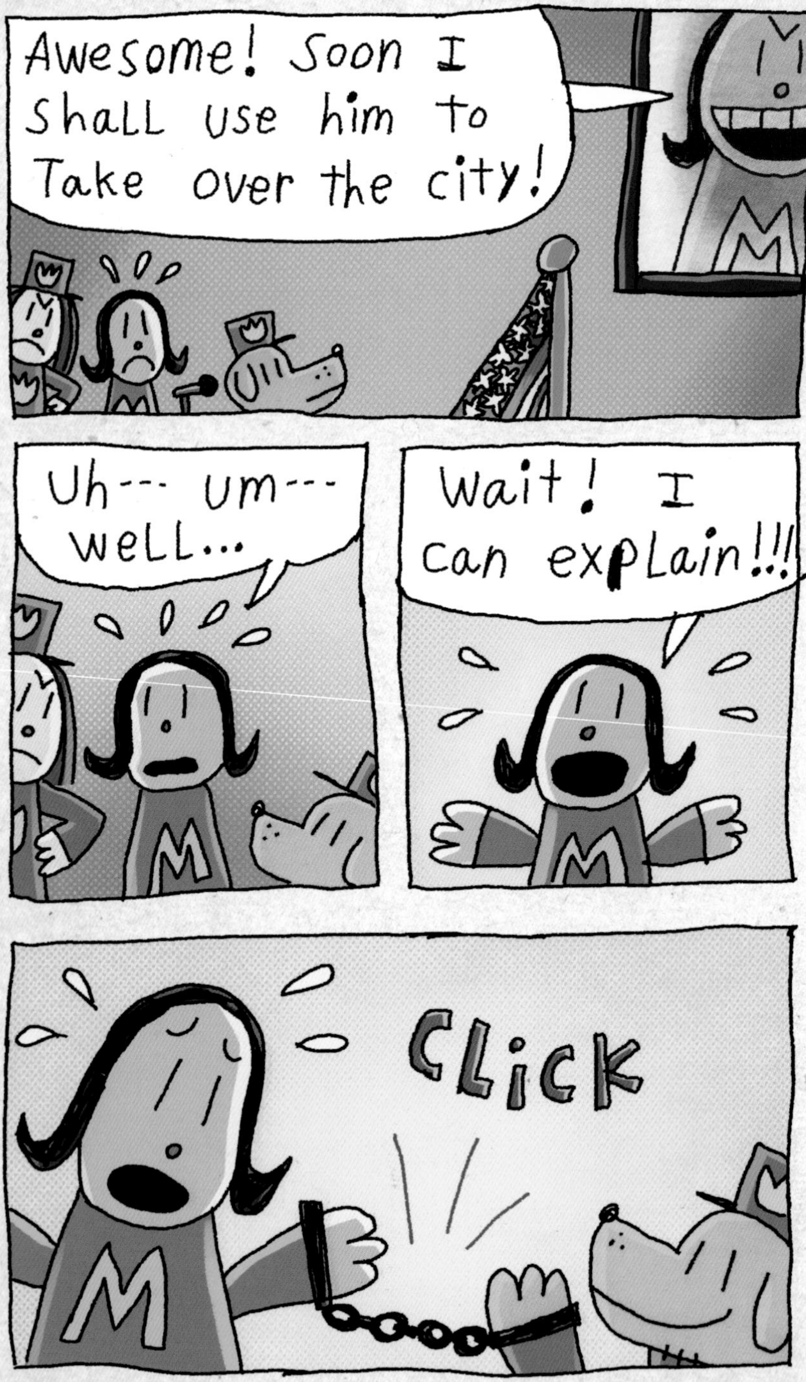
Awesome! Soon I Shall use him to Take over the city!
Uh--- um--- weLL...
Wait! I can expLain!!!
CLicK

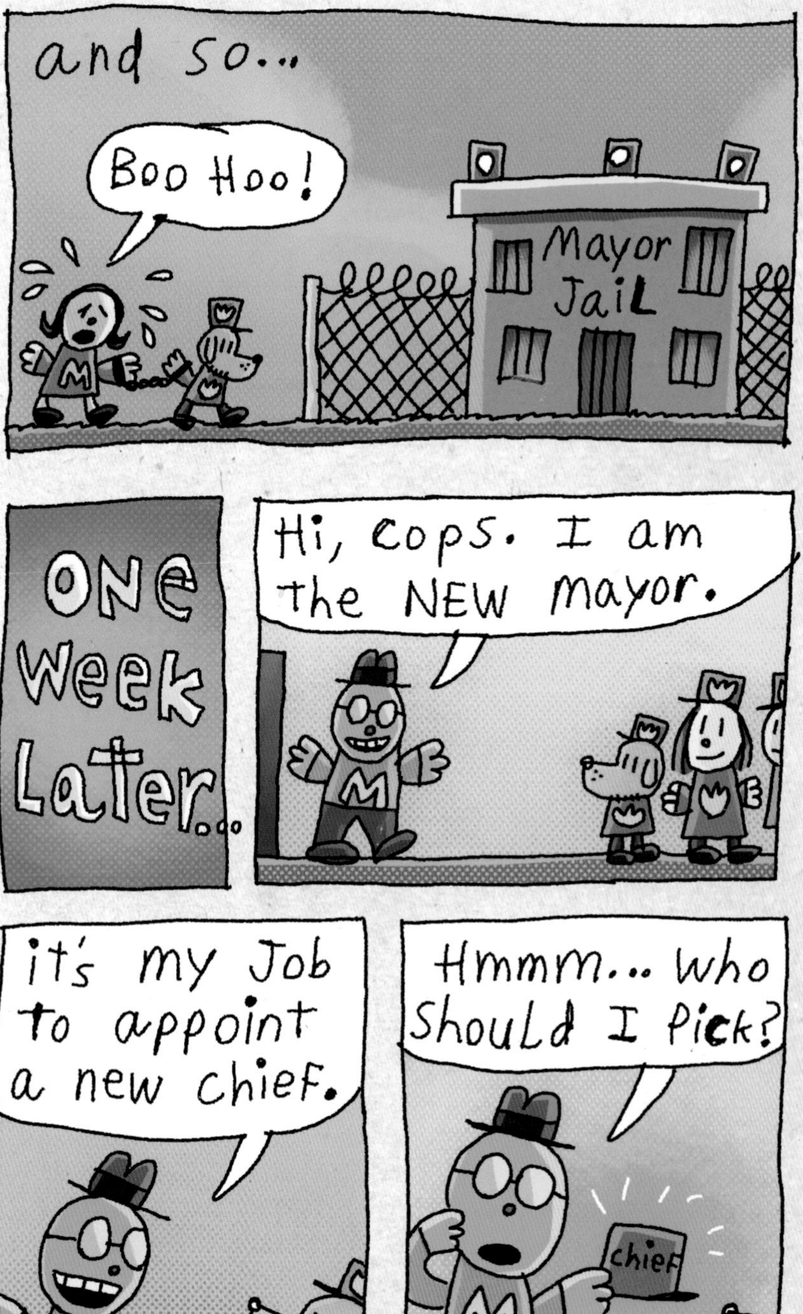
and so...
Boo Hoo!
Mayor Jail
One Week Later...
Hi, cops. I am the NEW mayor.
it's my Job to appoint a new chief.
Hmmm... who Should I Pick?
chief

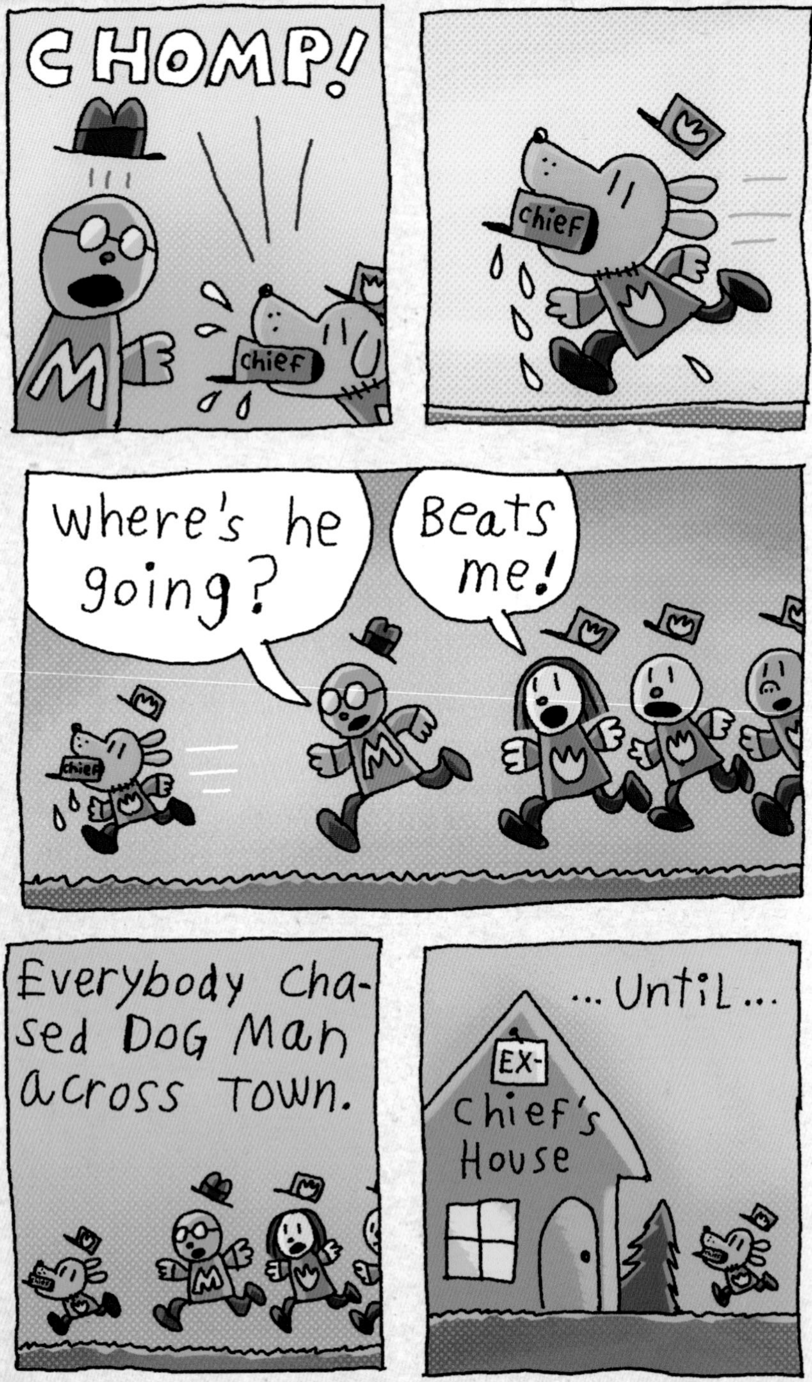
CHOMP!
chief
chief
Where's he going?
Beats me!
chief
Everybody Chased DOG Man across Town.
...UntiL...
EX-
Chief's House

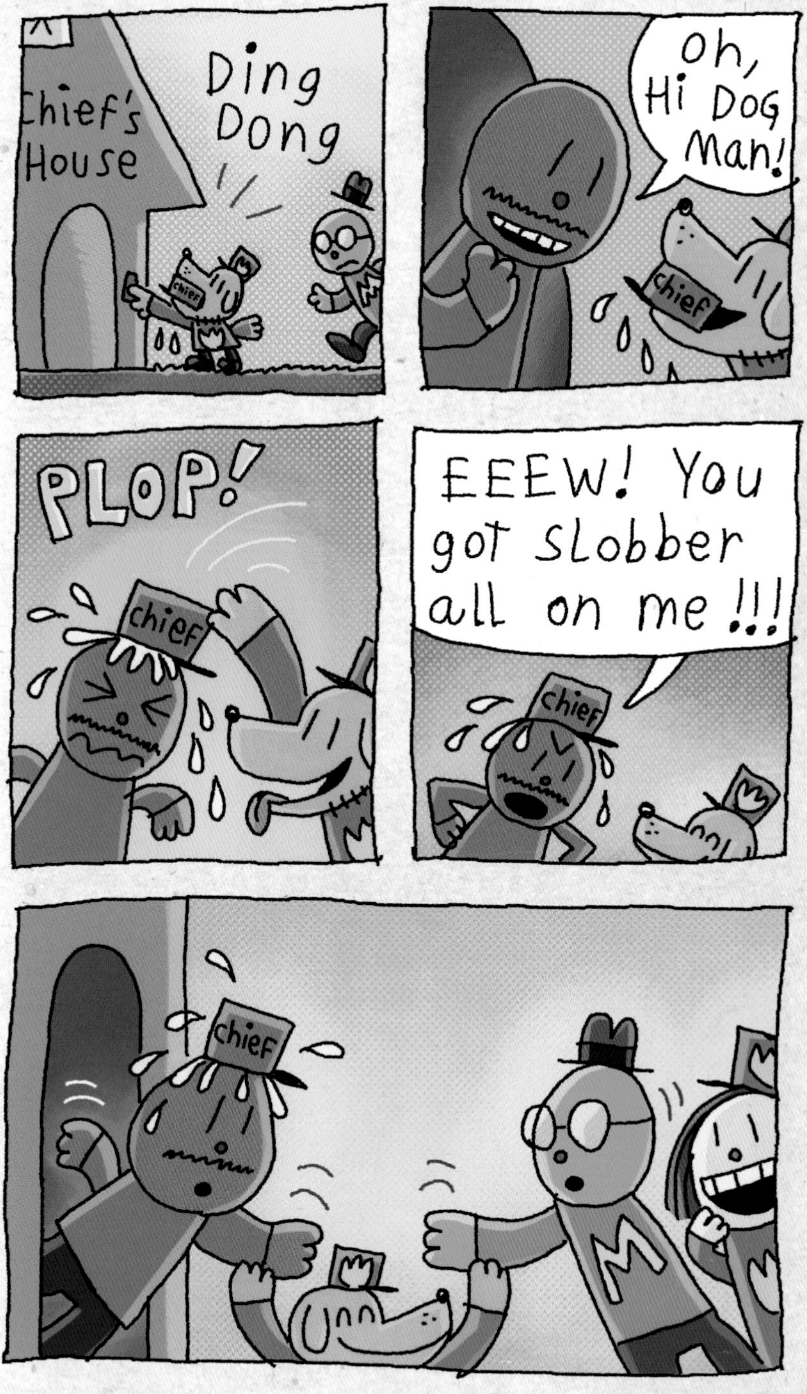
Chief's House
Ding Dong
chief
Oh, Hi Dog Man!
chief
PLOP!
chief
EEEW! You got slobber all on me!!!
chief
chief

CHAPTER 3

Jerome Horwitz Elementary School

We put the "ow" in Knowledge

Dear Mr. and Mrs. Beard,

Once again I am writing to inform you of your son's disruptive activity in my classroom.

The assignment was to create a WRITTEN public service message to promote reading. Your son and his friend, Harold Hutchins (I am sending a nearly identical letter to Harold's mother), were specifically told NOT to make a comic book for this assignment.

As usual, they did exactly what they were told not to do (see attached comic book). When I confronted George about his disobedience, he claimed that this was not a comic book, but a "graphic novella." I am getting fed up with George's impudence.

I have told both boys on numerous occasions that the classroom is no place for creativity, yet they continue to make these obnoxious and offensive "comix." As you will see, this comic book contains multiple references to human and/or animal feces. It also features a very questionable scene of disregard for homeless/hungry individuals. There are scenes of smoking, violence, nudity, and don't get me started on the spelling and grammar. Frankly, I found the little trash bag "baby" at the end to be very disturbing. I mean, how is that even possible?!!?

George's silly, disruptive behavior, as well as these increasingly disgusting and scatological comic books, are turning my classroom into a zoo. I have spoken to Principal Krupp about Dog Man on numerous occasions. We both believe that you should consider psychological counseling for your son, or at the very least some kind of behavior modification drug to cure his "creative streak."

Regretfully,

Ms. Construde

Ms. Construde
Grade 1 Teacher

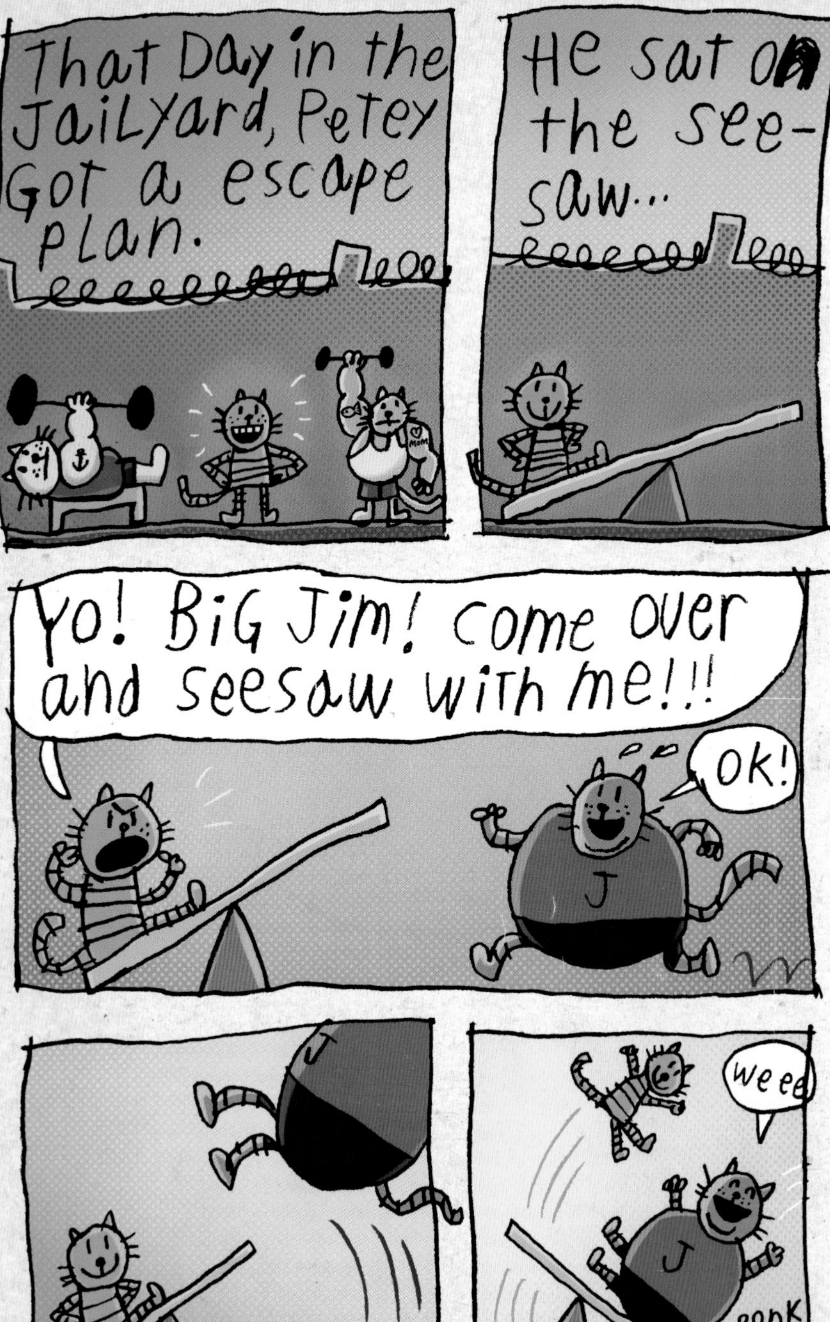
That Day in the JaiLyard, Petey Got a escape plan.
He sat o
the see-saw...
MOM
Yo! BiG Jim! Come over and seesaw with me!!!
OK!
J
J
weee
J
BONK

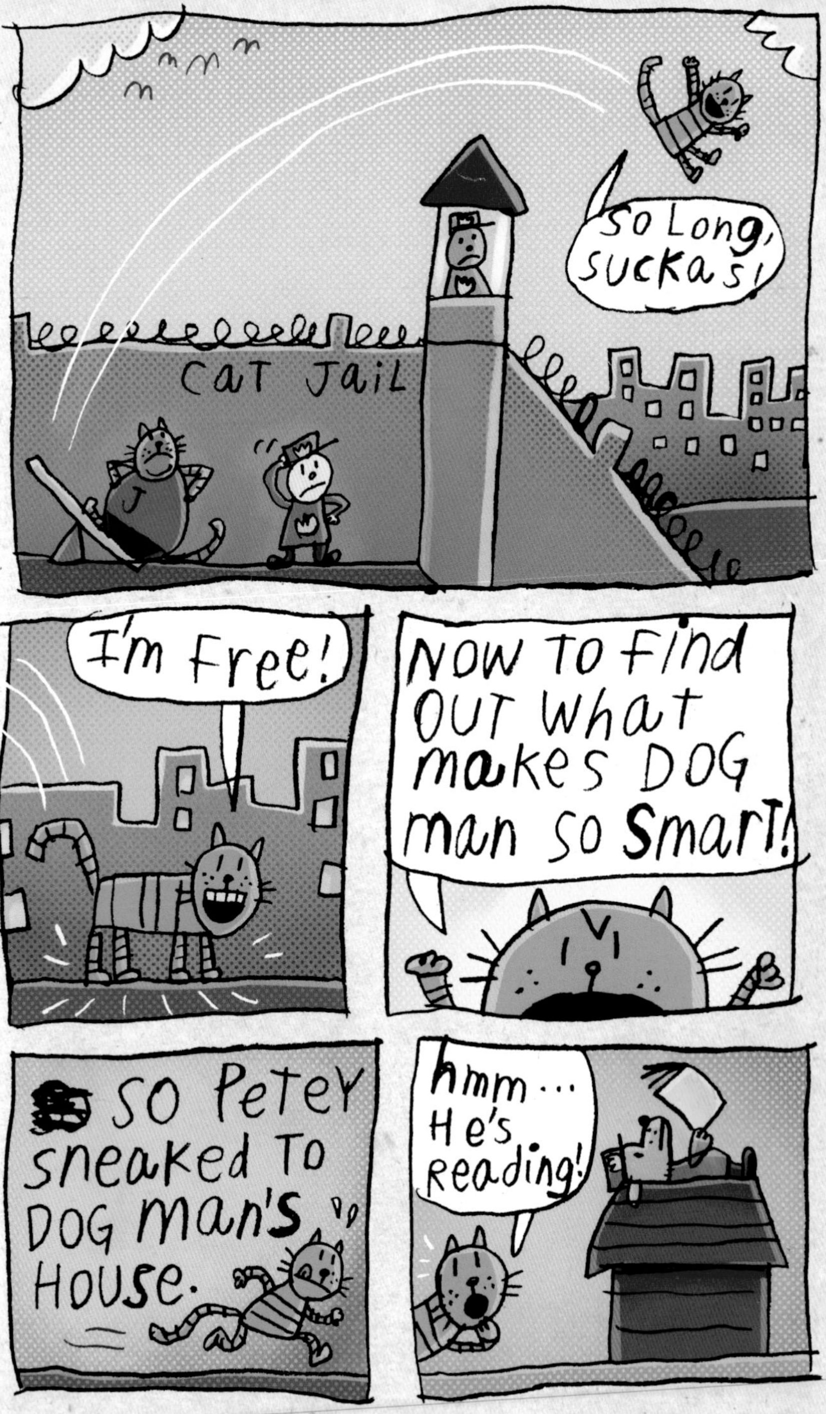
CAT JAIL
So Long, Suckas!
I'm Free!
NOW TO Find OUT What makes DOG man so Smart!
So Peter sneaked to DOG man's House.
hmm... He's Reading!

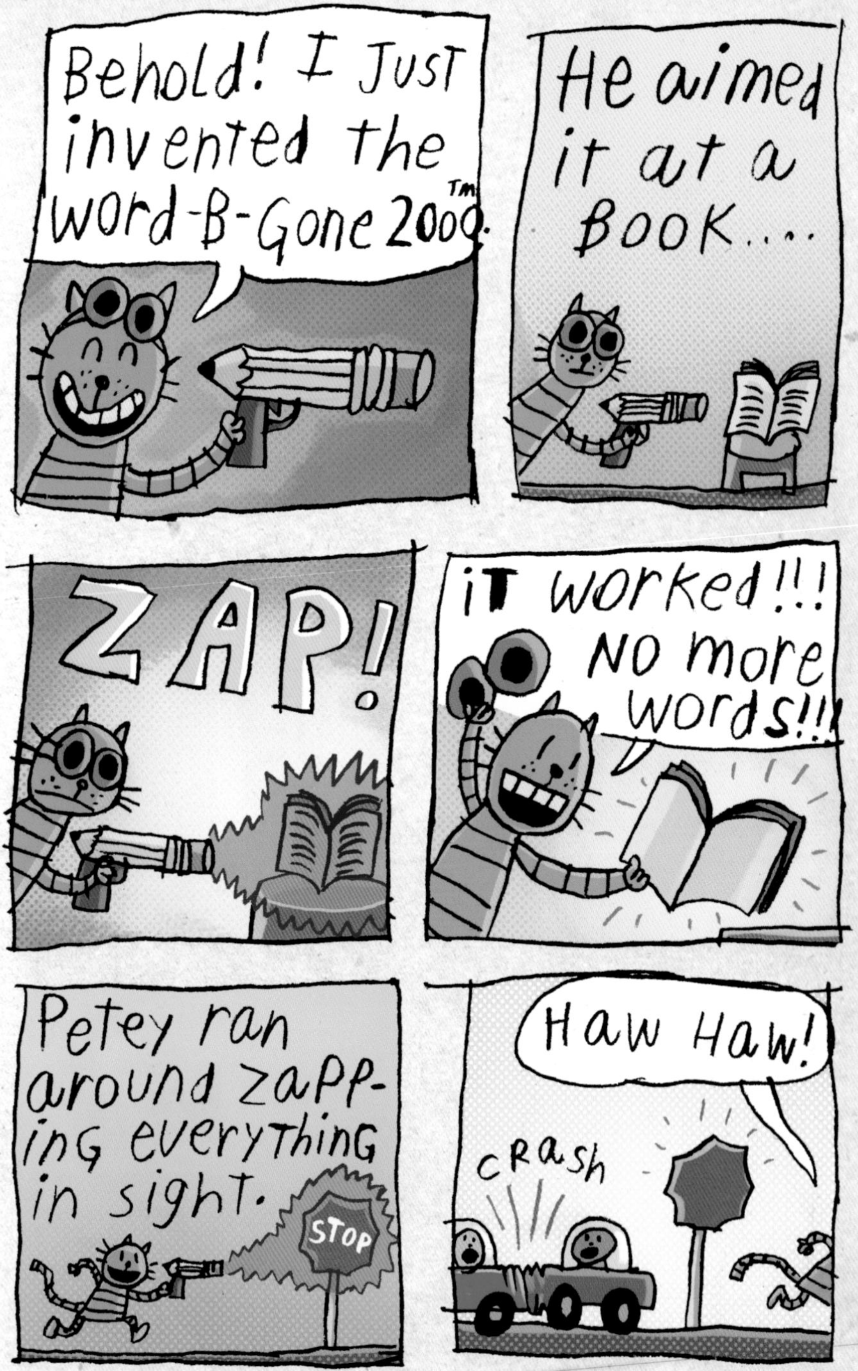
Behold! I JUST invented the word-B-Gone 2000™.
He aimed it at a Book....
ZAP!
iT worked!!! No more words!!!
Petey ran around zapp-ing everyThing in sight.
STOP
Haw Haw!
cRash

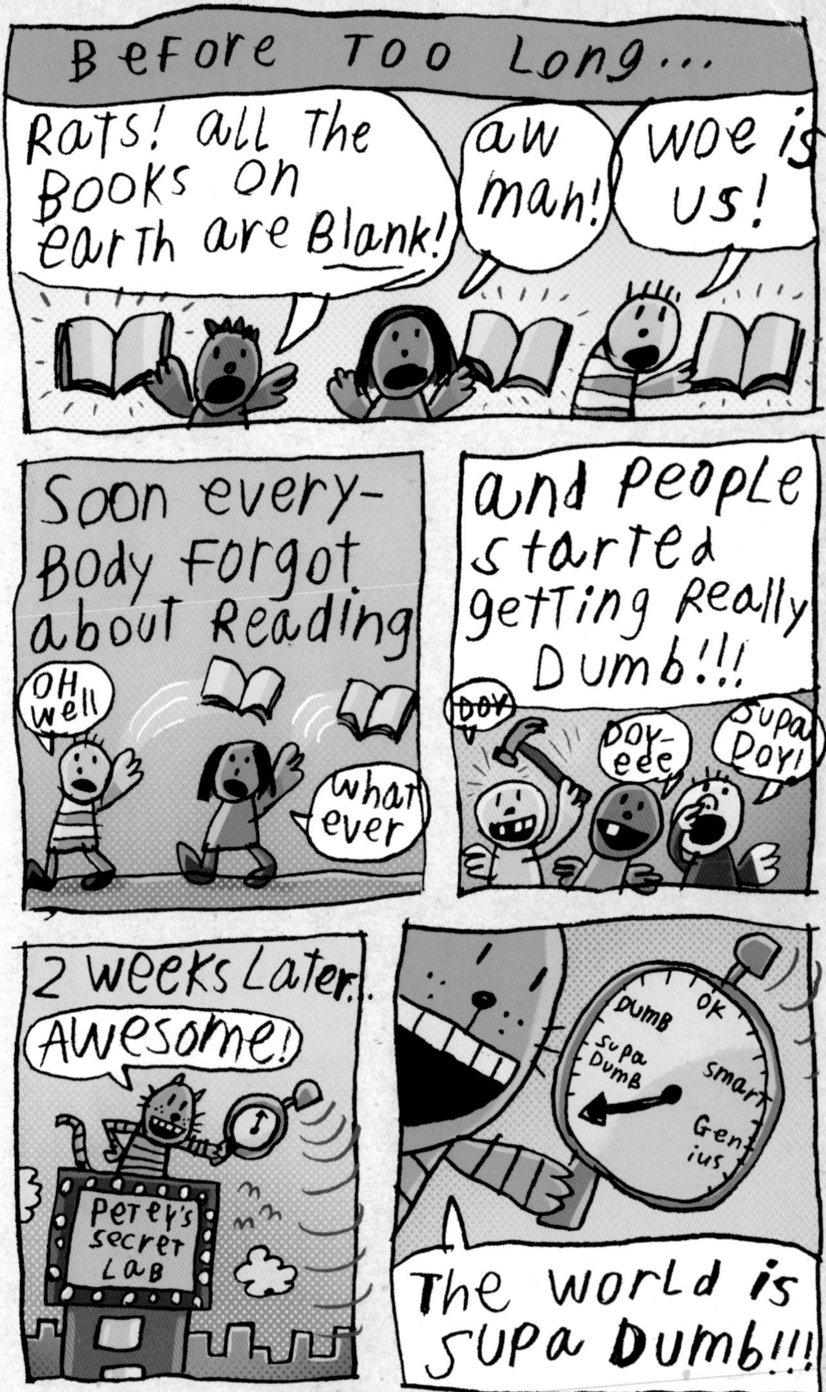
Before Too Long...
Rats! all The Books on earth are Blank!
aw man!
woe is us!
Soon every-Body Forgot about Reading
OH well
whatever
and People started getting Really Dumb!!!
DOY
DOY-eee
Supa DOY!
2 weeks Later...
Awesome!
PETEY'S SECRET LAB
DUMB
OK
SUPA DUMB
SMART
GENIUS
The world is Supa Dumb!!!

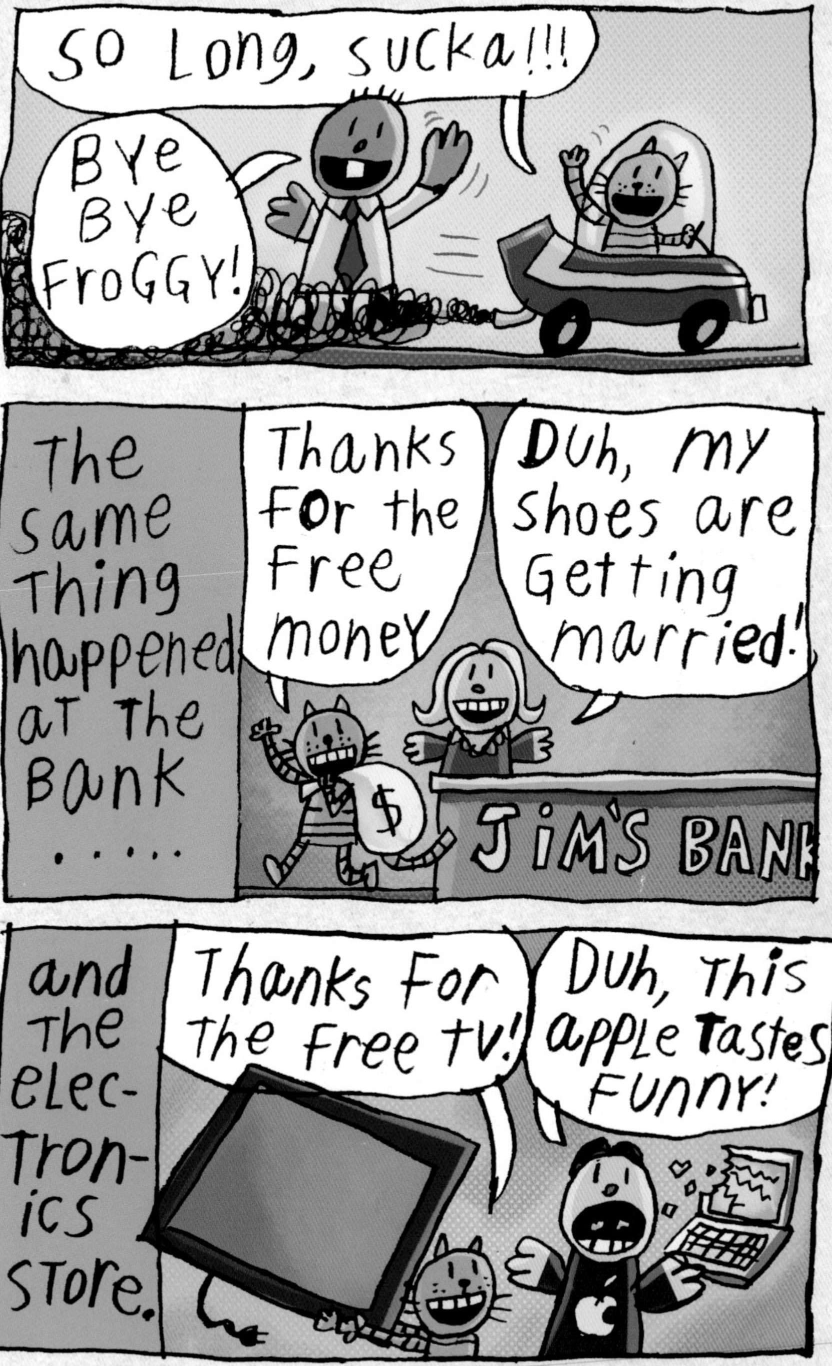
SO LONG, SUCKA!!!
BYE BYE FROGGY!
The same Thing happened at The Bank .....
Thanks For the Free money
DUh, my Shoes are Getting married!
JIM'S BANK
and The elec-Tron-ics Store.
Thanks For The Free TV!
DUh, This apple Tastes FUNNY!

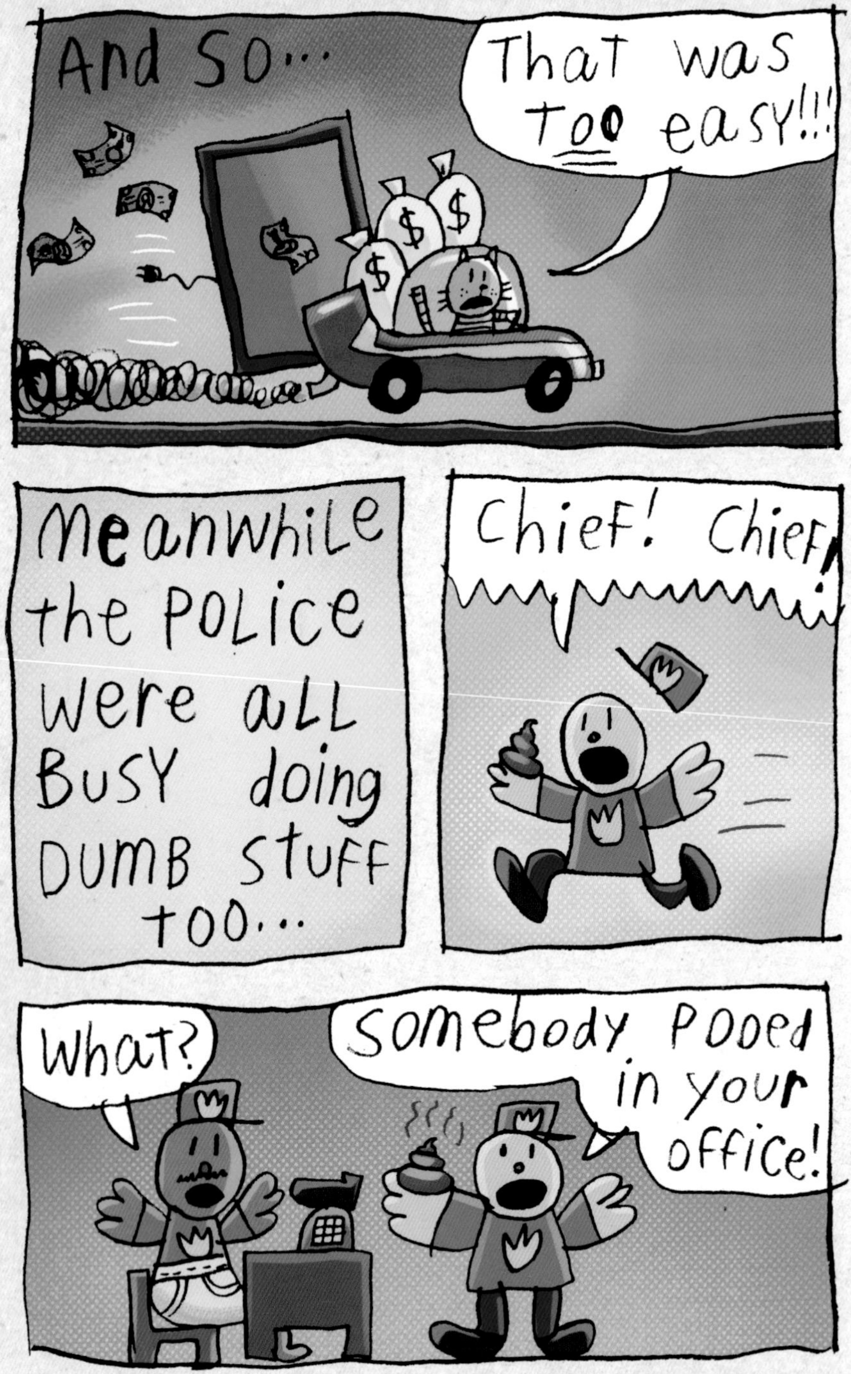
And so...
That was TOO easy!!!
Meanwhile the POLICE were all BUSY doing DUMB STUFF too...
Chief! Chief!
What?
Somebody Pooed in your office!

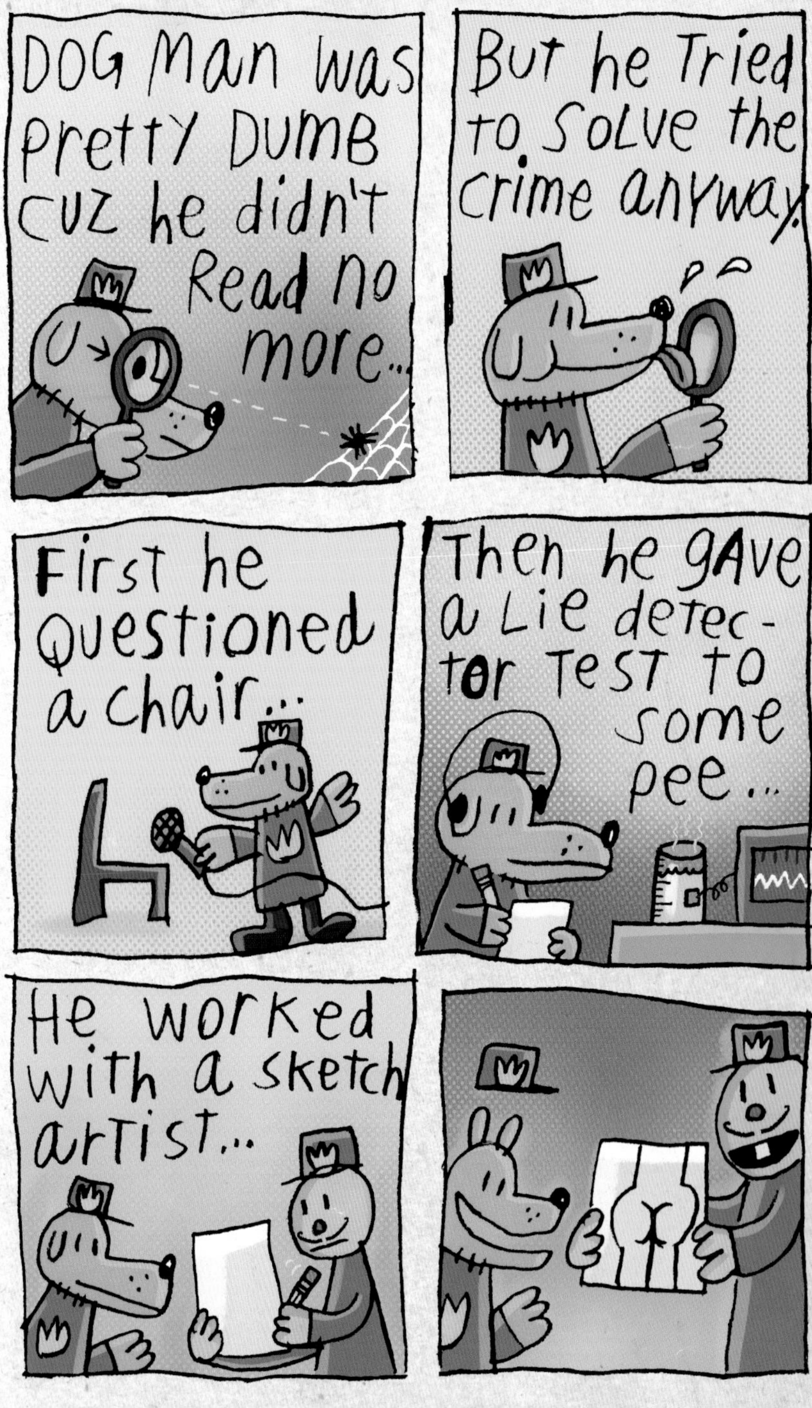
DOG Man was pretty DUMB cuz he didn't Read no more...
But he Tried to Solve the crime anyway.
First he Questioned a chair...
Then he gAve a Lie detec-tor TEST to some pee...
He worked with a sketch artist...

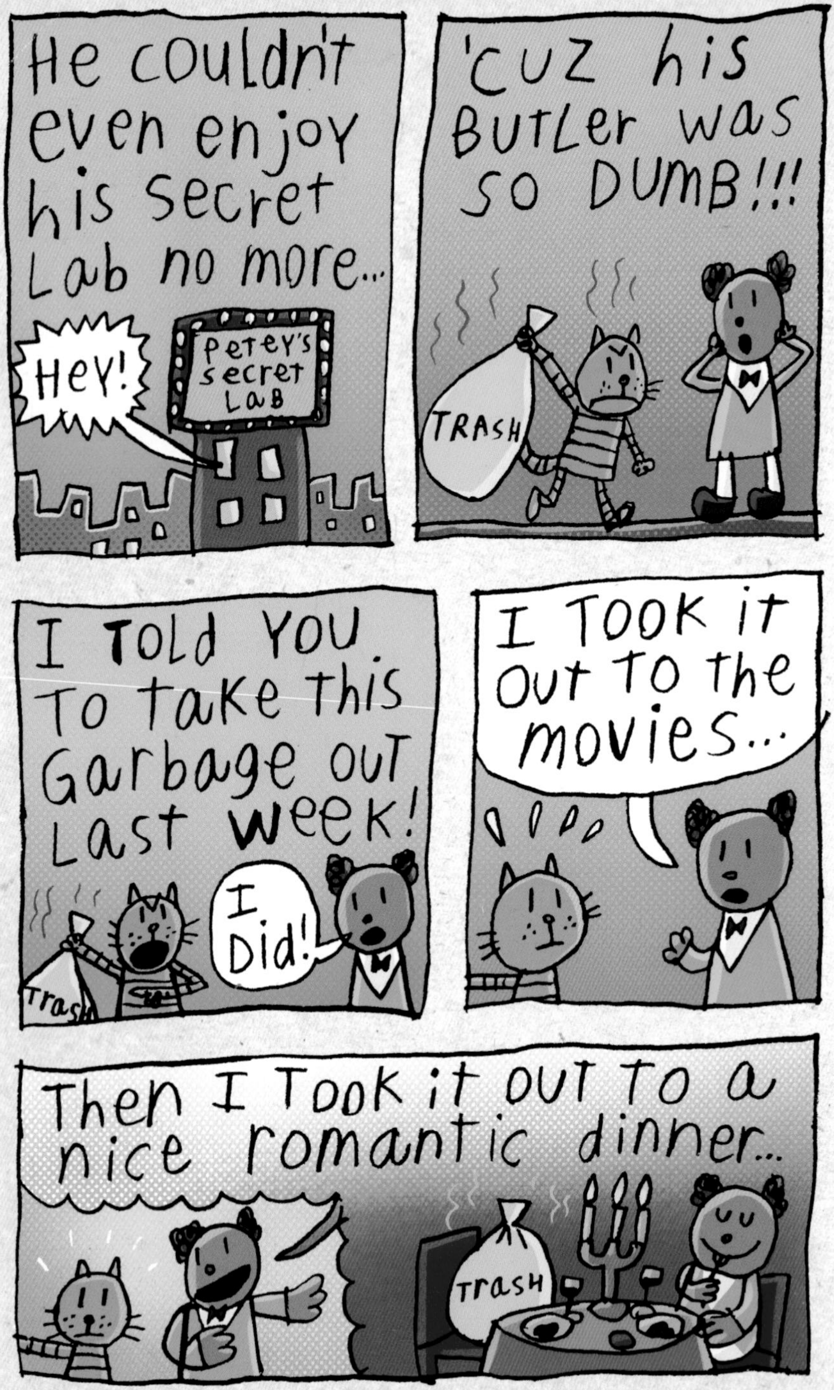
He couldn't even enjoy his secret Lab no more...
HEY!
Petey's secret Lab
'Cuz his Butler was so DUMB!!!
TRASH
I Told You To take This Garbage out Last week!
I Did!
Trash
I Took it out To the movies...
Then I Took it out To a nice romantic dinner...
Trash

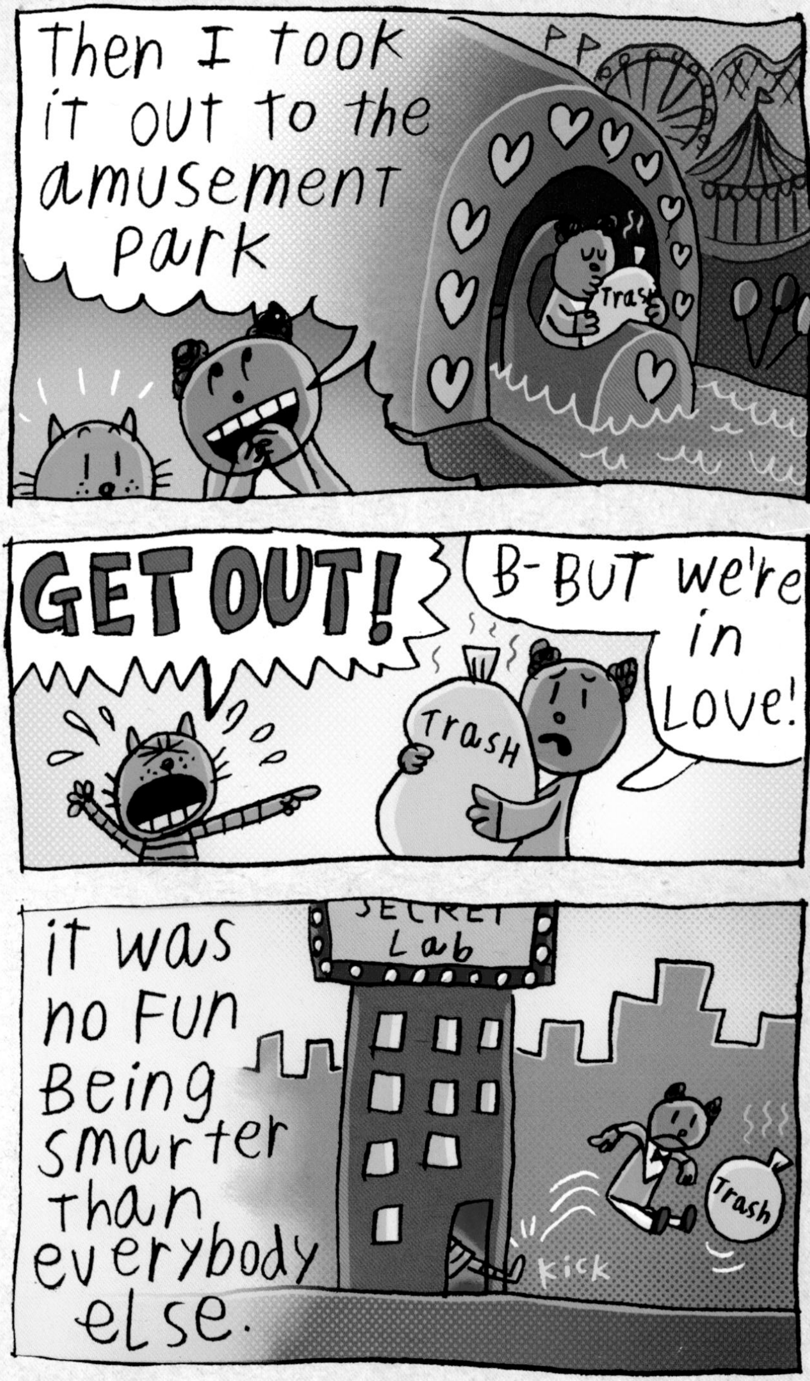
Then I took it out to the amusement park
GET OUT!
B-BUT we're in Love!
Trash
it was no Fun Being smarter than everybody else.
Lab
Kick
Trash

132

134

135

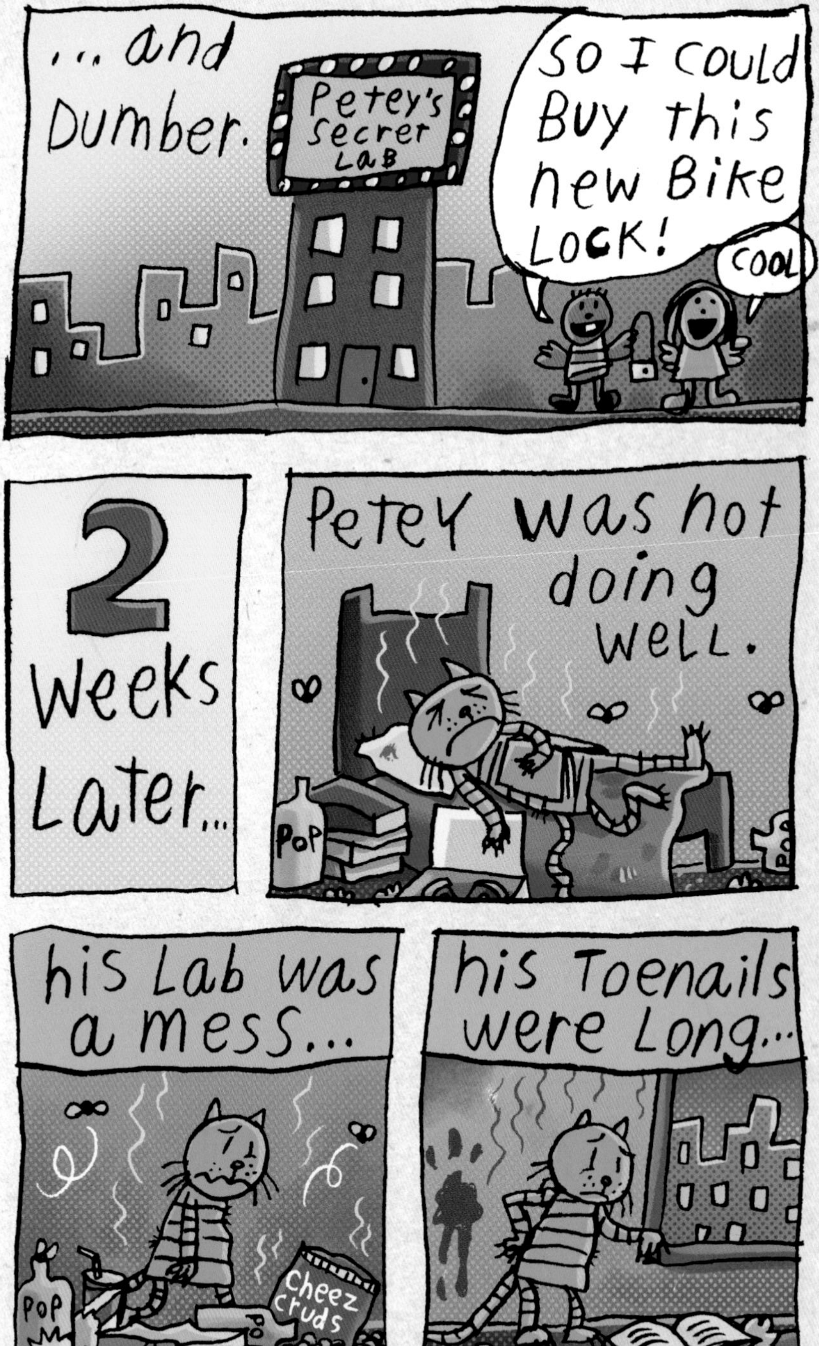
... and Dumber.
Petey's Secret Lab
So I could Buy this new Bike Lock!
COOL
2 Weeks Later...
Petey was not doing well.
POP
his Lab was a mess...
POP
POP
Cheez Cruds
his Toenails were Long...

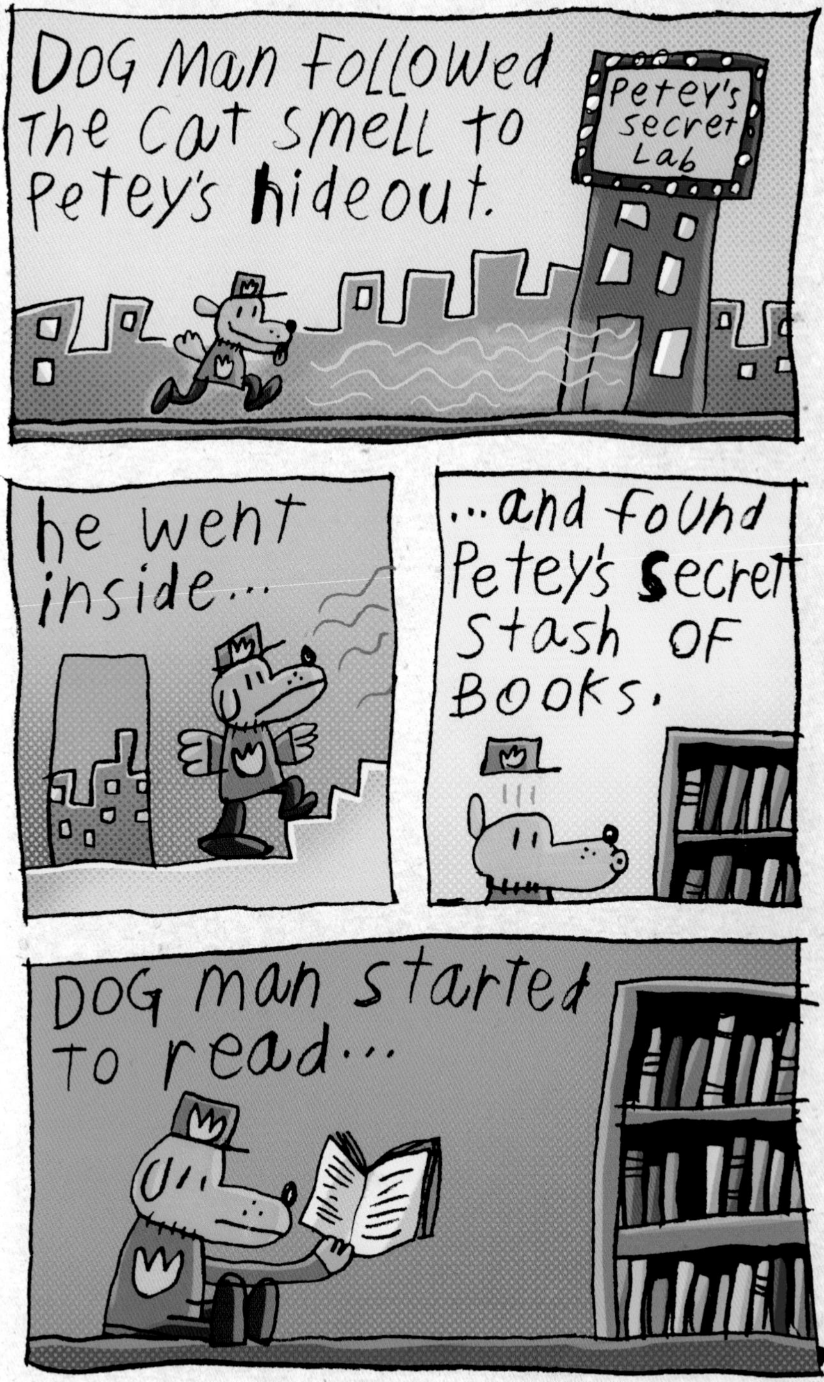
DOG MAN FOLLOWED THE CAT SMELL TO PETEY'S HIDEOUT.
PETEY'S SECRET LAB
HE WENT INSIDE...
...AND FOUND PETEY'S SECRET STASH OF BOOKS.
DOG MAN STARTED TO READ...

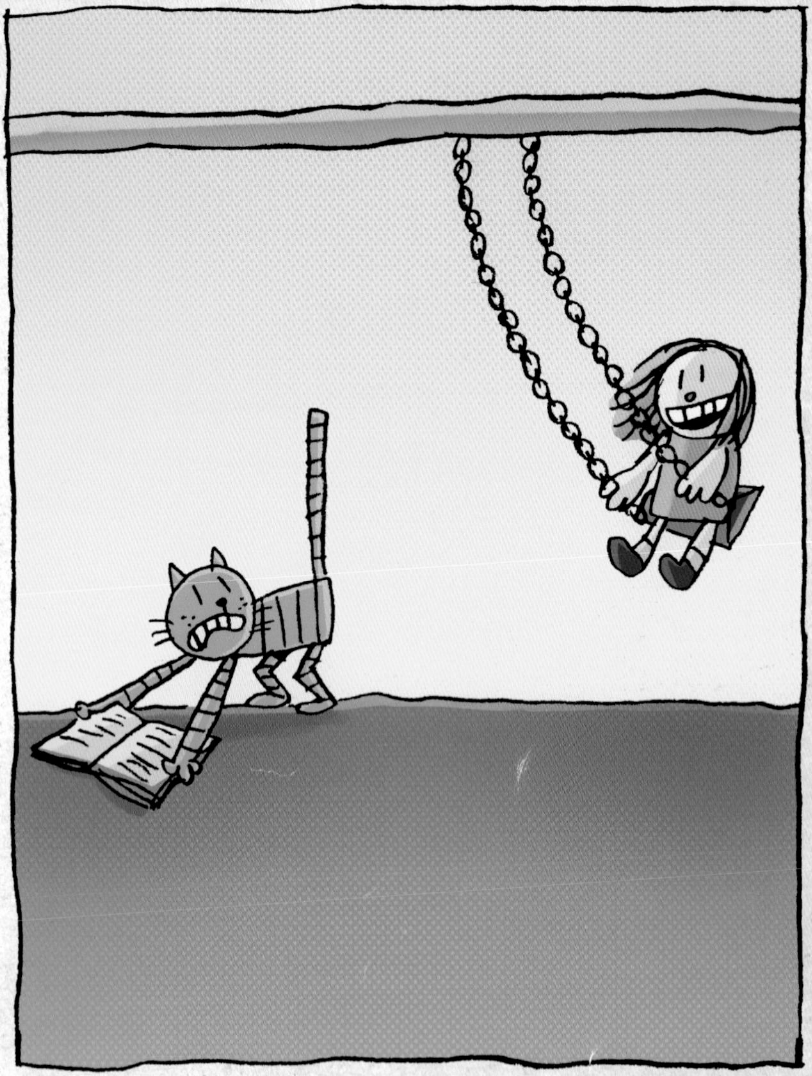

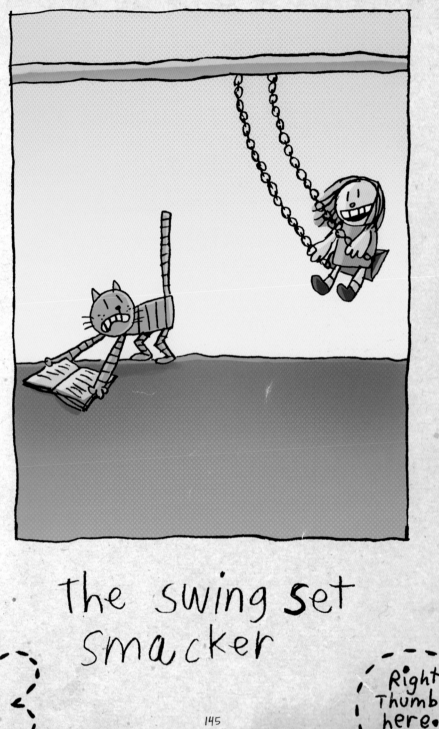

The Swing Set Smacker

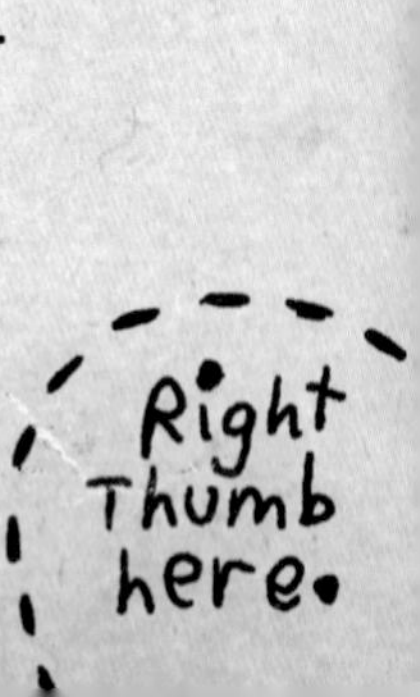
Right Thumb here.

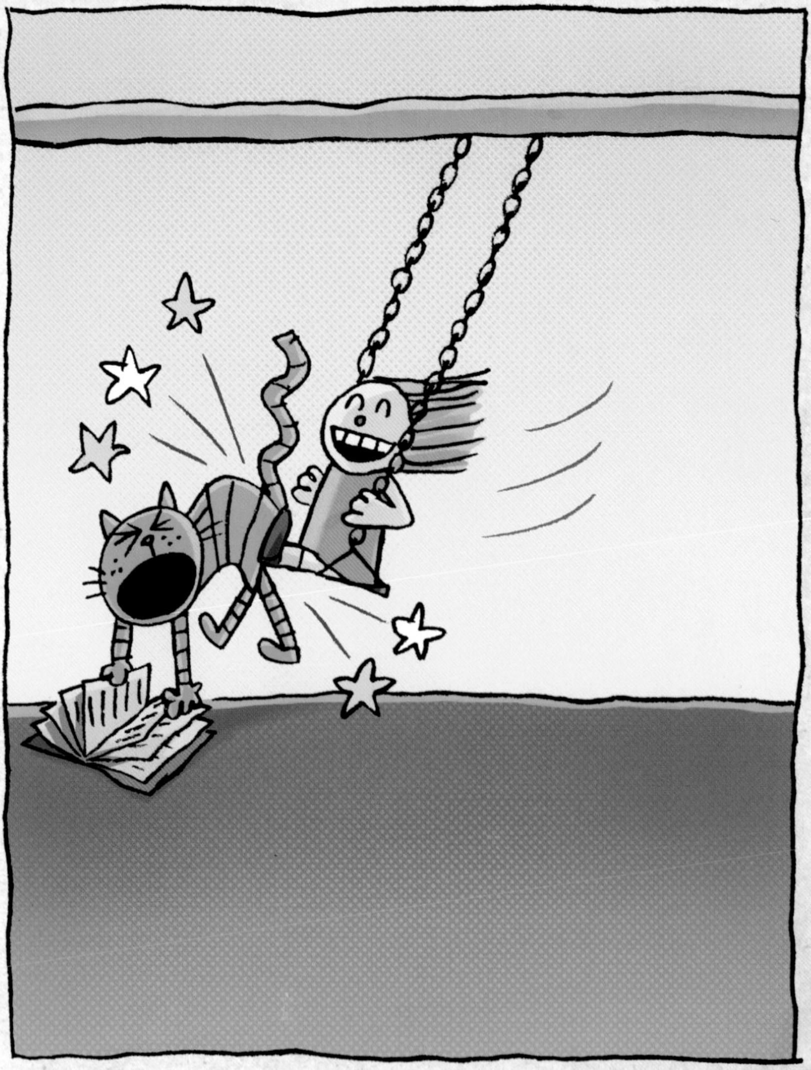

The Swing Set Smacker

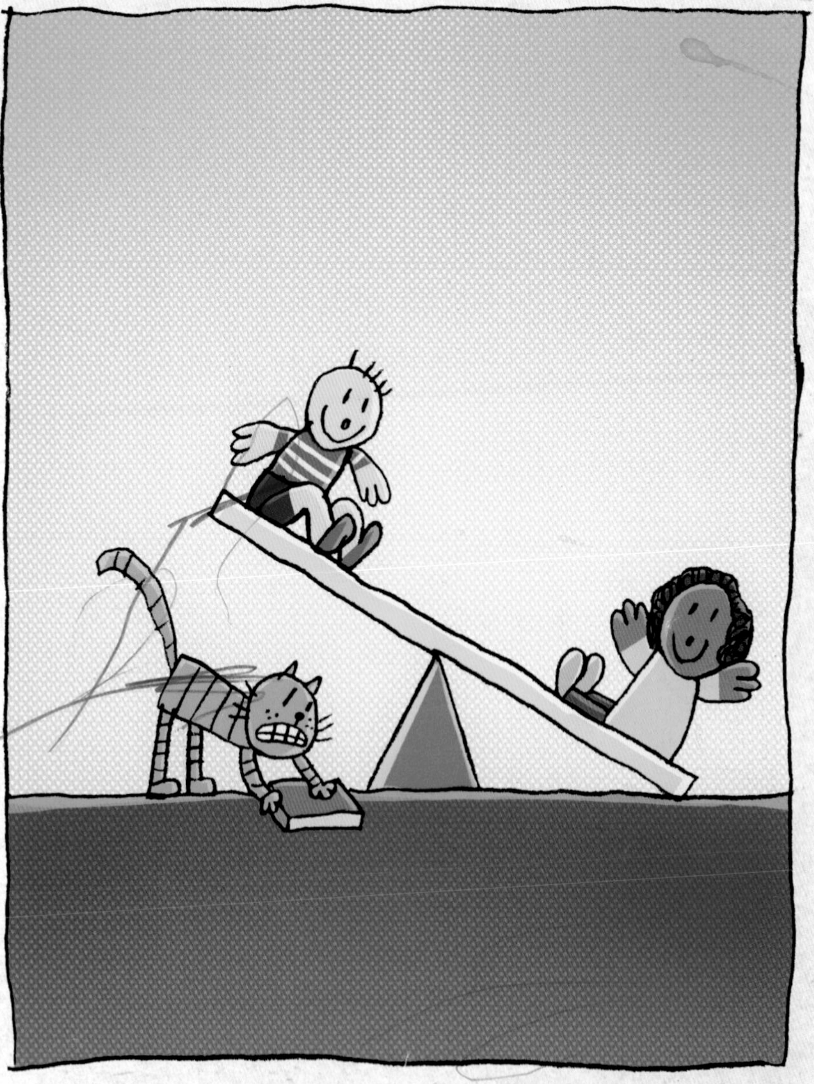

The Seesaw Smoosher

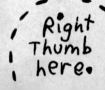

Right Thumb here.

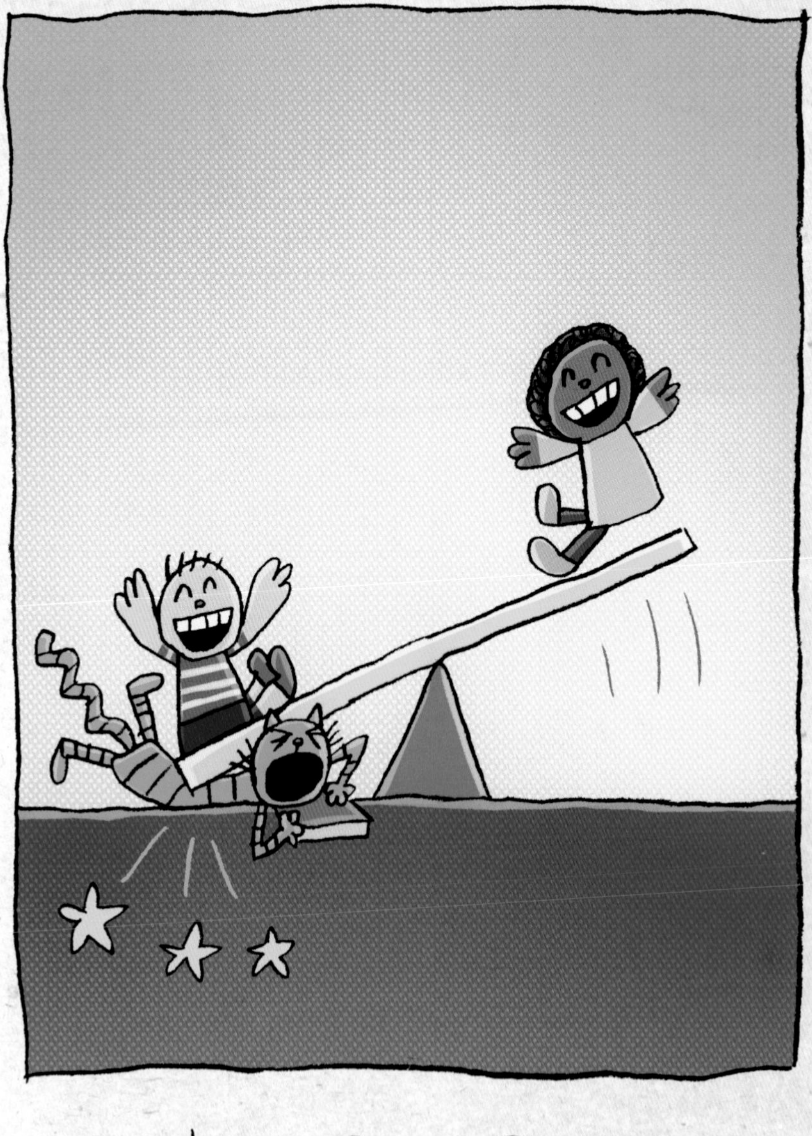

The Seesaw Smoosher

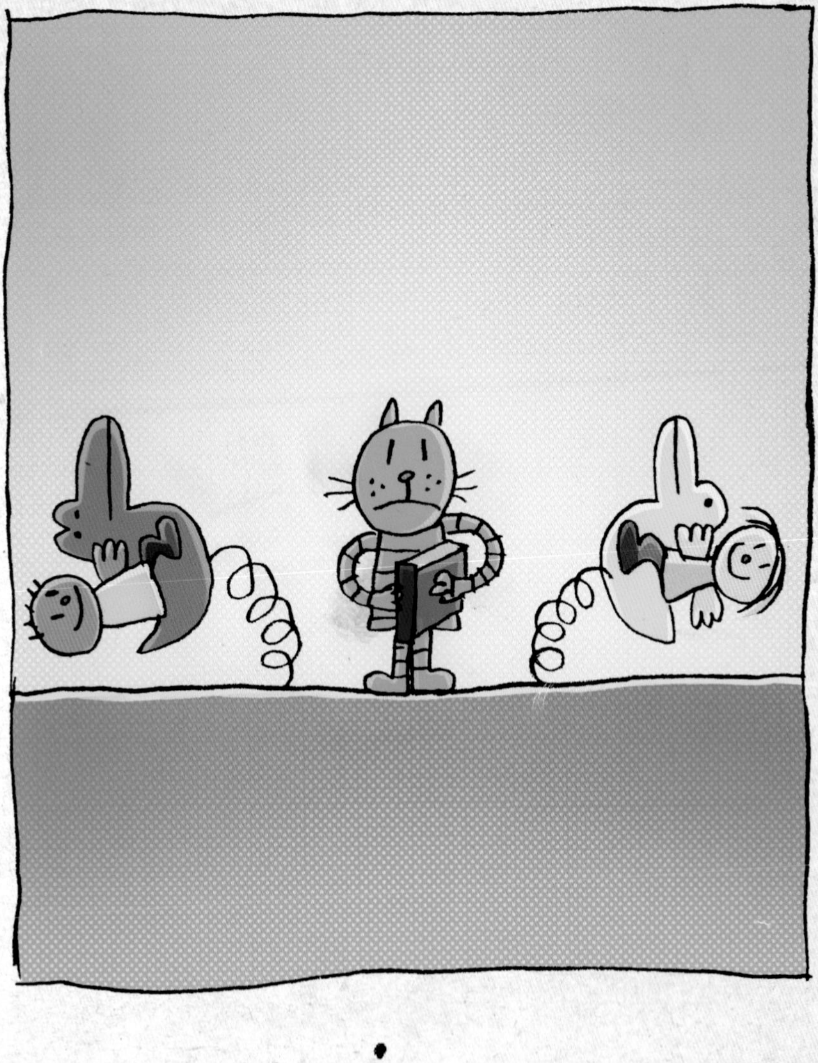

Spring Break

Right Thumb here.

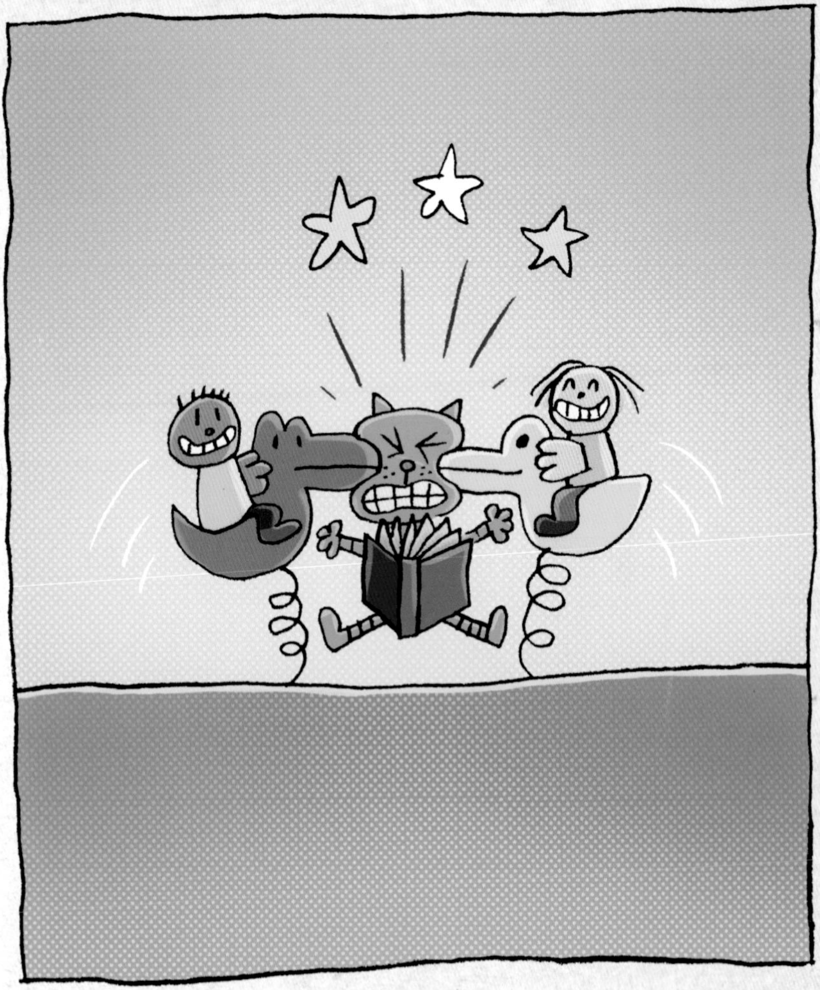

Spring Break

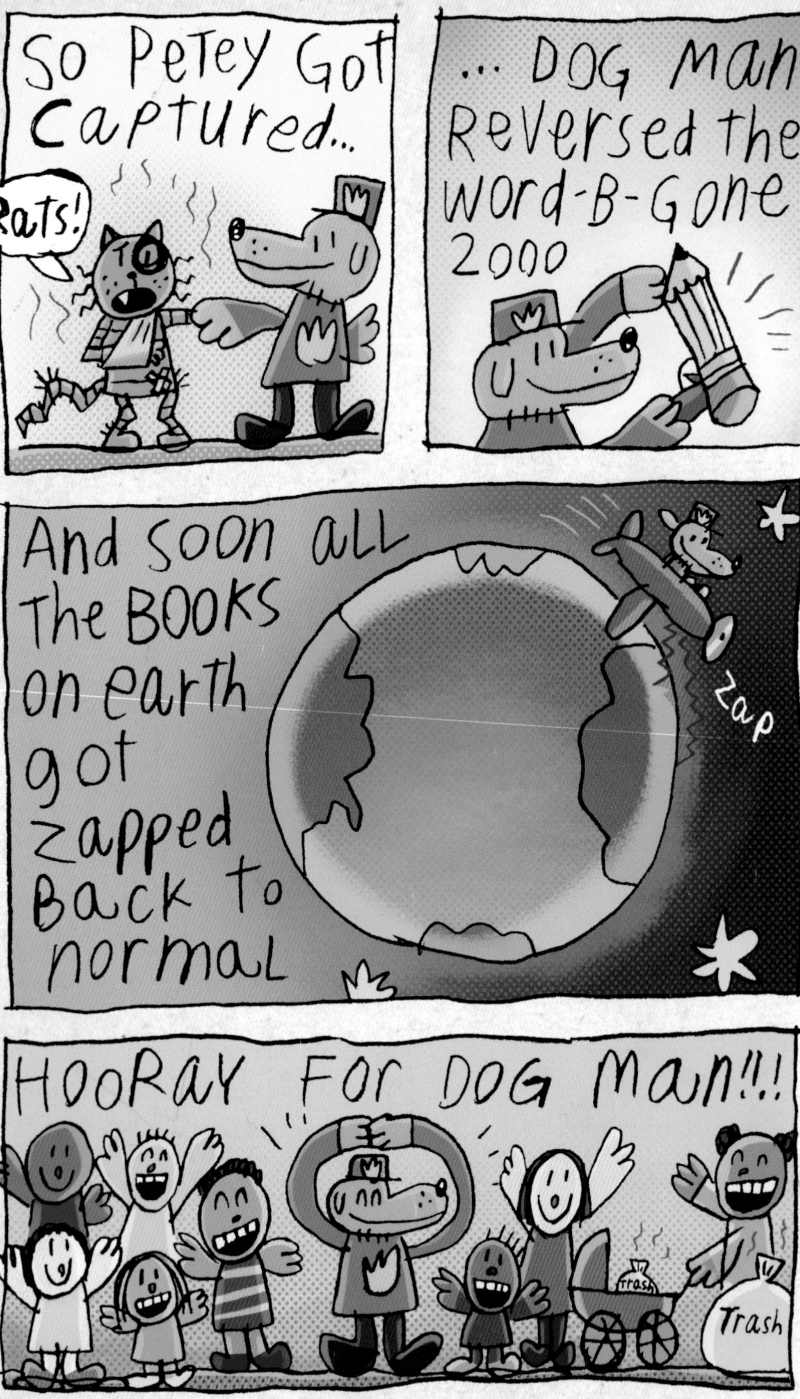
So Petey Got Captured...
Rats!
... DOG Man Reversed the word-B-Gone 2000
And soon all The BOOKS on earth got zapped Back to normal
Zap
HOORAY FOR DOG MAN!!!
Trash
Trash

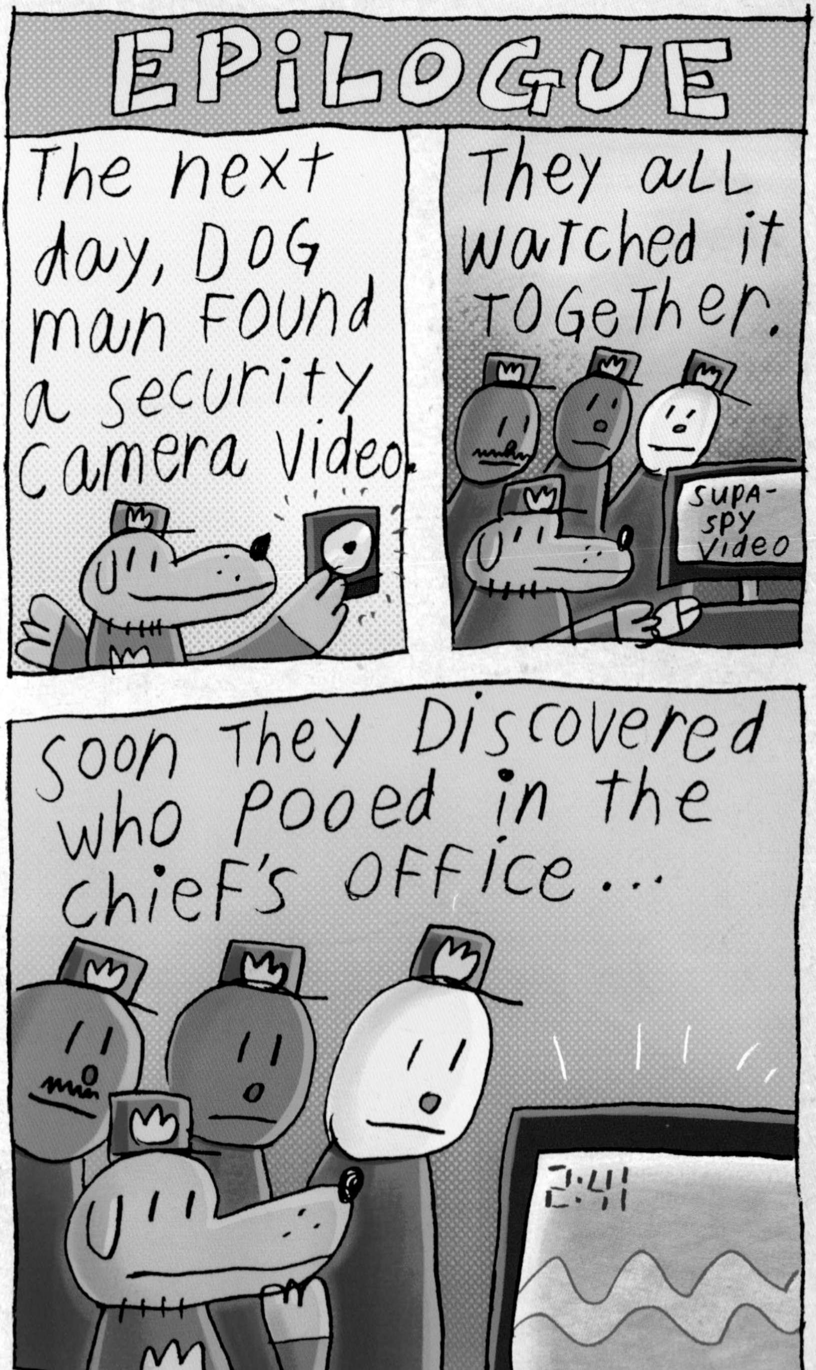
EPILOGUE
The next day, DOG man FOUND a security camera video.
They all watched it TOGether.
SUPA-SPY Video
Soon They Discovered who Pooed in the chief's office...
2:41

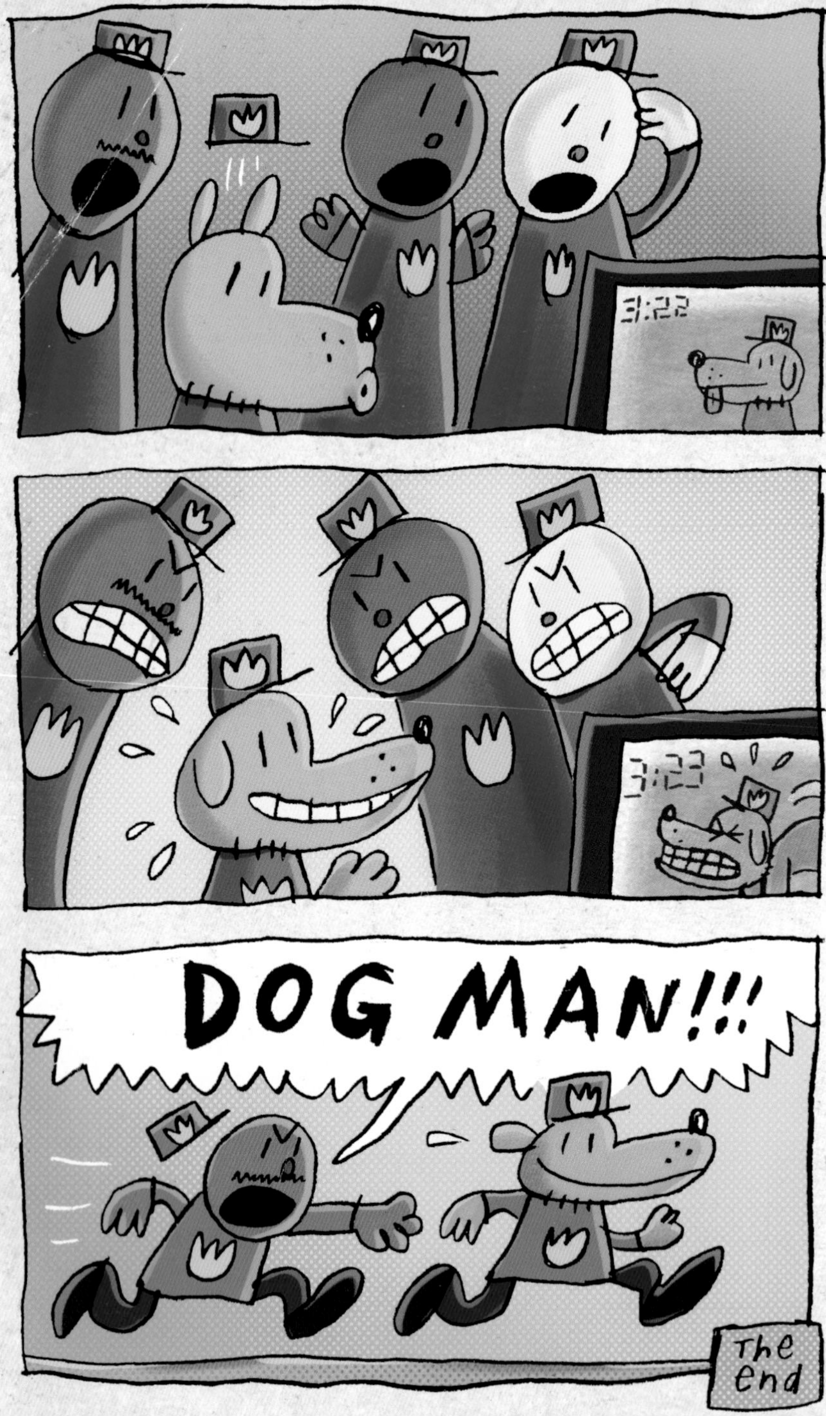
3:22
3:23
DOG MAN!!!
The end

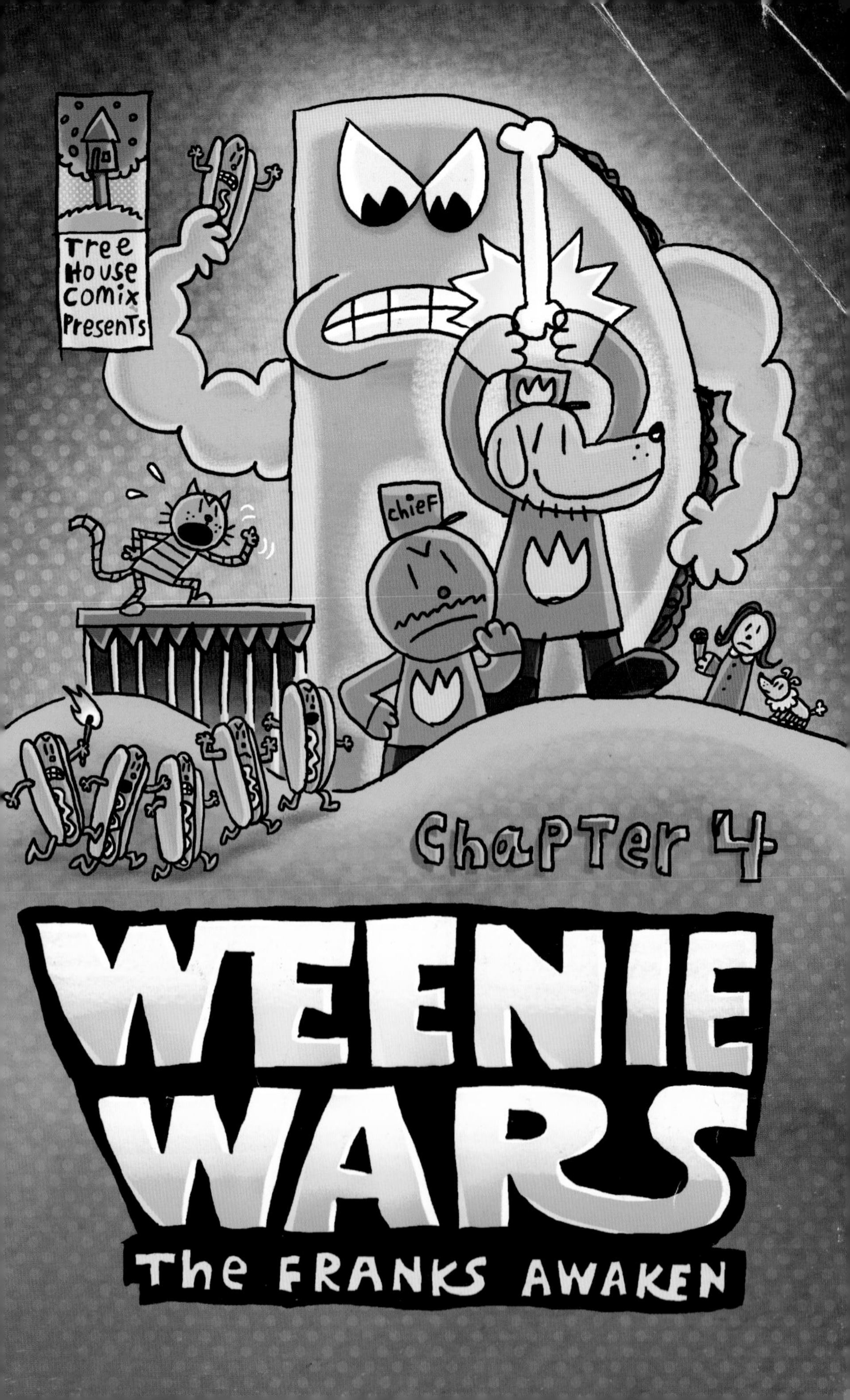

Tree House Comix Presents
chief
Chapter 4
WEENIE WARS
The FRANKS AWAKEN

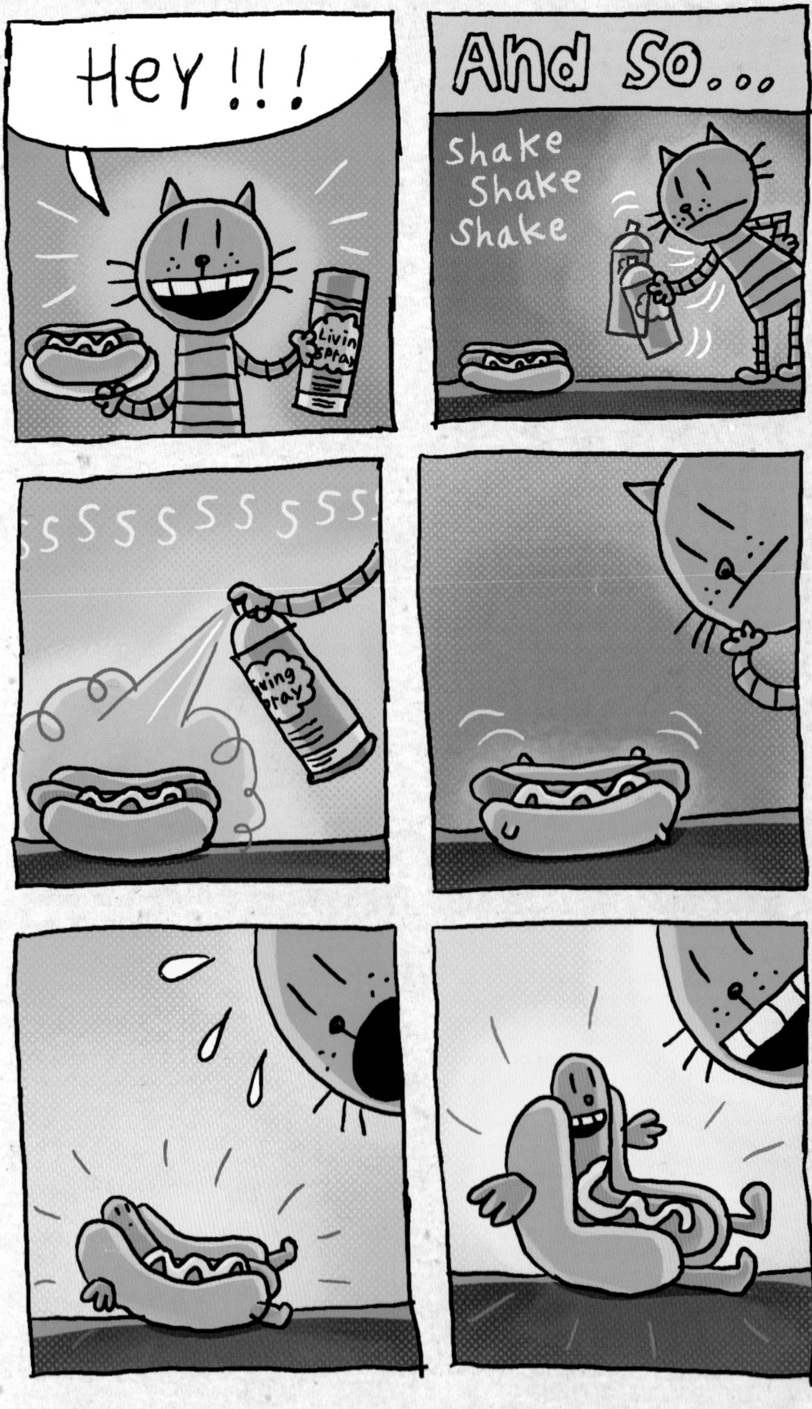
Hey!!!
And So...
Shake
Shake
Shake
SSSSSSSSSS

164

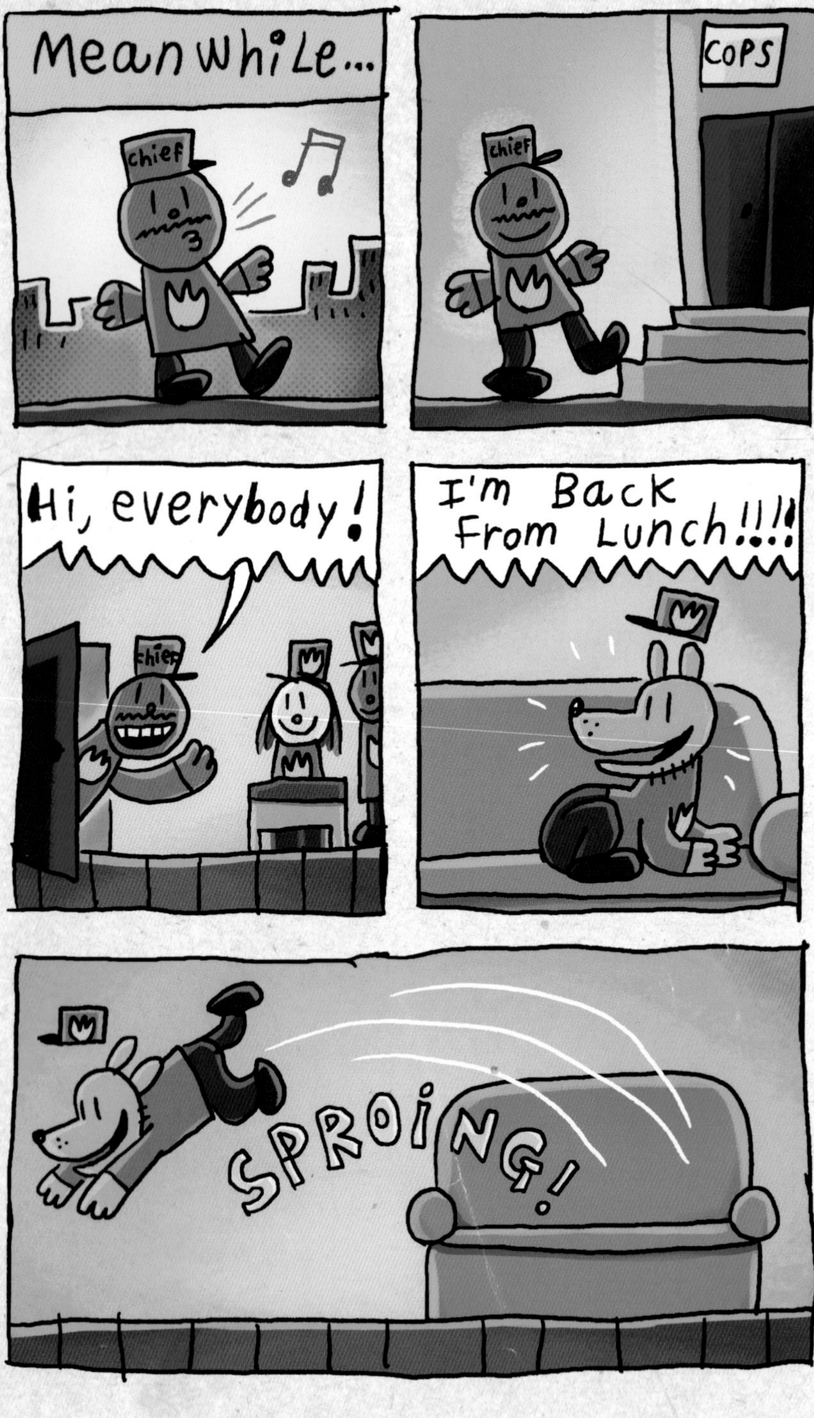
Meanwhile...
COPS
chief
Hi, everybody!
I'm Back From Lunch!!!!
SPROING!

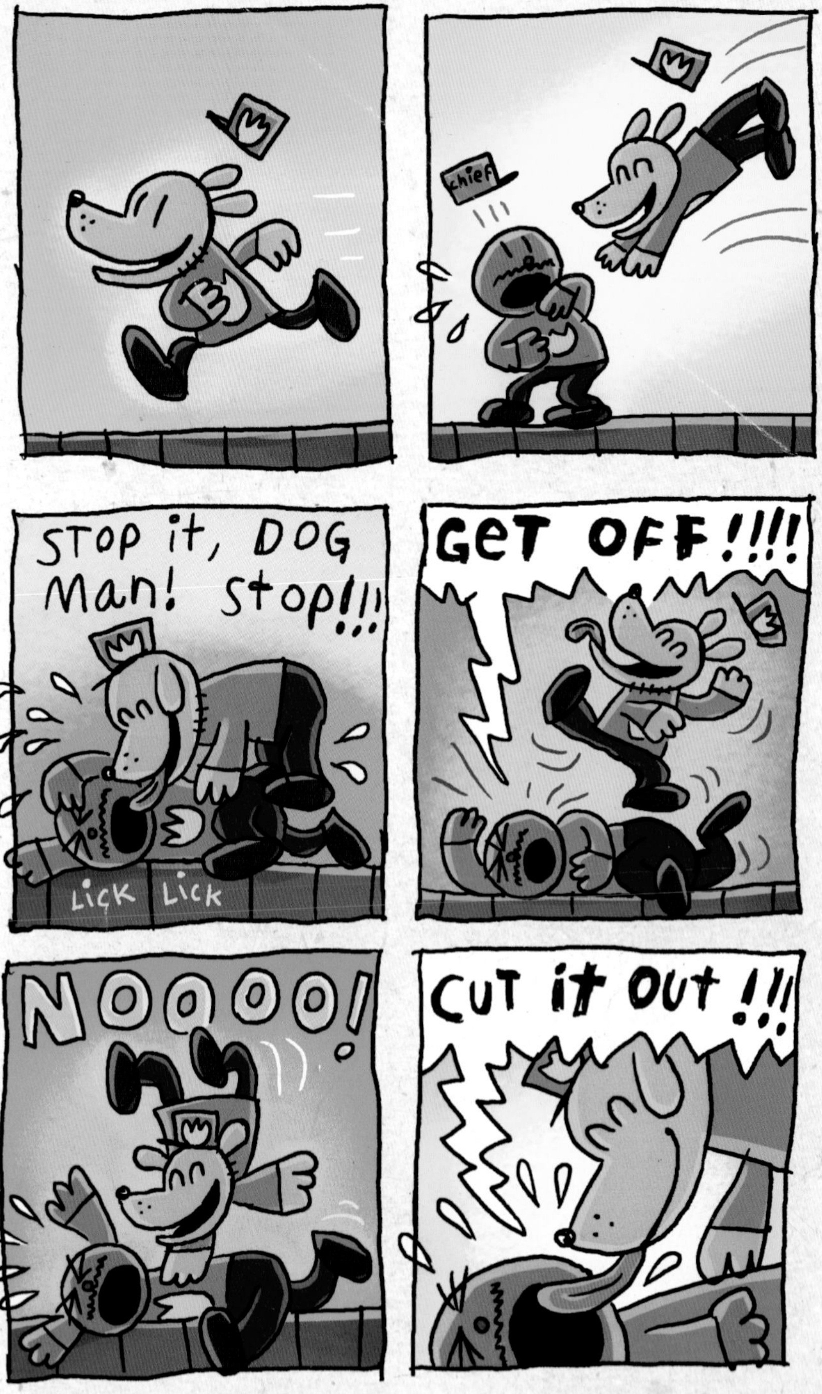
chief
STOP it, DOG Man! Stop!!!
LICK LICK
GET OFF!!!!
NOOOO!
CUT it OUT!!!

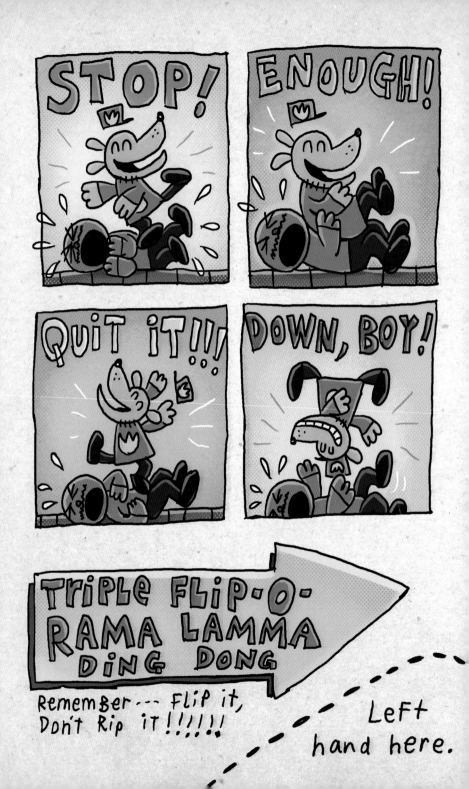

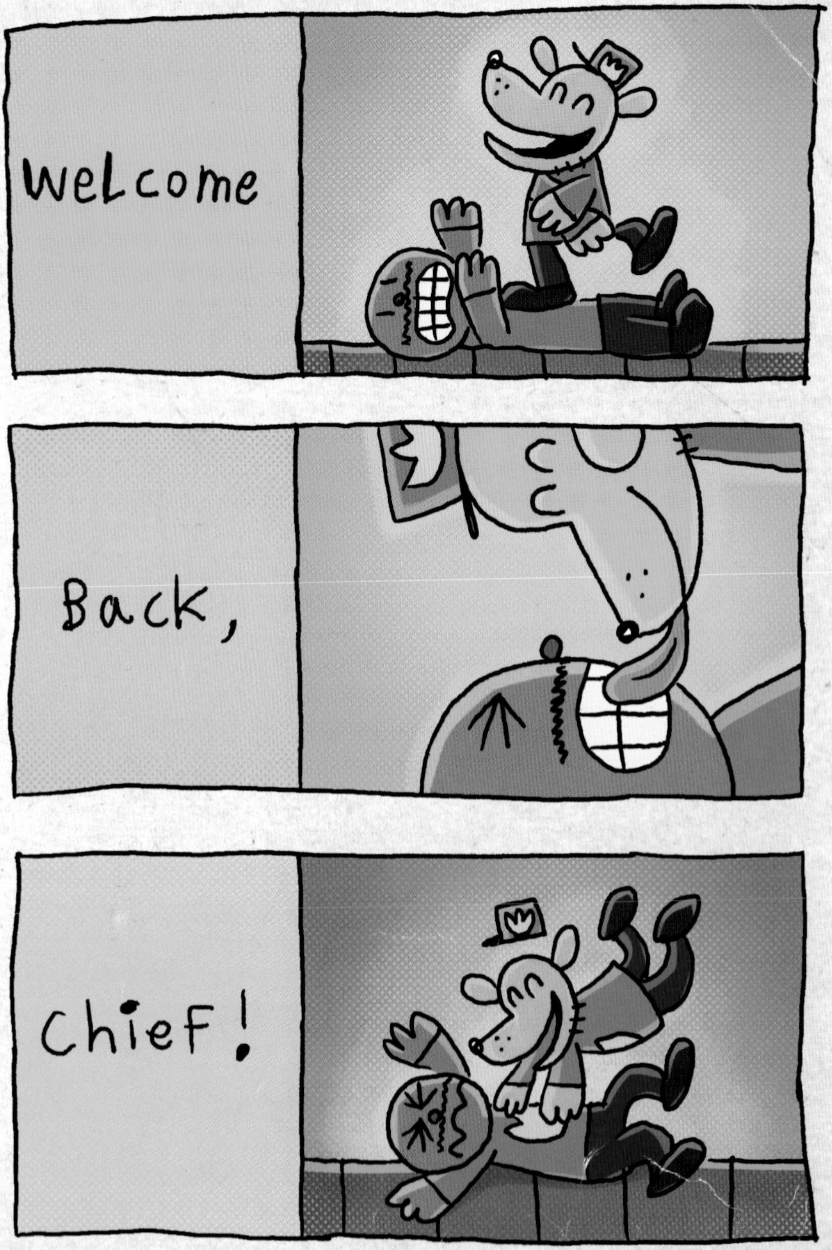
Welcome
Back,
Chief!

Right Thumb here.

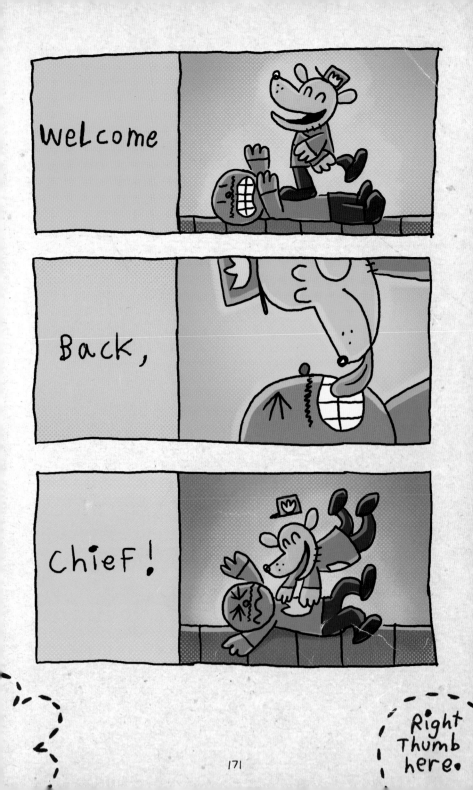

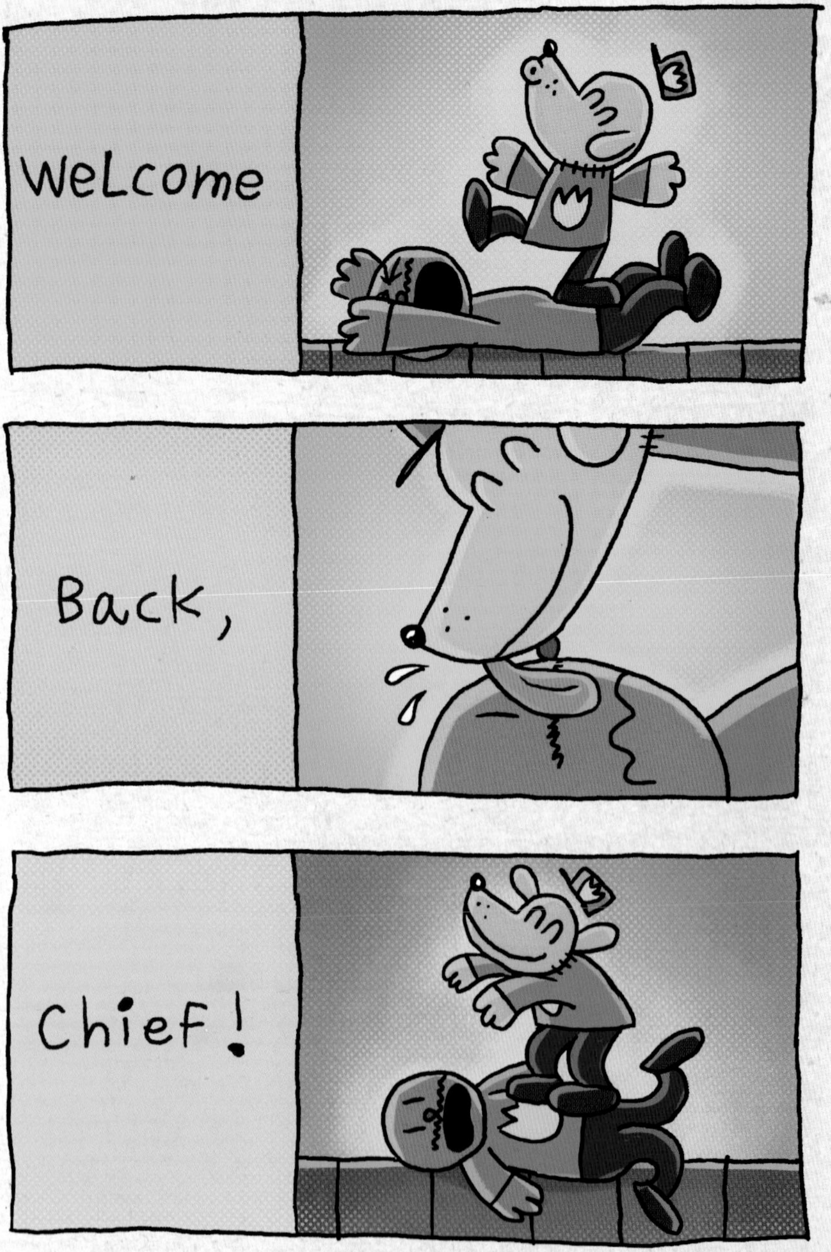
Welcome
Back,
Chief!

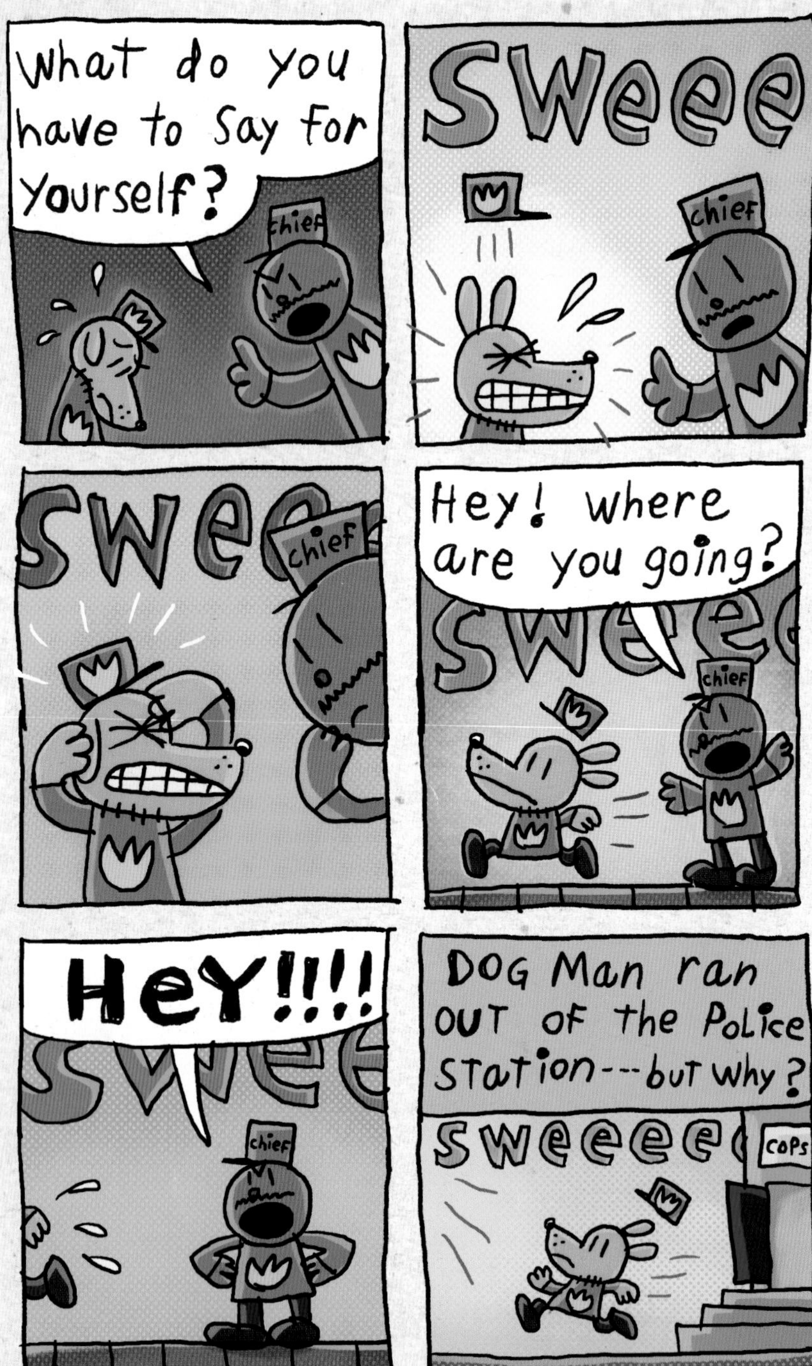
What do you have to Say for yourself?
chief
SWeee
chief
SWee
chief
Hey! where are you going?
Swee
chief
HeY!!!!
Swee
chief
DOG Man ran OUT of the Police Station---but why?
Sweeee
COPS

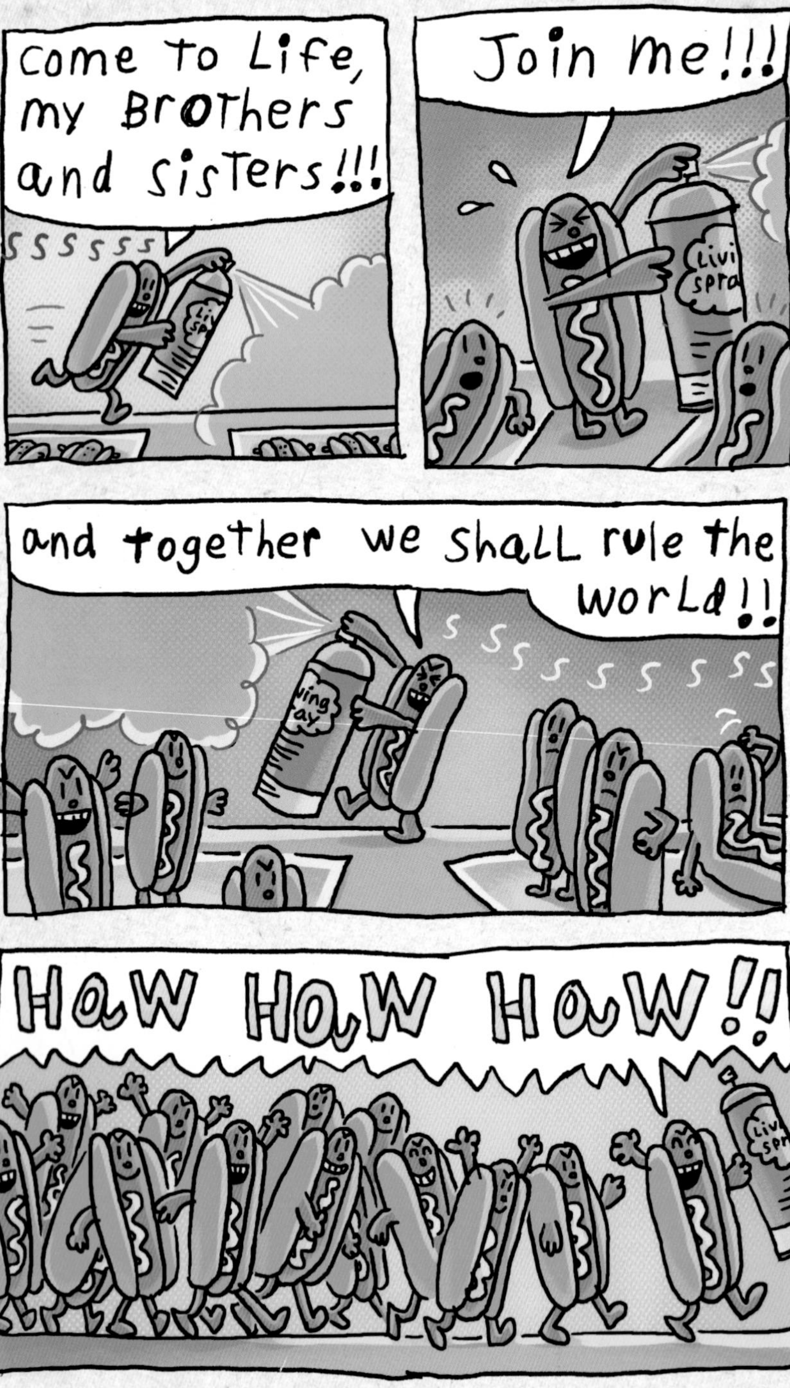
Come To Life, my BroThers and SisTers!!!
SSSSSS
Join me!!!
and together we shall rule the worLd!!
S S S S S S S S S S
HaW HaW HaW!!

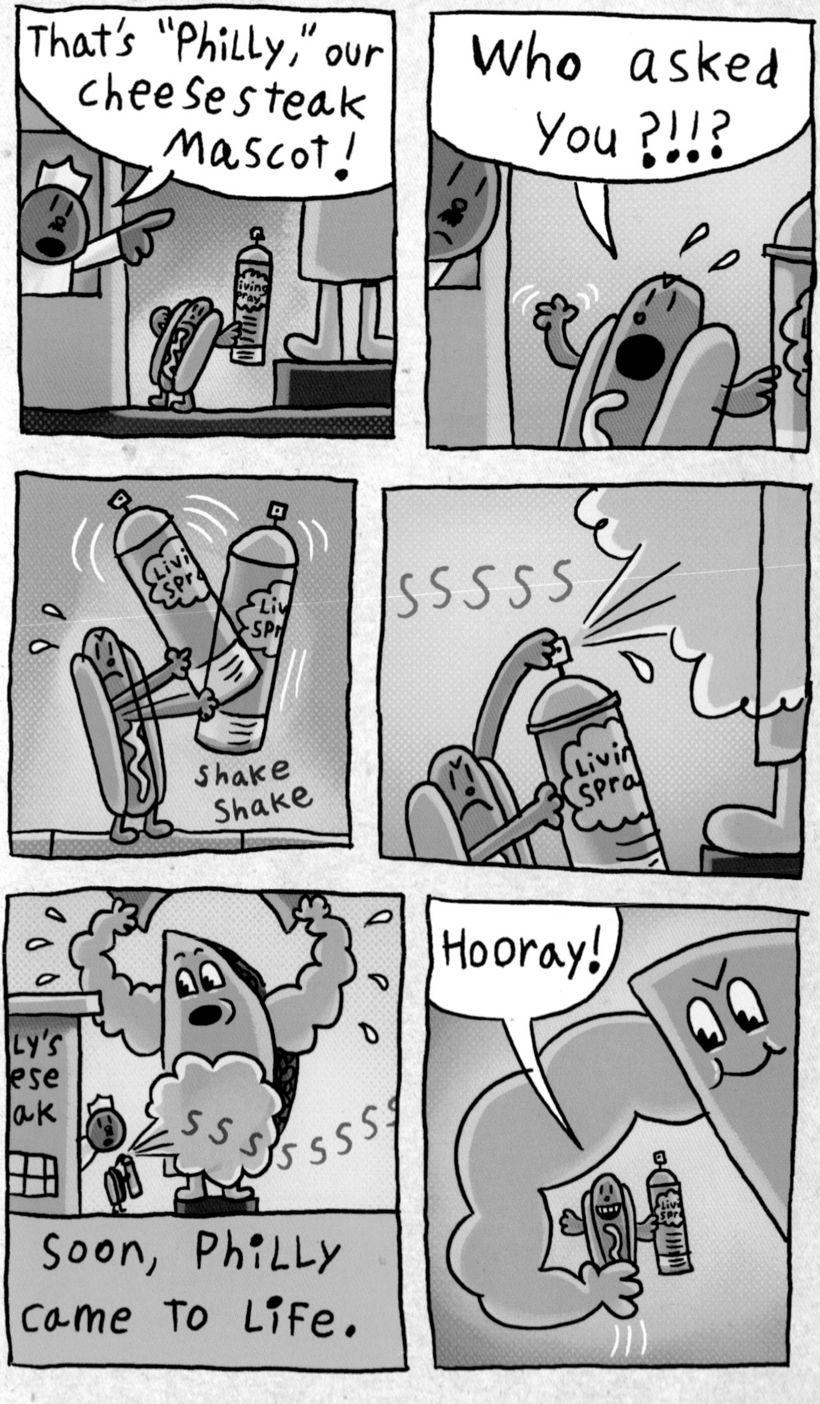
That's "PhiLLy," our cheesesteak Mascot!
Who asked You?!!?
Living Spray
Shake Shake
SSSSS
Living Spray
Soon, PhiLLy came to LiFe.
Hooray!

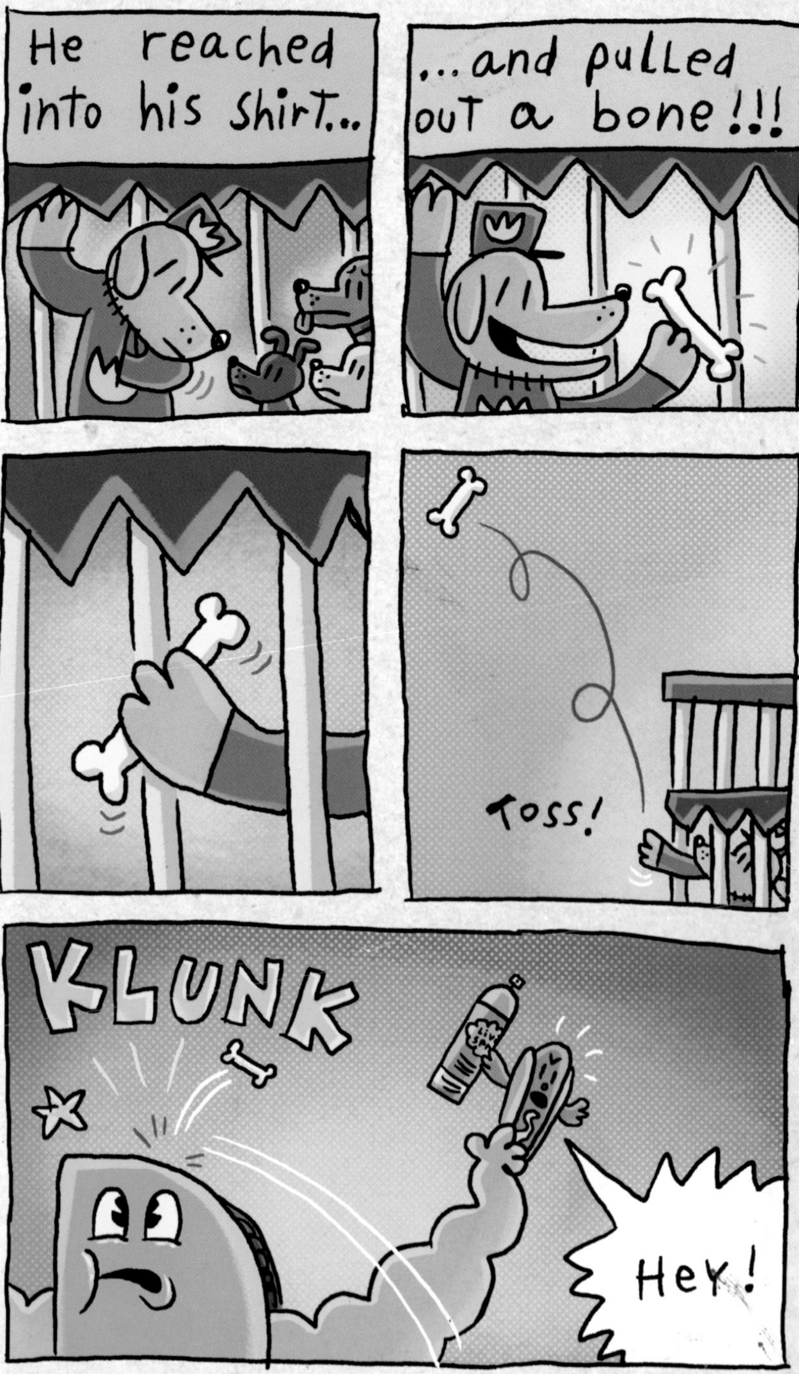
He reached into his shirt...
...and pulled out a bone!!!
TOSS!
KLUNK
Hey!

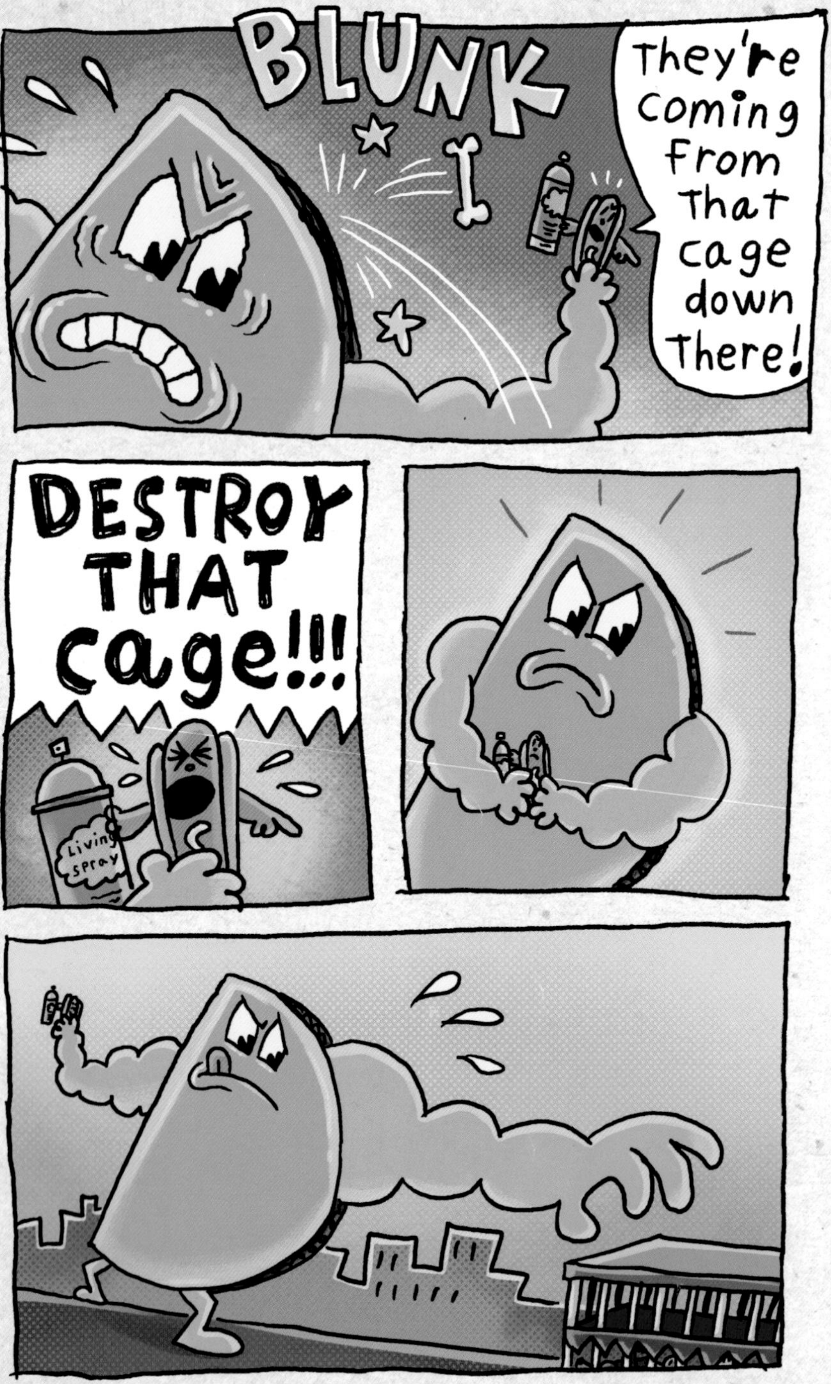
BLUNK
They're coming from that cage down there!
DESTROY THAT cage!!!
Living spray

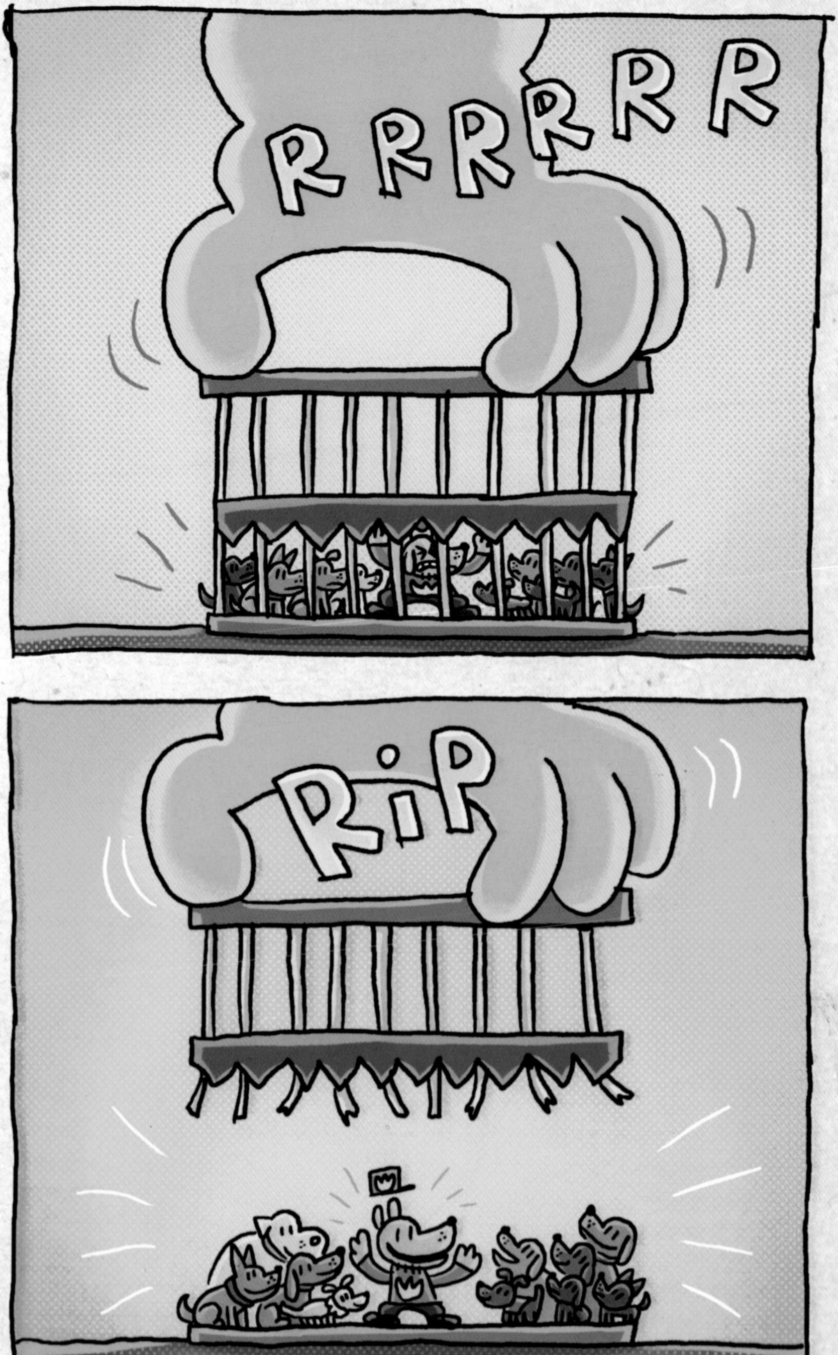
RRRRRRR
RIP

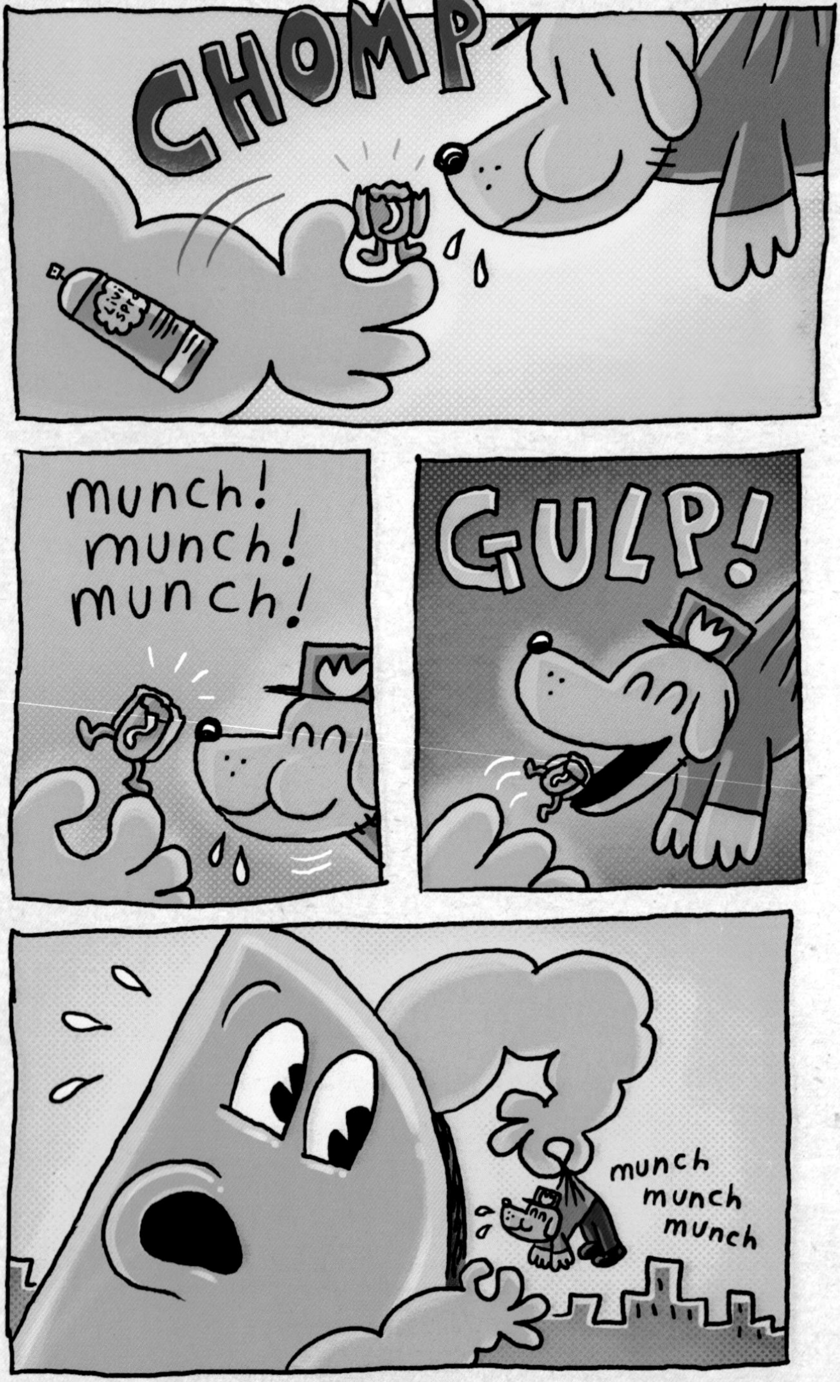
CHOMP
munch! munch! munch!
GULP!
munch munch munch

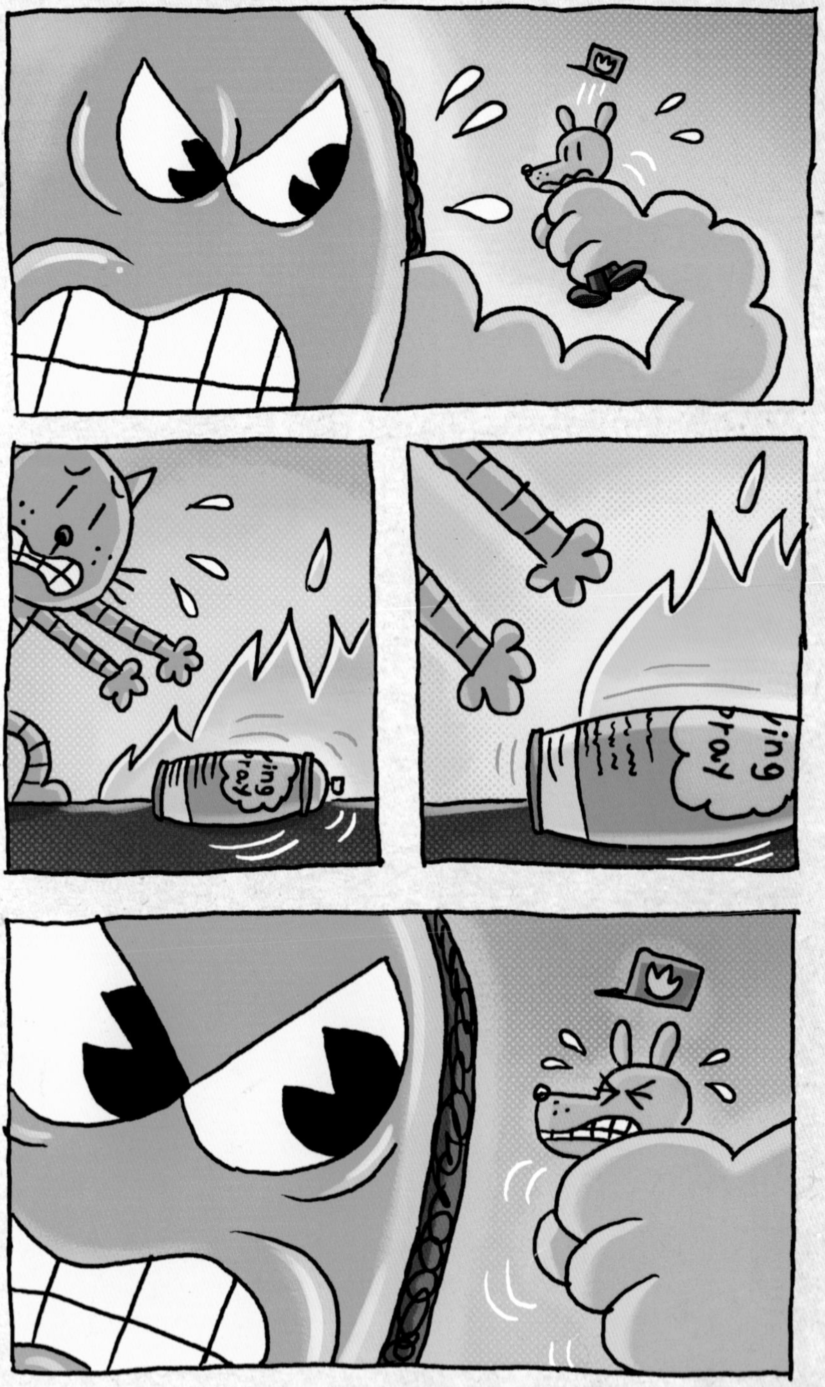
ving
pray
ving
pray

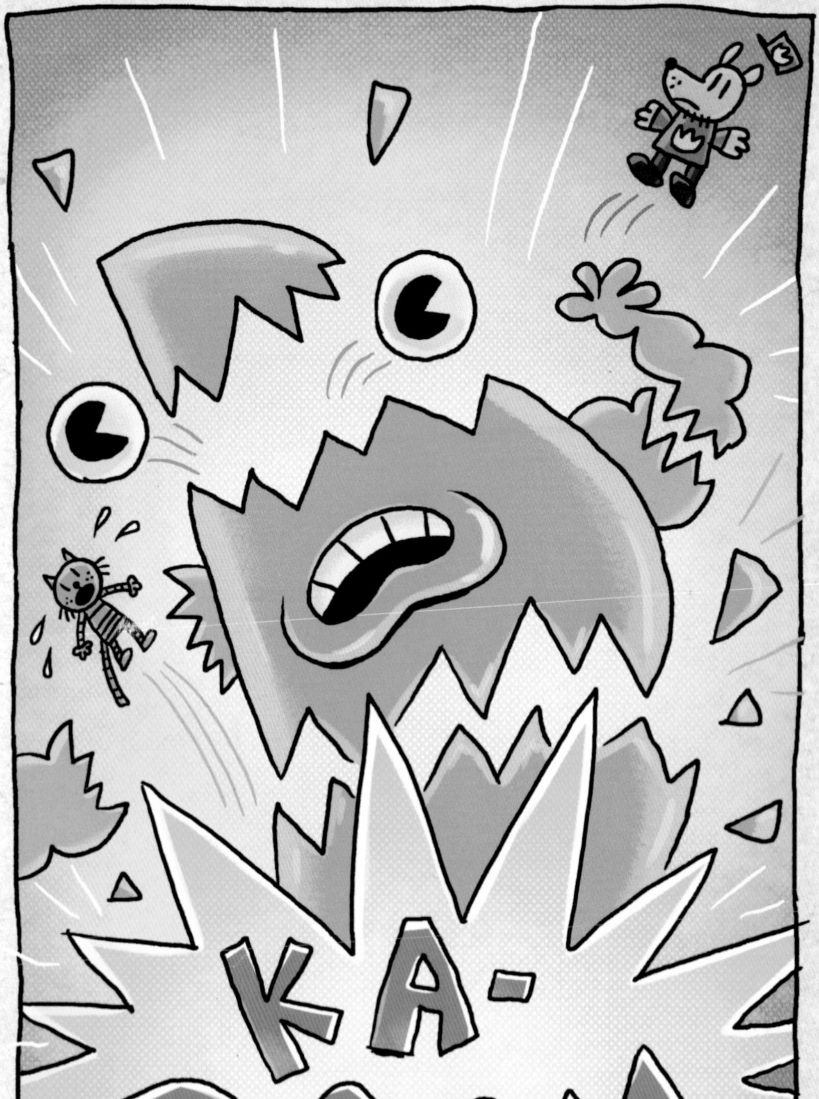
KA-
BOOM

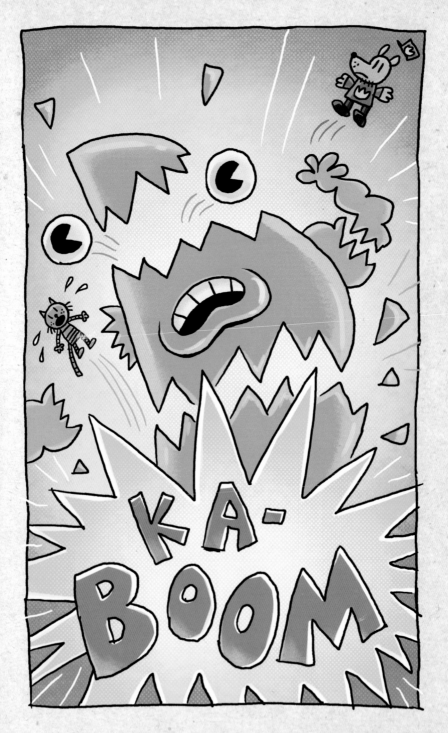

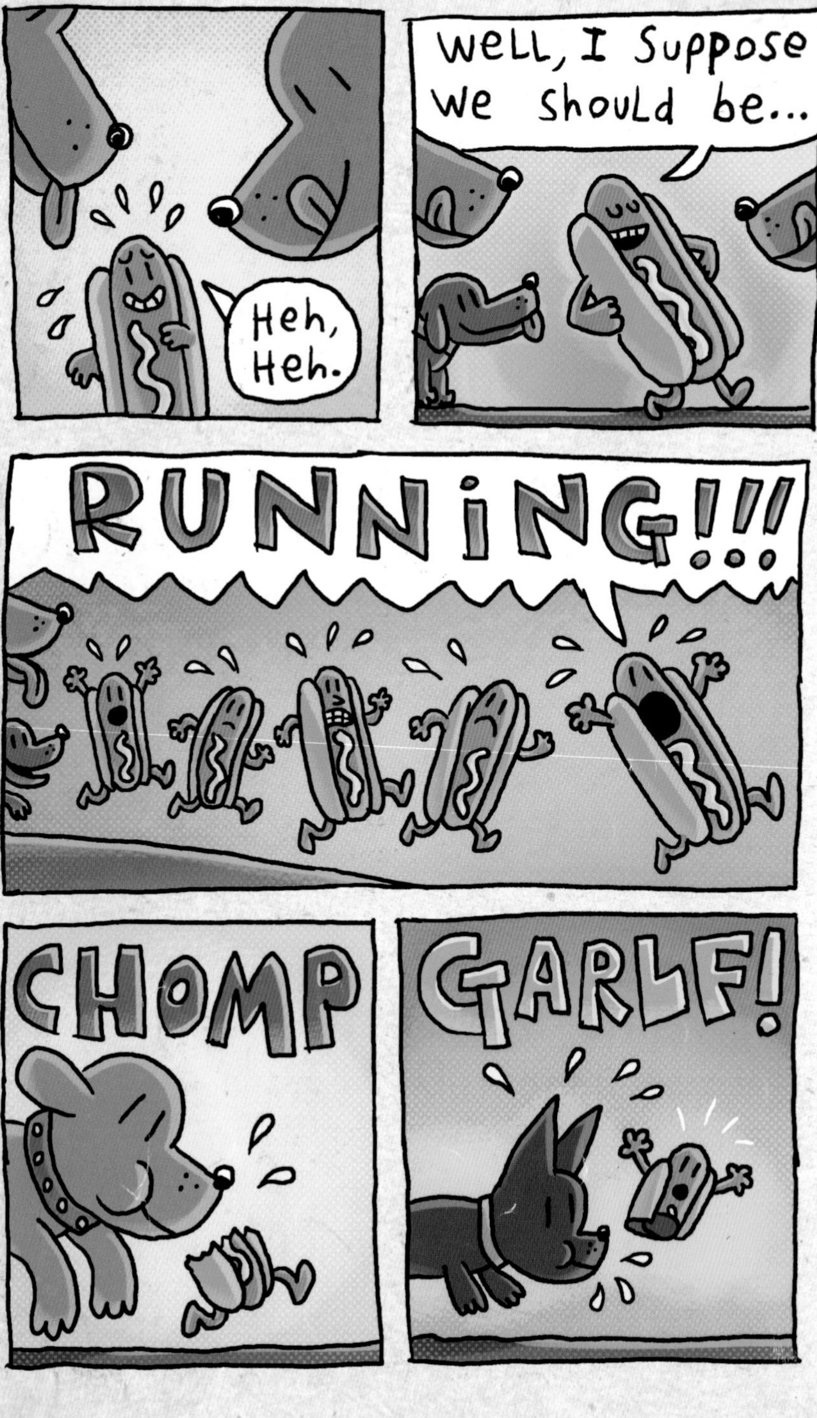
Heh, Heh.
WELL, I Suppose we should be...
RUNNiNG!!!
CHOMP
GARLF!

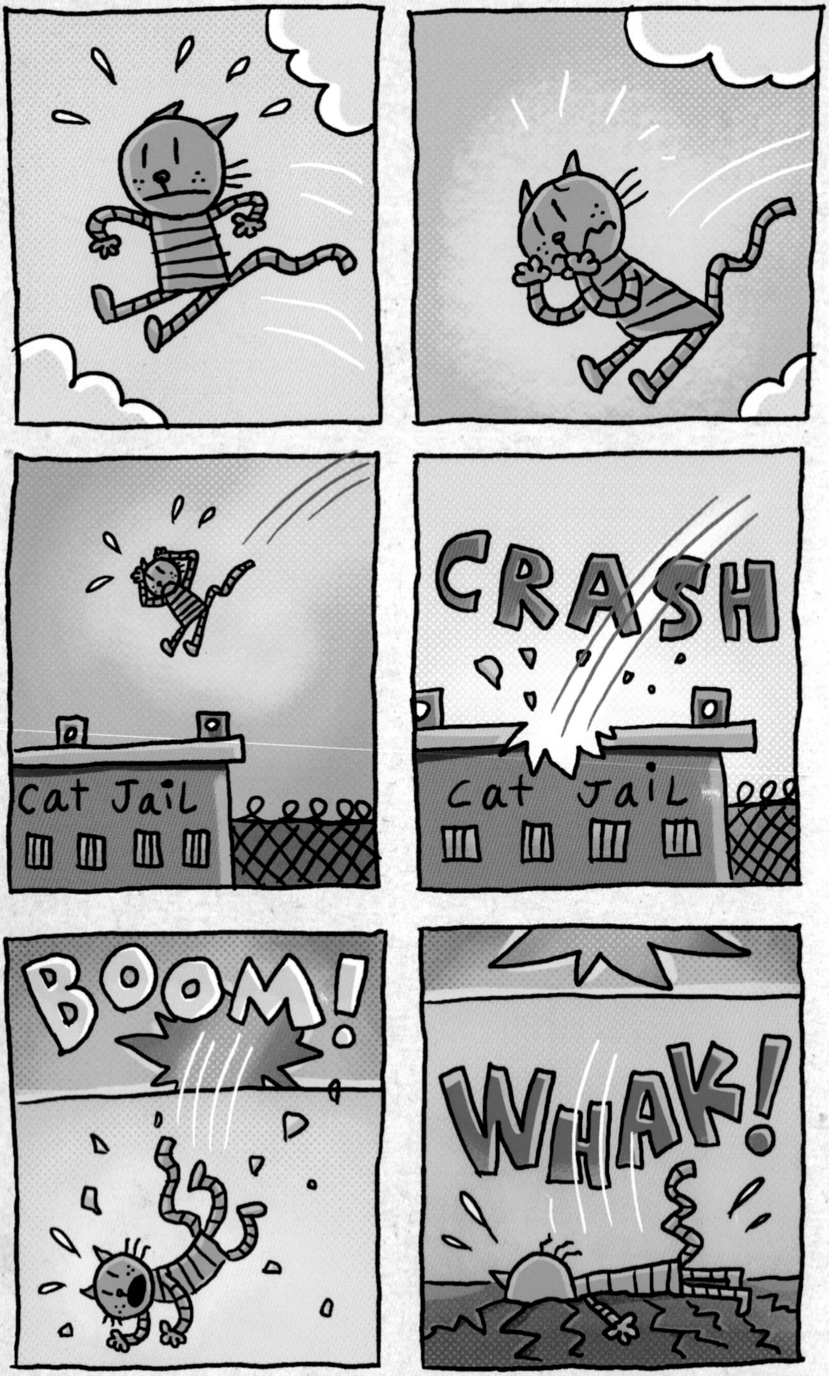
Cat Jail
CRASH
Cat Jail
BOOM!
WHAK!

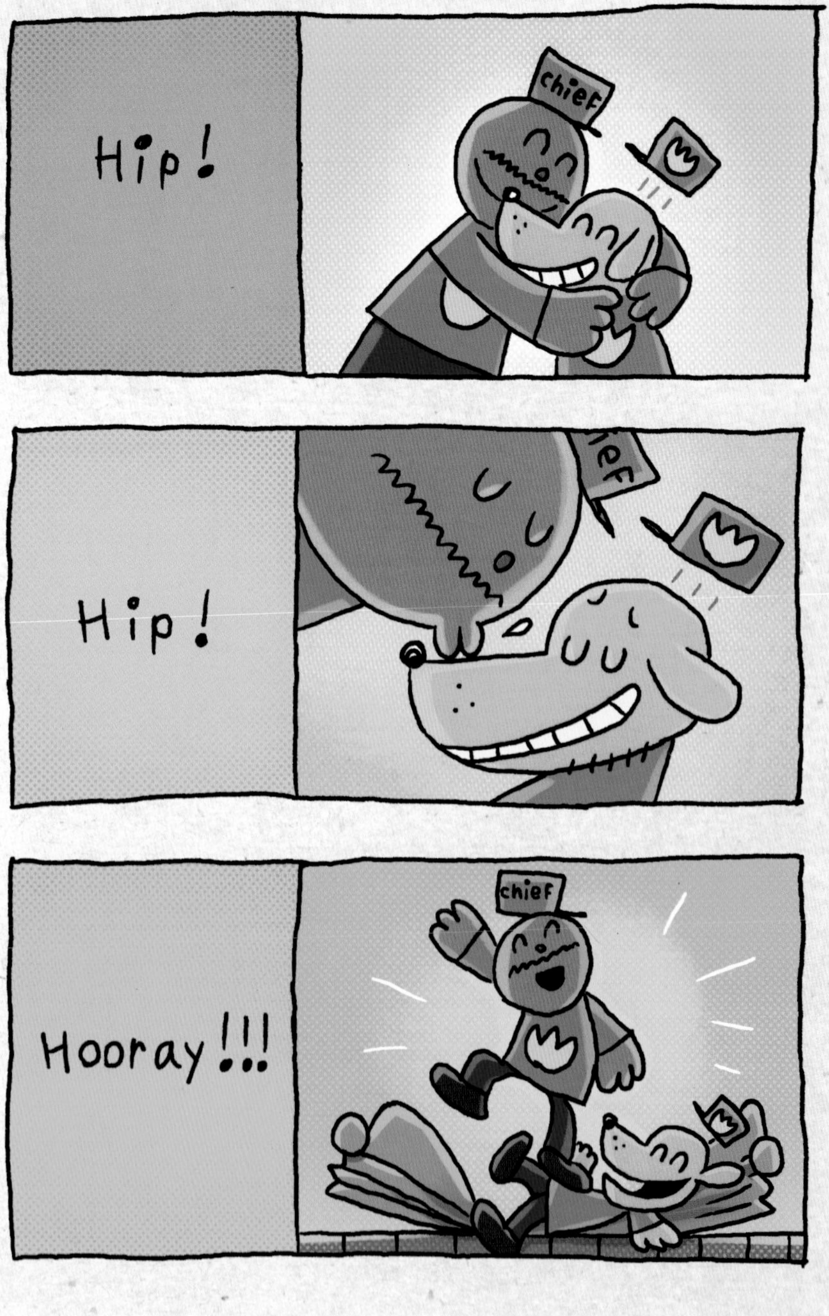
Hip!
chief
Hip!
Hooray!!!
chief

ain't you glad chief ain't mad at DOG MAN no more?

I sure amn't!

HOORAY FOR DOG MAN!

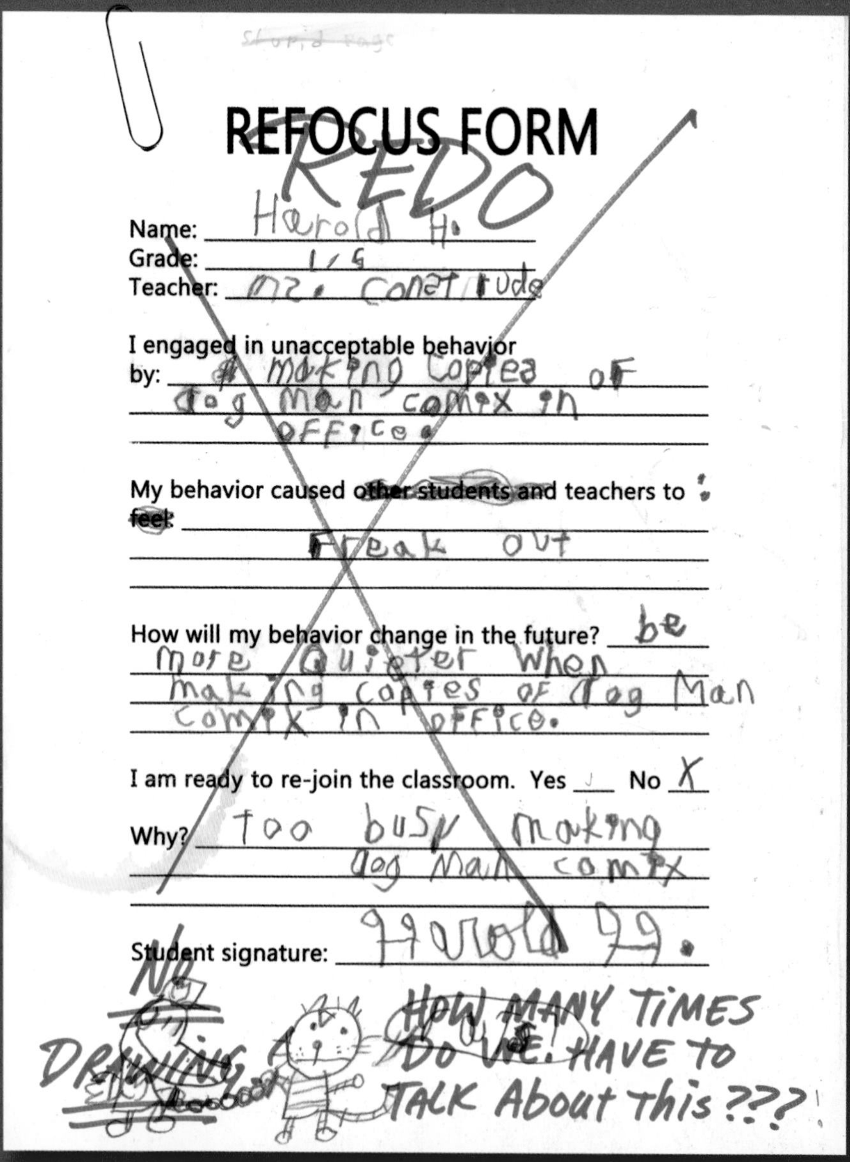

REFOCUS FORM

REDO

Name: _Harold H._
Grade: _1/2_
Teacher: _Ms. Construde_

I engaged in unacceptable behavior
by: _# making copies of_
dog man comix in
office.

My behavior caused other students and teachers to
feel: _freak out_

How will my behavior change in the future? _be_
more quieter when
making copies of dog man
comix in office.

I am ready to re-join the classroom. Yes ___ No _X_
Why? _too busy making_
dog man comix

Student signature: _Harold H._

NO
DRAWING

HOW MANY TIMES
DO WE HAVE TO
TALK About this ???

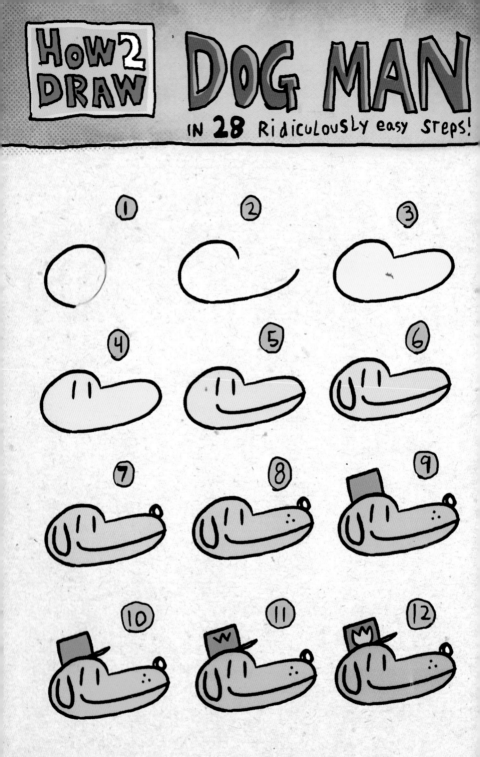

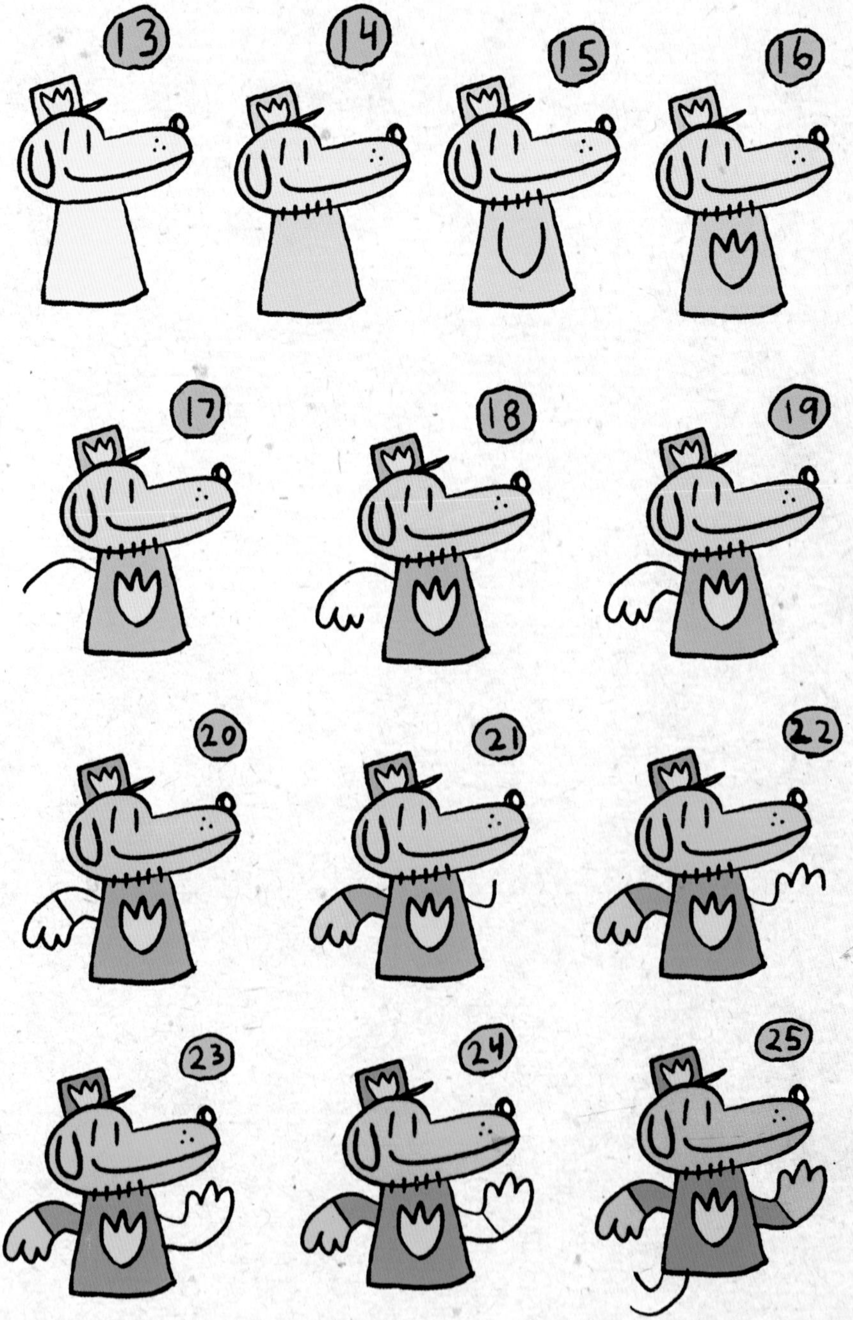
13
14
15
16
17
18
19
20
21
22
23
24
25

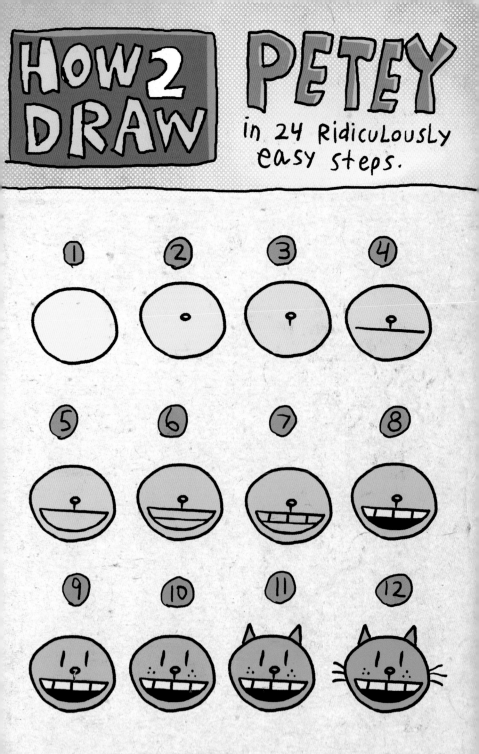

225

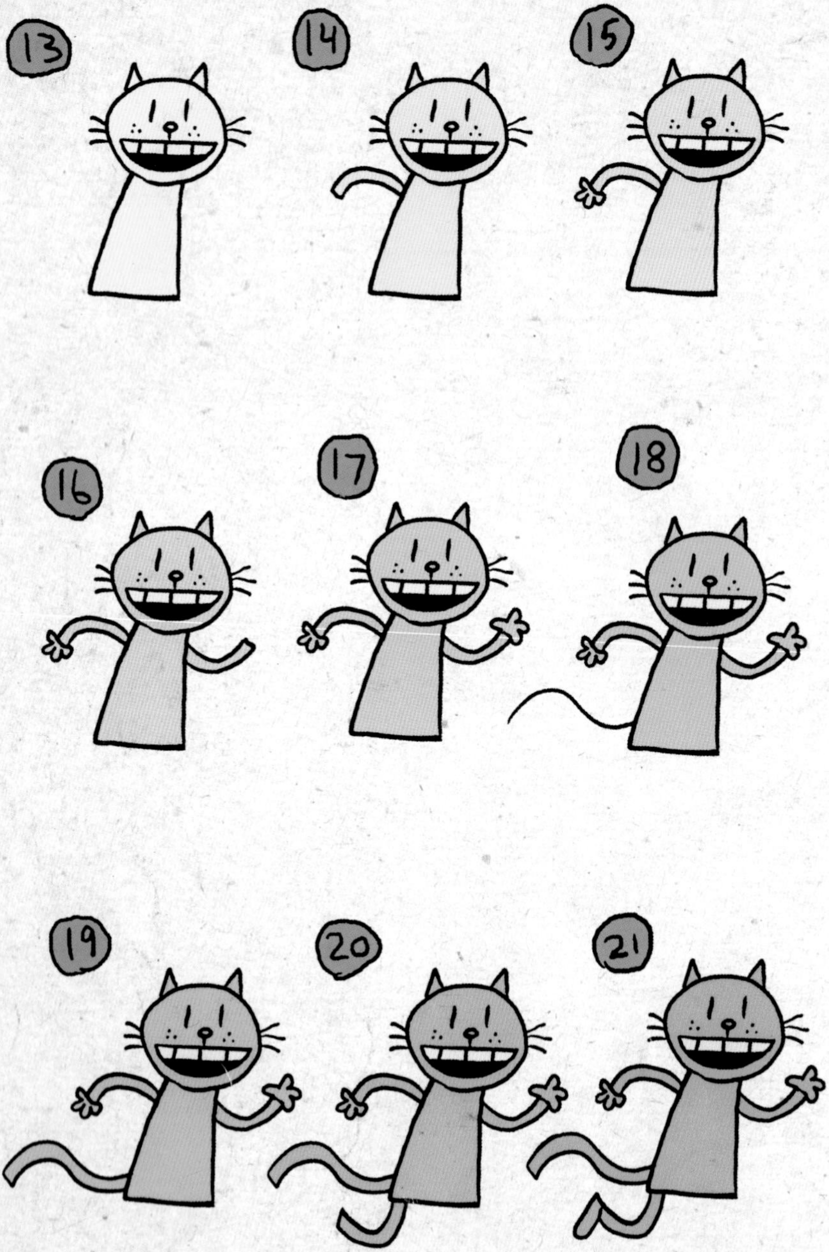
13
14
15
16
17
18
19
20
21

BE EXPRESSIVE

evil   Diabolical   Supa Sinister

Sad   Angry   Supa angry

Supa, supa   Surprised   sleepy
   angry

① ② ③ ④

⑤ ⑥ ⑦ ⑧

⑨ ⑩ ⑪

⑫ ⑬ ⑭

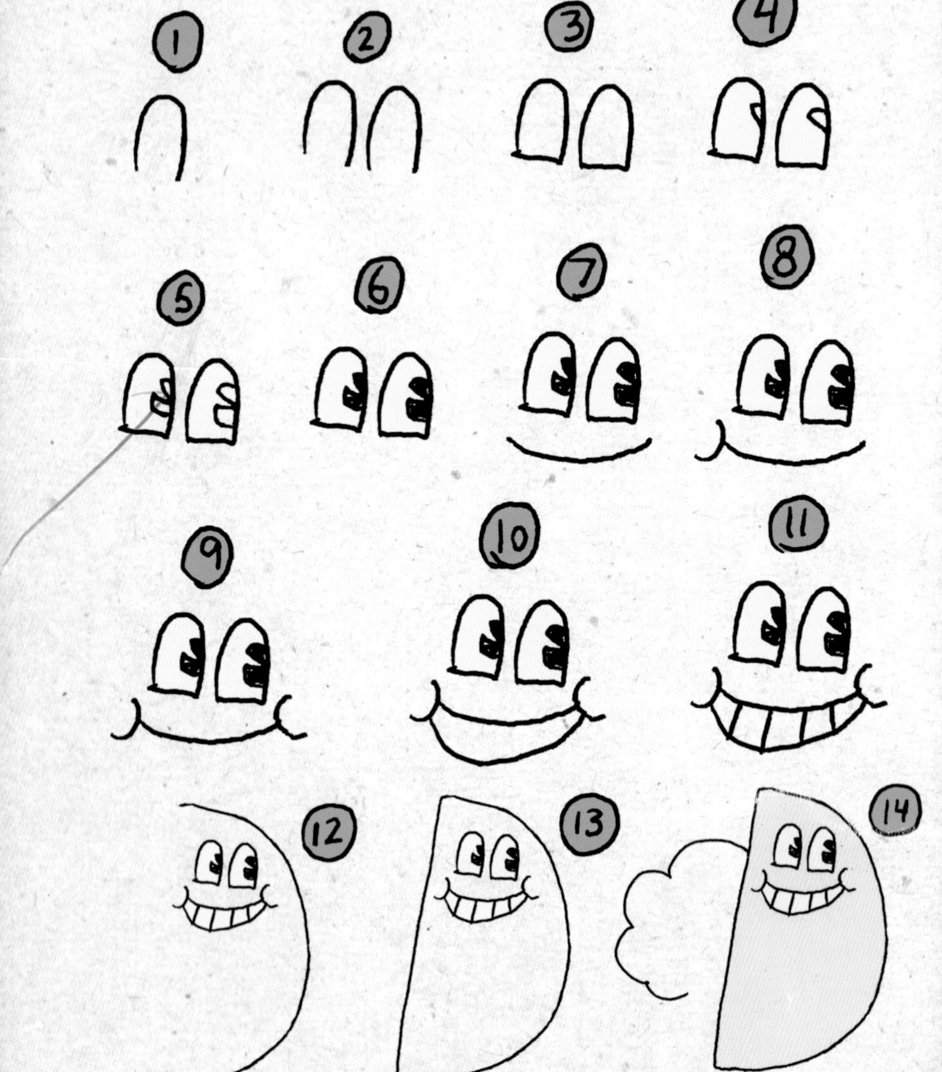

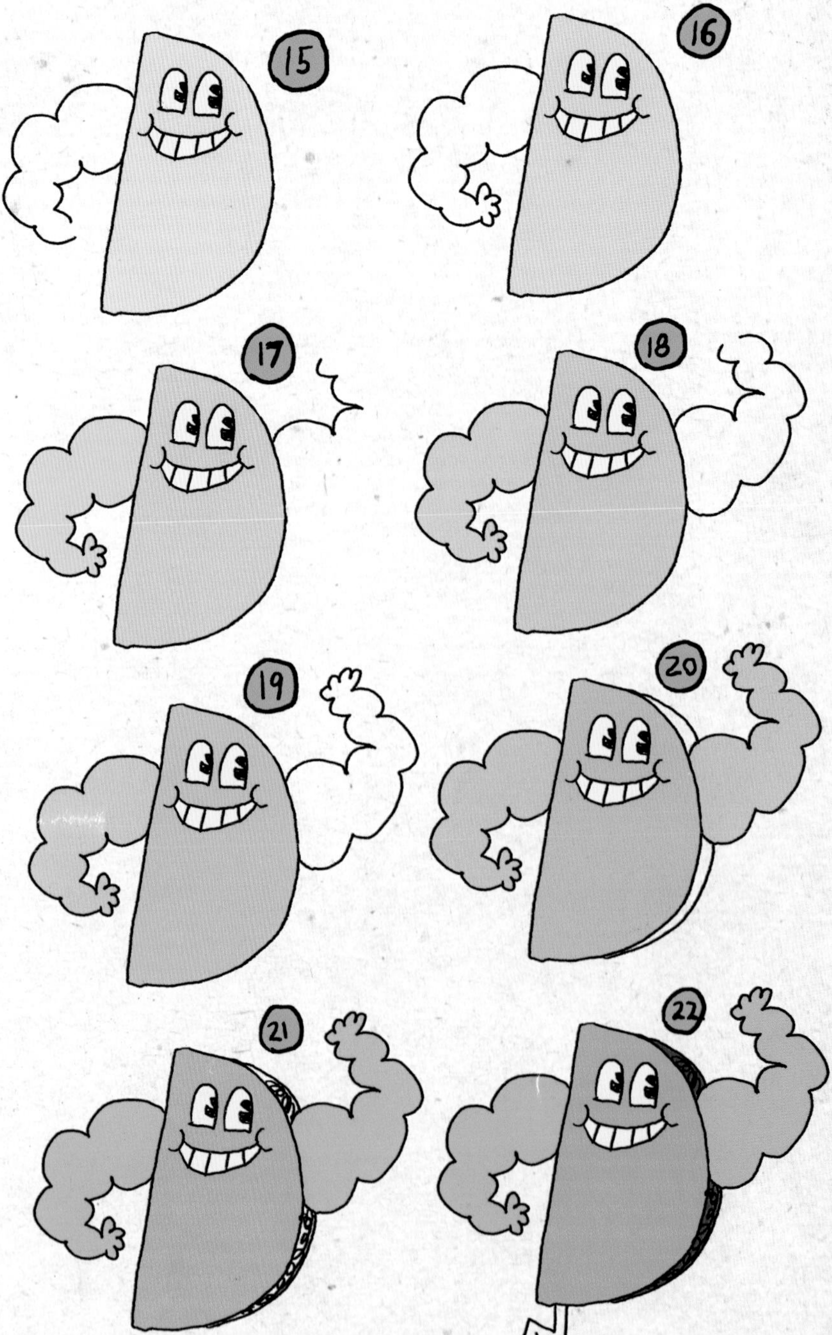
15
16
17
18
19
20
21
22

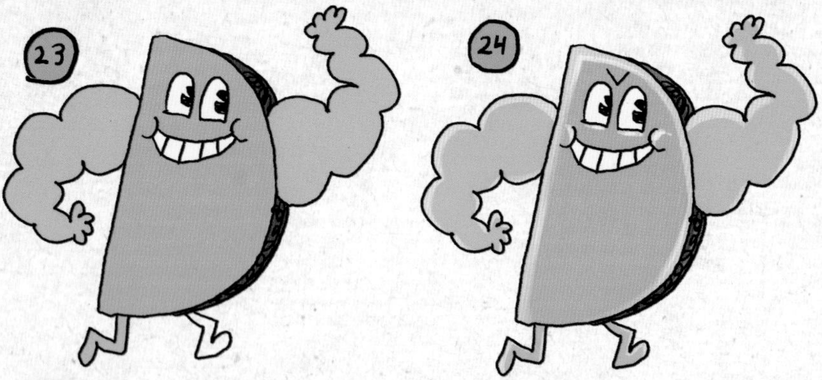
23
24

BE EXPRESSive!!!

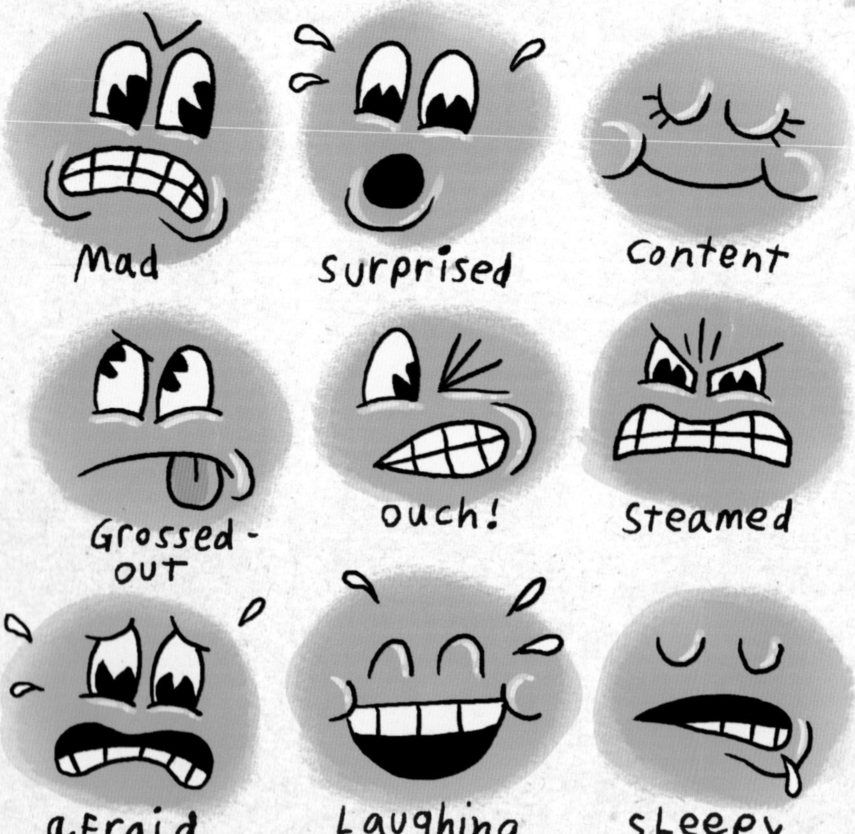
Mad
Surprised
Content
Grossed-out
ouch!
Steamed
afraid
Laughing
sLeepy

HOW 2 DRAW 2 INVISIBLE PETEY

in **8** easy steps.

① ② ③ ④

⑤ ⑥ ⑦ ⑧

BE EXPRESSiVE!!!

Happy   angry   sad   oBsequious

ABOUT THE AUTHOR-ILLUSTRATOR

When Dav Pilkey was a kid, he was diagnosed with ADHD and dyslexia. Dav was so disruptive in class that his teachers made him sit out in the hall every day. Luckily, Dav loved to draw and make up stories. He spent his time in the hallway creating his own original comic books.

In the second grade, Dav Pilkey made a comic book about a superhero named Captain Underpants. Since then, he has been creating books that explore universally positive themes celebrating the triumph of the good-hearted.

ABOUT THE COLORIST

Jose Garibaldi grew up on the South Side of Chicago. As a kid, he was a daydreamer and a doodler, and now it's his full-time job to do both. Jose is a professional illustrator, painter, and cartoonist who has created work for many organizations, including Nickelodeon, MAD Magazine, Cartoon Network, Disney, and THE EPIC ADVENTURES OF CAPTAIN UNDERPANTS for DreamWorks Animation. He lives in Los Angeles, California, with his wonder dogs, Herman and Spanky.

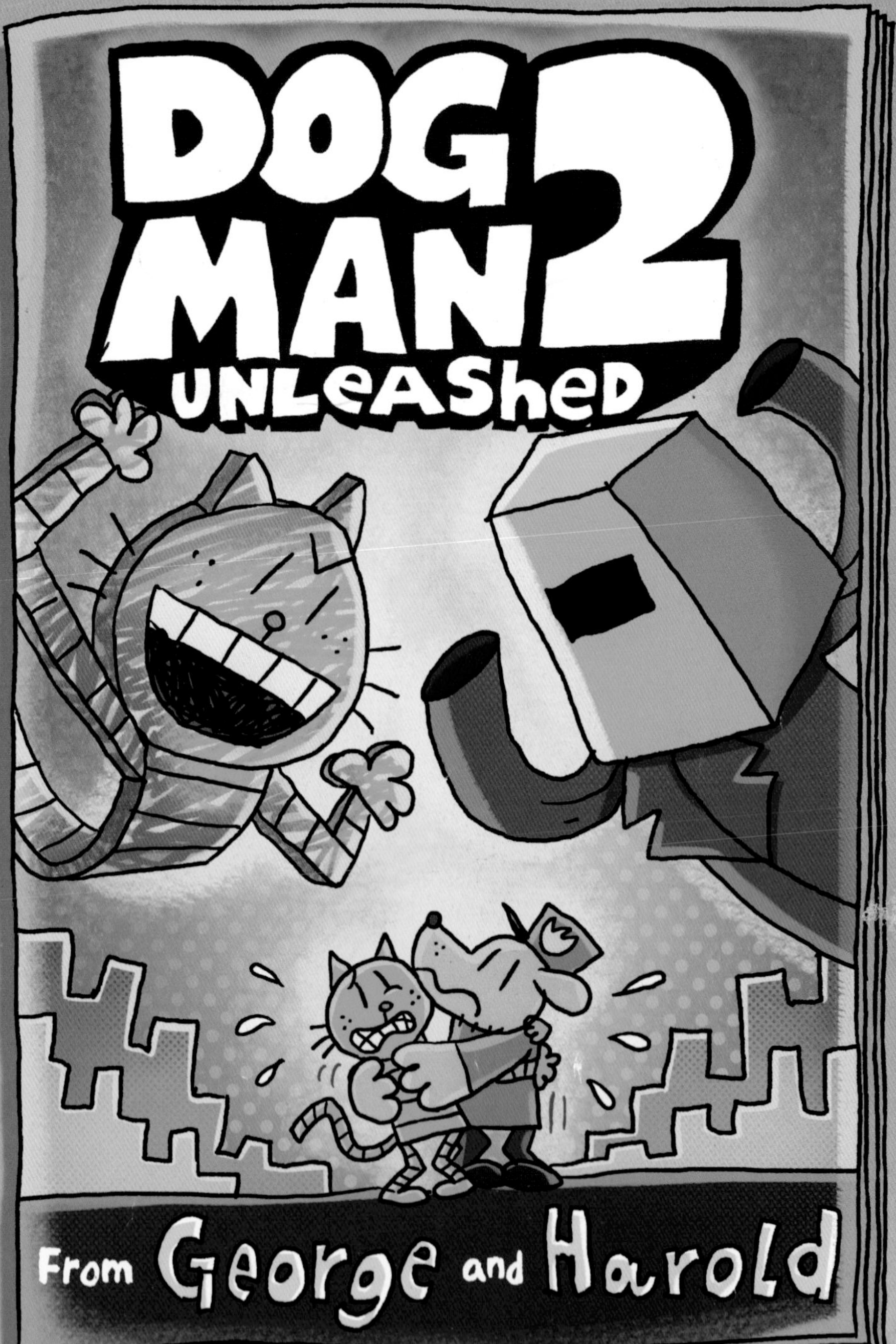
DOG MAN 2
UNLEASHED
From George and Harold